EverSweet

Other books by Sue Chamblin Frederick
The Juan Castillo Spy Series

The Unwilling Spy

Madame Delafloté, Impeccable Spy

The Ivy Log Series

Grandma Takes A Lover

The Boardinghouse – Return to Ivy Log

VISIT THE AUTHOR AT: www.suechamblinfrederick.com

Ever Sweet

Sue CHAMBLIN Frederick

ISBN: 978-0-9852104-4-1

Word Jewels Publishing

Acknowledgments

To my four brothers and sisters who thought my wild imagination was dangerous – see, you guys, I've channeled that imagination into terrific novels.

To ROBERT (ROB) L. BACON of **"The Perfect Write"** who tirelessly contributes his wisdom of the writing world to both published and unpublished authors. His manuscript evaluation and editing are solid gold! You're still the smartest guy I know, Rob.

To STEVE W. JOHNSON, the best layout person in the world; screenwriter and author of *Not Much Of A Crime, Pier Pressure, Bare Essentials* and others.

To JAY METZLER of **Idle Hands Bread Company**, Richmond, Virginia, who is positively the best baker this side of the Mississippi. Thank you for your baking genius!

To the folks at **JIM'S SMOKIN' QUE** in Blairsville, Georgia. They do barbecue just right!

To the eagle eyes of the proofers: GARY FREDERICK, BRENDA COCHRANE and SALENE JUSTICE – *you never miss a thing*!

And, to the folks of Ivy Log, Georgia, for letting me take literary liberties in building their fictitious town. To ensure authenticity, I traveled to Ivy Log to get a feel for the town...*but there was no town!* Ivy Log is a wide spread community of wonderful mountain folk who live at the top of Georgia. So, I gave them a town with a Main Street, The Church of Ivy Log, The Boardinghouse and a town square with the tallest blue spruce in Georgia. *Thank you, Ivy Log!*

VISIT THE AUTHOR AT: www.suechamblinfrederick.com

Prologue

The screams came from a quarter-mile away, the mountain winds carrying the desperate cry to a ridge jutting out over a deep Appalachian valley. When she heard the pitiful sounds, Lula Starling was sitting on her cabin porch, snapping beans. She pushed the heavy enamel pan from her lap and stumbled down wooden steps that led to the narrow mountain trail which would take her to Hattie Murphy's cabin.

Panting for breath at the top of the ridge, the thin woman slowed and called out, "Hattie?" Only a few feet from the small two-room shack, she called again, "Hattie? You in there?" There was no reply, and warped slats creaked as she stepped onto the porch and moved toward what was now soft whimpering. Easing through the half-closed front door, she announced, "It's me, Hattie. Lula."

A weak voice drifted through the shadows of a small room at the back of the house. "Oh, Lula. Help me. Come help me." Hattie reached out her hand to Lula as she rushed in. "I done had this baby, Lula. A tiny little thing. And I think there's another one comin'!"

"Two babies . . . you havin' two babies, Hattie?" Lula leaned over the bed. "Oh, my. Look at that little thing. No bigger than a mountain trout."

"I already done named her EverSweet," said Hattie. "Pyune EverSweet Murphy." She closed her eyes.

"Where's Vernon," Lula asked.

"I ain't seen Vernon. Left yesterday afternoon, lookin for one of our pigs."

Lula ran to the sink and returned with a wet towel.

A moment later a scream split the air, followed by, "Here it comes, Lula. Here it comes." Hattie grasped the protruding wooden rail on the headboard and raised her hips, groaning and gasping for breath. "Oh, God in heaven," she cried as the second baby spilled out into Lula's hands.

"Another girl, Hattie. So tiny." Lula stared. "Oh, my. Two of them. Now, ain't that somethin'."

Lula hummed as she wrapped the squirming little girls tightly. A self-taught midwife in the remote high peaks of the Appalachians, Lula had no children of her own. She snuggled both babies in the crooks of her arms and grinned at Hattie. "Just let me hold these babies a minute. Then I'll get you fixed up."

Hattie, her eyes still closed, spoke softly. "Lula, I can't take care of two babies." She opened her eyes, tears flowing freely. "You take one,." As exhausted as she was, she rose onto her elbows. "You got to take one, Lula. You just got to."

~~~

Chapter 1

Time is measured differently in the mountains, this love story beginning long ago, way before mountain man Wiley Hanson came down from his beloved peaks and sat in The Boardinghouse in Ivy Log, Georgia, just a stone's throw from the North Carolina line, eating Pyune EverSweet Murphy's lemon pudding cake. If it hadn't been for something else beckoning him, Wiley would have stayed on the high ridge at the edge of the Chattahoochee-Oconee Forest, just a knob or two from Brasstown Bald, and lived out his life hunting and fishing.

But everything changed when the mountains sent him secret words; hushed words that floated over the peaks and found him one cool autumn day hunting squirrels near Wolfpen Ridge. It was a heart thing: *Put down your gun for a while and see what the world holds for you.* It was then that he meandered down from the rugged hills and ambled into Ivy Log, a hamlet that rested so quaint and still in the early morning mist that he stopped in wonder at the smoke curling from the chimney of a two-story white-shingled house whose windows glowed with yellow light and called to him like nothing ever had before.

"Hello, House," he yelled, as if the building were a proper name. He cocked his head and listened, fully expecting a reply. He got one.

"What you hollerin' at?" a female voice called from behind an open door. "Don't you know it's 'fore sun up?" The door slammed shut—but not before a day-old biscuit, duly hard, flew across the porch and found Wiley's head.

"That's some welcome I get, my first time in this here town," he yelled back as he picked up the rocklike biscuit and threw it at the closed door, a loud clunk attesting to his good aim. "No need to be unfriendly like that," he added as he turned and found a trail out of town, looking over his shoulder just in time to see the face of a lovely young girl in the window, watching him.

~~~

Chapter 2

Years later, the spring that followed one of Ivy Log's most ruthless winters in memory came slowly; the sun hesitant and perhaps unwilling to acknowledge the end of so many endless dark evenings. It was the warmth at the end of March, however, with the soft green leaves budding out on bare-limbed trees and the return of birds migrating from the south that made it clear that winter had lost its grip on the tiny community.

There were other changes in the air that spring, and how those changes began, even Ivy Log's long-time residents couldn't say. There must have been some small moment that started the swell of events, and whatever it was must have happened around the edges. But it was at the center that the changes fermented and spilled out into the souls of those who lived in the small town nestled below a ridge at the foothills of the Appalachians. Of course, anyone with any wisdom at all would say it was all about *love* and nothing else.

At The Boardinghouse, where for years the venerable country kitchen had provided Union County's folks with the most delicious food imaginable, Wiley leaned over the documents placed in front of him and examined each paragraph, one by one. His doctorate in environmental engineering from Georgia Tech was no help at all as he strived to interpret the meaning of a formal invitation with all sorts of instructions. His Scottish-flavored Elizabethan English was buried deep inside his mountain self as he quietly struggled to put together exactly what was expected of

Pyune EverSweet Murphy.

"Okay," he proclaimed at last. "I think I got it. You have to be in New York City on Wednesday, the twentieth. Then you catch a return flight on Sunday night, the twenty-fourth."

"You needed all that time to tell me that?" Pyune threw a dishtowel across her shoulder and sat down at her worktable. "I think I'm just going to leave the twenty-five thousand dollars with those people."

"Like heck you are!" Wiley refilled his favorite coffee cup, the one with the faded image of Roy Rogers and Trigger on the side. "This kitchen needs a new stove and larger refrigerators, and that twenty-five thousand dollars will be a big help. You're going to New York, get that check, and then come back to where you belong—in Ivy Log, Georgia." Wiley bobbed his head up and down. "Enough said about that! You got four days to get yourself together. You ought to start packing now."

"Can't you come with me?" Pyune asked, her soft eyes pleading better than her gentle voice.

"No, I can't. We've talked about this all we're goin' to. This is your time. Pyune EverSweet Murphy is the queen of Bakers' World Magazine, and you're going to be the belle of the ball. Just think, yours was the number-one recipe of all! It beat out thousands of entries!"

"I know . . . I know." She closed her eyes and shook her head. "Except for where I was born, I've never been out of Union County." She jumped up and began pacing. "Check that paperwork again. Can't they just send me the check?"

"Not from what this contract says." Wiley waved the papers back and forth. "It's spelled out—to get that twenty-five thousand dollars you got to go to New York. And that ain't all. You have to attend a reception on Wednesday night, where all the magazine's board members will honor you. On Thursday you have a big photo session, and on Friday you and three of New York's celebrity chefs will compete in a fundraiser to benefit the city's homeless. You finish up on Saturday night at a big awards banquet when you get the check. How good is that?"

"Oh, not good at all. I just want to get the check and come back here."

Wiley licked his lips. "Oh, Lordy. Says here you'll be on 'The Today Show,' Thursday morning. Reckon you'll be interviewed by that bald-headed fella?"

"'The Today Show'!" Pyune drew her hands up to her face. "There's no way, Wiley! I just can't do it!"

Wiley left his chair and pulled Pyune into his arms. "You can do it. You're Ivy Log's most prominent citizen. This whole town is proud of you, and you've got to go to New York for all the folks who've supported you and The Boardinghouse for all these years." He rubbed her back and rocked her gently back and forth. "That's all there is to it, my little EverSweet."

Wiley was right, it was Pyune's time. She had walked bare-footed on the mountain trails that led to Ivy Log when she was two years old, one hand holding onto her mama, the other sucking her thumb. In Ivy Log, they'd come upon a deserted Main Street, but when she and her mama heard music they walked toward it and found the town square.

Everyone had gathered around picnic tables, where watermelons lay split open and lemonade flowed from big glass pitchers. Atop a flagpole, an American flag flapped in the breeze. It was the Fourth of July Festival, and the most beautiful sight Pyune had ever seen. Her little feet began tapping to the fiddle music, and she laughed her way to the red juicy watermelons, climbing onto the table and plopping a big slice of melon in her lap and eating it and a few more like it until her mama told her to quit 'fore she got a tummy ache.

This faint glimmer of time had remained in her mind even after forty years had passed. Ivy Log's town square continued to be the gathering place for all events, important or not, the flagpole the very same one that stood so many years ago when Pyune had first arrived. Nothing much had changed, not even The Boardinghouse, except for a coat or two of paint now and then, and maybe an occasional board replaced on the porch. Pyune's place in Ivy Log was one of grace, enhanced by a soft refinement that belied her origins in the remote peaks of the Appalachians. She was a mountain woman, true, but beneath her shy, unassuming character, the rest of her lay ready for an awakening. She just didn't know it yet.

~~~

Chapter 3

Ivy Log's warm spring, with its early flowering dogwoods, created the perfect setting for Pyune Murphy's grand send-off to
New York City. The Boardinghouse overflowed with well-wish-
ers, and they in turn benefited from some of the finest country
food in the Appalachians—or anywhere in the South, for that
matter. But they would have been fed in that manner even if
Pyune wasn't going away, and they all knew it.

Lizzie Lindquist, her broken arm healed from last winter's
fall on thick ice along the sidewalk in front of Patton's Drugs, arrived carrying a big bowl of chicken salad. "Look out, everybody!
You're in my way."

"Come on through, Lizzie," farmer Doyce Conley said, his
thickly calloused hand held high as he waved her toward a table
that sagged with platters of food. "Hope there's room on that table over yonder."

At the bay window, wearing a new mint-green dress, Paula
Jennings sat in quiet repose while roiling inside, drinking coffee
and nibbling on Pyune's warm yeast rolls. She was still smolder-
ing over the perceived theft of her family's lemon pudding cake
recipe. *I'm the one who should be going to New York City to
collect the check for $25,000. Pyune won't look half as good on
television as I would.*

Ah, Paula. She was a true testament to the adage that leop-
ards don't change their spots. After an apparent epiphany a half-
year earlier when she pulled in her claws and accepted William
Johnson as pastor of The Church of Ivy Log, the first black man

to assume this role in the almost century-and-a-half history of the parsonage, she methodically moved back to being her old self. Which meant spewing venom and vitriol whenever she believed that only she knew what was best for the community—and of course herself.

Across from her, Sam Cobb, the prior pastor's son, who had returned to Ivy Log after his father's passing, fiddled with the salt and pepper shakers. Next to Sam sat Wiley, who seemed distracted, his eyes on the door to the kitchen. Every once in a while he'd look out the window, as if to ask *Where is Pyune?*

"I understand Pyune doesn't want to go to New York City," Paula remarked, as if sensing what was making Wiley a nervous wreck. "Poor thing. First time away from Union County." Paula waited until Lizzie started refilling cups at a nearby table where Dr. Casteel sat with Pastor Johnson before she added in a louder voice than necessary, "Never flown before either, has she? Must be scared to death."

Without looking her way, Wiley thumped his fist lightly on the table. "You're right about that. Girl is scared to leave this town. Afraid she'll never come back. Says it's just a feeling she has." He nodded toward the kitchen door. "Bet she's hiding upstairs in her bedroom. She didn't want this big celebration, and she sure doesn't want to go to New York City."

Sam nodded, rubbing his square chin. "I can't imagine her leaving this place for five whole days. Folks will starve to death."

"Not hardly. Lizzie and Vallie will be doin' the cookin'." Wiley smiled. "Even though we all know it's not possible to fill Pyune's shoes, nobody's gonna die of hunger."

"What?" Paula wrinkled her nose. "Have you ever eaten Vallie's cooking? Her pie crust is the worst ever."

Sam shushed Paula. "Here comes Vallie now."

Vallie Thomas pulled a chair away from the large round table and plopped down, a long breath escaping her smiling mouth. "Hey, folks. I reckon you done heard. Me and Lizzie are running this place while Pyune's in New York."

Paula cringed. Sam looked away. Ivy Log had its share of colorful characters but few with the mystique of Vallie Thomas. The ageless, plump woman wandered the streets of Ivy Log like a homeless vagabond despite living in an old but comfortable house on the edge of town.

"We heard all right," Sam said, chuckling softly but seeming ready to break into a full-fledged guffaw. "Pyune says it's up to you and Lizzie to keep things going."

"That's true. Only, I ain't cookin'. I'm good at washin' pots and stuff. You know, clean-up work. Pyune says I cain't even salt anything right." Vallie grinned, her crooked teeth falling over each other as though confused about where they belonged. "Pyune says I cain't get near her lemon extract. Says it's eighty-five percent alcohol. Course, Formula 44 Cough Syrup is enough for me—it's only twenty percent." She let out a raspy laugh, as if her throat was in need of the soothing remedy at that very moment.

"So Lizzie is going to do all the cooking?" Paula said and glanced over at the subject of her disdain, who stood guard over the buffet table, making certain Harley Bradley didn't take all the sweet-potato fries.

Vallie's brown eyes, as large as stewed prunes, widened. "If she can stay away from those soap operas she likes to watch."

"Soap operas?"

"Oh, she's addicted to them all right. Especially the one with that handsome fella—what's his name? The one with the scar on his chin. She says he's sexy as all get out."

From across the room, The Church of Ivy Log's pastor stood and raised his hands just a bit to get everyone's full attention. "Hey, folks! Glad you all are here to give Pyune a big send-off. But before we get started, there's something I've got to tell you." William Johnson, tall with tinges of gray in his close-cropped dark hair, looked out across the crowd. "Last night, around nine o'clock, I heard something at the back door of the parsonage. Thought it was Delilah wanting in." He paused and smiled. "You all know my cat, Delilah? Fierce when she's ready to go to sleep and wants inside."

A few laughs could be heard and Doyce clapped.

The pastor moved into the center of the room, his preacher hands now up and moving while he talked. "When I opened the door, there stood a young boy. Hair as red as the feathers on Doyce's Rhode Island Reds. Lad was dirty, hungry, and as wet as could be from that big shower we had last night."

"Redheaded?" yelled Doyce. "He must be kin to those people over on Rocky Top. All Irish over there."

"Could be," Pastor Johnson said. "Not sure, though. Boy says he's fourteen years old, and his name is B.T. I told him that his was an unusual name. He said it's the only name he's ever had." More laughs. "Hasn't got any brothers or sisters. Said his mama died two weeks ago, and he'd come down the mountain looking for food."

"Where's he now?" Harley Bradley asked while popping a sweet-potato fry in his mouth.

"Sleeping. I fed him all the leftovers in the parsonage's refrigerator, showed him the bathtub, and gave him some clean clothes. He's been sleeping ever since."

"What's goin' to happen to him?" Lizzie asked as she moved across the room, her eyes still on the chicken salad and the few remaining sweet-potato fries.

"Not sure," said the pastor. "Right now, unofficially, I'd say he's a ward of the church." He looked slowly around the room, taking in the familiar faces. "And probably all of Ivy Log."

Heads turned, and whispers floated around the room but settled quietly. Sam Cobb stood from his place at the bay window. "I think I speak for everyone, Pastor. We'll help in any way we can. Perhaps a few of us can go over to Rocky Top or thereabouts and poke around a little. See if we can learn something about the boy. Did he say anything more about his family?"

"Not a thing. He was so worn out, it was all he could do to hold his head up and eat. Thought he was going to fall asleep on the way to the bathtub."

From her seat across from Sam, Vallie leaned forward and whispered, "I'm thinkin' I might know that boy." Before he could ask her what she thought she knew, she left her chair and waddled into the kitchen.

~~~

Chapter 4

Aand there she was—coming through the kitchen doorway. Her hair was pulled back, held by a satin ribbon the color of a mountain sunset, orange with wisps of yellow throughout. Her eyes, the color of dark rum, searched the room. A slight flicker came and went, a nervousness running through her that was impossible to shield.

She was a girl born on a ridge in the Chasteen Mountains in North Carolina, near Old Billy Top in the southern Appalachians. Ivy Log was the first town she had seen when her mama tugged at her little hand and said, "Come on, Pyune. This is gonna be our new home."

Forty years later, she lived in the same little hamlet that she and her mother had walked to on that hot July day, leaving behind all they had known. She had never gone back to the Chasteen Mountains, not even to get the bones of her father, which purportedly lay at the bottom of the ridge where she and her mama had lived. He'd disappeared the day before she was born, and when her mother watched the buzzards circling a few days later, she could only assume he was somewhere on the rocks below. And when he never returned home, she was certain of it.

Pyune forced a smile when Doyce hollered across the room, "There's the famous Pyune EverSweet Murphy!" He stood and began clapping. Everyone in the room joined in, and the festivities began.

"Speech! Speech!" yelled Lizzie after things quieted a bit.

Pyune laughed. "I cook, I don't make speeches!" She pulled

her apron straight and held on each side. "But I will say that I appreciate all of you coming . . . to wish me well." She wanted to say more but had to stop talking. She was leaving the only place she'd ever known. Her eyes found Wiley. Her Wiley. If he would go with her to New York, she'd be fine. But he said he wanted her to fly by herself, as if to spread her own wings. Well, she was happy right where she was—at The Boardinghouse, in front of her stove and stirring a pot of hot cinnamon apples.

From his seat by the bay window, Wiley felt his beating heart. In a few days he would drive Pyune to Atlanta, put her on a plane, and wait. Wait for her return. Or would she? He cleared his throat, trying to say something to calm her. He was nervous himself, a feeling of loss overcoming him. But she'd be back. He needn't worry. And he'd be waiting. He managed to aim a smile her way.

Since Wiley wasn't saying anything, Pyune volunteered, "I'll be on 'The Today Show' on Thursday morning. Don't know what time, but I'll let Wiley know as soon as I find out." She let her apron fall as it may. "I've got a peach pie in the oven. I'll bring it right out. Lizzie, would you get some vanilla ice cream out of the freezer?"

Wiley left his place at the bay window and walked out into the cool spring air. Something in his mind made him fidget, something he didn't want to think about. He passed Dr. Casteel's office and crossed Main Street to the town square, where the tops of evergreens swayed gently back and forth. The sound of a train's whistle blew softly and made him think of a song about leaving. What was it? "I Heard That Lonesome Whistle Blow," by Jimmie Rogers? He lifted his chin and strained to hear the song in his head. No, not Jimmie Rogers; Hank Williams, Sr., that's who'd sung it.

He turned around and looked down the hill to The Boarding-house, its windows brilliant with yellow light. He saw Pyune walk onto the porch. She had taken off her apron and stood watching the ink-blue sky. He wondered if she'd heard the train's whistle—and if she would miss him as much as he would miss her.

~~~

Chapter 5

William Johnson's life as the new pastor of The Church of
Ivy Log was a far cry from his church of three thousand in
Atlanta, Georgia. He had left behind the woes of big-city life and
the heartbreak of losing his wife of fifteen years. Childless, he
was alone except for Delilah and the church congregation, the
latter filling his need for a family—somewhat. But the handsome
preacher found solace in the simplicity of small-town living—
and the peace for which he'd been searching since his wife's
passing.

Well into Saturday morning, and after a much-too-large
breakfast at The Boardinghouse, he'd returned to the parsonage,
fed Delilah, and settled in his study to prepare Sunday's sermon,
a task he savored more than anything he did. Earlier, he had
peeked into the small spare bedroom in the back of the parsonage to check on the young boy who had sought refuge during the
rainstorm the night before. The boy was sleeping soundly, his
skinny body twisted in the sheets and his mouth agape in a soft
snore. William tried to remember himself at fourteen years old,
where he was, what he was doing, and who loved him. He felt his
eyes mist over and gently closed the door.

At his desk, he picked up his worn and tattered Bible, mas-
saged the soft leather and opened it to where a faded red ribbon
divided the pages. The pages were heavily marked and carried
with them his memories of past churches and congregations. His
six months at The Church of Ivy Log had already been filled with
many memorable events: the marriage of Frank and Adela and

their extended honeymoon in Europe; the rescue of Wiley from the side of the mountain; the return of Sam Cobb, the son of Ivy Log's past preacher, Adelpheus Cobb; but, best of all, The Boardinghouse. The Boardinghouse had become his own "living room" of sorts, a place for long-winded conversations with the townsfolk and warm fellowship with his parishioners. However, as he recollected the experiences that came to mind without thinking too hard about them, he couldn't be fair to himself if he didn't include the redheaded harridan in the mix, as Paula Jennings had made his life interesting in ways he hadn't imagined possible. Of course, he hadn't imagined anyone like Paula Jennings, either. And, please, Heavenly Father, just one per lifetime.

For all of his warm feelings for The Boardinghouse, William Johnson had quickly discovered that it would be nothing without Pyune Murphy, who, well before daylight, began making berry pies and fresh squash with Vidalia onions. Upon the reverend's arrival in Ivy Log the previous December, it was Pyune who had befriended him, a friendship the widowed pastor valued beyond words.

As to maintaining his waistline, it was Pyune's prized lemon pudding cake that was forcing him to continue to exercise vigorously. A dessert that created a stampede to The Boardinghouse every Tuesday. It was also the lemon pudding cake that would take her away from Ivy Log and to New York City. The pastor would miss her, even for just five days.

His musings were interrupted by the rush of a skinny body, all arms and legs, that filled the doorway to his study. The redheaded boy, heavily freckled, stared at him, wide-eyed. "Who are you?"

The preacher smiled and closed his Bible. "Pastor William Johnson. I live here. This is the parsonage of The Church of Ivy Log."

"That's where I am? Ivy Log?" His eyes darted around like a cat in a strange room. His fingers fidgeted and his knees jerked.

"That's right, Ivy Log."

"I heard of Ivy Log before."

"Son, where exactly did you come from?"

"Up the mountain," the boy said after a pause, clearly confused by the obvious question.

The preacher grinned and nodded. "Where up the mountain?"

The blue eyes sitting in the mass of freckles flitted back and forth to the ceiling, as if measuring its height. "Pretty high up, I reckon."

Pastor Johnson leaned forward and patiently clasped his hands together, forcing back a laugh. "If I showed you a map, could you point out where you lived for me?"

"Can't read a map."

"Can't read a map? Didn't you go to school?"

"I did."

The pastor's brow wrinkled, and he narrowed his eyes. "Then you should be able to read a map."

"Nope."

"Why not?"

"The lines are all squiggly and don't make no sense."

"You can read, though, right?"

"Not great, but I can make out most words—if they ain't too long."

The clock chimed twelve noon, and the pastor settled back in his chair. "You said your name was B.T. Is that right?

"Yep. That's me."

"What does the T stand for?"

"Nothin'."

"Does your last name begin with a T?"

"Nope."

"Young man, if you're called B.T., the T must stand for something."

"Cain't you tell?" He grinned wide, his lips pulling upward to reveal enormous bucked teeth. "B.T. is for Buck Teeth." He closed his mouth and blinked several times. "My last name is Hickel. Buck Teeth Hickel. That's me." He jerked his thumb toward his chest.

The pastor remained quiet for a moment, studying the red hair that poked upward and out of control as if looking for a home. From its appearance, it was cut in various lengths by something other than a sharp pair of scissors. He noticed the tops of B.T.'s ears were skinned and crusted with scabs. The long boney fingers on his hands, scuffed and red, fiddled with the edges of his too-big shirt, which the pastor had given him.

"Looks like you've been in the woods awhile, B.T. That so?"

"Why, sure I have. Ever since mama died and was buried, I been walking the trails all over the Bald."

"Who buried your mom?"

"Some women on the mountain came and washed her real good and put her best dress on her. Then, some men put her in the ground." He hesitated. "Preacher said a few words, and then everybody left."

"Did you contact the authorities?"

"The what?" B.T. scrunched his face, his teeth protruding like kernels of corn before resting on his bottom lip.

Pastor Johnson pulled out a notebook and picked up a pen. "Did you call the sheriff or 911 when she died?"

B.T. shook his head. "Mister, we don't got no sheriff, and I sure as heck don't know nobody named 911."

Becoming slightly exasperated, the reverend left his chair and sat on the edge of his desk. "Do you think you could show me the way back to where you lived?"

"Back where I lived? Now, why would I want to do that? I'm not leaving here till I find my aunt."

"Your aunt?"

"That's right. My aunt."

"Who's your aunt?"

"My mama's sister."

William Johnson closed his eyes. "Son, what's her name?"

"Can't remember—but I'd know her if I seen her."

The pastor of The Church of Ivy Log felt a rumbling inside his stomach that he seldom experienced; a buzzing noise that made him shake his head and lick his lips. "What about your father?"

"What about him?" The young boy jerked back and raised his fists as if in a boxing ring. The thinness of his face hollowed out as he puffed his lips and stared at the pastor. The boy was obviously malnourished, and this bothered the pastor.

The pastor rose from the edge of his desk. "You can put your hands down. How about you and I go over to The Boarding-house and get us some lunch."

The boy ducked his head and glared at this man who was trying to befriend him. "Sorry, don't got no money. Besides that, I ain't never ate nobody's cookin' but my mama's."

"I didn't say you needed any money. What if I buy your lunch?"

"What if you do? And what if I bathe that old stinky cat of yours. It slept with me last night and I about puked from the smell." B.T. hung his head. "Mighta been me smellin', though."

"Delilah? You're talking about the most beautiful cat in the world. She always smells like spring itself, even in winter." He grinned at his cat, finding her spread out on a bookcase shelf.

"Your cat done either had gas or it rolled in a dead animal of some kind. I thought only dogs did that, but it seems like your ol' cat thinks it's a dog."

"Oh, no. Not Delilah. Delilah knows she's a cat. I guarantee it."

B.T. looked sideways at the pastor. "How can you guarantee somethin' like that?"

Pastor Johnson took his jacket from the back of his desk chair. "Why don't we discuss this over some of Pyune's fried chicken?" He took a step toward the door.

"Who's Pyune?"

"You're about to find out." The pastor paused. "But how about you run a comb through your hair before we go over to The Boardinghouse."

"I don't like it slicked down."

"Why not?"

"Mister, you sure do ask a lot of questions." The boy spied Delilah sleeping on the top shelf of the bookcase and pointed a crooked finger at the animal. "That cat got gas—real bad."

~~~

Chapter 6

Pyune sat on the side of her bed in her small bedroom above The Boardinghouse kitchen and listened to Vallie and Lizzie argue about which pot to use to boil potatoes. *Oh, what have I done?* Leaving town for five days and putting the care of The Boardinghouse in Lizzie's and Vallie's hands was a mistake. Wiley had assured her time and time again that things would work out, but a voice kept telling her that it would end up a catastrophe. Vallie drank too much Formula 44, and Lizzie watched too many soap operas. The citizens of Ivy Log would perish from hunger or food poisoning, and The Boardinghouse would surely be closed down.

Her flight was scheduled for 7 o'clock on Wednesday morning, and she had yet to pack. Clothes were strewn across the bed, on the floor, on the backs of chairs; not one stitch of anything had made it into her borrowed luggage. Oh, what she'd give for some Formula 44 herself. All this for $25,000? It wasn't worth it. No woman in her right mind would go to New York City by herself, especially if she'd traveled only fifty or so miles from her birthplace during her entire life.

Hearing the familiar sound of Wiley's boots coming up the stairs, she brushed a beginning tear from her cheek. When his tall frame filled the doorway she smiled and trilled a long, "Hey."

"Hey, to you. I'm here to help you pack." Wiley glanced at the mess of clothes. "Looks . . . looks like you need to do a little more work." He put his hands on his hips and scrunched his eyebrows. "Let's see, five days, two outfits a day—with a couple to spare. We got to get a dozen outfits into those two suitcases. That seem right to you?"

Pyune stared at Wiley, mouth open, and squealed, "Nooooooo! I don't even have a half-dozen outfits!" She jumped from the bed and began flinging things across the room. "Oh, I got plenty of clothes, all right. Why, I have dozens and dozens of . . . aprons." She stomped to the closet and threw open the door. "Just look in here, Wiley! Do you see any New York clothes?" She turned around and glared at him. "I reckon you don't!"

She went from her closet to her dresser and yanked open a drawer. "See any diamonds and furs in this drawer?" She slung out a pair of flannel pajamas. "Tell you what," she snapped, her eyes large and crazy, a gleam that caused Wiley to take a step backwards. "We'll just run over to the Dollar General in Blairsville and pick up a few fabulous outfits—one for the reception and one for the awards ceremony. Oh, and what about "The Today Show"? Why, I'll be the toast of New York City." She collapsed on the floor and began whimpering as if ready to drown in a puddle of her own tears.

Wiley, stunned by an outburst from the most calm, reasonable person he'd ever known, sat down beside Pyune and patted her head. "Now, now, everything's gonna be just fine. I'll just give Paula a call and she can come over and help you. Maybe even let you borrow some of her things."

Pyune lifted her head, and through the narrowest of eyes stared at Wiley. Her words came out snarling and in a high-pitched whine: "So help me, Wiley Hanson, you bring that redhead in here and I'll get my sharpest butcher knife after her. And you next!"

Wiley shrank back. "Bad idea?"

"The worst idea I ever heard of. Ever, ever, ever."

Wiley found himself easing out of the room. "You want we should run over to the Dollar General in Blairsville and find you something to wear?"

Pyune's arm shot up, with something in it. "Get out!"

Wiley hastily shuffled backwards and through the doorway, but not before a shoe sailed across the room, just missing his head and reminding him of the biscuit she'd thrown at him so many years before.

~~~

Chapter 7

An April breeze as sweet as fresh-picked peaches swept down Main Street and whistled through the new church steeple. Last year's blizzard had toppled the original structure onto the pastor's car, and the church board had authorized replacing the ruined tower with a taller white sphere with copper trim, making The Church of Ivy Log whole again.

The pastor and B.T. left the parsonage and walked to The Boardinghouse, the young boy chattering faster than the squirrels that played on the sidewalk, his scuffed hands moving through the air as if leading a choir. "Ain't you afraid that there cat a yours will pee on everything?"

"Not Delilah. Delilah's a lady. She'd never do anything like that. What makes you think she would?"

The boy snickered. "I ain't never seen no cat that didn't pee on stuff. We had a cat one time peed all over mama's sewin' basket. She throwed the furry thang in the fireplace." He spit across the sidewalk. "Were a fire a going too."

The pastor cringed. "That so?"

"Sniddle-snot if it ain't," he said and skipped up the steps of The Boardinghouse.

"Hold on a minute. Let's see what Monday's lunch special is." The pastor studied the menu on the chalkboard nailed to the wall on the front porch. It wasn't Pyune's handwriting, and he wondered if it was Lizzie or Vallie who'd printed the hardly legible words. "Looks like meatloaf's the special today. You like meatloaf?"

"I like everything, 'cept liver. Liver's like eatin' puke and—"

"Whoa," said the reverend. "There are lots of fine folks inside, and we don't want to offend anyone with our language."

B.T. looked at the preacher as though he was the one who'd spoken out of line. "My language? I speak English."

"I know you do, but let's be a little more . . . genteel." B.T. gave the pastor a nonplussed look and the man quickly clapped him on the back and added, "You know—let's be gentlemenlike."

The Boardinghouse's oak door opened wide, and it seemed to William Johnson that half the folks in Ivy Log sat bellied up to the scattered wooden tables. Dr. Casteel waved from his chair. "Afternoon, Pastor."

The pastor nodded and headed toward the large round table in front of the bay window. Sam Cobb and Wiley Hanson sat together, their laughter heard above the conversations buzzing throughout the restaurant. "Who you got there?" asked Wiley, looking B.T. over from head to foot.

The pastor clasped the boy by his shoulder. "This is the young man I told you about. Full name's B.T. Hickel."

The pastor and B.T. sat at the table with Wiley and Sam. Lizzie came by right away, and everyone ordered the same thing—meatloaf and iced tea.

"So you're a Hickel," Wiley said after Lizzie took the order and poured the tea. "Don't reckon I know any Hickels."

"Well, welcome to Ivy Log," Sam said as he squinted and began studying the boy. Wiley chuckled to himself at Sam's too obvious inspection. *Okay, Sam, you're wondering why he's so skinny, why his ears are scuffed up, and who in the world cut his hair.* While he was being examined, the boy seemed lost, his eyes darting around the room as if looking for someone.

"Where you from," Sam asked after the longest time. Wiley remembered when Sam had told him about how lonely and neglected he'd felt during his youth, and he assumed that the boy's slow reaction was due to somber memories regarding his own upbringing.

"I'm from up in the mountains." B.T. said as he fingered a menu he'd taken from a holder on a ledge by the table.

"Where's up?"

"Pretty high," he said, raising his eyebrows.

Wiley grinned at Sam's questioning going nowhere and decided to give it a try. "Young fella, your place got a name?"

"Why, sure. It's Standing Indian Mountain."

"Standing Indian Mountain? Up in North Carolina a ways?"

"I reckon thereabouts."

"You come through the Chasteen Mountains?"

"'at's right. Say, how'd you know?"

"Hunted up there all my life. How'd you get to Ivy Log?"

"Walked. How else? Cain't fly." The boy licked his lips. "That meat-loaf ready?"

"Be here in a minute. You walked through the Nantahala forest all by yourself?"

"Heck, no. There was wolves and bears . . . and a few deer."

No one laughed as three sets of eyes stared at B.T. The young boy had traveled at least forty miles through difficult forest, probably followed Kimsey Creek to Deep Gap and on south to Ivy Log. *But why did he want to get to Ivy Log?* "Where's your family?" Wiley asked.

"I'm it. Me. B.T. Hickel." He scratched his head. "I'm tired a waitin' for that meatloaf."

Wiley hollered to Lizzie, who said, "Hold your horses. It's on the way." Lizzie backed through the swinging kitchen door, using her wide hips to make her way before she disappeared.

Wiley smiled at B.T. "Pretty hungry, huh?" He couldn't help but notice the boy's thin face and hollow cheeks. And the abrasions on his face could use some attention.

"Course I'm hungry. Pastor here cain't cook a lick, I guess."

William laughed and nodded. "He's absolutely right. If it weren't for Pyune, I'd starve."

"How'd you get those cuts around your face and ears?"

"Climbing a tree. Thought I heard something coming through the woods. But it weren't nothing but a flock of wild turkeys." He scratched his head again. "Probably got me some lice while I slept in them woods."

The boy's face turned to the window as he saw Paula Jennings walking down the sidewalk. He rose a few inches from his seat and peered through the window as she came closer. "I'll be danged," he said, his words husky. "Her hair's the same color as mine."

Wiley said under his breath, "I hope that's the only thing you two have in common."

~~~

Chapter 8

Paula Jennings charged through The Boardinghouse doors and right away spied Wiley, Will and Sam, all of them looking her way. She called out to Lizzie, who'd just stuck her head out of the kitchen, "Bring me some iced tea," and proceeded to click her way to what had been her table for over thirty years. She felt her skin bristle a little as she maneuvered around Wiley and plopped down. "Well, what have we here, a pow-wow about something?" She placed a napkin in her lap. "And just who is this young man?"

Wiley smiled at the boy and noticed his eyelashes were also red. "Why, this here is B.T. Hickel, from Standing Indian Mountain."

"That right?" She eyed the boy for a long moment, especially the whacked up red hair that jutted in all directions. "Who's your mama?"

B.T. seemed to study Paula, her face, her clothes, and especially her hair. "Mrs. Hickel."

"You don't say? She got a first name?"

"Mama."

Paula rolled her eyes. "Of course you call her mama, but what about her legal name, like Mary or Martha?"

The boy thought a moment, his gaze lifting up to the ceiling as if he was seriously considering Paula's question. "I reckon it would be Bernice. Yep, that's it, Bernice Hickel."

"Hmmmm. I'm thinking you've run away from home or something. You look to be about fourteen or so."

"I ain't run away from nowhere. But you got it right. I'm fourteen."

"Well, you must be running from something. You steal something from somebody?"

The boy flushed and glared at Paula. "Cain't a body just do what he wants?"

The pastor placed a hand on B.T.'s arm. "Hold on, Paula. There's no need to be so harsh. B.T.'s mama died, and he's here looking for his aunt."

"His aunt?" She turned to B.T. "Who's your aunt?"

"He doesn't know her name—but says he'd know her if he saw her," the pastor said.

"Well, Lordy, that's a crock. How come he can't contact the authorities and let them find her. Especially since he's evidently homeless."

B.T. threw his hands up in the air. "Ain't I ever gonna get some of that meatloaf?"

Wiley left his chair and hurried across the restaurant to the kitchen. He stuck his head inside and grabbed some biscuits. "Lizzie and Vallie, you better hurry up. We got a hungry boy out there. Where's that meatloaf?"

"Comin' right up," Lizzie said. "I had to make some more gravy and watch the cornbread." She wiped her hands on her apron, yanked open the oven door, and pulled out a tray of cornbread. It smelled a little burned and it was—more than a little.

Oh, my. Pyune will be gone five days. Five long days. Already he could see the major catastrophes waiting to happen. If he had to, he'd take over the kitchen and get things done the right way—or at least he'd try. "Lizzie, how about I get Pyune down here?"

Lizzie cut the cornbread and spread butter extra heavy on top to cover the burn. "That girl is packing, you leave her alone. Vallie and me got this just fine."

Wiley grabbed a plate of cornbread and a dish of jelly and returned to the table with everything, including some biscuits. "Here you go, fella. You fill up on biscuits and cornbread for a few minutes. That meatloaf is comin'."

Paula raised her voice. "I think I'll call the authorities and report this boy. He's either a runaway or running from something."

"You'll do no such thing," Sam said, giving her a sideway's glance. "The pastor has everything under control. He'll do whatever is necessary to help B.T."

Paula's face hardened. The fake black beauty mark above her

left eyebrow seemed to darken. "Well, the last time I checked, the parsonage was not a bed and breakfast."

"I can't believe you just said that." Sam put down his tea glass, a tenseness washing over him. "That's exactly what a church is—a place to seek refuge. And to feed the hungry." Sam's relationship with Paula had cooled. After her fierce resistance, which was really a prolonged attack waged against the hiring of a black pastor for the 147-year-old Church of Ivy Log, he'd found himself rethinking his feelings for her. It was true that they had been lovers a long time ago, but this and other major differences between the two had surfaced after his return to Ivy Log.

William Johnson, his voice calm, reached out and put his hand on B.T.'s shoulder. "I hereby make this boy an unofficial ward of the church . . . and of Ivy Log, for that matter. Together, we'll figure out what should be done regarding his future."

"Great idea, Pastor Will." Sam smiled around the table and turned to Wiley. "Why don't you and I go to Standing Indian Mountain and take the boy with us. We'll find out as much as we can about his home and any relatives who might be around."

"A ward of the church!" Paula yelped. "You can't do that without the board's approval." Paula threw her napkin on the table. "I'm calling a board meeting right now."

"You can do whatever you want," Pastor Johnson said. "But no board meeting is going to keep this boy from being fed and given a warm bed." The reverend squared his shoulders and leaned back in his chair.

Paula stood, her face flushed, her eyes flashing. In the florescent lighting, her turquoise eyeshadow glowed harsh, much like the words that came forth: "As long as I'm the chairperson of the board of directors of The Church of Ivy Log, there'll be no unilateral decisions made. Is that clear?"

Paula grabbed her handbag and headed for the door, leaving a wake of the worst huffiness this side of Chattanooga.

The table remained quiet for a few moments. Wiley cleared his throat. Sam rearranged his napkin. The pastor sipped his iced tea. And B.T.? "Where in all get out is my meatloaf?"

~~~

Chapter 9

Wiley drove Pyune to Atlanta on Tuesday morning. After a fitful night crying and stomping around her bedroom, she fell asleep at daylight. They left before noon and traveled in silence, a deep sigh every few minutes the only indication Pyune was awake. He took her to Macy's, and she spent well into the afternoon looking at dresses, skirts, blouses, pants, and jewelry. She stopped by the Estee-Lauder counter, and a make-up artist asked Pyune to sit for a glamour makeover she referred to as a movie star look.

Pyune hesitated before climbing onto the stool and giving the woman permission to turn her into anything. "What's a movie star look?" Pyune asked.

"A movie star look eez glamorous. You're just about there, but we need to get some color on your face. Your skin is absolutely perfect. And your cheekbones are fabulous." Pyune glanced in the mirror and saw nothing but plain and homey. But this woman was lovely, having sleeked-back blond hair, flawless skin, and lips as red as an overripe strawberry. And her foreign accent gave her an air of sophistication. German? French? Italian? She continued, "I promise you, if you'll let me put a little definition on your face, you'll stop traffic! You're a beautiful woman already, but you'll be an absolute knockout with the right coloration."

Pyune thought the woman just wanted to sell her make-up, and she was about to say no when Wiley moved next to her.

"Pyune, honey, what would it hurt to have this nice lady put some make-up on you? You're beautiful without it, just like she says, but wouldn't it be fun to go to New York City with some fancy-colored lipstick on those lovely lips of yours?" Wiley's words soothed her anxiety. He smiled at the blond woman. "This here lady is going to New York City for a big reception and awards ceremony." He patted Pyune on the shoulder. "I'll be back in an hour or so."

"Please don't go too far." Pyune's eyes became wide and expressed real fear.

Wiley hesitated and found himself tearing up. "I'll never go too far away from you." He squeezed her hand before meandering to the Macy's Men's Department and trying on some sport coats. He didn't buy one but the salesman didn't seem to mind, and Wiley found a belt that said, "Buy me."

The blond make-up artist's name was Celeste, her perfume French—Tocade by Rochas she told Pyune at her asking—and everything she did was skillful and professional, her perfectly manicured fingers pushing back Pyune's hair and smoothing soft creams onto her honey skin.

"Your skin is warm, like Italian skin," Celeste said. "Are you Italian?"

"Oh, no. My granddaddy was a Cherokee Indian."

"Oh, my. So that's why you have these lovely cheekbones and glorious brow lines. Have you ever been a photographer's model?"

Pyune twisted on the stool and looked up at Celeste, incredulous. "Goodness, no. I've never even been out of the mountains."

"Ah, my dear, I think you have come to the right place to get you ready for New York City." Celeste stepped in front of Pyune and lifted her chin with her long finger and studied her for a long minute. She smiled. "Now that the foundation is in place, shall we begin?"

Pyune nodded but wished once again that she'd stayed home.

~~~

Chapter 10

The skies above Atlanta were overcast, with thunder rumbling in the west as Wiley walked a few blocks down Peachtree Road after leaving the upscale mall at Lenox Square. A flag in front of an office building snapped loudly, while across the street rapidly increasing winds buffeted the ornate awning covering the entrance to a bookstore. Wiley stepped off the curb and crossed the street to a deli just in time to miss the big drops of rain that began hammering everything. The deli was crowded but he found a stool at the counter and pulled himself onto the red plastic seat.

"What ya havin'?" a large fellow with split front teeth asked, a white paper toque slipping on his very bald head as he wiped the counter in front of him.

Wiley could smell the beerwurst and corned beef. His mouth watering, he said, "How about a pastrami on rye—with lots of mustard."

"Comin' right up, and you put all the mustard you want to it," the big man said as he slid a mammoth squeeze bottle of French's toward Wiley. "What to drink?"

"I'm in Atlanta, so I believe I'll have me a Coca Cola."

Wiley smiled at the man before slowly twirling around on his stool and looking around the deli. The two big glass windows across the front pinged with rain, and the sound of hail soon followed. In what seemed like just seconds to Wiley, the noise became loud and he watched an awning fly down the street, perhaps from the very bookstore he'd just passed, the wind whipping the metal framework along like tumbleweed. "Would you look at that?" he hollered to the guy behind the counter. "And there goes somebody's umbrella."

The counterman walked closer to the window and said to everyone within earshot, "Y'all, I ain't believing this. It's like a tornado out there." At that moment the deli went dark, all mechanical sounds grinding down to nothing, the only noise provided by the storm. "Good Lord!" the man said, "I think y'all better duck under something." Wiley stepped away from his stool, ready to take cover under a table—regardless of who was sitting at it. But after a few tense minutes the storm ended, and other than the power still being out everything else was okay.

Wiley went back to his seat. He was staring out the picture windows behind him when he heard a plate rattle on the counter. "Here ya go, bud," the man wearing the paper hat said.

Wiley sat in the deli, which was illuminated by the light passing through the front windows, watching the now light rain and eating his pastrami sandwich. He'd overdone the mustard, and it squeezed out from the rye bread and stuck to the corners of his mouth. He wiped it away, not remembering when he'd been this happy. A pastrami sandwich fixed all problems, cured all ills, and made his stomach jump for joy.

The rain eased into a light drizzle, fast-moving clouds opening a little and revealing a piece of lonesome blue sky. Soon as the rain quit, Wiley left the deli and crossed the street and walked back to Macy's, a tune in his head. Something about beautiful brown eyes. He thought of Pyune. The rain-swept streets glistened as the sun spread an orange glow across this beautiful section of Atlanta known as Buckhead.

He was forty-eight years old, a mountain man who possessed a Ph.D he'd earned from right down the street, but in another life, a life he called his city life. He'd gone back to the mountains. Back to the mountains where he'd been born. When he was a little boy he told his mama he wanted to be a mountain, standing tall over the land, hearing the wind blowing through the trees and listening to the magic words of the rocks. At forty-eight, he still wanted to be a mountain and sometimes had dreams in which he'd leave his body and float above the high peaks and watch the earth below. He chased the icy streams and galloped on the backs of deer, all the while singing in a language only he knew.

He thought he knew love. Love was what made the heart swell with happiness and created that little tingle in a person's chest that was called giddiness. He got that when he was around Pyune. A giddiness that made him want to pick her up and take her with him when he left the mountains and floated through the clouds. How could he be complete without the woman who made him feel this way?

Marry me. That's what he would say to her. *Marry me,* and let's spend the rest of our lives together. We'll fish for trout in Kiutuestia Creek. Afterwards we can snuggle in my grand-pappy's old feather bed and make love until sunup. Yes, that was the way it was supposed to be. When Pyune returned from New York, he'd ask her to marry him.

He returned to Macy's, and no one seemed the slightest bit affected by the bad weather. Power had stayed on, the mall's generators apparently making sure of that, and he found Pyune still sitting at the make-up counter, her back to him and with a beautiful green scarf now tied atop her shoulders. Catching sight of her like this, he couldn't breathe, a hand pressing his chest, a ringing sensation filling his ears. Just then, as if she could see from the back of her head, she spun around to him. A smile spread across a movie star's face, a face that could have been on the cover of Cosmopolitan or Allure. Large gold hoop earrings sparkled in the light as they dangled from her ears, and a gold herringbone necklace hung elegantly around her neck.

He was tongue-tied when he reached her, muttering, "You . . . I . . . Pyune! You . . . look amazing!"

Pyune dipped her chin and stared up at him. "I'm glad you recognized me."

He lifted his hand, and with one finger slowly circled her soft cheeks and then her lips. "Watch out New York City. Here comes Pyune EverSweet Murphy."

~~~

Chapter 11

Wiley insisted on paying for Pyune's glamour makeover, and arm in arm they walked slowly to their hotel, which was directly across the street from the mall. Along the way he hummed a favorite tune of his: "You were in my arms, right where you belong . . . and we were so in love . . . it was almost like a song."

Later, from their hotel window, Atlanta's skyline sat along a peach-colored horizon as the April sun eased its last rays behind the hills to the west. In the east, a new quarter moon chased the night, along with Jupiter and the pinprick stars of God's great universe. The storm had left the air cool and clean and the sky devoid of clouds. They made love and were asleep by half-past nine. But at the very stroke of midnight Pyune sat straight up in bed and proclaimed, "I am *not* going to New York!"

~~~

Chapter 12

B ut she did. Her plane left a few minutes late, at 7:20 that morning., soaring into the misty gray Atlanta haze. It headed due east, took a gentle turn north, and followed the coastline of the Atlantic, leaving behind all she had known. She trembled when she looked out the window and saw the tiny specks of cars and trees and scattered lakes, which sat like ill-shaped pancakes along the edges of valleys and endless pastures. She held her breath, certain her life would never be the same.

In their hotel room, Wiley had soothed her as she wailed with her face in a pillow, her back shaking with sobs: "Okay, okay. Stay. I'll take you back to Ivy Log, and you can pick up where you left off—in your tiny town in the Appalachian mountains."

"And just what's wrong with my tiny town in the Appalachian mountains?"

"Not a thing. Not a dang thing." Wiley turned out the light and pulled her close. "But here's what I'm gettin' at. When I left the mountains and went to school, I was just like you. Scared of anything new. But, later, I was so glad I did what I did—because I came back a better man. Things became clear to me about who I was. It was a life experience. And that's what I want for you. Think of it as an adventure outside of Ivy Log." He paused and rubbed her back. "Just think of the things you can tell your grandchildren."

"My grandchildren?" She flipped on the light that Wiley had just shut off.

"That's what I said, Pyune. Your grandchildren." He pulled her under the covers and made love to her again.

~~~

Chapter 13

Bakers' World Magazine functioned under the umbrella of a huge media conglomerate, TWS, which focused on commercial broadcasting, publishing, and television production, with most of its operations in the United States. However, with a market cap of $30 billion, TWS's many business ventures stretched far and wide. Robert D. Larson, president and CEO of the company, was also its majority shareholder. Its headquarters were located in midtown Manhattan.

Bakers' World Magazine was the whim of Robert Larson's wife, Tess. But while Tess Starling Larson's husband may have called her idea for taking over the struggling magazine a lark, Mrs. Larson referred to it as her baby. From day one, ten years earlier, she oversaw the pages one by one, always with the same care as if designing the circuitry for a rocket to the moon. Her gut was her guide, and her uncanny feel for what women liked and wanted had boosted the magazine to the top echelon of all food- and cooking-related publications. To her, the success formula for the magazine was simple—engage the magazine's readers, who, just like herself, were women.

"Good morning, Ms. Starling," her administrative assistant, Linda Richardson, said as she hurried from her desk and handed Tess a handful of messages.

Tess took the notes and said, "Thank you," and nothing more. But when she reached the doorway to her office she turned back to Linda. "Today's the day our contest winner arrives, right?"

"Oh, yes. Miss Murphy's flight lands at ten after nine at La-Guardia. Frandy is of course meeting her."

Tess smiled. "Very good. Be sure all goes well."

"Yes, of course." As soon as the door closed to Tess's office, Linda checked to see if the flight from Atlanta was on time. Their limo driver, Frandy, would already be on his way if not already at the airport. For years Frandy had ferried celebrity guests to TWS's towering glass building, always assuring their safe arrival through the busy streets of New York City. He was known for his affable personality, which after his handsome face and brilliant white teeth was the other thing everyone remembered about him. How could they not? His lilting Jamaican patois had cajoled many a curmudgeon into loving New York City almost as much as he did.

"Frandy, I just checked flights," Linda said after calling him on his cell. "Looks like Ms. Murphy's plane from Atlanta is on time. You well on your way?" Linda was from a small town in central Ohio; a tough, attractive blonde who was efficient and trustworthy, and more than anything loyal to a fault to Tess Starling Larson. She had worked at TWS for twenty-two years, and in ten years of being Tess's right hand from the very first day she took the reins of the magazine, not once had she ever called her by her first name. It was always "Ms. Starling," and in the presence of Mr. Larson she referred to her "Mrs. Larson."

"I be very early, Miss Linda, for flight one zero seven three" Frandy said from his dash-phone hookup as he eased the limo into traffic and crossed the Brooklyn Bridge and onto the Queens Expressway. He was listening to 93.5 WVIP and thumped his fingers on the steering wheel as the reggae music bounced off the limo's windows.

"Turn down that noise!" Linda yelled into her phone as she brushed her hair away from her forehead and looked at a list she always made whenever a VIP came to visit. "Did you get the sign I left in the lobby for you?" she asked after the music quieted.

"Sure did. The one that reads 'Free Sex.' Oh, and I noticed it has your phone number." Frandy's laughter came bellowing over the phone. "I'll hold that sign up real high so everybody can see it. You gonna be one busy girl, Linda!" Again, the laughter rolled.

"Frandy, would you please straighten up? I'm going to get

you for sexual harassment one of these days." She couldn't help herself and laughed. She checked her watch. "If you're just getting on the Queens Expressway, you've got just thirty minutes to make it to the terminal. I don't want Miss Murphy to be looking for you. There's a tour of Bakers' World scheduled for one and a small reception with employees in the conference room on the twenty-ninth floor at two. Call me just before you get back here. I'll meet you in the lobby."

"Ah, don't worry, Miss Linda. Frandy do this just fine. Miss Murphy no different than any other Bakers' World celebrity." Frandy increased his speed and the limo whizzed over Astoria Boulevard and down the exit ramp to LaGuardia.

Linda had to give him something in return for his earlier insolence: "Did you wear a clean suit? Tie? Cap?"

"Sure did. Frandy good-looking as they come, Miss Linda. You never have to worry about Frandy."

"What about your name tag?"

"On my lapel as we speak!" He turned up the radio and sang along to Bob Marley's "No, Woman, No Cry."

Linda sighed. "You remember the time you were supposed to pick up Jennifer Lopez for her interview—and you didn't recognize her? How embarrassing was that for TWS? Be a good boy and make a good impression for us. Please."

"Oh, Miss Linda, I always make a good impression. I be handsome, I be so smart, I be so tall and lovely. Frandy deliver Miss Murphy right on time."

~~~

The long, sleek MD 88 readied for landing, approaching from the southeast toward LaGuardia. The skies were clear, a light wind from the west. Beneath the airplane, New York City spread out like an out of control garden—buildings and roads touching each other as if multiplying into the horizon. The landing gear clanked into place and the plane descended toward the runway.

From Row 34, Seat A, Pyune gasped. Her stomach flip-flopped and her mouth became dry. She leaned her head back on her seat and closed her eyes. She had grasped Wiley's hand at the security gate. "I'll call you as soon as I land," she'd said, a hush of words that came out breathless and weak. "You'll be back in Ivy Log by the time I land, right?"

Wiley had squeezed her hand. "Yep. I'll be sittin' at The Boardinghouse and eatin' lunch, you can bet on that. Guess Lizzie and Vallie are busy in the kitchen right now."

Pyune's eyes filled with tears. "This isn't easy, Wiley. I just want to get my money and come back home."

Wiley rubbed her shoulder. "You'll get your money all right, but best of all you'll have the time of your life. You'll be like one of those butterflies inside a cocoon just waitin' to come out. You'll never forget this."

That's what I'm afraid of. And she'd retained those same dire thoughts throughout the entire flight.

~~~

The tires screeched as they hit the tarmac, followed by a swoosh of air and then a quick slowdown and turn toward the gate. Seat belts clicked open, and passengers stepped into the aisles. Pyune, however, sat still as a statue, unable to move no matter how hard she tried. Her body felt like lead, and she experienced a shortness of breath that made her think she was going to faint. She heard her heart beat in her ears, and a fog of hot air surrounded her as well.

Leaning toward her, a flight attendant smiled. "Everything okay?"

"Yes, I'm fine," Pyune managed. "Just a little nervous."

"The plane's about empty, so let me help you." The woman reached out and took Pyune by the arm.

"I . . . I'm okay." She stood on wobbly legs but followed the flight attendant down the aisle without faltering.

On the way to the front of the plane, the woman chattered about something Pyune didn't understand. But just before Pyune was to step onto the portable walkway, she said, "You look familiar. I'm thinking I've seen you before—maybe on one of those soap operas." She laughed. "Sorry. I know you celebrities like your privacy."

Celebrity? "I . . . no, this is my first time in New York City."

"Really? You'll love New York City."

Pyune forced a smile out of courtesy, doubting her immensely. Her ticket was stuck in a pocket on her purse. It had popped up and she pushed it back.

"I see you have a claim check. Just follow the signs to Baggage Claim." She smiled warmly. "You're going to do just fine, dear."

Pyune felt herself relax a little. She found Baggage Claim, spotted Delta Flight 1073 on a digital readout above a carousel, and waited for her luggage—just as Wiley had told her to do.

The Bakers' World instructions had explained that she should look for someone holding up a sign with her name on it. Her eyes swept the baggage area, and sure enough, across the way, she spotted a tall, dark-skinned man with a big grin on his face, holding up a sign: "Ms. Murphy, BWM." He was scanning the crowd, nodding, smiling, winking, waving, shuffling his feet. She found him amusing, acting like a windup toy, grinding out movements that would attract the attention of anyone passing by.

Pyune followed the carousel around until she located the borrowed deep-purple suitcase. She'd decided to take just this one piece of luggage. She lugged it off the deck, pulled out the rollers, and headed for the man who held up the sign. She approached him and watched his smile fade, until his mouth hung open; the sign, as if once alive, virtually wilted by his side.

"You've got to be kidding," he blurted. "This some kind of joke, right?" He backed up a step and stared at the petite and now very frightened Pyune.

Pyune stuttered. "I . . . I . . . is there a problem?" *Oh, why couldn't Wiley be here?*

Frandy slowly shook his head. "Please, madam, you must excuse me just a minute. I must make a phone call." The sign with her name on it disappeared into a large trashcan by the door as Frandy traipsed outside, tapping two numbers into his phone. Once outside the terminal, he barked at Linda when she answered her phone, "You playing a funny joke, right?"

"I don't know what you're talking about. What's going on?"

"Ha! Like *I* know."

"Are you at the airport?"

"Of course Frandy is at the airport."

"Miss Murphy arrive?"

"Yes, Miss Murphy has arrived."

"Then what's the problem?"

"Linda, you are just so funny! I be downtown in about forty

minutes. Then you can see for yourself soon enough." He hung up, took a deep breath, and walked back inside the terminal. He stopped by the trashcan and retrieved the sign with Pyune's name on it. He held it with his long fingers and shook his head slowly before stuffing it back in the can and heading her way.

Bewildered, Pyune wanted to shrink and die. The noise in the airport hammered her ears as the rush of people seemed to suck the air from her lungs. To make things worse, she had lost sight of the driver. She stood on her tiptoes and looked for the black suit and the tall dark man who wore it. He had abandoned her. She would indeed be going right home.

However, from behind her, she felt a soft touch on her shoulder. She turned and Frandy lowered his chin to her. "Miss Murphy, let me take your luggage, and please follow me."

Pyune did as she was asked, trailing the purple suitcase and the tall black man, whose shoulders slumped as he trudged to his limousine as though walking in quicksand.

~~~

Chapter 14

They sped along the expressway, New York City coming in gi-
ant waves, each one taller and wider than its predecessor,
every glass and concrete and steel building spiking higher into
the sky. She watched as each object on the ground moved—
wheels, feet, hands, arms, legs, flags, lights, mouths—all in constant motion. Pyune felt dizzy as the limo glided along. Frandy
kept looking at her in the rearview mirror, which unnerved her
even more. She wanted to talk to him, but the raised glass partition between the front and rear seats made this a fruitless idea.

She noticed how Frandy's eyes darted into the backseat and
onto her face, but every time she made eye contact he would
look away. She reached in her handbag and pulled out a small
mirror. She had applied her makeup exactly as the Estee Lauder
consultant had shown her, worn the large gold earrings and
necklace and brushed her hair upward into a sleek French twist.

So why wouldn't Frandy look at her? No blood was coming
out of her eyes, and she didn't have fangs for teeth. She looked
up again and there he was, staring at her but quickly averting
her eyes the moment hers found his.

She returned her mirror to her handbag and pulled out her
phone. It was a good time to call Wiley. She pressed in his number and in just two rings he answered, "Well, hot dang, you
made it okay." There was laughter in his voice.

"Yes, I did." she said softly. "I'm in a limo, on my way to Bakers' World headquarters."

"My, my. You're in New York City and all in one piece. How

do you feel? How is everything?"

"I feel fine. Everything is just fine." She had rehearsed the words over and over. *Everything is just fine. No problems. Just give me my money and put me back on the plane.*

"Well, I sure as heck miss you," Wiley said. "And so does everybody in Ivy Log."

"I miss you, too, Wiley, and tell everybody I said 'hey.' I'll call you later, when I find out what time my 'Today Show' interview is tomorrow. Goodbye." She hung up before Wiley could ask another question, before he heard her voice tremble, before she begged him to come get her.

~~~

Chapter 15

The lunch crowd at The Boardinghouse had thinned out. Lizzie and Vallie plopped themselves into the weathered rocking chairs on the front porch, where they watched an afternoon shower sweep the pollen off the rails of the porch and color the puddles yellow. Farther down Main Street, the American flag snapped to attention in what had become a brisk wind, the standard's red and blue colors deepened by the rain.

Vallie lifted the edge of her apron and wiped her brow. Her curly gray hair, damp and in ringlets, drooped onto her forehead. Her cheeks, flushed and puffy, glistened. "You reckon there was too much salt in that pot a beans, Lizzie?"

"I'm a thinkin' so. But I don't believe nobody complained, though. You hear somebody sayin' somethin'?"

"Not a word. I think they was just so shocked that the carrot salad had so much mayonnaise in it, they was just speechless." Vallie reached in her apron pocket and pulled out a fresh bottle of Formula 44. "We got to do better tomorrow. Pyune done trusted us, and we cain't even salt the beans." She screwed the top off the bottle and tilted it upward.

Lizzie watched her friend lick her lips after a long swig. "How come you always have a cold, Vallie? Seems to me you drink too much of that stuff."

Vallie grinned and twisted the top back in place. "You really ought to try this. You do, you won't never cough again. Why, with all this here pollen in the air along with everything else, if I don't have my Formula 44, I cain't even swaller half the time."

Lizzie scrunched up her face. "How much of that stuff do you drink?"

Vallie leaned back in her rocker and closed her eyes, a smile tickling the corners of her mouth. "As much as I want, Lizzie. As much as I want."

They rocked in silence while the rain tapered off. Lizzie looked at her watch. "It's about time for my soap opera. You gonna watch it with me?"

"Now why would I want to watch those folks do the things they do? Why, they're immoral folks on them shows. They do things they ought not to do."

"Like what?" Her words hadn't come out too sweetly, and she slapped Vallie's arm good-naturedly.

"Oh, Lizzie. Life ain't like that show. Them people is livin' in a fairy tale. You don't see none a that stuff goin' on here in Ivy Log."

Vallie took another sip of her "medication." Lizzie watched a mockingbird bathe in a puddle, its wings fluttering wildly.

Suddenly, Lizzie puffed up. "Course they's stuff like that going on in this here place. Reckon you done forgot about Paula."

Vallie stopped rocking. "What about Paula?"

"Woman, get your head outta the sand! They's stuff going on right here in Ivy Log—just like in them soap operas."

Vallie, huffing and sputtering, sat up in her rocker. "Well, if there is, I sure don't want to know about it."

"That's 'cause you're always sippin' your Formula 44." Lizzie laughed and propped her feet on the railing. "Yes, ma'am, we got our own little soap opera right here in Ivy Log."

Vallie narrowed her eyes at her friend. "So, you gonna tell me about it?"

~~~

Chapter 16

Wiley slipped his phone in his shirt pocket, the call from Pyune way too short. He'd wait until she called again to ask her more questions about her trip to the big city.

Across from him, Sam Cobb fiddled with the newspaper from Blairsville— The North Georgia News. He looked up and said to Wiley, "I think I'm going to establish a newspaper here in Ivy Log—you know, a little weekly paper that covers the north side of the county. What do you think?"

"A newspaper for Ivy Log?" Wiley squeezed lemon juice into his iced tea. "What have we got to write about in Ivy Log?"

"Why, I've been back home for five, almost six months now, and there's news everywhere." He ran his hand over his fore-head, as if for inspiration, and his eyes got wide. "What about you flying off the side of Rabbit Top? And Ivy Log's new preacher? Adela and Frank getting hitched and their long hon-eymoon in Europe is big news for us folks."

"News? Do you mean gossip or real news?" Wiley looked out the window and watched Lizzie and Vallie rocking furiously, their mouths going at the same speed.

"Real news but also human interest stories about the people in Ivy Log. Maybe an editorial column where opinions can be voiced. We've got a national election coming up this year, you know?"

"Oh, Ivy Log's got lots of opinions, that's for sure." Wiley eased out of his chair. "Be right back. I want some pie. Want a piece?"

Sam shook his head. "I'll pass."

Wiley returned with a slice of lemon meringue pie, the meringue a little wobbly and browned too much. He stuck his fork in it and the filling slipped all over the plate and onto the table, oozing toward Sam. "Dang it! I see why you didn't want any pie. Who made this meringue?" He stared out the window at Lizzie and Vallie.

Sam laughed and reached over with his fork and pushed the squiggly slab of meringue back toward Wiley. "Like I said, I'll pass."

Wiley wiped his mouth. "What about this newspaper? What would you call it?"

Sam rubbed his chin. "How about The Ivy Log Reporter. It'll come out every Wednesday."

"Okay. But what do you know about running a newspaper?"

"Not a dang thing. I can learn, though."

Wiley laughed. "I know one thing you can put in your newspaper."

"What's that?"

Wiley leaned forward, his voice dropping to a near whisper: "I'd like to know who that redheaded boy is." He took a moment to let Sam finish a sip of his iced tea. "You reckon his long-lost aunt is really anywhere around here? or if he even has an aunt he's lookin' for?"

"Why don't we run up to Standing Indian Mountain tomorrow, take the boy with us, poke around a little bit?"

"Good idea." Wiley pushed the sorry excuse for lemon meringue pie farther away from him. "I hate to admit it, but Paula's right, we need to alert the authorities at some point. He's underage—and homeless. I'm sure it won't matter if the pastor and the church oversee his well bein' for a while, but sooner or later we've got to find out who he is and figure out somethin' permanent."

"I don't disagree with that at all. Just wish we could find his aunt—if he has one. Maybe our trip up the mountain will give us something to work with. Let's run this by Will and see what he thinks."

Wiley nodded. "One thing's for sure. The red hair on that boy is a dead giveaway to who's in his family."

"Really? His red hair is the clue to his family connection?"

"That's exactly what I'm sayin'."

"Well, heck, if that's so, then Paula could be his aunt!"

Wiley hadn't considered that and broke into a guffaw. He calmed himself and said, "That's true, but he's seen Paula and didn't do anything beyond ogling her. Here's the thing." Wiley pulled closer to the table. "That boy says he's looking for his aunt. Says he doesn't know her name but would recognize her if he saw her. All we got to do is take him around these parts, and he's bound to find her if she's for real."

"And we start at Standing Indian Mountain?"

"I'd say so. Even if we end up right back here."

The front doors of The Boardinghouse swung open. Lizzie and Vallie, with their aprons wrapped around their ample bodies, each fell into a fit of laughter when they saw Sam and Wiley.

"What's so funny?" asked Wiley.

Lizzie's fat face beamed. "That meringue—it's alive, ain't it? Why, we fought that stuff all mornin'. You got to be a juggler to git it on a fork." Both ladies waddled into the kitchen, their laughter surrounding them like a too-tight corset.

Wiley watched them go off and shook his head. "Maybe we should close this place down until Pyune gets back."

Sam didn't argue.

~~~

Chapter 17

Frandy took the Queens Midtown Tunnel, the ramp to East 37th, right on 3rd Avenue and left on East 45th. The dividing window in the limo slid down as Frandy once again glanced in his rearview mirror. "We're about there, Miss Murphy. Just a few more minutes." The offensive glass rode up before Pyune had a chance to respond.

The limo slowed at Broadway and 56th Street, where Bakers' World Magazine was located. A gleaming 32-story building, with a parking garage underneath, housed the 732 employees of TWS's New York operation. Bakers' World Magazine occupied the top five floors, which included the penthouse set of offices on the 31st floor where Tess Starling Larson and her elite group of subeditors and production teams worked. Accounting was on the 28th floor, publishing on the 29th floor, and the Bakers' World kitchens, conference rooms and auditorium were situated on the 30th floor. The 32nd floor housed the massive apartment Tess and her husband, Robert, enjoyed. This floor was strictly off limits to anyone but Tess and "Robbie," as she affectionately called him.

The limo eased into its designated parking space next to the elevators. Frandy opened the car door for Pyune and waited until she stepped out and into the garage. "We can leave your luggage in the car for now. Miss Richardson is in the lobby waiting for you." His words were formal, almost aloof, his eyes wandering everywhere but on her. He nodded his head slightly and headed to the elevator.

Pyune dutifully followed Frandy. She had to hurry to catch up with his long strides, her eyes on his shiny, black, patent-leather shoes, at least a size 12, as he raced to the elevator.

The elevator opened to a lobby ceiling that soared high into the air, the spacious area sparkling with glass and chrome. A sprawling aviary housed trees and plants and dozens of colorful, flitting birds, their little bodies zooming through the air as if chased by flying cats. Through the thick glass of the lobby walls, the hubbub of pedestrian traffic was silent, the traffic noiseless. A bell dinged on a set of elevators across the lobby. Pyune turned to see a short blonde, about her age she guessed, step into the lobby. She wore a dark business suit and held a clip-board.

When the woman looked her way, Pyune caught her eyes as they widened along with her mouth. As she walked slowly in her direction, the woman's gaze never left Pyune's. The closer she got, the wider her eyes became. A smile, ever so slightly, formed on her thin lips, followed by a look of utter confusion. The woman glanced back and forth between Pyune and Frandy.

"Miss Murphy?" she asked, her words froglike, needing oil.

Pyune smiled and held out her hand. "Yes, I am. It's so nice to meet you."

Frandy stepped back a few steps and folded his arms, rocking back and forth on his heels, a little squeak from his shoes the only sound in the awkward moments that followed.

Linda opened her mouth but no words came out, as if they would not form in her throat and pass her tongue and her lips and fall upon Pyune's ears. The efficient Midwesterner, who was the right hand of Tess Starling, stood paralyzed, squeezing the clipboard as if it were a life preserver and she was drowning in the waters of a very rough ocean.

Pyune found herself trembling. There was something wrong, very wrong! Was she not the winner of the Bakers' World Magazine recipe contest? Did she not fly to New York City at the magazine's behest to receive the $25,000 check? Was she not going to be on "The Today Show"? Was she not going to attend a grand reception to be held in her honor?

A bird squawked noisily above them. The air in the lobby seemed freezing cold, as though they had been transported to Antarctica. Frandy, the affable Frandy, leaned toward Linda and whispered too loudly, as Pyune could make out every word: "Oh, yeah. Knew it would be like this. Uh, huh. Saw this coming. Sure did." He grinned wide, showing his enormous white teeth. "Thing is, Miss Linda, what we do now?"

The spell broken, Linda grasped Pyune's arm. "Come. We have to talk."

~~~

Chapter 18

The walls in the parsonage study were lined with shelves that sagged from the weight of many books. The former pastor, Adelpheus Cobb, reined for more than forty years at The Church of Ivy Log. His impressive knowledge of theology was evident in the pulpit each and every Sunday morning. He had devoured the church's library as though it were a feast—and he had been eternally starving. After the death of the illustrious preacher, when William Johnson arrived as the new pastor he was delighted by the library at his fingertips. The lamp on his desk burned long into many nights as he voraciously read from books that begged to be opened once again.

Sam Cobb, who was the deceased pastor's only child, waited in the parsonage's study, his feet propped on the desk while the reverend made coffee. Wiley sat opposite and rubbed Delilah's sleek fur. The cat purred and arched her back, occasionally turning her body around and looking at Wiley as if he were there to do her biding—and slacking off.

Pastor Johnson returned with three coffees and eased into the worn leather chair he'd inherited from Adelpheus Cobb. His duties as prelate of The Church of Ivy Log were widespread, but he never dreamed he would serve Sam and Wiley coffee. To put more pressure on him, they asked if he had some cookies or something sweet to eat.

"Heck, no. Go over to The Boardinghouse if you want something to eat."

Wiley's head came back. "Pastor, are you kidding? When we

saw the meringue on Lizzie and Vallie's lemon pie, we decided to get us a candy bar from the gas station for dessert." Wiley dumped two teaspoons of sugar in his coffee and stirred slowly. At least the pastor had cream and sugar.

Sam laughed and blew into his cup. "Wiley's right. It's not quite the same over there with Pyune gone and all."

Pastor Johnson swiveled around in his chair and reached for the bookshelf behind him. He pulled out a book and handed it to Sam. "Found this cookbook the other day. It was your mom's. Her name's written inside the front cover, along with the date."

Sam flipped the cover back and read the inscription: Erma Jean Terry (Cobb) April 26, 1942. "Oh, my. This was before she was married." He turned the pages. "Her handwriting is all over the place."

The pastor nodded. "It's quite a keepsake. I hope you'll take it with you."

Sam was quiet for a moment. "My mom was a good cook. I liked her hushpuppies."

"That recipe is in there—on a card in the back."

"That right?" Sam flipped through the pages and found a yellowed index card stuck near the rear of the book. He studied it a moment and read out loud: "One cup self-rising flour, one cup cornmeal, two eggs slightly beaten, two tablespoons sugar, one teaspoon salt, one-half teaspoon baking soda, one-quarter cup chopped onion, one cup buttermilk." His words were soft as he gently touched the edge of the card. "Maybe I can give this to Pyune and she can make these hushpuppies at a Friday night fish fry."

"She'd do that in a minute," said Wiley, nudging Delilah from his lap and onto the floor.

The window in the study was open, the April air sweet with the flowering jasmine that ran up a large oak shading the parsonage. Across the yard, B.T. had his legs wrapped around a rope swing, the same one that Sam had played on as a boy.

Sam watched the rope swing past the window and then back again. "What about the boy, Will? You got any ideas?"

He closed his bible and propped his feet beside Sam's. "I'd like for us to help him find his family. That aunt of his must be somewhere in the area. I don't think he'd make up a story like that, especially since he just about killed himself getting here.

Only wish we knew her name."

"Sam and I thought we'd ride up to Standing Indian Mountain and see what we could find. Want to go too?"

"Nah. You two run up there on your own. I'll stay here and keep an eye on The Boardinghouse." Delilah jumped in his lap. "I assume you'll be taking B.T. with you."

Wiley stood and drank the last of his coffee. "I'm thinkin' he'll be able to show us around a bit. Not too many folks live up that way. From what B.T. says, he'd go months without seeing anybody except his mama."

"Can't get too much out of that boy," Sam said. "Seems to be in a world all his own."

Wiley opened his wallet and pulled out a card. "This here card has the number of the sheriff of Union County. Went to college with him. Could be we'll end up making some inquiries through him." He handed the card to the pastor.

While passing the card back to Wiley, the pastor caught the blur of B.T. as the boy and the rope passed the window. "You got plenty of money on you?"

Wiley found himself going through his wallet. "Some. Why?"

"Because that boy is hungry—all the time. And if you don't feed him, he gets quite irritable."

"That's no problem. We'll keep him fed." Wiley put his wallet back into his pocket. "See you later, William."

"We'll check in with you when we get back." Sam tucked his mother's cookbook under his arm.

"Hold up," said the pastor, not looking at them, rubbing his chin as if in deep thought. "There's one other thing I should mention."

Both Wiley and Sam hesitated at the doorway. "What's that?" Wiley asked.

William started to speak but paused and smiled. "Oh, nevermind. You'll find out soon enough."

"What? Why can't you tell us?" Wiley saw the swing pass the window again, B.T. hanging on, grinning, and wearing floppy socks, likely given to him by the pastor.

"It's, ah . . . rather delicate." Will turned and began straightening a bookshelf that didn't seem to need it.

"Delicate?" Sam asked. "What the heck does that mean?" Sam and Wiley exchanged glances.

Will turned and eyed his friends. "Trust me. You'll know very quicklike."

Sam and Wiley shrugged and left the study. Once outside the parsonage, Sam hollered, "B.T., we're heading up to Standing Indian Mountain. Maybe we can find a Dairy Queen somewhere along the way. Get your boots on."

The boy jumped from the swing, jammed his feet in his boots and walked toward them, his face sweaty, his hair resembling a bale of forked hay. "What's a Dairy Queen?"

Wiley squinted at B.T. "You ain't never been to a Dairy Queen?"

"Not that I knowed of."

"Then maybe this'll be a first," Wiley said.

Wiley's new red truck pulled down the parsonage's driveway. Wiley and Sam sat in the front and B.T. in the seat behind them.

From Main Street and onto Highway 129, the truck headed north and crossed into North Carolina, past the town of Murphy and up into the Appalachians. The ride was quiet, a Hank Williams song playing on WKRK, ". . . your cheatin' heart will tell on you."

Suddenly Wiley hollered, his hand flying to the window button as he glanced over his shoulder at B.T. "Good God Almighty, did you have to do that?"

Sam hit the button on his window. The mountain air rushed in as he leaned his head out, but it wasn't enough. "Pull over, Wiley. I got to get out . . . of this truck."

Wiley braked hard, the tires not catching the gravel on the side of the road very well as the vehicle zigzagged to a stop. Both men were out of the truck in no time, gasping for fresh air.

"What the . . . ." Wiley observed B.T. looking through his window, which he'd left rolled up, a big smile on his face, his teeth protruding as if in defiance.

Both men glared at B.T. Wiley shook his head. "Delicate? They ain't nothing delicate about it." He cleared his throat. "We got to do something about that—or he's gonna ride in the truck bed the whole way up and back."

~~~

Chapter 19

"**A** where do you think you're going?" Linda skidded to a stop at the elevator and looked up at Frandy. There was no smile on her face.

Frandy shrugged. "Thought maybe you might need Frandy." He hung his head and straightened his cap. His nametag was crooked, and Linda reached up and smoothed it.

"I'll call you if I need you. Just stay nearby. Go have some lunch or something." Linda turned and entered the elevator, her hand still grasping Pyune's arm.

The two women rode silently to the 29th floor. They walked down the long hall from the elevators, Linda holding Pyune close to her side. They seemed to be the only two people on the floor, an eerie quiet preceding the talk Linda was going to have with Pyune. They reached a conference room that sat tucked in a corner, a view of the city stretching out across Central Park.

"Have a seat, Miss Murphy." Linda sat across from her, a gleaming walnut conference table, polished to a rich shine, separating them. Linda placed her clipboard on the table, where a pitcher of fresh water and several glasses had been neatly arranged on a tray.

Linda took a sip of water and began: "Miss Murphy, I apologize for my . . . my rather—" she searched for words, her eyes roaming around the room and then back to Pyune— "my rather abrupt reception in the lobby."

Pyune nodded without understanding anything.

"Perhaps you and I can figure this out between us," Linda

said, her words softer.

"I'm very confused," Pyune said, leaning forward in her chair —and waiting. What they had to figure out, she had no idea. She just knew, from the moment she'd arrived, something was not at all right.

"When I first saw you, I thought a joke was being played on me. Now, I realize this is no joke."

"What is *no* joke?" Pyune wrinkled her brow, not at all liking the way this conversation was going and not caring if she sounded a little tart.

"Miss Murphy, you are the spitting image of Tess Starling."

"Excuse me? What are you saying?"

Linda took a deep breath. "Miss Murphy . . . may I call you Pyune?"

Pyune lifted her chin, her eyes wide and questioning. "Of course."

"Pyune, except for the hairstyles and subtle differences in make-up, you and Tess Starling, the head of Bakers' World Magazine, are identical twins, even in height. What I'm trying to figure out is *how*?"

"Identical? I—"

Linda's phone chirped. She took it out of her purse and read a text. "That was Miss Starling, wanting to know if you arrived safely." She pressed the microphone and spoke into the phone. "Miss Murphy arrived safely and is preparing for a tour after a quick lunch. See you at five." Linda touched "Send" and placed the phone on the table.

"Perhaps we can determine a few things before you meet Miss Starling. There's an informal reception with the board at five o'clock. Cocktails." She went to her water again, this time taking a gulp. "Do you drink?"

Pyune smiled. "I had a sip of Champagne one time—on New Year's Eve."

"A sip of Champagne. And that's all?" Linda grinned. "Pyune, I want to hear all about you. I have a feeling that things are getting ready to change around here, and I want to be on the ground floor."

"What would you like to know?" The room brightened when the sun moved above the tall windows and sent soft light across the room. Pyune found herself wanting to laugh. The idea of coming to New York to get her $25,000 check was beginning to become less important. There seemed to be a slight tilt of the earth, causing a misalignment among the planets, and she was right in the middle of it. The past was the past, and everything was beginning anew at this very moment—in New York City, twenty-nine stories high up in Manhattan—and only a floor or so away from the woman who supposedly looked just like her.

"I'd like to know whatever you'd like to tell me about yourself." Linda poured another glass of water and handed it to Pyune.

Pyune let out a short sigh. "There isn't a whole lot to tell. I was born on a ridge high up in the Appalachians, in the Chasteen Mountains. My mama had me in the house we lived in." She paused and closed her eyes. "Mama didn't know it at the time, but the day before I was born my daddy fell off the side of the mountain, trying to hunt down one of our pigs. Nobody ever recovered his bones. She said she watched the buzzards for days, circling above the ridge."

"How did she know it was your father?"

"He never came back home after that day."

"So your mother raised you by herself?"

"That's right." Pyune sipped her water and stared out the window at what she assumed was Central Park, which she'd read about in magazines.

"When I was two, we walked the trails down from the mountain we lived on. Ended up in Ivy Log. Been there ever since." She smiled. "The end."

She leaned back and shrugged slightly, leaving Linda to frown somewhat as she searched Pyune's face. Pyune was unaware of her beauty; it had been hidden away in Ivy Log her entire life, kept there along with her love for the mountains. The women were quiet for a long moment, Pyune's thoughts wandering to places they'd never been before, the consequences of their conclusions a tad unsettling.

"You had no siblings?" Linda asked after writing some notes.

"No siblings. Just me and mama."

Linda leaned forward and propped her elbows in front of her and rested her chin in her hands. She smiled at Pyune. "That's not possible."

"What's not possible?"

"The woman on the thirty-first floor is your identical twin. I don't know how she got to be your twin, but trust me, she's your double in every way."

The words were said with such conviction that Pyune jerked back. "I don't want to offend you in any way, Miss Richardson, but—"

"But nothing. And call me Linda. It is what it is." She let out a long breath. "Perhaps when you and Miss Starling meet, this mystery will be solved." She stood and waved her hand through the air as if willing everything to be okay. "Let's go have some lunch. There's a Bakers' World tour scheduled for one o'clock."

Pyune picked up her handbag. "I have a question," she said, her words timid. "Where was Miss Starling born?"

Linda, her hand on the doorknob, turned around slowly. "I know just about everything there is to know about Tess Starling, but I have no idea where she was born." She stared at the floor, biting down on her lower lip as she lifted her eyes to Pyune's. "As soon as you see her, I'm sure that's the first question you'll want to ask her—or vice versa."

~~~

Chapter 20

The three had just entered a section of the mountain that could only be traversed on foot. B.T. told them this would be the quickest way to the cabin where he lived. With Sam in the lead, they hadn't walked more than a hundred yards into the woods when Wiley heard sounds he knew all too well. And he'd left his rifle in his truck!

"Run, Sam! That hog can tear a man to pieces!" Wiley took off and jumped the fence in front of him in one leap, scrambling along the roadside until he could hop up into the bed of his truck. He landed right beside B.T., who'd had sense enough to scramble back into the truck at the first sound of trouble.

They stood together, sweating and breathing hard, watching Sam run through the brush and flailing his arms. Not far behind him, the loud, high-pitched sounds of a wild boar filled the air: a squeal, a grunt and then another loud squeal. Sam cleared the fence even better than Wiley, sailing over it like he was an Olympic high jumper using a scissor technique. Sam was exhausted when he reached the truck, so Wiley and B.T. each grabbed an arm and pulled him up and over the side.

"Holy shit!" Sam wheezed. "Nobody said anything about wild hogs around here." Sam swatted at a horsefly buzzing around him.

B.T. shook his head. "I done told you two fellers that they was wild hogs in them woods. But nobody listens to a mountain boy, do they?"

Exasperated, Wiley turned to B.T. "Here's the thing." He held up his hands like he was preaching a sermon. "When you said there were hogs in the woods going to your cabin, you didn't say they were all over the place. I'd a brought my gun if I'd known that."

"Wild hogs is wild hogs, no matter where they might be livin'. Shouldn't had to told you to bring a gun." The boy paced the truck bed, obviously disappointed with the two grown men who stood breathing hard and wiping sweat from their brows.

Wiley plopped down on his toolbox. "I got a Winchester .30-30 under the seat. It's loaded and ready to walk, but I didn't come up here to go hog huntin'. Let's just rest here a minute and forget about that wild hog." He hung his head over the side of the truck bed and closed his eyes.

"Forget about that hog?" Sam yelled. "Look over there, Wiley. That damn thing is spread out like he's going to stay awhile." Sam pulled out his shirttail and wiped his face.

Wiley raised up and spied the hog in the shade of an old sycamore tree. "All I gotta do is make it inside the cab. I can get a shot off way before he gets here, if he's that aggressive."

"What about the cabin?" asked B.T., his red hair glowing like embers in the noonday sun.

"What about it? It ain't going nowhere." Wiley eased himself over the side of the truck, one eye on the hog.

"I thought we was hikin' up there." B.T. nodded toward the summit.

"We *will* walk up to your place—if we can get past that hog." Wiley unlocked the truck door and pulled his rifle from under the seat. He climbed back up in the truck bed and checked the sights on his rifle.

Sam began brushing stick-tights from his pant legs. "I'm not moving from this truck for as long as that hog's out there."

B.T. rolled his eyes at Sam and said to Wiley, "Just shoot that gun. The noise will scare that hog way back into the hills. He won't want no part of us."

"Not a bad idea." Wiley levered in a shell and fired into the ground not far from the boar, the loud boom echoing across the valley. Sure enough, the hog gave one long squeal, sprang up, and thrashed through the woods, soon well out of sight.

Wiley chuckled. "Whew! Close call, Sam. Never knew you could run so fast. Or jump so high."

"Never thought I'd have to run like that ever again. Brought back my college days." Sam legs visibly trembled for all to see, and he started laughing.

"That hog weren't very big," B.T. said. He threw his leg over the side of the truck and eased down to the ground, his eyes on the brush in front of him. "You scaredy cats ought to be ashamed of yer-selfs. That hog ain't weighed more 'an two-hundred pounds. Don't think he woulda hurt us." He snickered through his protruding teeth.

Wiley glared at B.T. "Then why'd you beat me to the truck?" The boy looked away and Wiley lifted his rifle to his shoulder. "Come on. Let's go."

Sam found the courage to leave the truck bed and followed Wiley across the fence. "Why's this barrier here?" he asked B.T. as he checked the spot where he'd high jumped to safety.

"This here used to hold the cows. Kept gittin' out. But they still got away one day, and I ain't seen 'em since. At the end there was just two of them anyways. An old mama cow, and a steer we was gonna butcher."

"So your family had a farm way up here in these woods?" Sam asked.

B.T. grimaced. "I wouldn't call it no farm. Just a few chickens and not much else." He looked wistful for a moment but his face hardened just as fast, his freckles moving into the shadows of his cheeks. B.T. Hickel, mountain boy, skinny and scuffed from head to toe, swiped his hand across his eyes and walked on.

Wiley slowed at the top of a high ridge, shading his eyes with his hand as he scanned the valley below where he'd parked his truck. "How far did you say you lived from a regular road?

"Road? They ain't no road that's close to the cabin. What we come to is a part of the Appalachian Trail."

Sam stood alongside Wiley, his eyes following the line of the mountains to the north, which seemed to stretch on forever. "And just exactly where is it you live?" Sam asked B.T.

"We're getting' closer." B.T. pointed. "See that there big yellow birch on the ridge? Just around the bend is my house." The boy moved forward, a quickness in his step. He passed Wiley and Sam and released a mountain yodel that carried in the wind. Nearby, a hawk left the top of a sugar maple and caught a draft of cool moun-tain air. The bird swooped down into the valley below, letting out a cry that was shrill and long.

Wiley lingered on the ridge and watched the back of the redheaded boy until he disappeared around the bend. He felt a kinship with him, knew his heart, understood that deep inside him there existed a need for love. Maybe B.T. would discover it in Ivy Log—just like he had when he found Pyune.

Around the next ridge, almost hidden by rocks and trees and runaway vines, a weathered structure the size of a rail car leaned against a large rounded rock, the building's tin roof rusted and covered with forest debris—a woodland hideaway only someone who lived here could find. Fifty feet from the backside of the shack, a stream poured over rocks and down the mountain, making its way to merge with a river perhaps far away. Wiley thought it might be the start of Cartoogechaye Creek, one of many such rivulets flowing throughout the Appalachians.

He looked into the sky, trying to find his bearings. He figured they were at an elevation of about 5,000 feet, just off the Appalachian Trail south of the Smokies. His eyes searched for the boy and found him sitting on an old rocking chair on the dilapidated front porch.

"Hey, B.T., where did you say your mama was buried?" Wiley asked with somber compassion for the boy's loss.

B.T. gestured and said, "Over yonder."

Both Wiley and Sam scanned the area of B.T.'s point and saw a small clearing on a rise east of the cabin. They walked through the brush, finding yellow daisies growing alongside a rocky path. Rhododendrons dotted the woods around them, their sweet fragrance mixing with the earthy smell of the mountain itself.

In the clearing, a small mound was covered with rocks a person could carry without need of a cart. At the head of the grave, a white wooden cross poked out from the ground. Across it, neatly painted block letters read: "Bernice Hickel, Born 1950, Died March 16, 2016."

Sam sniffled. "Gravesites are lonesome places. This woman endured a hard life. Probably a sad one too. Can you imagine living up here, in a shack like that, especially in winter?" Sam squatted beside the grave and replaced a few rocks that had fallen off to the side or been knocked away by animals.

"Yeah, it's a mighty lonesome place, all right—for an adult." Wiley moved beside Sam. "But think about a young boy like B.T. No wonder he's the way he is."

"What do you want to do? This place is obviously deserted."

Wiley glanced at the horribly warped wood holding up the front porch. "Let's see if he wants to get any of his things from the house. We should also give him some private time with his mama before we head back down the mountain. We get out of here with enough light left, we can check around Deep Gap and along Highway 64. The pastor said B.T. mentioned a church. Surely there's someone who knows the boy—or of him."

Sam gave Wiley a wary look he couldn't quite read.

"Hey, B.T.!" Wiley hollered. "Get everything you want out of the house so we can saddle up. We figure you might want some time with your mama 'fore we leave, but I don't want to be up here too late."

"I'll go by her grave. But I ain't got nothing to git except maybe a comic book I got for Christmas last year."

Wiley stepped up to the porch. "Let's get it and—" From inside the house, a shadow crossed the window for only an instant, but long enough to halt his speech. He eased his rifle from his shoulder. Sam nodded to Wiley that he'd also seen movement. Wiley motioned to B.T. to move aside, and he inched his way onto the porch.

"Hello, anyone in the house!" Wiley called to the closed door, which he now stood beside. Silence. He leaned over and knocked on the door. "Anybody in there?"

A creaking, from rusty hinges that needed oiling, sounded as the door opened. A girl stepped out. Tall and lean with hair bunched up on top of her head, she appeared to be in her mid-twenties. The bottoms of her jeans were stuffed into knee-high snake boots. A shirt the color of a Halloween pumpkin hung loose across her hips, the sleeves tied in a knot at her waist. Underneath, a black T-shirt hugged her chest. She, too, had a rifle, holding the weapon firmly in her hands.

"Who the heck are you?" Wiley asked, squinting at the girl.

She studied Wiley with a great intensity, then Sam, then B.T.

"I'm his sister," she said, pointing to B.T.

Wiley jerked his head around to B.T. "Sister? B.T., you told us you didn't have any family except for an aunt."

B.T. sent out a loud guffaw. "I ain't never seen that girl before in my life."

~~~

Chapter 21

It was high noon, a breezy day on the streets of New York City, where the cool fragrance of spring coupled with the smell of sizzling hot dogs, hot pastrami, and the ever-present aroma of frying onions, seeped from the doorways of busy delis.

At the entrance to the garage elevators, Frandy stood guard, arms folded and eyes narrowed. He'd followed Linda and Pyune to the lobby doors that exited 56th Street. "Where you ladies off to?" he asked as they began walking away.

Linda ignored him before turning left out of the building and calling over her shoulder, "Are you stalking us?"

Frandy quickened his pace and slid in beside Linda. "Not stalking you, Miss Linda. Just want to know what you gonna do about . . . " He jerked his head toward Pyune. ". . . about Ms. Starling number two."

Linda skidded to a stop. "Frandy, how many times do I have to tell you that your duties for Bakers' World Magazine are to drive people to and from wherever I tell you to—and nothing more? You are not—I repeat—*not* in charge of solving this company's problems." She huffed forward, pulling Pyune along with her.

Frandy followed. "Ha! So you admit this is a problem! Miss Linda, Frandy knows perfectly well what his duties are in this corporation. He also knows that his opinions are very educated because he sees and hears everything there is to see and here around here. Eh?"

Linda stopped again. She put her hands on her hips. Pyune

was at her elbow, her eyes darting back and forth between the woman and Frandy. Linda was grinning when she lifted her chin and addressed the tall limousine driver: "And just what is it that you see and hear, Frandy, which you feel is worthy of your *educated* opinion?"

Frandy puffed up and straightened his tie, his piano-key-white teeth spread across his lips. "I've thought about this a lot, and Frandy think you should schedule a brief meeting with Miss Starling prior to the five o'clock cocktail reception with the board. That way, she can meet—" nodding to Pyune, seeming not quite sure how to address her— "she can meet Miss Murphy. And by the time the cocktail party begins, the shock will be over with. She will know there is another beautiful lady who looks exactly like her."

"And that's your *educated* idea."

He paused, clearly proud of what he thought was a brilliant idea. "Think about it, Miss Linda. Can't you see the look on Miss Starling's face when she sees Miss Murphy? You don't want that to happen in front of dozens of people at the cocktail reception, now do you?"

A look of contemplation spread across Linda's face, and it remained while everyone intermittently watched the clouds scud across the New York City sky. A flock of pigeons flew overhead and landed on a ledge on a building across the street. Linda pulled out her phone and punched in a short message to Tess Starling. They all waited in silence until Linda said, "Okay, Frandy. I'm on Tess's calendar for three o'clock. Happy?"

Frandy touched his cap. "Be seeing you later, Miss Linda. Call Frandy if you need a ride back to BWM." In midstride, he turned and faced Linda, walking backwards as he spoke. "Yes, I am happy. You need Frandy, Miss Linda." He jerked his thumb into his chest. "Yes, ma'am, I'm the man." Having said that, he turned and whistled Bobby McFerrin's reggae song "Don't Worry, Be Happy" on his way down the sidewalk, his black patent-leather shoes blindingly reflecting the noonday sun.

Linda touched Pyune's arm, guiding her across 55th Street and heading toward Broadway and 51st. "Where are we going?" Pyune asked, more than a little curious about what a sophisticated New Yorker ate for lunch.

"Ellen's Stardust Diner has the best chicken potpie on the

planet."

You've never eaten mine. And this is what a New Yorker dines on for lunch. There might be hope for me yet! Pyune Ever-Sweet Murphy, born and bred in the peaks of the Appalachians and plunked down in the middle of New York City, found herself in the shadows of tall buildings instead of the lofty yellow birch and sugar maples towering over the ridge where she was born. Below her feet was concrete, not the soft earth and the lushness of wild ginger and yellow ladyslipper. Nor was there dogwood or mayapple to remind her it was spring. She hurried along in a trance as her mind tried desperately to absorb all that was new, all that was sure to change her life forever. She considered hailing a cab, just like in the movies, and hightailing it back to Ivy Log, devoid of the $25,000 prize money.

They crossed over to Broadway, the antlike movement of New Yorkers almost laughable compared to the slowness of an April afternoon "crowds of three" in Ivy Log, Georgia. Her thoughts found Wiley, and she wondered if he missed her. In her mind's eye, she saw him ambling down Main Street and across the town square, on his way to a trail that led to a small ridge above Ivy Log. He went there sometimes at midday and napped in the shade of a sycamore, his hat pulled down over his handsome face. She had found him there once, had spied on him and told herself she'd like to get to know him better. And she had done just that.

Wiley eased into her life like a slice of pie after dinner, nothing fast and passionate but smooth and slow like that first bite into a tender crust. She was comfortable in his presence, so much so that she hardly noticed when he peeled a bucket of potatoes or shucked corn in The Boardinghouse kitchen. She marveled as the mountain man's calloused fingers slowly pulled at the corn silks as though he were exposing the heart of a hummingbird.

He never hurried with anything, especially when he made love to her. He had found her one day in the smokehouse and helped her pull down a big country ham. It was there that he'd kissed her for the first time. She wasn't surprised, yet she'd been more than a little curious about what it would feel like. But the bigger question was, what did a man with a Ph.D. want with a woman who'd spent her life in a kitchen, cooking for others?

They entered Ellen's Stardust Diner to the tantalizing aroma of fried bacon, grilled mushrooms and onions, steaming bowls of spaghetti, sizzling steaks, and last but not least the chicken potpie for which Linda was so enamored.

"Shall I order a potpie for you?" Linda asked, not waiting for an answer and licking her lips. "You'll absolutely love it!"

"Can't wait." Pyune couldn't help but smile, yet her answer was sincere. She'd never eaten a potpie other than her own, and she was naturally interested in comparing it to hers.

Pyune had seen her reflection in the restaurant windows when they arrived. The woman at Macy's had dressed her perfectly: a light linen jacket in navy, silk slacks the color of buttermilk, and an emerald-green silk camisole. During the ride in the car with the silent Frandy, she'd switched to a gold necklace inlaid with large green stones the color of an Irish meadow. Her large oval drop earrings provided the perfect complement to the ensemble. Would anyone looking at her have the slightest indication she was a mountain girl from Georgia? Never!

A waiter rushed over and placed bottled water on the table. Linda ordered for both of them. "And would you please set aside two pieces of coconut pie for dessert?" Linda smiled at Pyune. "Oh, I know what you're thinking, it's all about food. But that's my life, —" sipping her water— "after all, I work for the largest food magazine in the world."

Pyune nodded and grinned. "That's my life too. Food."

"What about *your* restaurant? What do you serve?"

"Restaurant?" Pyune chuckled. "The Boardinghouse is mostly a big old country kitchen. Lots of home cooking—that's what folks seem to want."

"How long have you been serving that lemon pudding cake?"

"Since I first started working at The Boardinghouse. I was probably fourteen years old."

Linda clapped her hands, her eyes glistening. "And, here you are, in New York City! Did you ever dream your recipe would end up the grand-prize winner?"

Pyune placed her napkin in her lap and toyed with the edges a moment. Dreams? She certainly never had any involving this. "It was a big surprise when I got that certified letter telling me I'd won." It truly had been a surprise. What had prompted her to enter the recipe in the first place, she didn't know. Her mother had taught her how to cook, and that was as far as it went.

Linda leaned forward and squinted at Pyune. "I'm so glad you won. I . . . well . . . just think, if you hadn't won and come to New York City, you would have never known about Tess Starling."

Pyune felt lightheaded. "I still don't know about Tess Starling."

"Ah, that's true. But you're going to find out at three this afternoon when we meet with her."

"Are you sure that's what we want to do?" Pyune slipped her jacket from her shoulders and placed in on the back of her chair. The restaurant had suddenly become warm, stuffy, and airless. She found Linda watching her with questioning eyes.

"You okay?" Linda asked.

"I'm thinking that Miss Starling is not my identical twin. It's just a fluke that we seem to look very much alike. Perhaps when we're side by side, you'll see we're not that close at all."

Linda placed her chin in her hands and stared at Pyune for a long moment. "I spend seventy-five percent of my time with Tess. I know her better than anyone else on Earth. You are Tess. Tess is you." Her voice rose. "Why would having a twin sister be so bad?"

"Bad? I didn't say it would be bad. It's just that I think you're wrong. I'm an only child. I have no brothers or sisters. If I did, my mother would have told me about them." Pyune's eyes misted over. "Why would she not have told me, especially if I had a twin sister?"

Linda pulled a tissue from her handbag and handed it to Pyune. "Wipe those tears. Everything is good. Let's just take one thing at a time. You'll meet Tess, and both of you will have lots of questions for each other, I'm sure."

Steaming chicken potpies arrived, the waiter placing them carefully on the table and stepping back. Linda winked at him. "You didn't forget about that coconut pie, did you?"

He gave her a thumbs up. "Got them set aside, just like you asked."

She turned to Pyune before she had a chance to break the crust on her potpie. "I haven't mentioned it yet, but you're going to love the fundraiser with three of New York's most famous chefs on Friday afternoon."

"I saw that in the letter, but I don't understand what it involves."

Linda smiled. "It's a fundraiser arranged by BWM's marketing department, namely Monty Reynolds. Seems he wants to get as much press as possible out of this year's winner—which would be you—and have a little fun too. It will be live, of course, but filmed for presentation on one of the cooking shows, and it will serve as the lead article in the twenty-fifth anniversary issue of Bakers' World Magazine."

"I'm more than a bit overwhelmed," Pyune said, sticking a spoon in her potpie.

Linda blew on a steaming spoonful of chicken. "Fundraisers are nice. The event will raise money for New York's homeless, and we'll receive a lot of publicity for it. Oh, and *you'll* get a lot of publicity!"

"I don't understand what's expected of me?" Pyune slipped a spoonful of "the best potpie in the planet" in her mouth. *There's not enough sage in this pie.* "And what do you mean by *fun*?"

Linda said between bites, "Oh, it will be a fun cooking contest between a prize-winning cook from the Appalachians—which would be you— and three of New York's top celebrity chefs." She added matter-of-factly, "Now, won't that be fun?"

Pyune didn't answer. Linda continued talking while eating, her hands flitting this way and that as she described how the BWM state-of-the art kitchen had been arranged to accommodate the four participants, with every conceivable utensil an arm's length away—and of course the necessary food items. What a delight that would be! To top it all off, the judges would be other celebrity chefs from renowned New York restaurants.

Stunned, Pyune felt herself wilting. "What will we cook," she asked in a whisper.

"Ha!" Linda slammed her hand on the table. "Would you believe it? Chicken potpie!"

They ate in silence, the fork in Pyune's hand trembling as she moved the plate of coconut cream pie toward her. This was too much: New York City, a cocktail reception, an appearance on "The Today Show," a cooking contest between three renowned chefs and little Pyune EverSweet Murphy from Ivy Log, Georgia, and an awards dinner. Yes, she would sneak away from Linda and hail a cab as soon as she finished her pie. Tell the cabbie to rush her to LaGuardia. Call Wiley and tell him to come and get her at the Atlanta airport.

"Oh, my goodness," Linda said, interrupting Pyune's escape plan, her eyes wide as she looked across the restaurant. "You're not going to believe this, but Monty Reynolds, the producer of our show, just walked in." She hunched over toward Pyune. "He's heading this way."

Monty Reynolds had been one of New York's most beloved celebrities for over twenty-five years. Tall, thin, gray-haired and voted one of the most handsome men in the city, he was fifty-two years old, unmarried, and came from old money. He was known for many things, one of them being that his character was above reproach. He was charitable and kind, and best of all —to his many women admirers—he could dance like Fred Astaire. Remarkably, he was from a small town in North Carolina, near the mountains so beloved by one Pyune EverSweet Murphy.

"Linda!" he called out from behind Pyune. "How are you?" He moved forward and leaned into her, planting a kiss on her cheek and lifting her hand in his. "So good to see you." He pivoted to Pyune and opened his mouth to speak but nothing came out. He stared as if frozen in place, blinking just once. He slowly turned back to Linda and lowered his eyes to hers. "Is . . . is there something you need to tell me, my dear?"

In the chair across from Linda, Pyune felt a loud ringing in her ears, a sudden flash of light in her eyes, and a rapid heartbeat that seemed to pound in her chest like a drum. In slow motion, Monty picked up her hand and said, "Hello, my name is Monty Reynolds. Tess Starling never eats here, so you are . . . if I may be so bold to ask?"

~~~

Chapter 22

O n the mountain, the wind had picked up. To the west, rain
clouds mounted, one on top of the other, beginning a steady
march toward the east, to where Wiley and Sam stood looking
back and forth between B.T. Hickel, the buck-toothed boy whose
favorite word was sniddle-snot, and a tall, rather striking
woman who claimed to be his sister.

B.T.'s declaration that he'd never seen her before had been
shouted across the rocky knoll with such vehemence that Wiley
and Sam stared at the boy who had delivered the harsh words.
B.T. glared back at them and said, "Well, now, she don't have no
red hair, does she?" B.T. contorted his featured into a smug look
that reinforced his open hostility.

Wiley swatted his knee with his hat, his words twanging in
reproving syllables: "B.T., no, she does not have red hair, but
that doesn't mean you're not related." His words softened as he
turned to the girl. "Hello, my name is Wiley Hanson." He flicked
his hand at Sam. "This here is Sam Cobb. We're both from Ivy
Log, down the road a piece." He pointed to B.T. "This boy
showed up last Friday at The Church of Ivy Log, wetter than a
drowned rat and about starved to death. Preacher took him in."

The woman moved closer to Wiley and Sam, not hesitating to
hold out her hand. "I'm Eva. Eva McIlwain from . . . down the
road a piece." Her smile was pensive, bordering on apologetic. "I
didn't mean to cause dissension among everyone." She glanced
at B.T. and back to Wiley and Sam. "It's a long story."

The woman was older than she'd first appeared. Maybe

thirty-five or so, perhaps even closer to forty. Her hair wasn't red like the brilliant flames of B.T.'s, but hints of bright copper glistened from beneath the large clasp that held her long dark tresses. Sam saw an educated woman, well-spoken, reserved, with a soft humility in her voice. "Perhaps we can sort this out between us," he said and nodded to Wiley, who was also eyeing the woman as she held a rifle with obvious calm, maybe even a mountain-bred knowledge.

"I reckon we need to sit down and talk this out, but not right here and not right now," Wiley said as he gestured at thick black clouds moving fast overhead. "We're gonna get caught in what looks like a good storm if we don't hurry along. Any reason you can't follow us to Ivy Log? It's about forty or so miles southwest, through Murphy, on one twenty-nine."

Eva grinned, her straight teeth shining against her skin. "I know it well."

"Good. We'll have us some food and see if we can determine just who B.T. belongs to." He paused and held Eva's dark eyes and laughed. "And exactly who you are."

Eva laughed and placed her rifle across her shoulder, resting her free hand on her hip. "Mr. Hanson, it may surprise you—" nodding in Sam's direction — "and Mr. Cobb, but there's no question about who *I* am. Truth of the matter is, I'm amused that neither of you recognize me."

Wiley and Sam both narrowed their eyes and found themselves scrutinizing Eva with long, hard stares. "Ahhh," said Sam after a half-minute, a blush coming to his cheeks.

"Who?" asked Wiley. "Who is she?"

From across the knoll, B.T. snickered and swiped his hand cross his brow, pushing his sweaty hair back on his head. His fourteen-year-old voice croaked, "Sniddle-snot. Even this here buck-toothed, redheaded mountain hillbilly knows who *she* is."

~~~

Chapter 23

The tour of Bakers' World Magazine, scheduled for 1 o'clock, began on the 29th floor, where the printing presses noisily churned out the latest edition of the most-celebrated food magazine in America. Pyune dutifully followed Linda around the floor amid stares and smiles and nods from the dozens of people who tirelessly worked to assure that the periodical was released on time and in the finest quality. It was obvious to Pyune that Linda was quite knowledgeable about the publishing industry, having been employed at BWM for over twenty years. The respect her peers had for her was apparent the moment she stepped from the elevator, and Pyune saw firsthand the workings of a large publishing enterprise.

Linda chatted with everyone; knew the names, the job titles, the work responsibilities, where each person lived and what he or she liked to eat—even an employee's kid's name on occasion. Everyone acknowledged Pyune with silent questions, looking curiously at her as if to ask: *Who is this woman? Really, who is she?* Though not one person dared to ask, *"Are you Tess Starling and this is some joke? Maybe a segment for Undercover Boss?"*

After a tour of the design department on the 30th floor, where Pyune viewed a plethora of displays, storyboards, set designs, and a myriad of new products having to do with all-things-cooking, Linda said, "Come this way, I want to show you our state-of-the art kitchen. This is where you'll work with the three chefs we've got lined up for the show." She arched her eyebrows at Pyune and grinned. "New York Cuisine Meets Appalachian Delight." She led Pyune through a set of double doors and opened her arms to the gleaming kitchen. "Well, what do you think?"

Pyune was awestruck. This was no ordinary kitchen, its layout no less opulent than what would be found in the palace of a queen. From the extraordinary lighting to the gleaming stainless-steel fixtures, the kitchen was astonishing. Pyune shook her head and said, "When I first began cooking at The Boardinghouse, it was on an old woodstove in the back corner of the kitchen." She became wistful, the memory of her roots making her long for the simplicity of that time in her life.

Linda looked at her watch. "We'd better get going. Almost three on the dot, and Tess will be expecting us. I need to stop in the lobby for just a minute to pick up a FedEx for Tess. You can ride along." She pushed the elevator button for the lobby, where she locked the elevator in place when it stopped. She left and came back with the FedEx, and in less time than it took to brown a biscuit they were off to Tess Starling's suite of offices on the 31st floor.

The elevator seemed to glide on air. Quiet, subtly lit, and smelling of lavender, it rose as if on its way to anywhere but Heaven. Pyune felt herself floating outside her body but wishing she were back on the ridge above the valley that stretched a mile across the Appalachians; and, if she jumped off the edge, the air currents would catch her and take her anywhere she wanted to go. On that glorious ride she would breathe cool mountain air and soar to a place that wasn't . . . wasn't . . . New York City!

Just as she began wondering if the elevator ride would ever end, the doors opened and light from the large executive suite shimmered around her. A thirty-foot high ceiling seemed to swirl overhead, with chandeliers the size of hot air balloons, their lights small but in rows of hundreds, maybe even thousands, all twinkling and beckoning anyone to step inside this magnificent room.

Pyune stepped off the elevator but abruptly turned around and walked back inside it. Stricken with anxiety, her body slumped as she placed her face in her hands. "Can we wait for just a moment?" she entreated.

"Of course," said Linda, placing both her arms around Pyune's shoulders. "Tell you what, I'll brief Tess on what's going on. Prepare her a little. She knows nothing about any of this. I'll come back and get you." Linda guided Pyune to an expanse of chairs and sofas, all surrounded by ornate tables and gleaming brass lamps.

Pyune nodded and sat on a plush brocade sofa the color of a red chili pepper. She watched Linda scurry to a set of double doors trimmed in gleaming brass. She pulled them open, stepped forward, and the doors closed behind her. Pyune took a tissue from her handbag, sniffled once, shut her purse—and ran to the elevator. She pressed "L" for lobby and waited for the ride that would take her away from New York City and back to the safety and sanctity of her life in Ivy Log, Georgia.

~~~

Chapter 24

Wiley threw his hat to the ground and stomped over to B.T. "Okay, wise guy, who is she?"

"Cain't you tell? She's a movie star." B.T. covered his protruding teeth with his hand and giggled.

Wiley wasn't in the mood for humor. He didn't follow the lives of too many celebrities, and here was one right in front of him and he had no idea of her name. He glared at B.T. "Okay, which one is she?"

Laughter this time came from the woman. "I'm no movie star," she said, pulling her orange shirt away from her hips and shoving her arms though the sleeves. "We better get a move on! Here comes the rain!" They trotted down the mountain for about a quarter of a mile before the rain caught them, the drops hitting them hard just as they reached Wiley's truck.

"Jump in everybody!" yelled Wiley as he opened the driver's door and pressed the unlock button. He started the engine and let it idle, the windshield wipers working furiously. "Miss McIlwain, where's your vehicle?"

Eva wiped her face with her shirttail and shivered. "Don't need that air conditioning on, do you, Mr. Hanson?" She unclasped her hair and smoothed it back, breathing hard. "A ways back down the mountain. I'll show you, but it's about six miles by road."

Wiley turned the truck around and they followed the winding road that hugged the uppermost ridge of the mountain, slowly circling downward until it flattened out before heading in a

steep decline. It was slow-going, the rain battering the windshield with relentless fury, the noise at times becoming a roar
like a freight train was going by.

"I'm gettin' hungry," announced B.T. "Didn't you fellers say
something about a Dairy Queen?"

Wiley said, "That we did, B T., but right now we've got to get
off this here mountain in one piece. So just hang in there." He
added in a low, stern voice, "And you be sure to hold back your
delicate condition. You don't, you'll be ridin' in that truck bed no
matter how hard it storms. You got it?"

B.T. said nothing, and they rode a few minutes in silence until Wiley looked in his rearview mirror at Eva. Sam turned
around and smiled at her, a knowing look on his face. This close,
he was able to take her in, and he saw a quiet beauty and found
himself wishing he was sitting in the back seat next to her.

"So if you're not a movie star, who are you?" Wiley asked.

"She's the governor of North Carolina," Sam said before she
could answer.

Wiley braked the truck, bringing it to almost a standstill.
"Whaaaa . . . you got to be kidding." He whipped his head
around to her. "Well, I'll be danged." Wiley blinked several times
in rapid succession. "I do recognize you now. You *are* the governor."

"Former governor," Eva corrected both him and Sam.

"Republican, right?" asked Wiley, his eyes holding hers as he
smiled.

Eva returned his smile. "Absolutely."

B.T. snorted and said, "Well, sniddle-snot, I know'd who she
was. But what's all this got to do with the Dairy Queen?"

"We're gonna feed you," Wiley said. "Just hold on a few minutes longer."

The rain had not hit where they were now, and as the truck
whizzed around a highly banked curve, Eva's squeal was followed by laughter as she held fast to her seat. In a few minutes
they were on the other side of the mountain. Wiley spotted a car,
which Eva said was hers, and he parked his truck alongside a
gray Lexus and turned around to face her. "Well now, Ms. McIlwain, we do indeed have lots to talk about."

"That we do," she replied. "I'll follow you back to Ivy Log,
and we can stop in Murphy for a bite to eat. I'm about to starve,

myself."

"ShoeBooties, I hope," said Sam, just as the rain started and soon began to pour.

The rain had followed them, and even harder than at any time before, so everyone waited in the truck for the storm to let up. Eva found herself watching B.T. *Her brother. Really? Yes, he was.* Their mother was the same; the father, she wasn't so sure. She studied his profile and noticed his high forehead, which matched hers, and their eye color was the same. She didn't have near as many freckles, but she did have them—even if they weren't nearly as pronounced. The biggest difference was their teeth. Evidence of serious thumb sucking had pushed his teeth forward, resting them on the top of his bottom lip when his mouth was closed. She felt a pang in her heart. It was obvious the boy lived in poverty. She smiled at B.T. "You will love their bacon cheeseburger."

B.T. gurgled and said, "I could eat a whole cow right about now." He leaned over and tapped Wiley on the shoulder and half-whispered, "Might want to get out of the truck for a minute or two, Mr. Wiley, if you don't want everybody to keel over."

"What's he talking about," Eva asked Wiley.

Rain or no rain, Wiley opened his door and jumped from the truck, followed by Sam on his side. "Come on, Eva," Sam said quickly as he pulled her door open. "If it's okay, I'll ride with you and we can talk about a few things along the way." He grimaced. "I'll explain B.T. . . . best I can."

When Eva got in her car, she reached over and tossed a brief-case from the passenger seat to the back, and Sam slid into her Lexus. They pulled away and followed Wiley's red truck, B.T. sitting in the front seat, all the windows open, his red hair blowing in the wind. Sam thought he saw Wiley frowning. In a few minutes the rain lightened up, but dark clouds continued to roll in from the west, typical April showers that sometimes seemed endless. But on this afternoon the sun came out just as the highway turned south toward Murphy, past trees whose leaves were bright green with new spring foliage.

The radio jumped on when Eva had started the car, a country music station playing Eddie Arnold ". . . I'm sending you a big bouquet of roses, one for every time you broke my heart." Eva turned down the volume but Eddie continued singing his sad love song, a guitar twanging softly in the background.

Sam broke a long silence between them: "You don't really have to tell us anything—Wiley and me. We have no legal authority at all regarding B.T. We're just trying to help out. William Johnson, the pastor of The Church of Ivy Log, is a good friend of ours and asked for our help. Or maybe it was the other way around, come to think of it. Regardless, we all want to help the boy." He paused and glanced at Eva. He noticed some mascara had smudged on her cheek, and he almost reached over to wipe it off. He laughed at himself.

Eva nodded and he continued, "It was our plan to contact the authorities about B.T—him being only fourteen. Didn't know if he was a runaway or what. Just showed up on the back step of the parsonage during a fierce rainstorm last Friday night. Of course the pastor took him in. That's what churches do, right? take in the poor and hungry? And the boy sure was hungry." Sam laughed. "Will took him to The Boardinghouse for lunch, and all of us watched him devour four big slices of meatloaf and all the trimmings." Sam pretended to zip his mouth shut. "I'm talking too much. Sorry."

Eva shook her head and smiled. "No, you aren't. This is all good to know. I'm glad he showed up in Ivy Log and y'all were there to help him." Her voice was soothing, calm, and, as expected, more than a hint of a southern accent touched lightly here and there.

"May I ask you something?" Sam pulled out his phone, tapped into it for a moment, and put it away.

"Of course."

"What were you looking for at the cabin? B.T. or something else?"

"Both. Didn't see him there but went inside to see if I could find anything that might lead me to him." She played her fingers on the steering wheel a moment and turned to Sam. "Maybe I'm the one who should start at the beginning."

"No pressure here, I can promise you. Tell me whatever you're comfortable taking about. If anything."

The trees whizzed past while Eva continued tapping the steering wheel, the radio playing softly and Sam watching Wiley's red truck in front of them. In a few moments, in a half-whisper, Eva began the long story she'd mentioned on the mountaintop:

Eva's mother had her when she was thirteen, unmarried, and living in the heart of the Appalachian mountains, where life was unbelievably hard every single day. Her parents, poor and uneducated, were devoutly religious and took the baby, conceived in unspeakable sin by their holy standards, to the pastor of the church in the valley below them. The reverend and his wife promptly gave the baby to a childless couple who happened to be visiting the church one morning—and seemed to have the means to care for a newborn. The couple left the mountains with the baby, never to be seen again.

Eva's life with the couple was happy and materially quite abundant. When Eva was twelve, they sat her down and told her she'd been legally adopted by them. When her last remaining parent died, the mother just two weeks ago, Eva had found a journal, more like a diary, written in detail about a young girl of thirteen who lived on Standing Indian Mountain. Eva had stared in amazement at the names of the people who had given her to her adoptive parents.

"So, after having the names, it was fairly easy to conduct a search. Incredibly, my first hit was Bernice Hickel's death notice, who was my mother."

"Amazing timing. But how does that make B.T. your brother."

Eva dropped back a little from Wiley's truck, slowing down as if to pace her story. "It was indeed amazing. A puzzle really. Once I put one piece in place, another one came up. In the end, I learned that my birth mother had another child, some thirty-two years later." She shook her head. "Can you imagine that? I'm forty-six, and I have a brother who's fourteen. A half-brother, but a brother, and as far as I know my only living relative."

"And your real father?" Sam quietly asked.

"I know nothing about my real father, at all. It's possible B.T. will have some knowledge, not only of my mother but also my father."

Sam let out a sigh he wished he'd held back. "He's a quirky kid. No telling what he'll tell you." Sam took a deep breath. "You need to know something. B.T. came to Ivy Log looking for his aunt."

"His aunt!" Eva turned to Sam, her smooth forehead now creased. "What's her name?"

"He doesn't know but said he'd recognize her when he saw her."

"Why did he think she was in Ivy Log?"

"None of us have the slightest clue. And he won't say." Sam drummed his fingers on his knee. "Guess I should tell you another little tidbit about B.T."

"Oh, my. What else?"

"The pastor said—and confidentially I might add—that B.T. said his aunt was a woman of means."

"Was what?"

"A wealthy woman."

Eva shook her head. "I'm sorry, I know what it means. I'm just shocked at his contention. If he doesn't know her name, or where she is, why would he think she's worth any money?"

Sam shook his head. "I don't know, but stranger things have happened."

They caught up with the red truck in front of them, and in less than a mile both vehicles pulled into Murphy, North Carolina, and ShoeBooties Café. B.T. bounded from Wiley's truck. "This ain't no Dairy Queen, is it?"

"What's that mean?" asked Wiley, slicking his bald head with his hand and tucking his shirt into his pants. "If you ain't never been to one, what's a Dairy Queen supposed to look like?"

"Well, I reckon it would be a queen sittin' on a cow or somethin'. You know, lady with a crown on her head and all." He seemed to deliberate a moment. "Aw, heck, maybe the cow got a crown on its head."

Wiley laughed and slapped the boy on the back. "B.T., you're the funniest young feller I know."

B.T. trotted into ShoeBooties, taking a seat before anyone else in their little party had made it through the doorway. When the waitress came by, without even a peek at the menu, he ordered two of the bacon cheeseburgers Eva had promised were so good.

~~~

Chapter 25

Her heart beating wildly, Pyune waited for the elevator that would take her to the lobby of BWM—and freedom. She pressed the down button again, willing the elevator to magically appear. When the doors finally opened she charged inside, only to skid to a stop. Leaning against the wall of the elevator, Monty Reynolds smiled at her. His arms were folded against his chest, his feet crossed as though he had been waiting for her. Yet how could he be waiting for her? He had no idea she would be scrambling to get out of the building.

She stood wide-eyed and speechless, hearing the elevator door close gently behind her. The one man she did not want to see again had essentially captured her. Her encounter with him in Ellen's Stardust Diner had unnerved her, left her panting for breath. Romance novels had claimed bells would ring, harps would play, and bodies would float through the air when you were in love. All those things had happened to her at the restaurant as she reached out and placed her hand in his, but she certainly was not in love with Monty Reynolds.

Wiley. She must get back to Wiley. Her beloved Wiley, who would hold her and put her life back in the place where it should be—with him and in Ivy Log.

"Miss Murphy," Monty said, casually nodding to her. "I see I have again found the most beautiful woman in New York." His hydrangea blue eyes held hers. "Ah, my wish has come true."

Pyune said nothing. She squeezed the tissue in her hand and looked at the control panel on the elevator where the "L" button beckoned her finger.

"You're on Tess's floor." He unfolded his arms and pressed the lobby button himself. *How could he know where she was going?*

"Yes, I . . . I . . . I am . . ."

"Bailing out?"

"Wha . . . what . . ." Like a trapped animal, Pyune began to frantically turn her head from side to side.

"Settle down," Monty said, smiling warmly. "I knew when I saw you at the diner that something was going on. I called Linda after lunch and she told me everything. At least, everything she knew." He looked at his watch. "You're scheduled to meet Tess at three." She checked her own watch, and it was exactly 3 o'clock.

Pyune rose on her tiptoes. No matter, she was nowhere near the height of her elevator companion, which she estimated at 6-feet-2. "Mr. Reynolds, I feel as though I'm under some sort of . . . of questioning like a criminal receives. It's really none of your business where I'm going. Or, for that matter, what I'm doing." She held his eyes for as long as she could before looking away from his penetrating stare.

His laughter began as a quiet rumbling and soon erupted into a guffaw that resonated loudly in the enclosed elevator. "Oh, Miss Murphy, how funny you are."

"What do you mean?" She'd spoken more politely this time. She was never rude, and her previous tone had bothered her even though she'd meant every word.

He grinned. "You have no idea, do you?"

"Idea about what?" She heard anger in her words. The elevator reached the lobby, and the doors opened. The first sound came from the dozens of birds that flitted back and forth in the aviary. She stepped out and looked up at Monty. "Well?"

He cocked his head and studied her for a moment. "You have no idea that you are about to take New York by storm."

"Take New York by storm? I don't understand." Pyune started to walk away when her phone chirped. She pulled it from her bag and flipped it open. "Hello."

"I hear those damn birds, so you must be in the lobby," Linda shouted into the phone. "Please go back on the elevator and get up here, pronto. Tess is ready to meet you. I've already briefed her about what to expect."

Monty carefully took the phone from Pyune. "Hold on, Linda. She'll be there in a minute." He handed the phone back to Pyune and pressed the elevator's "Up" button. "Go up there and meet your sister," he said softly. When the elevator doors opened, he reached out his hand and brushed his fingers lightly across her cheek. "Five o-clock, at your cocktail reception," he said and walked away.

~~~

Chapter 26

Pyune EverSweet Murphy had no intention of taking New York City, or any other city for that matter, by storm. The $25,000 check—that was why she was here. No other reason. She would go to the 5 o'clock cocktail reception, appear on "The Today Show," prepare chicken potpie with three of New York's top chefs, go to the awards dinner, but she'd be *damned* if she'd take New York by storm.

With a sharp jab, she punched the button to the 31st floor. Her ride was filled with anxiety, becoming more so the closer she got to Tess Starling. This was all so ridiculous. As soon as the two women were side by side, the differences would be evident—and glaringly so—of this she was certain. She would go through the motions of meeting her and not say *I told you so* when it became clear there was no familial relationship whatsoever between the two women.

Pyune took a deep breath and watched the lights: 27th floor . . . 28 . . . 29 . . . 30 . . . and, at last, the 31st.

When the elevator door opened, Pyune saw the silhouette of a woman across the lobby, the light from a backdrop of long windows framing her petite frame. She couldn't see her face. Continuing to stare, she watched the figure move toward her, one slow step at a time. The woman took a few more steps, her deliberate gait faltering even more, but the space between them closed.

Tess, with her hands together and with a glow in her eyes, reached out and gently touched Pyune's face.

Stunned, Pyune breathed hard in the silence, all the while looking into a face—identical to hers. Only a moment more passed before Tess Starling folded her arms around Pyune, who heard muffled cries released into her shoulder and felt the speeding, thudding heart of the woman who embraced her. Tess clung to her and wailed like a baby. When she leaned back, tears ran down her cheeks and her lipstick was smeared. She cried out, "Oh, my God. Oh, my God."

All Pyune could do was smile and shake her head. She said softy, "I don't know how this happened."

"Neither do I," Tess said amid sniffles and in a voice that sounded just like Pyune's, "but it was meant to be! This is the most wonderful thing that's ever happened to me." She grasped Pyune's hand and tugged her out of the elevator.

Beside them, with tears in her own eyes, Linda stepped onto the elevator. "See you gals later," she said and waved, her voice breaking up.

Pyune followed Tess into the executive offices; followed the woman who was in every way an image of herself. They were truly identical, from their petite frames, dark hair and luminous skin, to their large dark eyes. Pyune, with the realization that she might indeed have a sister, was lightheaded and overwhelmed—but unable to shed her doubt, which remained considerable. Tess, however, acting jubilant and accepting of everything, was not indicating the slightest reservation regarding their relationship. "Come, sit here with me, Pyune." Tess went to the sofa nearest her, tossed two huge pillows on the floor, and plopped down on one.

The room seemed to spin as Pyune sat down and waited. For what, she didn't know. All she could do was wonder how all of a sudden she had a twin sister. How was it that she had won a baking contest, come to New York, and now sat opposite a sister she didn't know she had? It was too much.

Pyune relaxed enough to find Tess Starling exquisite. From her perfectly coiffed hair to her lavish jewelry to the designer dress she wore, she projected culture to match her beauty. She possessed a naturalness that was rare among women who were rich and powerful and enjoyed celebrity.

Tess Starling's stunning looks had certainly played a part in her rise to the top, but her intelligence and drive were the major factors. She wore her position as CEO of Bakers' World Magazine well, as she was known for putting in sixteen-hour work days. Her moxie was respected throughout the publishing industry, the philanthropic endeavors she administered always drew rave reviews, and her role as the wife of one of the world's top business leaders was considered complementary and not subordinate. What wasn't known was her history before the extraordinary person she had become. This she had always kept private.

Tess picked up Pyune's hand and held it in hers. "Tell me who you are, Pyune. I want to know everything about you. Every single detail."

The buzzing in Pyune's head became louder. Tess was asking her who she was. Wait: *Who am I?* Her throat tightened while her eyes roamed the room before again settling on the woman who sat next to her. She spoke about what she remembered of her early childhood, feeling her voice quiver as she spoke. When she was about finished, she added, "Well, it was just mama and me all those years. Mama died seven years ago, doing what she loved to do, tending her flowers out behind her little house. She died with a hoe in her hands." Pyune fiddled with the buttons on a cuff. "I never married. I've been in Ivy Log since I was two years old." In a barely audible voice, she ended her monologue by saying, "There's really nothing much else to tell."

Tess listened with rapt attention, leaning back and folding her arms and staring at Pyune in a long, contemplating gaze. Pyune stared back and waited, when like a probing journalist Tess dipped her chin and asked *the question*. The question that would hopefully propel them onto a path that would solve the mystery: How were the two of them separated after they were born?

Pyune jerked back, her eyes wide and her mouth open, and all she could offer was, "I don't know."

Tess didn't hesitate. "We have the same mother, Pyune. The woman who raised me was not my birth mother." She stood and paced slowly around the room, coming back to the sofa and leaning on the armrest closest Pyune. Tess uttered a soft sigh and clapped her hands twice. "Things are now beginning to make sense. All we have to do is determine when we were separated."

"How could we ever find out?" Pyune asked. "There's no one

alive who would know anything about that."

Tess's face seemed to light up. "There might be one person."

Pyune could only shake her head, something she'd been doing a lot lately.

~~~

Chapter 27

Wiley and B.T., followed by Eva and Sam, rode on Highway 129 to Ivy Log. B.T. had pounded down two of Shoe-booties's fabulous cheeseburgers in record time and now slept in Wiley's truck, his head leaning against the door, a soft snore that sounded like the purring of a dozen kittens escaping his open mouth. A touch of saliva glistened at the corner of his wide lips.

The boy had scoffed at the idea that he was related to Eva McIlwain. In his young life, his exposure had been limited to the mountains and a small country school where children just like him attended. They carried a cold biscuit for lunch and went home to a sparse dinner, hungry throughout the night. It was obvious he'd endured a life of abject poverty. If Eva were his half-sister, Wiley wondered how the boy's life would change and if this prominent woman/politician would assume responsibility for him and bring him into her life.

Crossing the Georgia state line from North Carolina, Wiley hummed an obscure melody and thought about Pyune. She was to call him after the cocktail reception with the Bakers' World board of directors. He looked at the clock in his truck. *Only an hour or so and he'd hear from her.* He was comforted with the knowledge that in only a few days she'd arrive back at the Atlanta airport. Perhaps he would take her for a romantic dinner with candles and soft music. It's there that he'd ask her to marry him. He grinned in the quiet of his truck—he would buy her the most beautiful ring in all of Atlanta.

Wiley eased his truck around the curve at the top of the ridge above Ivy Log. He looked down at his blessed community, the town square with the liberty oaks, the American flag and the tall spruce that the folks in Ivy Log decorated each Christmas; this haven where the citizens of the small hamlet were his family, his friends, and the heartbeat of his life.

Something caught his eye on Main Street, around the location of The Boardinghouse. Coming closer, he made out the red flashing lights of an ambulance, the message clear. He drove nearer to find a crowd gathered on the sidewalk, everyone shuffling back and forth at a nervous pace.

Wiley pulled his truck along the curb. He glanced in his rearview mirror and saw Sam and Eva parking behind him. He quickly reached over and tapped B.T. on the shoulder. "Hey, fella. We're here." The boy didn't respond so he gave him a good shove.

Wiley jumped down from his truck and ran to the emergency vehicle, sleepy-eyed B.T. staggering along behind him. Doyce and Harley walked beside two paramedics who rolled someone on a gurney toward the ambulance. "What happened?" Wiley asked, eyeing the oxygen mask fitted over the nose and mouth of the sick or injured person's gray face. "Oh, no, poor Vallie," he lamented after getting a better view. "She looks awful."

"Yep," Harley cried out. "Looks terrible. Believe she done had a heart attack." Harley, his eyes red, squeezed his big hands together. "They're taking her to Blairsville."

Wiley saw tears in Doyce's eyes as well as Harley's. B.T. eased beside Wiley and looked down at Vallie. "Well, I'll be danged," he said. "That there's my aunt."

~~~

Chapter 28

The delirium of New York City's roistering nightlife was far removed from the elegant cocktail reception scheduled for five o'clock in Tess Starling's apartment in the Bakers' World Magazine building. Thirty-two stories above the city, the apartment's quiet elegance always welcomed its visitors with an aura of warmth and love.

At a quarter-to-five, Tess dimmed the lights and personally lit candles. Music from Broadway's "Jersey Boys" played softly, and she sang along ". . . I can't give you anything but love . . ." A bartender and a server had arrived at four. Both worked efficiently and effortlessly behind and in front of a tavern-length antique bar made of mahogany and trimmed in brass.

Bakers' World's board of directors were in for a surprise. Not only would they meet the winner of the $25,000 grand prize, Pyune EverSweet Murphy, they would also learn that Tess had a twin sister—namely, one Pyune EverSweet Murphy. The board members, who numbered six, and their spouses, had anticipated the reception for several reasons, the most prominent being that they had been invited to Tess and Robert Starling's apartment. Guests of the Starlings were always doted upon, fed gourmet food, and provided with fine wines from all over the globe.

Tess and Robert had been married twelve years, with him being the first man Tess had ever dated seriously. She had always been mentored in private all-girls' schools, her life shaped around business as well as the arts, the former providing the skills that had propelled her to present-day success. Tess, however, believed that whatever she'd achieved was the result of a well-grounded upbringing. It's what made her genuine, and she was respected for this as much as for being a powerhouse of publishing acumen and physical energy.

Tess would not have to introduce Pyune to anyone attending the reception. Everyone would simply look at Pyune and . . . and gasp! Then, the questions would begin. Questions that, at the moment, could not be answered. Tess would simply smile and nod her head. "We're not sure." "I don't know." "Well, that remains to be seen." What could she say? She knew nothing about her and her sister's history. But she was determined to find out —not only for herself but for Pyune too. After all, the two sisters shared the same mystery.

Upstairs, Pyune stood at a window that enabled her a view of much of Manhattan. Tess had insisted she cancel her reservations at the Marriott Marquee, the expense of which Bakers' World was covering, and stay in the guest suite at the apartment instead. "It would be so convenient," she had said. "We'll be able to spend much more time together. Talk until three in the morning, just you and me. We're sisters, you know." Tess had laughed and hugged her for the hundredth time after her last remark.

The joy of having a newfound sister was overshadowed by questions. What nettled her most—since she had never been told she had a twin sister—what else had been hidden from her? For once, her life was not what it seemed. It was as though pieces of her lay everywhere, especially in New York City, where the strangeness of the place and the people she didn't know made her want to hide in a closet and close her eyes. She must get back to Ivy Log, to a place where she knew who she was. She had heard about people getting lost in New York City. Now she was one of those people.

The knock at the door seemed to come from a faraway place, a soft beckoning that, once answered, would make things okay. The knock was followed by Tess's voice: "Pyune? May I come in?"

Tess. Her sister. Still so strange. *How could this be?* "Yes," answered Pyune. "I'm almost ready."

The door opened and a smiling Tess entered the room. "Ah, how gorgeous you are!" Tess beamed. "That is the perfect dress for you." Tess crossed the room and reached inside her jacket, gently removing and placing a pearl bracelet around Pyune's wrist. "This is a very special piece of jewelry. It's from India—a trip I made some years back. I want you to wear it . . . and I want you to have it. I want you to keep it forever."

Pyune gazed at the three rows of lustrous pearls, held together by an intricate filigree clasp made of silver. "Oh, my, how can you part with such a lovely piece of jewelry?"

Tess stepped back, her breathing quiet and even as she said, "You've given me a great gift, and that gift is you—a sister. I don't have to know how or why this happened, I just know it has." She reached out her hand. "Come. It's time to let the world know who you are—and that I have a sister. I already called my husband, and he said he can't wait to get home to meet his new sister-in-law."

"He believed you," Pyune had to ask.

"Always," Tess replied without the slightest hesitation.

~~~

Chapter 29

Although eccentric and laden with a peculiar personality to match, Vallie Thomas held a distinctive place in the hearts of Ivy Log's citizens, and as far as they were concerned she was an integral part of the small town's population of just under 600 kindred souls. She was family as much as any of them. Within minutes of her departure in the red ambulance and its wildly flashing lights and blaring siren, Doyce drove over to Vallie's house to feed her cat. Lizzie Lindquist went along with him and gathered a couple of Vallie's nightgowns and some undergarments and other personal items, which she packed in a small suitcase.

Doyce and Lizzie went back to The Boardinghouse. Lizzie handed Vallie's pocketbook to Wiley. "Guess she'll be needing her identification and such. Got a bag of her underclothes and stuff in Doyce's truck. I'll stay here and look after things." She wrinkled her brow and looked away and then back to Wiley. "You reckon we ought to close The Boardinghouse for a spell?"

Wiley took Vallie's handbag and tucked it under his arm. *Close The Boardinghouse?* He felt his throat tighten. The Boardinghouse had been an Ivy Log fixture for more than forty years and not once had closed its doors. Even on Christmas day a body could sneak in the backdoor of the kitchen and get a piece of pie and a cup of piping hot coffee. He wasn't going to allow Pyune's kitchen to go cold—that was all there was to it.

"I'm thinkin' you'll do just fine, Lizzie. Get Paula over here and she'll help you out."

"Paula? You got to be kiddin', Wiley Hanson. Paula ain't cooked a thing worth a dang in all her life. How could she help?" Still scowling, Lizzie shoved her hands in her apron and stepped up on The Boardinghouse porch. "Paula Jennings wouldn't know how to turn on a stove!" She spun her big frame around and tramped inside.

Wiley felt a tug on his sleeve. He turned and found the red-haired boy watching him, a half-smile on his face. "You look funny with that there purse under your arm."

"You heard, it's Vallie's. Come on. We're going to Blairsville." Wiley found Sam and Eva in a crowd, everybody talking at once. Pastor Johnson, Dr. Casteel, and Harley were among the same group.

Dr. Casteel eyed Wiley and called to him. "Can you come over here a minute?"

Wiley handed Vallie's pocketbook to B.T. and pointed to Doyce. "Go over to that feller and get a bag he's got for Vallie. Put that bag and this purse in my truck and wait for me there." B.T. rolled his eyes and trudged off. Wiley eased into the circle of folks as Sam was writing in a small notebook. Wiley said, "I'm heading to the hospital. Taking the boy with me. Anybody else going?"

Sam and Eva both nodded, as did Dr. Casteel, the preacher, and Harley. Dr. Casteel, his voice low, asked Wiley, "You're the executor of Vallie's estate, aren't you?"

"Ah . . . yeah, guess I am." Wiley hadn't thought about this and found himself breathing hard. "Hope it won't come to that, though. For now, I'm anxious to get to the hospital." Dr. Casteel nodded.

"We'll follow you," Sam said, tugging gently on Eva's arm as Dr. Casteel hustled to Harley's truck, the big farmer already in the driver's seat. Pastor Johnson headed to the parsonage to get his car and Bible. It seemed as though half of Ivy Log would be close behind the ambulance that carried Vallie Thomas to Union General Hospital in Blairsville.

In Wiley's truck, the freckled face of B.T. Hickel swiveled around to Wiley. "Yes, sir, that there's my aunt all right. Just like I remembered her. 'Cept her hair used to be red. It's all turned nasty gray, like the color of mildew. Frizzy, too. Don't remember her being so fat and ugly neither. Maybe—"

"Hold on, boy. Let's be respectful here. Your aunt, if she really is your aunt, is on her way to the hospital with Lord knows what kind of problem. You don't need to go calling her fat and ugly. She might think you ain't so pretty either."

"Least I ain't fat."

B.T. had him on that one. Before long, as Wiley settled in on the drive to the hospital, his jaw began quivering, something that seldom happened. He had known Vallie his entire life, yet he didn't really know very much about her. No one did, it seemed. She was just *Vallie*, a town enigma, a woman with zero fashion sense as evidenced by her routinely wearing a combination of plaid pants and checkered shirts, and layering these garments even in the summer. The scarf she tied around her head, usually purple or bright yellow, could be seen all up and down Main Street and across the town square. She was a true character in the gentlest sense.

She hummed to herself throughout the day, the sound rising and falling and offering no recognizable melody. About nightfall, she'd disappear into her old rundown house at the end of Monroe Street on the outskirts of town, a new bottle of Vick's Formula 44 deep in her pocket. Her cat, Bandit, followed her most everywhere she went and sometimes even had a little piece of scrap cloth tied around his neck, matching the one on Vallie's head.

"How do you know that's your aunt?" Wiley asked B.T. after many miles of dead silence except for the road noise.

"Well, sniddle-snot, it's as plain as day for everybody!" The boy slapped his knee and sat upright, a surge of energy seeming to push through his gangly body.

Wiley gripped the steering wheel and groaned. "It can't be as plain as day for everybody, because I sure as heck cain't see it."

"Ha! Then you must be blind, Mr. Wiley. Blinder than a newborn puppy." B.T. turned away and mumbled, "Besides that, now you ain't gonna know unless I tell you."

Wiley felt his face turn red. This skinny, freckled boy had riled him, kept him agitated, and worst of all—delighted him to no end. There was no denying it, B.T. reminded him of how he'd comported himself when he was a teenager. Mark Twain had said that the only thing to do with a young boy was to put him in a barrel, hammer on a lid, and drill a hole in the side of the barrel the size of a quarter. Then, when the boy was sixteen years old, plug up the hole!

Wiley sighed heavily, and in his most wheedling tone he said, "Now, B.T., I'm a askin' you to tell me how it is you know that Vallie Thomas is your aunt."

The silence that followed lasted for three miles, past the heavenly cool spring that seemed to explode from the trees that lined the road, past a field of freshly planted tobacco seedlings, and past the peach trees in full bloom at the base of the mountain. It was only then that the boy spoke.

"Reckon you ain't seen Aunt Vallie's gold tooth," B.T. said, his range starting high and going low. He grinned, and when Wiley didn't answer continued in his boy-man voice. "I saw it when the medic pulled open her mouth and stuck some kinda hose in it." The boy leaned his head back on the seat and closed his eyes. His words now came slowly, soft like the wings of a butterfly fluttering in the air. "Last time I saw her, she let me hold that tooth. Reached back in her mouth, pulled it out, and said, 'Here you go, boy. Look at this here gold. Your great, great, great granddaddy done worked the Georgia gold rush, and this is just one small dribble of that gold.'"

"That so?" Wiley said, not knowing what to believe.

B.T. cleared his throat. "I held that tooth in my fangers, and I swear it felt hot—like it were on fire. Then she grabbed it from me and popped it back in her mouth and grinned real big." He turned to Wiley. "How could I ever forget somebody like that? A woman who'd just yank her tooth out and hand it to me."

Wiley said nothing, trying hard to remember if he had ever seen Vallie's gold tooth. He couldn't recall and turned to say so just as B.T. hollered, "Yep, that's my Aunt Vallie all right. When we get to the hospital, we'll take a look in her mouth and I'll show you that tooth, long as she don't bite me. Big ol' gold thang in the back a her jaw."

Wiley cringed and the truck weaved and crossed the centerline. Union General Hospital was still a mile or so away, but he was ready to get out of the truck and walk the rest of the way. The only good thing was that B.T. had controlled his delicate condition the whole way.

The parking lot was crowded, hardly a space left because of the influx of cars from Ivy Log already at the hospital, Wiley as-

sumed. Luckily, he found a spot near the emergency room entrance as someone was just leaving. He grabbed Vallie's handbag, along with the small suitcase Lizzie had packed. "Let's go,
boy. We've got to see what's goin' on with Vallie."

B.T. followed a few steps behind Wiley as they entered
though the wide automatic double doors. Across the room, the
admissions/information desk sat near more double doors, these
leading to the treatment rooms Wiley had visited a few times for
others, and just this past year for himself when his truck slid off
the side of a mountain—with him in it. Only a few people sat in
the chairs that filled the waiting room. Most stood or paced. He
recognized about half the people; the others there for folks other
than Vallie. Regardless of who had fostered the visit, all the faces
displayed the same high level of anxiety.

Wiley eased up to the large desk and a woman sitting behind
it, her hair gray and a widow's peak at her hairline. "Hello,
ma'am. I'm here on behalf of Vallie Thomas. I'm her legal advocate, or whatever it's called. She was just brought in from Ivy
Log." He stared into the somewhat vacant eyes of the woman,
who sat stiff-backed, a pen in her hand and a telephone nearby.

"Your name?" She pulled a form onto a clipboard and in
black ink wrote "Vallie Thomas" in big block letters.

"Wiley Hanson is my name."

"You're related to Ms. Thomas?"

"No, ma'am, I'm not. But I've been assigned her power of attorney and I'm executor of her estate. She has no family I know
of." Wiley was not going to confuse the issue by discussing B.T.'s
claim.

The woman placed the clipboard and pen on her worn desk.
"Do you have documents with you showing you hold that position?"

"Yes, ma'am, I do. . . I mean . . . I have them, just not on me
right now. There's a copy of everything over at Collins and Dyer.
This just happened, and I hurried over here." Wiley thought a
big smile might work, so he gave her his widest effort and added,
"My own papers are all back in Ivy Log."

"May I see your identification?" The woman asked and
smiled back at him.

He reached into his back pocket and pulled out his wallet.
His driver's license was four years old, almost ready for renewal.

He looked at his picture. He hadn't changed much. "Here you go." He handed the license to the woman, whose nametag read: "Doris."

Doris studied the license a moment and made a phone call. When she finished she stood. "Come with me, Mr. Hanson."

"Ma'am, I need just a few seconds to do something first." Wiley walked over to B.T., who was sitting and studying the freckles on his arm. "You stay out here in the waiting room. Here's some money for a cold drink." Wiley pulled some ones from his wallet. "Should be enough for a while. Get a candy bar, too, if you want one." He handed B.T. the dollar bills. "I won't be long. Sam and Eva will be here shortly if you get lonely."

"I won't be goin' nowhere." He glanced around the area before leaning close to Wiley and whispering, "Don't forget to look for that there gold tooth I done told you about."

Wiley nodded and followed Doris through the double doors and into the cool, brightly lit emergency room where the pungent smell of Betadine and the beeping of machines caused him to have to gather himself. A man with a stethoscope protruding from a lab-coat pocket approached him and Doris.

"Mr. Hanson, this is Dr. Meyer," Doris said. "He'll discuss Ms. Thomas's condition with you." She turned and left the area, her nurse's shoes squeaking on the tile floor.

Dr. Meyer reached out his hand. "I do believe we've met, Mr. Hanson. You drove off the mountain at the end of last year. About froze to death in a blizzard, if I recall."

"Yes, sir. That was me. You patched me up real good."

"There was really no patching to do. You're a mountain man. Few bruises here and there are nothing to you."

Wiley smiled. "Miss Thomas?"

Dr. Meyer, tall and slender, his brown hair graying around his temples, rolled over a nearby stool and motioned for Wiley to sit down in a chair that was behind him. The doctor eased himself onto the stool. "Mr. Hanson, I'm sorry to have to tell you this, but Ms. Thomas didn't make it. Massive heart failure." Dr. Meyer reached out and squeezed Wiley's shoulder. "I wish we could have done something for her, but she wasn't breathing when she got here. We tried everything but she didn't respond. Poor gal's heart just gave out on her, I'm afraid."

The crowd that had gathered in the emergency room stilled as Wiley walked through the double doors, his eyes searching for B.T. The boy's possible aunt, the woman he had come down the mountain to find—at considerable peril to himself—had died. Wiley hesitated halfway across the room. What would he say to the boy? The orphaned child, barely a teenager, who'd walked forty miles through the Natahala Forest in search of family? He found B.T. by a vending machine, doing a messy job of eating a candy bar.

"Look here, B.T., I'm afraid it's not good news. Your Aunt Vallie has passed on." He patted B.T. on the back and felt a lump in his own throat.

He reached out and put his arms around the boy's bony shoulders, expecting to have to console him.

Instead, the boy squinted hard at Wiley and asked, "Did you get a look at that gold tooth I been tellin' you about?"

~~~

Chapter 30

Tess Starling's living room filled by five o'clock. Monty Reynolds arrived late, but not too late to see Pyune Murphy descend the stairs hand in hand with Tess. Greg Martin, a vice president at BWM, and his wife, Gwendolyn, would be helping Tess entertain the various board members and their spouses since Robert couldn't make it back from the West Coast in time for the cocktail party.

All heads turned to the stairs and an eerie quiet fell across the room. "Oh, my," said Gwendolyn, her wine glass held in midair and an expression of utter confusion on her face.

Monty grinned and watched the two identical women as they reached the bottom of the stairway. "Unbelievable, isn't it?" he whispered.

Tess, smiling and radiant, tugged on Pyune's hand and led her into the room. "Hello, everyone," she said in a raised voice. "We're so glad you've joined the Bakers' World family for an evening of celebration." She paused, her smile even wider. "I personally have something to celebrate. You're all wondering why the winner of the grand prize for our baking contest looks so much like me?" She laughed out loud and gazed at Pyune.

As one, everyone in the room moved a step closer, not wanting to miss a word.

"We don't have any of the answers as to how we've never known about this until now. For me, a few hours ago to be exact. Chance, serendipity, whatever one would want to call it, but when Pyune EverSweet Murphy won our annual baking contest and came to New York, it was unbelievable that she also turned out to be related to me. As you all can see, she's my twin sister." Tess smiled lovingly at Pyune. "This is a miracle, wouldn't you all agree?" There was a loud round of applause, and after the noise subsided she turned to Pyune. "I'd like to present you to the BWM Board of Directors, who also happen to be our friends and a huge part of the BWM family."

A formal rumble of welcome spread across the room as glasses were raised and toasts made. Pyune could do nothing but smile and nod her head as one person after another wished her well. When the last of the toasts ended, Tess stepped back so Pyune could have the "stage."

With a slight tremble in her voice, Pyune said, "My, what a warm welcome." She folded her hands together, pausing to gather her thoughts. "From the moment I received the letter from BWM announcing that I was the winner of the baking contest, my life has been a whirlwind." A slight giggle escaped her shiny lips, on which red lipstick had been meticulously applied by Tess minutes earlier. "I'd never even been outside Union County, Georgia . . . much less on an airplane." She took a deep breath. "And here I am—in New York City."

Monty applauded and the others followed. Her voice dropped. "Who would have thought, waiting here for me, was a sister I didn't know I had. I . . . I am so grateful . . . I . . . . " A tear rolled down her cheek, and she made a swipe at it with just a finger. "Oh, dear, my eye make-up will be ruined."

Tess handed Pyune a tissue. Leaning on one end of the magnificent bar, Monty sipped a Scotch and wondered how Pyune would cope with the discovery of a sister, especially one such as Tess, and have this coupled with the celebrity that would attend her selection as BWM's grand-prize winner. What kind of person loomed inside the soft loveliness of this small-town woman, whose exposure to the outside world had been limited to a life in the Appalachian Mountains?

He meandered closer to the chair where Pyune now sat, an untouched glass of wine in her hand. He passed Tess, who was talking with Guy Madison, BWM's financial guru and no relation in looks or lineage to the man who'd played the first Zorro on television. Monty nodded and eased onto the end cushion of a nearby couch, placing himself only a foot or two from Pyune. He crossed his legs and placed his elbow on the plush arm of the sofa. "At last you're alone, and now it's my turn to bask in your glow."

Pyune turned to him, her dark eyes laughing, but not for the reason he thought. "Your socks don't match," she said.

His James Bondish black dinner jacket cut to perfection, the black bowtie perfectly arranged, Monty leaned over and studied the socks he was wearing. "I'll take your word for it." He looked at her and gave her a crooked smile. "I guess my secret is out— I'm colorblind. Indeed, those must be navy socks." He glanced around the room. "Should I leave?"

Pyune shook her head. "Please don't. I can't imagine this room without you. You saved me twice."

"Ah. I assume that is a compliment. I'm not sure I deserve it though."

"And why not?" Pyune shifted her wine glass to her other hand and leaned in closer to Monty, waiting for his answer.

Monty tilted his head and nodded as if remembering something. "My ride on the elevator with you. You were free to do whatever you wanted. You didn't have to stay, you know, despite my prodding."

"That's true. But now I'm glad I did."

"Are you sure about that?"

"Why not?"

His voice hardened somewhat. "I'm not so sure of what effect New York will have on you. As the metaphor goes, you're a fish out of water. A beautiful fish, but on land nonetheless. I told you, before it was over, you'd be the toast of New York City. But then I thought about it." He took a sip of his drink. "Maybe that's not what you really want."

Pyune found herself considering Monty's words. It was true, she was a fish out of water. Upon her arrival in New York, all she had wanted was to get her $25,000 and rush for the airport and return home. However, here she was with a sister she didn't know she had, holding a glass of wine in one of New York's plushest apartments, wearing one of Tess's designer dresses, and she'd been gifted a genuine pearl bracelet. Just then she thought of Wiley and felt a shiver up and down her spine. She must remember to call him the moment she returned to the guest suite.

"Mr. Reynolds, I—"

"Please, I'm Monty." The James Bond jacket and bowtie leaned back, the navy blue socks exposed for the world to see as the legs crossed again.

The room seemed warm even if it wasn't, possibly due to on overabundance of fragrances—perfumes, wines, and delectable hot hors d'oeuvres recently brought out by a chef and two servers. Adding to the effect, a rustle of taffeta drifted past her as a guest swished by in a long gown. "Okay, *Monty,* you have to understand what my life is like in Ivy Log. There are no sky-scrapers, no limousines—" glancing at Monty's jacket— "no tuxedos."

Monty arced his brow. "Are you happy with your life in Ivy Log?" The long legs uncrossed and Monty placed his elbows on his knees and clasped his hands together. His expression was in-tense; it was a personal question, one that perhaps she didn't want to answer.

Pyune might be a simple mountain woman but her intellect ran deep, as did a quiet sophistication, providing a complexity to her that belied her small-town upbringing. It's possible her an-swer to Monty's question would reveal an inkling of who she re-ally was, and she weighed her response carefully.

She gently cleared her throat. "How can I answer that ques-tion when I have nothing else to compare it to? I know what I know—based on where I come from. So everything is relative, isn't it? Yes, I'm happy with my life in Ivy Log. Could I be hap-pier somewhere else is a question I can't answer?" She smiled, leaving Monty Reynolds with a bemused look on his matinee-idol face and nothing more to say.

Monty finished his Scotch and stood. He took Pyune's un-touched glass of wine and asked, "How about a ginger ale or a cola? You're obviously not a wine drinker." He smiled and she noticed a dimple for the first time. "I'll be right back. There's lot to talk about."

"Not about me, I hope."

Monty paused and looked down at Pyune's glistening eyes. "You're all I want to talk about."

He left Pyune and headed for the bar. Behind him, Tess called out, "Hey, handsome man! What are you up to with my sister?" Monty and Tess ended up together along the sleek edge of the bar, each watching the goings-on in the room as if casual observers.

"And what would you like, madam?" the bartender asked Tess.

"Oh, you know how much I like German wine. How about a glass of that special Riesling everyone thinks is good only for cooking?" The man chuckled, immediately coming up with what she'd requested.

"And you sir," the bartender asked Monty after he handed Tess her wine. Monty ordered another Scotch for himself and a ginger ale with lots of ice for Pyune. Tess could see Pyune across the room, surrounded by some of the crème de la crème of New York society. She was a novelty—a true Cinderella at a ball just for her.

"Quite a woman, isn't she?" Tess remarked.

"That she is. I'm still having a hard time believing this. Not in a million years did I think there was another one just like you out there." Monty laughed and touched his glass to Tess's.

"Hmmm," she said, sipping her wine and not making it clear what the "hmmm" was about until she continued. "I'm sure we're different in many ways—just don't know which ones yet. How could we in such little time together? But I'm going to work on changing that. I'm hoping she'll delay her departure for a few days so we can get to know one another. Find some answers."

"Do you know where to begin?" Monty asked.

"Not really." Tess pressed her lips to the side of her wine glass. "But how was it that I went to the best schools, lived in a fine apartment in Manhattan—while all this time Pyune was left in the mountains of North Carolina to fend for herself? Nothing makes sense about this."

"Somebody surely must have the answers to those questions."

Tess sighed. "Perhaps."

Monty set his glass on the bar. "By the way, I see I have a meeting tomorrow morning with you and your staff on Friday's fundraiser. Nine o'clock, right? You planning to go over 'The Today Show' with Pyune?"

Tess nodded. "Tomorrow morning, before she leaves, I'll brief her. Cover the standard interview questions. Shouldn't be too complex. I think she'll do fine. She seems like a natural."

Tess found herself looking into the mirror behind the bar, at the image of her sister, who seemed quite at ease in her new surroundings. She studied Pyune's profile, her mannerisms. They were her own.

"You seem distracted," Monty said. "What are you thinking?"

Tess turned around and faced the room, her back to the mirror behind the bar, her wine glass empty. Again, she studied Pyune's profile. "I'm sorry, Monty. My mind is running a million miles an hour." Tess was beginning to piece things together. Sooner or later she would know everything there was to know about her and her sister—but she wasn't sure she'd like what she'd find out.

~~~

Chapter 31

Except for a single light over the large gas stove in the sprawling kitchen, The Boardinghouse sat dark at the end of Main
Street. In the dimmed room, Wiley, Sam, and Will drank luke-
warm coffee from a pot on the stove. The crumbs from a piece of
chocolate cake remained sprinkled over the wooden table where
they sat. At the parsonage, B.T. slept with Delilah entombed in
his arms, the cat apparently not smelling so bad after all.

The death of Vallie Thomas lay heavily on the minds of all of
Ivy Log, but especially on Wiley Hanson. He had piled firewood
behind her little house for years, picked pecans from the vast
spread of trees in the field south of her house, but best of all he
enjoyed her wild stories about the big Georgia gold rush in the
early 1820s, her ancestors becoming prospectors during what
was known as the second-largest event of its kind in the States,
surpassed only by the California stampede for gold in 1849. Vallie had shocked him one cool October evening when she pulled
out a cigarillo, a Havana Honey, and entered into a long monologue on the joys of smelling cigar smoke.

"We got to write an obituary for Vallie," Wiley said, putting
another teaspoon of sugar in his coffee and stirring his coffee re-
lentlessly, his eyes on Roy and Trigger, their stenciled picture almost faded to oblivion on his favorite cup. "You're good at writing, Sam. How about you doin' it?"

"I hardly knew Vallie, but I'd be honored to, I don't know,
put the finishing touches on it." He pulled a small notebook
from his pocket and saw what he'd written earlier that evening:

Eva's telephone number—underlined twice. "Maybe between the three of us we can come up with something appropriate. Will, would you mind getting us started?" Even though Sam and William Johnson had roomed together in college and become best friends, when the latter received his doctorate in theology and was ordained, from that point forward he was Pastor Will in Sam's mind, and no longer just plain Will. The humble pastor insisted on remaining just plain 'Will.'

"Of course." The pastor held Vallie in high esteem, as he did all members of his flock. Her simple life had humbled him, had reaffirmed his belief in Christ's Sermon on the Mount in which the Beatitudes presented a set of Christian ideals that focused on a spirit of love and humility. *Blessed are the meek, for they shall inherit the earth.* In the few short months he had known Vallie, she personified Christ's teachings in the way she conducted her everyday life. "Why don't we start with this: "Vallie Gertrude Thomas, Ivy Log, Georgia, passed away—"

"Wait a minute, pastor." Wiley stood and walked across the kitchen, his steps slow and deliberate, and he pulled open the back door to The Boardinghouse kitchen. To his left he could see the towering steeple of The Church of Ivy Log, the usually gleaming white spire darkened to soft gray by the long shadows of the setting sun. He tilted his face to the sky and felt the soft April breeze, not quite summer warm but mixed with cooler air, like green clover in a wet meadow. He felt his throat squeeze and let the memories of Vallie Thomas fill his head.

"You okay?" called Sam through the dark kitchen.

Wiley didn't turn around, just held up his hand. One day he'd seen Vallie feeding squirrels and birds in the town square after a big snowstorm. Her sweater thin, she wore no gloves and the scarf wrapped around her head was made of light cotton. He slowed his pickup truck and parked along Main Street, right in front of the flagpole. "Hey, Vallie, where's your coat?" he'd asked. "It's fifteen degrees out here."

"Them boll weevils got my coat. Ain't nothing but holes now. Why should I wear me a bunch of holes?" She turned away and continued scattering handfuls of corn.

"Boll weevils? I thought boll weevils only lived in Texas. Don't matter none. We need to get you a coat." Wiley blew his horn. "Come on, Vallie. Let's go over to The Boardinghouse. You can eat some hot grits while I find you somethin' to wear so you won't freeze to death."

She looked up and grinned at him and began trudging through the snow, leaving a trail of corn behind her as she wedged herself into his warm truck. She pulled the scarf from her head and wiped her runny nose. "Hot grits, you say? I'd like a slice of ham, too, if you don't mind." He bought her a big meal and watched as she cleaned her plate.

How many years had it been? Didn't matter, she was gone now. Wiley watched the last of the sun move behind the darkening peaks while The Boardinghouse rooster jumped on top of the smokehouse, settling in for the night as he placed his head under his wing. It wouldn't be the same without Vallie. He walked back inside and saw Will and Sam watching him.

"I reckon I'll be writing that obituary myself, if y'all don't mind," Wiley said. No one objected.

Later that night, in the quiet of a sleeping Ivy Log, Wiley poured a small glass of bourbon and began writing. At midnight, he lay down his pen.

Vallie Thomas, perhaps the most kindred spirit in Union County, began her Heavenly journey out of Ivy Log, Georgia, yesterday afternoon. She left in a hurry, certain that what lay ahead was full of marvelous adventures and glorious endeavors. The grin on her face was touching as she waved goodbye with her purple handkerchief and faded into the blue mountain sky. She took with her the hearts of Ivy Log, a small box of Havana Honey cigarillos deep in her pockets, and an old coat covered with Bandit's long gray hairs. And, of course, a bottle of Formula 44.

Her friends Wiley, Harley, Doyce, Lizzie, the doc, the pastor, and Sam didn't want her to go—they would miss her almost bawdy laugh and stories of times gone by. *Stay a little longer*, they all said. *The 4th of July fireworks won't be the same without you.* Pastor Johnson understood her passage from earth: *Vallie, you've got a mansion just over the hilltop in that bright land where you'll never grow old. And some day over yonder you'll never more wander but walk on streets that are purest gold.*

Now Bandit will sit in the shade on top of the porch railing at The Boardinghouse, waiting for his loving owner to return. Everyone in Ivy Log will pet him, but he will have a yearning in his eyes, certain that Vallie will be along any minute.

If Vallie had to leave us, we're glad she left in the spring when the fragrance of peach and apple blossoms fills the air, and the trout in the mountain streams are starting to move. We can never walk Main Street again without looking for her, that purple scarf, the bottle of Formula 44 in her hand and Bandit piddling along behind her.

Vallie Gertrude Thomas was born on October 8, 1951, and left this earth on April 21, 2016. A memorial service will be held Monday, April 25, at 1:00 p.m., at The Church of Ivy Log. Vallie leaves behind her nephew, B.T. Hickel, and her beloved cat, Bandit.

Wiley turned out the light, sat in the darkness, and watched the hands of the clock move to 2 a.m., his worried mind leaving him restless. *The boy. What about the boy?*

~~~

Chapter 32

BWM's limousine eased through the early morning traffic, down West 72nd Street and the Avenue of the Americas. Bakers' World Magazine headquarters stood only fifteen minutes from Rockefeller Plaza and Studio 1A, where "The Today Show" staff was preparing for its Thursday broadcast. Pyune EverSweet Murphy would be their special guest, the winner of BWM's 25th annual baking contest.

Pyune sat in back of the limo and listened to Frandy hum Adele's new song "Hello." He belted out the last line in his Caribbean lilt ". . . hello, can you hear me?" waving his arm in the air as his voice lifted. The glass between the front and back was lowered and Pyune smiled as she watched him rock gently in his seat and navigate New York City traffic. There were Yellow Cabs everywhere, honking, pulling to the curbs, and merging into traffic. Had Pyune been in Ivy Log, she would already be serving breakfast at The Boardinghouse—hot biscuits, ham, grits, and of course a pan of warm cinnamon rolls.

Though pleasant enough, last night's cocktail reception with the BWM board members was exhausting. She fell into bed at 11:30, only to jerk awake at 3 a.m., realizing she had not called Wiley. She fretted until 5 a.m. when Tess tapped softly on her door. "Pyune, coffee's ready. I have an outfit laid out for you in my dressing room."

Both women hurried through the morning before Pyune was off to "The Today Show" after a briefing with Tess in which she gave her a few pointers on her live television appearance. A meeting with Tess's marketing group on the upcoming celebrity chef fundraiser planned for the next day was scheduled for 9 a.m., right after her "Today Show" appearance. Talk about hectic!

Frandy trilled, "Hey, Miss Pyune, it's a lovely day, isn't it? Your first time in New York City, and now you'll be on 'The Today Show.'" Frandy rocked some more in his seat. "You gonna be famous, I say. Famous like those celebrities out in Hollywood. A diva, all right. Everybody can't cook like you and be beautiful too." Frandy chuckled and smiled wide in his rearview mirror. "I say you're gonna to be one hot mama when this is all over."

One hot mama? "Frandy, I cook, and that's all I do. How can that be so special?"

"Oh, Miss Pyune. Frandy'll teach you all 'bout this celebrity stuff. You got to walk like a queen, you know, just hold that chin high, sway them hips and pout those lips. Yes, Miss Pyune. Those photographers will be snapping your picture day and night. You listen to what Frandy say because it be true—as true as anything I ever tell anybody about anything."

Pyune shook her head, "I don't want to disappoint you, but on Sunday afternoon I'll be on a plane headed back to Ivy Log. I'll be a celebrity only three more days, then it's back to making biscuits." Pyune saw the reflection of the sleek limo in the glass windows along Central Park West. *Surely, I can last another three days in New York City.* She dialed Wiley's number and he answered on the first ring.

"Pyune! Everything okay? I waited for your call until past midnight."

"I'm so sorry, Wiley. Things are so hectic here. I'm on my way to Rockefeller Plaza and 'The Today Show.' I'll be on the eight-thirty segment, if you want to watch."

"What are you talkin' about! Course I want to watch. All Ivy Log wants to see you."

"How's everything going? Vallie and Lizzie handling everything okay?"

Wiley was ready for this, and he didn't hesitate for a split second. "Everything's fine, Pyune. Just have fun and I'll be turning on the television in a few minutes. I love you. You know that."

"I love you too. And *you* know that." She closed her phone and smiled.

Frandy grinned into the review mirror. "Ah, Miss Murphy,

you love a man, eh?"

"Yes, I do, Frandy. Wiley Hanson. A mountain man, handsome as can be."

Frandy pulled to the curb, and a Today staff member met the car and held out his hand. "Ms. Murphy, I'm Scott. I'll be taking you to a dressing room to prepare for your segment." He squeezed her hand and glanced at Frandy. "Hey, Frandy. Come back a few minutes before nine for a pick-up."

"Will do," Frandy said and waved. He smiled at Pyune. "Knock 'em dead, pretty lady."

Scott directed Pyune into the building, touching her shoulder lightly and steering her to an elevator. "On behalf of 'The Today Show,' I'd like to welcome you to NBC, Miss Murphy."

"Thank you, Scott. It's my pleasure to be here." Pyune felt her heart flutter. Goodness, *The Today Show.*"

Pyune was led to a dressing room and to a chair in front of an expansive table full of cosmetics. "We want to be sure your make-up is camera-ready," a pleasant-sounding woman with long blond hair said as she came over and carefully inspected Pyune's face. Pyune wrinkled her nose when she began applying some powder. The woman backed away and laughed.

"This won't hurt, Miss Murphy. Just need to tone down a couple of areas. Sometimes the television process can accentuate undesirable attributes in a person's face." The make-up artist brushed back Pyune's hair with her slim hand. "With your face, there's certainly nothing undesirable to have to worry about, but heat from studio lights can cause a shine, so let's use some face powder, okay?" She smiled. "By the way, I'm Tara."

Pyune nodded and leaned back in her chair, her head resting on a support. Tara worked quietly and efficiently. "When we get through, we'll look at you under a color-balanced monitor to check the results."

Another woman, introduced as Tara's assistant, held brushes and a tray of lipsticks and blushes and hovered above Pyune. A heavy fragrance of perfume drifted from her body.

"You'll most likely have some good close-ups, so let's make sure your ears, hands and nails are ready for the studio light."

After a few minutes of "touch-ups," Tara scrutinized Pyune closely and pronounced, "I think you're camera-ready, my dear. Step over here, and let's look at you in the monitor."

Pyune got up from her chair and stood in front of a camera. She could see the monitor across the room. *Was this her? Or Tess?*

"Perfect!" Tara and her assistant left the room and two members of "The Today Show" staff moved in with clipboards and pens. A short, pudgy man with a mustache reached out his hand. "Miss Murphy, we're delighted to have you on our show. I'm Alex, an associate producer of the show, and this is Jennifer, also an associate producer." Alex was full of energy, rising up on his tiptoes as he spoke. "We want to go over the script and some information you'll need to know."

"Whatever you need to do," mumbled Pyune.

"I see you've been in make-up, Miss Murphy," Jennifer said as her eyes scanned Pyune faced before settling on her dress, which was a deep royal blue. "Perfect color dress for you. Good style for television too. You'll be on camera in a sitting position for about three minutes, then standing for about five minutes. You'll be filmed from your right profile, across from your interviewer, in your first segment."

"Who is my interviewer?"

"You've got Natalie and Savannah this morning. Matt's on assignment. Al might step in for a moment also."

Pyune nodded and looked up as Alex flipped the pages on his clipboard. "Here's how the run will go, Miss Murphy: Savannah will preface your appearance with an introduction and rundown of who you are—a woman from a small town who won an international baking contest sponsored by America's favorite baking magazine, Bakers' World."

Alex circled Pyune's chair, his hands moving through the air as if clicking off pieces of the planned segment. "You'll be asked the following questions by Savannah: What made you enter the baking contest? How did you decide on which recipe to use? What were your feelings upon hearing you had won?" Alex stopped in front of Pyune and made a note on his clipboard.

Jennifer stepped in. "Natalie will take over with these questions: What do you plan to do with your prize money? How do you like New York City?

Altogether, these questions will take approximately three minutes, then a commercial break. Afterwards, the three of you will walk to 'The Today Show' kitchen, which is just a few steps away, and you'll discuss your restaurant in Ivy Log."

Alex, looking up from his clipboard, took over again: "I believe that's The Boardinghouse, right?"

"Yes, sir."

Alex said rapidly, "Next, you'll show Savannah and Natalie how to make a perfect piecrust and—"

"Piecrust? I'll be making piecrust?"

"That's right—is there a problem?"

"I . . . well . . . what about the ingredients I'll need?"

"Oh, you'll have everything you need, Ms. Murphy."

Pyune felt herself perspiring—with palpitations coming on as well. "You have lard?"

Jennifer and Alex looked at each other. Alex blurted, "Lard? What is lard?"

"I make my piecrust with pure lard."

Alex raised so high on his tiptoes that Pyune thought he might lose his balance. He said, "All we have is butter—I'm sure that will do." He looked at his clipboard. "You'll talk about—"

"I don't mean to be any trouble, but I use lard for my piecrusts." Pyune's eyes darted from Alex to Jennifer and then back to Alex.

Alex placed his clipboard on a nearby table and folded his arms across his chest. Jennifer looked down at her shoes. "Why must you use lard?" he asked.

"Because if you make piecrust from scratch—using lard—and serve it to your guests, it's something they won't ever forget." Pyune raised her chin. "Ever." A very private little smile appeared at the corner of her lips.

Alex cut his eyes to Jennifer. "Can we send someone out for some lard?"

Jennifer nodded. "We'll have to hurry to make the spot."

Pyune raised her finger. "I'll also need superfine sugar, bleached all purpose flour, and cake flour."

"Two flours?" A pink flush now suffused Alex's cheeks.

"Yes, I make my own pastry flour for my piecrusts."

"*Really*?" Alex huffed his way to the door. "Jennifer, start a list of things Miss Murphy will need and send someone out for everything immediately." He looked at a big clock on the wall. "Thank goodness her segment is late in the show." He spun on his heels and left the room, once again demonstrating considerable balance.

"I don't mean to be any trouble," Pyune said to Jennifer. "It's just that a well-made piecrust has no equal." Pyune twirled around in her chair. She was beginning to act like a diva, just like Frandy said.

"You're no trouble, Miss Murphy. Just tell me everything you'll need."

At 8:25. Pyune was shown to a grouping of chairs on "The To-day Show" set. A microphone was attached on her collar, and she smiled when Savannah and Natalie entered and sat across from her. Both women welcomed Pyune, and she responded with, "Thank you so much. I love being here."

Seconds later, from the set: "Three, two, one. Live!"

Savannah began Pyune's introduction as she smiled and talked into the camera: "No doubt you've been hearing about a woman from a small town in the Appalachian mountains who climbed to the top of her own mountain when she won Bakers' World Magazine's top prize."

"That's right," said Natalie. "From within the warm kitchen of The Boardinghouse Restaurant in Ivy Log, Georgia, a recipe ex-isted that was so extraordinary that all six judges for the twenty-fifth annual baking contest rated it a ten."

Savannah said, "We'd like to introduce the special lady who entered this recipe—Pyune EverSweet Murphy—a woman who's been baking since she was fourteen years old." Savannah turned to Pyune and the camera zoomed in on her. "Welcome, Pyune, to 'The Today Show.'"

Pyune EverSweet Murphy was on national television. After her first plane ride, her first trip to New York City, and her first time out of Union County, she was being viewed by millions of people. *Oh, Lord, please don't let me stutter or mumble.*

"Thank you for having me on your show." There was no hesi-tation in Pyune's delivery—she was cool, calm and collected. Who would have thought it?

Natalie asked, "Pyune, tell us about the Bakers' World contest and what made you submit your recipe?"

Pyune laughed. "I received the December issue of Bakers' World Magazine, and it just fell open to the page that announced their twenty-fifth anniversary baking contest. I thought it was an omen, so I entered right away."

Savannah laughed. "Just like that, you sent in a recipe? Since you own and operate a restaurant—The Boardinghouse in Ivy Log, Georgia—you must have hundreds of recipes. How did you decide on a particular one?"

"Oh, that was easy. My mama taught me how to make lemon pudding cake when I was fourteen years old, and I've been making it ever since. It's my favorite dessert." Pyune tilted her head, her earrings catching the lights, her red lips glistening as she smiled.

Savannah followed up: "What did you do when you heard you'd won?"

"Oh, my goodness, I couldn't believe it!" Pyune took a deep breath, her eyes shining. "I'm so grateful to be the winner."

Natalie asked, "Do you have any plans for the $25,000 prize money?"

Pyune appeared thoughtful. "Well, The Boardinghouse needs a new stove."

All three ladies laughed.

Natalie asked, "How do you like New York City?"

"It's unlike anything I've ever seen. It's been so magical; everyone has been so kind. I appreciate very much the hospitality I've been shown."

Savannah said, "We'll take a short commercial break and be right back. Pyune is going to give us a quick lesson on how to make the perfect pie crust."

A staff member rushed in and powdered Pyune's nose, swiped a hair from Natalie's forehead, and put lip gloss on Savannah's pink lips.

"You did great, Pyune," Natalie said.

"Are you sure you haven't been on television before?" Savannah chided her. "You're a natural."

"Thank you both. I can't believe how easy it is. I hope I'm doing okay."

Savannah smiled. "You were perfect. Let's walk over to our Today kitchen and get ready for that pie crust lesson."

From the set: "Three, two, one! Live!"

Savannah said, "Welcome back to our interview with Pyune EverSweet Murphy, the winner of Bakers' World Magazine's twenty-fifth anniversary baking contest. Miss Murphy has been kind enough to offer to give Natalie and me a lesson on how to make the perfect pie crust." Savannah and Natalie laughed. "We don't know if we'll be good students or not, but we'll try."

All three women donned aprons with a bold red "BWM" logo on the front. Pyune stood at a large rectangular table, Savannah and Natalie on each side of her. "Making a perfect piecrust is quite easy," said Pyune, lifting a bowl. "I like to put my mixing bowl, flour, and lard in the freezer to have them all nice and cold."

Natalie gestured to the two different bags of flour. "I understand you like to make your own pastry flour. How do you do that?"

"You blend bleached all-purpose flour and cake flour to get a good pastry flour. Put about two parts all-purpose flour to one part cake flour. And, of course, mix well."

Pyune seemed to disappear into another world. Her hands worked swiftly, a dip and sweep of the flour—one-and-a-half cups —then one-half teaspoon of salt and one-eighth teaspoon of baking powder. In mere seconds she'd mixed one-half cup of cold lard into the flour and added a quarter cup of ice water, a small amount at a time. "It's necessary to put your hands into the dough." She smiled. "Hands-on experience is everything." She looked up. "Here, y'all try it."

Natalie patted the dough as if it were a pet of some kind. "What is an ideal pie crust?"

Pyune pulled the dough from the bowl. "It has light, flaky layers, is tender and golden brown when baked, and has a flavor good enough to eat by itself."

Pyune rolled out her piecrust and began placing it into a pie pan, crimping the edges with her thumb and forefinger. "Oh, if only we had some wonderful fresh blackberries—"

"And some vanilla ice cream," said Savannah.

Camera Three zoomed in on Pyune as she held up the pie pan. She was camera perfect except for a little flour on her chin. But she stood triumphant—the mountain girl whose first cooking lesson was on a woodstove back in the corner of a cold kitchen deep in the Appalachian mountains had demonstrated her skill for a national television audience.

"That's a wrap!" came a sharp voice as everything went to commercial with both co-hosts gushing over Pyune.

~~~

Chapter 33

A couple of hours before Pyune's television debut—eight-hundred miles and then some as the crow flies from New York City —Ivy Log, Georgia, lay in early morning repose; no skyscrapers, Yellow Cabs, or the sounds of horns and sirens. Bandit walked up and down the porch railing at The Boardinghouse, an occasional soft meow escaping through his long whiskers. He was restless, waiting —not for his breakfast but for the woman who wore the purple kerchief. Farther up the mountain, a soft gray mist hovered around the tall peaks, a prelude to an April sun that was rising like a jewel in the east.

Wiley Hanson, long awake, propped his long legs on the porch railing and watched Bandit pace. The cat knew Vallie was gone; he just didn't know why or how. "It's okay, you old tomcat, you ain't gonna miss a meal around this place. Or a back rubbin', for that matter."

He rocked in a chair that had been on the porch of The Boardinghouse ever since he could remember. The seat's shape was the result of years of various rear-ends that had eased themselves into the rust-colored hide of what appeared to be an old Hereford cow. Wiley rocked to sooth himself. He'd slept little the night before. He closed his eyes and tried to sort out the cause of his worry.

From the railing, Bandit navigated down Wiley's legs and curled up in his lap. "I know. I know, old boy. That sweet old woman's gone from us." He ran his hand up and down the soft fur on the cat's back. "Life's tough, ain't it?"

Wiley would go to Collins and Dyer in the afternoon and talk with Jesse about Vallie's will and resolve any possible issues. He'd decided not to tell Pyune that Vallie had died. He felt that her trip to New York did not need to be overshadowed by Vallie's death. She might get mad at him when she found out after she got back, but he believed this was the right way to handle it.

From the sidewalk, the pastor stopped in front of The Boarding-house and called up to Wiley. "Got any coffee made? You know there's going to be a big crowd here in a little while to watch Pyune's interview." He shuffled up the steps and took a seat in a newer rocker next to Wiley's relic.

"I made the coffee before you were even out of bed."

The pastor chuckled. "I believe you. I'll get a cup in a minute." Both men rocked slowly and watched the morning sun ease over the ridge.

"With Vallie dyin', things are going to be startin' kinda slow around here today, so don't expect any food right away. Where's B.T. this mornin'?"

"Left him in bed. He stayed up late last night reading. The boy likes to read."

"He said he's not very good at it"

"He's not. But he gets by. I'm teaching him how to use a dictio-nary when I'm not around so he knows what the words mean."

"What does he read?"

"You're not going to believe this, but he likes reading the Bible. I promise, I didn't say a word to him. He just pulled an old Bible off the shelf in my study and took it back to the bedroom I've got him sleeping in."

A mockingbird perched on the railing at the end of the porch. Bandit's eyes sprang open and his ears twitched.

Wiley said, "When things settle down a bit, let's talk with Eva. She claims she's B.T. half-sister, and I feel she'll want some say so in all of this. After all, Vallie was her aunt too. I'm hopin' that Vallie's will might offer a few answers."

"You've never read the will?"

"Nope. Although I'm the executor of her estate, I've never even seen a copy of the will. I just signed a bunch of papers a long time ago and went on my way. Old Jessie Collins will have to enlighten me."

"Vallie and Eva's mother were sisters, right?"

"So it seems." Wiley laughed quietly. "It's like a movie, ain't it?

Who woulda thought a young boy would show up in Ivy Log lookin' for his aunt and find out he has a half-sister three times his age?" Wiley jerked forward in his chair, spilling Bandit onto the porch. "You know what I think?"

"You're a complex man, Wiley. I'd hate to try to guess what you're thinking right now."

"Well, I'll tell you. A small town is not unlike a living being, exhibitin' birth, youth, maturity, old age, and death." He looked thoughtfully at the preacher. "I think Ivy Log and its folks are at the maturity stage, don't you?"

The pastor grinned. "I think Ivy Log is far past its youth—if gauged by both you and me especially." Both men laughed just as a loud clattering noise come from the kitchen, followed by something hitting the floor.

"I think Lizzie's back in the kitchen getting some things together. Guess she'll try to serve breakfast this morning." Wiley pretended to duck. "I sure don't want to be in there when Paula gets here. I called her last night and asked her to come over and help Lizzie out."

"Oh, my, Wiley. What have you done? You know that's not going to work." The pastor couldn't help himself. He turned his head so Wiley wouldn't see a grimace cross his normally serene features.

Wiley shrugged. "What else could I do—Lizzie can't handle it all by herself. I'll help her as much as I can. Surely those two can get along until Pyune gets back."

"Don't count on it."

At that moment Lizzie poked her head out the front door. "There's been some knockin' on the backdoor for about five minutes, and when I first looked through the window I seen Paula." She stopped talking and stomped her foot. "Wiley Hanson, she says you told her to come over here and cook. I ain't about to let that witch in the kitchen as long as I'm a runnin' it."

Lizzie's cheeks were flushed, flour was strewn across her face and arms, and her hair hung down in uncombed strands. She untied her apron and threw it across the porch railing. "If she comes in here, I go!" Lizzie charged back inside, the big door slamming behind her.

Lizzie's apron toss had disturbed a sleeping Bandit. Wiley stood, gently placing the old cat back on the railing. "I reckon I better go in and set down all the rules. If I don't, someone might get hurt."

"Could be you," the pastor said.

"That's what I'm thinkin'."

In the kitchen, pots and pans were everywhere, each of the stove's burners flaming high and water boiling with fury. Wiley didn't know what to do first—let Paula in the back door, keep the kitchen from catching fire, or stuff Lizzie in the pantry and lock the door. He dashed to the stove and turned down all the burners. He took Lizzie by the arm and sat her on a stool. "Sit. Don't move." He rushed to the back door and let Paula inside. "Good morning," he said as cheerfully as he possibly could.

"Why, good morning, Wiley." Paula pranced to the middle of the kitchen and twirled. "Well, what do you think?"

Wiley felt ill. What had possessed him to ask Paula to help in The Boardinghouse kitchen? He'd earned a Ph.D. in environmental engineering, held a full professorship at Georgia Tech, was financially independent and considered a man of sterling character. Yet he had asked the most troublesome woman in Union County—and perhaps the world—to assist in the running of The Boardinghouse while its owner was away. *Please, just shoot me. Throw my body off the highest mountain peak. I deserve no mercy.*

"Well?" Paula twirled again, her feet firmly planted in three-inch strap heels.

Wiley burst out laughing. "What the heck are you wearin'? That looks like one of Doc Patton's pharmacy jackets."

Paula tugged on the sleeves of the jacket. "It sure is. Looks just like a chef's coat, doesn't it? Last night, right after you called me, I had Doyce's mama embroider "Chef" right here above the pocket, along with my name. She loves to do that stuff. Cute, huh?"

"Yeah, *really* cute, and—"

"And, look here." She held up some papers. "I have some fabulous recipes. Here's chicken cordon bleu and an authentic French recipe for *Clafoutis*." Paula looked sideways at Lizzie, a smirk easing its way onto her mouth. "I'm sure Lizzie doesn't speak French, but *Clafoutis* is nothing but custard with fruit in it. Can you just imagine, The Boardinghouse serving French food?" Paula stopped for breath and clasped the recipes to her chest as if they were hundred dollar bills.

Exasperated, Wiley shook his head. "Paula, let's get some things straight. We ain't changing a thing on Pyune's menu. You're here to wait on a few tables and wash a few dishes. There's some high school younguns comin' in to prep for Lizzie, and you can help them if you want to—but no cookin'." Wiley backed up a step, knowing what was coming.

Paula's expression. The black beauty mark above her left brow seemed to smolder, and her eyes narrowed into a slit the size of a sharp-knife's edge. She took a few steps toward Wiley. "Wait tables?" Her eyes cut over to Lizzie, who hadn't moved from her stool. Wiley had said sit—and she wasn't going anywhere.

"Wiley Hanson, how dare you? I could be the best thing that ever happened to this place. All Pyune does is cook country food. I could add some class to The Boardinghouse menu. Why, folks would be coming from miles around to eat some French cuisine."

Wiley took a deep breath and spoke as calmly as he could. "Folks already come from miles around—to eat Pyune's cooking. I don't think folks in Union County are quite ready for—"

"Oh, hush. What do you know? I've been to France and to New York City, and I know what I'm talking about. The whole town of Ivy Log needs some class, and we can start with a fine French restaurant. We could change the name of The Boardinghouse to *Le Boardinghouse, Cuisine Francais* and—"

Wiley threw up his hands. "Enough. If you want to wait tables in your chef's coat, fine! If you want to wash dishes in your chef's coat, fine! But you're not changing one thing about this menu—even for a few days—and that's final. And you sure as heck ain't cookin'."

The kitchen fell silent. Lizzie swiveled around on her stool and faced Paula, a delightful, triumphant smile easing its way onto her face. Paula, elevating her chin in sinister defiance, slowly began unbuttoning her chef's coat. She slipped the sleeves of the coat off her arms and let the garment drop to the floor. "I'm afraid my innovative, brilliant ideas for The Boardinghouse have fallen on deaf ears. There are those of us—" raising up so she could look down at Lizzie from the highest possible angle—"who do not have the capacity to think outside the box. I, for one, have vision. I'm so sorry there is no one in Ivy Log who will jump at the opportunity to achieve bigger and better things."

Wiley and Lizzie watched Paula prance through the double doors and into the dining room, but not before calling back over her shoulder, "Coffee, Lizzie."

"There she is!" Someone shouted, followed by another voice, "There's our Pyune! The Boardinghouse regulars squeezed below the television on the wall in the main dining room and watched

Pyune Murphy's interview on "The Today Show." Wiley stood behind everyone and looked over the shoulders of Doyce and Harley. Lizzie clasped her hands tightly and kept saying, "Oh, my," until Paula told her to be quiet. Paula was the only person not smiling. She thought she was the one who should have been in New York City to receive the Bakers' World prize of $25,000. She would go to her grave thinking that the lemon pudding cake recipe was her very own family's and had been stolen by Pyune Murphy.

"That's a borrowed dress," said Paula, a sly smile on her face.

"Who cares?" Lizzie yelled at her. "Pyune is gorgeous." Lizzie glared at Paula until the redhead sidled behind Doyce. Lizzie sniffed. "I wish ol' Vallie was here to see this." Tears began to roll down her plump cheeks. Wiley patted her on the shoulder and moved aside to let Sam and the pastor take their places in the crowd and cheer for Pyune.

The camera zoomed in on Pyune, and Wiley's heart squeezed his chest. *His Pyune.* She was basking in the bright lights of New York City. He laughed when Pyune told Savannah and Natalie: ". . . *put your hands in the dough. Hands-on experience is everything.*"

Paula slid her way to the back of the crowd and nudged up to Wiley. This she-devil always found her tongue as easily as a flea finds a dog. She tilted her head toward Wiley's ear and quietly said, "You might not know this, Wiley, but I'm a very intuitive person." She nodded toward the television and the close-up of Pyune, then turned and faced him, her words now at a half-whisper. "I'm telling you, that woman is never coming back to Ivy Log." Paula moved away and added, "Or you." She sashayed through The Boardinghouse's front doorway, and left a bewildered Wiley watching her.

~~~

Chapter 34

From the 31st floor of Bakers' World, Tess Starling and Monty Reynolds watched Pyune's television debut on "The Today Show," the camera zooming in and caressing the mountain woman's loveliness as though she were a mountain sunrise. As the segment progressed, her voice was like melted butter and her movements both natural and poised. At the close of the spot, Tess muted the sound and turned to Monty, staring at him for a long moment before saying, "I don't know about you, but I think we just witnessed a star in the making."

Monty, with a look of pure delight on his face, threw his fist in the air and pumped it hard. "I knew it! I told her she'd be the toast of the town!" He jumped up and ran around the room, almost knocking over a lamp. "And just what are you thinking, my dear girl?" he asked when he came back to the big chair he'd been sitting in and rested against the back of it.

Tess leaned back in her chair and eased her legs to the corner of her desk, her blood-red shoes providing a striking contrast to the Max Mara black wool slacks she wore. Her eyes closed, her mind at once became the creative tool that had made her a legend.

"Okay, Monty, here goes. I'm not thinking Paula Deen, but . . ." Tess opened her eyes and made a wide sweeping motion with her arm. ". . . but, maybe . . . maybe . . . *Pyune EverSweet Murphy reveals all the romantic secrets of Appalachian foods . . . foods in which you can taste her mountain heritage.*" Tess sat up quickly. "Not your negative hillbilly persona, but Pyune can take foods that are native to Appalachia and bring them into a new culture and—"

"I've got it!" Monty slammed his hand on Tess's desk. "How about *Appalachia Gives You Her Heart—Cooking With Pyune EverSweet Murphy*?" His excitement unbounded, his hands drew in the air as if writing on a chalkboard. "Or, *A Gift From Appalachia—Pyune EverSweet Murphy Invites You Into Her Kitchen.*"

Tess ambled around the room, her index finger on her chin, pressing a dimple that didn't exist. Her gaze found the trees of Central Park and the clouds rushing across the April sky. When she turned around to face Monty, she'd settled on an idea of her own.

"Pyune may not be a formally trained chef, but she possesses a gift as well as a skill, that's quite remarkable—and marketable. Not only her looks, her demeanor, her voice . . . but there's something else too . . . something that's solid gold." Tess began nodding to herself.

Monty waited as Tess walked the length of her office again, past the glass windows that offered the view of Central Park, and finally back to her desk. When she sat down, her gleaming red fingernails pointed squarely at him.

"And that something is?" he asked, lifting his hands in question, almost impatiently.

Tess grinned. "She's believable, she exudes trust, and best of all her delivery is mesmerizing. I see something like *Around My Appalachian Table*. It's possible we could include The Boardinghouse in the show's marketing. Pyune's restaurant would be quite a draw, plus it would give her even more credibility as a cooking-show hostess." Tess placed both hands on her desk, as if to steady her resolve. "All of this has enormous potential. Let's sit on everything awhile and then get together with Pyune and pitch the idea."

"That will be the hard part, I'm afraid. Do you really think she's going to be interested? This is a real opportunity for her, but she might not recognize it as such."

Tess considered Monty's words. "You make a good point. I'm thinking that a cooking show might not be a very high priority for her right now."

"Now you've got me confused."

"It's clear to me that Pyune's main interests lie in finding out who I am, who she is, and exactly what our mysterious family history happens to be. Hell, I have the same interests." Tess moved away from her desk and sat next to Monty, who'd taken a seat on the couch in her office. "She's been in New York for only twenty-four hours, and there's been little free time. I plan to have lunch with her today and get some things out in the open."

Monty picked at the crease in his slacks. "What are your feelings about the whole thing?"

Tess raised her eyebrows. "I assume you mean the *sister thing*?" Her next words came softly, almost as though she were talking to herself. "Finding out I have a sister is the most wonderful thing I could imagine, and I don't want this new relationship tarnished in any way."

"Tarnished?"

"Yes, tarnished. I'm not quite sure how Pyune will fare with all of this."

"She seems to be rather savvy despite being isolated in a small mountain town all her life."

"Oh, savvy she is. I'm sure of that. It's just . . . . "

"Let me help. I have a feeling your separation was a . . . a sordid thing. Am I right?"

Tess's features became drawn. "I'm afraid I haven't been as truthful with Pyune as I should have been. I certainly don't know everything, but . . ."

"You still have an opportunity to be truthful, don't you?"

"Yes. It's just that I haven't been very forthcoming about something in particular."

"It can't be that bad, can it?"

Tess shrugged. "I'm not Pyune. I don't know how she'll feel about it."

Tess picked up her phone and called Pyune's cell phone. "Great performance on 'The Today Show'!" Tess said as soon as Pyune picked up. "I'm so proud of you."

Pyune was breathless. "It was fun! I loved it."

"Wonderful. How about we have lunch together. We'll have lots to talk about."

"Sounds great. Tess, you won't believe this, but when I finished the broadcast several people wanted my autograph. Really, can you believe that?"

"Oh, yes, dear sister, I can believe that. By the way, did Linda tell you that you're scheduled for a photo shoot at ten this morning?"

"Yes, Linda's meeting me. I assume we'll be finished by lunchtime."

"Let's make it a one o'clock lunch. I have an errand to run but should be back by then. I'll meet you in my office."

The call ended and Monty stood. "You're a good woman, Tess. I'm sure everything will work out fine—for both of you."

"Thanks. But don't leave just yet. We need to talk about the fundraiser."

The fundraiser: New York Cooks for Charity. Three of New York's celebrity chefs would be cooking along with Pyune in a competition in which all the proceeds went to charity. This "cook-off" was Monty's pride and joy. Every year he produced this gala event, which contributed hundreds of thousands of dollars to aid New York's homeless.

"Everything's set up for filming at one," Monty said. "It will be live and we'll tally contributions for three hours. Then we'll air it again in June nationally during our twenty-fifth anniversary show." Monty beamed. "And you'll have a huge spread in the June silver-anniversary issue of Bakers' World."

"Have you briefed Pyune?"

"Not yet. I'm waiting for her to settle in before I lay it all out."

"Who are the three chefs competing along with her?"

"We've got the dapper Dick Whittington. He's always a hit—so personable and a total delight with the ladies."

"Oh, yes. He'll bring some sparkle to the show. Wasn't he on last year?"

"Yes, he was, and he also brought in the most money. I can't remember the exact amount, but it was up there."

"I'm glad you're bringing him back, regardless of how much money he raised. Who else?"

"Next is George Fencik. You know him from The Silver Spoon. He adds a lot of class to the whole process. He's quite philanthropic in his own right. Donates heavily to New York's charities."

"I adore George! Is he still married to that model?"

"Oh, yes. They're quite the couple. She's pregnant, you

know?"

"No, I didn't. I'll be sure to send them a note." Tess scribbled on her notepad. "Who's next on your list?"

Monty hesitated and began writing on his own pad of paper, clearly stalling.

"Well? Who?"

"Joan Stone."

"Joan Stone! Please tell me that's not true! What an unlovely woman! Why in the world would you choose her?" Tess sighed heavily and swiped her hand across her forehead to further express her irritation with that choice.

"I know she can be awful, but she's done me a few favors and I . . . well, I owed her one."

"Oh, Monty, no favor is that big. She'll ruin the show!"

Monty held up his hands. "I promise, I'll keep her in line."

"You've got to be kidding. No one has ever kept her in line. Remember the scene she caused at the Restaurant and Chef Awards Dinner last year? She wore a totally inappropriate dress, boobs pushed up to her chin, even said the 'F word' while on a live mike. And what about her scandalous affair with . . . with . . . what's his name?"

Monty began laughing. "Come on, Tess, she's just what a show like this one needs. She brings a little bit of gossip with her, creates some good old-fashioned drama, and, guess what— she is a fabulous chef. She'll draw huge numbers no matter what she wears or says."

Tess remained quiet while she made a few notes. When she looked up, her eyes were dark. "I think you've made a mistake, but I won't overrule you. Let's get our marketing department in here to work out the details. Just try to soften Joan's appearance as much as possible." She stood and pointed one long red fingernail at Monty. "This better work."

"It will."

Tess went back to her desk. "There's one more thing." Monty raised his eyebrows. "I want you to look out for Pyune. She's in virgin territory. Brief her thoroughly, and make certain she's aware of the pitfalls of a competition like this, even though it's a fundraiser. And whatever you do, give her the complete lowdown on Joan."

"Will do!" Monty kissed Tess on the cheek and left her office, softly singing "Puttin' On The Ritz— . . . have you seen the well-to-do, up and down Park Avenue . . . ." He did a little shuffle as he closed her door. However, a moment later the door flew open and Monty stepped back in and yelled, "What about a Pyune Murphy Appalachian cookbook?"

Tess picked up a message from Linda. *Ms. Starling, the phone is ringing off the hook. Everyone who knows you and what you look like thinks it was you on "The Today Show" and not Ms. Murphy. Should I send out a mass media notification that you have a sister who looks and sounds exactly like you?* Linda's last statement held a tinge of sarcasm. Sooner or later everyone would know about Pyune. Tess had a lot of explaining to do . . . but how could she explain? She knew so little herself.

Frandy answered on the first buzz, his voice singing out "Helloooooo, dis is your most handsome and amicable chauffeur, Frandy. How may I serve you today?"

Tess couldn't help but smile. Frandy had been her driver for eight years and never once had she found him anything but jovial. He was 6-feet-4-inches tall, with skin as smooth and black as a vein of coal in a West Virginia mine. Yet despite his size he was gentle and humble. She'd once seen tears on his cheeks when he picked her up. She asked what was wrong and he replied, "Oh, not a ting, Miss Starling."

"I see that you've been crying, Frandy. What is it?"

Silence from the front of the limo. No singing, no chatter. Finally, in a choked voice he said, "Ah, Miss Starling, your Frandy has run over a little kitten on West 60th. I picked it up as tenderly as I could, but I could see it was dead."

"I'm so sorry."

"That's okay, Miss Starling. I will bury the little ting later."

"How kind of you, Frandy. Where is it now?"

Frandy nodded toward the passenger seat to his right. "Oh, the baby is right here, resting atop The New York Times."

"I see." Tess leaned forward and peeked over the seatback. A very small black and white kitten lay stretched out as though it were basking in the sunlight that streamed through the windshield and onto the seat.

They never talked again about the kitten, but some time later she did notice that the dirt around one of the big palms in the lobby at BWM had been disturbed, and a small white cross made of toothpicks protruded an inch or so above the soil.

"Frandy, after you drop off Miss Murphy for a photo shoot at ten, I'll be waiting for you in the lobby at BWM. I'd like you to drive me to Mt. Vernon and back. We need to return here by one."

"Your wish is my command, Miss Starling. See you at ten."

The light streaming through Tess's office windows suddenly dimmed. Dark clouds moved rapidly above Central Park, a stiff wind also blowing through the trees that filled the 843 acres. She spotted a few umbrellas, then some more. Rain. It was going to rain on her parade, and she didn't like it one bit.

~~~

Chapter 35

Wiley Hanson's first love had always been the mountains, which is why he said he'd never married. When he was a very young boy, he wanted to be a mountain. He told his mama that he would be strong as an oak and solid as a rock, and at night he would soar like an eagle over the high peaks and feel the winds of the past lift his body into the clouds. His mama said that was foolish talk, that he was just a boy.

Regardless of his wanderlust, Wiley was not just an ordinary boy. And he'd grown into a man who was not just an ordinary man. His strength of character had not been confined to those who knew him in the small town of Ivy Log. His character was evident everywhere he went, from the hidden hollows of the mountains to the august campus of Georgia Tech, where he'd held a professorship that filled his classrooms with students eager to learn more than what a college course normally provided.

Wiley was an enigma, filled with incongruities that baffled those who thought they knew him. Those incongruities were perfectly understood by Wiley himself however. So what if he possessed a genius-level IQ that enabled him to be an intellectual if he so chose. It was that same IQ that gave him the ability to stay centered; to remain the strong, grounded person he had become. Those words to his mama so many years ago still echoed in his mind. As far as the world was concerned as he knew it, he'd become that mountain.

In the grand scheme of things, perhaps he had neglected to admit his need for a wife and family; after all, the people of Ivy

Log had been his family. One of those especially dear to him had been Vallie Thomas. She'd been a big part of his life, and soon he'd be on his way to her funeral. He would see that the wishes in her will were carried out. He assumed there would be few requirements except to have a garage sale and then sell her house for what little it would bring, perhaps enough to cover the funeral. He'd pay the rest. But if there was anything left over, he'd already decided to give it to B.T., whether Vallie was or was not his aunt. She'd have liked it that way.

At the funeral parlor in Blairsville, Vallie would look about as good as any dead person as she lay in a beautiful silver casket with white linen around her chubby, almost smiling face. Wiley had written her obituary in the still of the night when the only sound had been a lonely whistle from the midnight train passing through Blairsville and heading to Asheville. He'd lost himself in his memories of Vallie while he committed words to paper. In the end he'd found himself grieving her death and having trouble wiping away his tears, they had come with such volume and so often.

He'd reach in his pocket and pull out one of her purple handkerchiefs, which he'd taken from her house. He wanted it wrapped around her gray hair, and he'd ask the funeral director to do this. Later on, when everyone was gone and just before the lid would be closed for good, he'd slip a bottle of Formula 44 in her hand as she lay prostrate in the brushed-silver casket.

At The Boardinghouse, when Pyune's television debut had ended, he'd given instructions to Lizzie to stand tall, keep her apron clean, and to remember not to add too much salt to anything she cooked. B.T. would come over and do whatever she asked of him. A loud harrumph had escaped her mouth as she chucked onions into a pot. "Ain't no youngun gonna know how to do anything that'll help me," she whined.

Wiley smiled. "Oh, come on now, he'll be a big help if you let him. And some high-school kids will be comin' by too. Let's get some biscuits made and a pie or two for later." Wiley patted her on the back, and at his touch she broke into tears.

"Vallie was my best friend," she cried, her shoulders shaking as she sobbed into her apron.

"I know. I know. Tell you what. Tonight, let's ride out to her house and sit on her porch. I'll bring my guitar and we'll sing her favorite song."

Lizzie looked up from her apron and squinted through red eyes. "Favorite song? I reckon I didn't know she had a favorite song. What was it?"

Wiley gave her his most beguiling grin. "Why, Lizzie, you don't mean to tell me you done forgot Vallie's favorite song?"

"Well, I reckon she never told me what it was." Lizzie's large frame belied the sensitive side of her, which was as big as her body. "But I'd sure enough like to know," she said softly and wiped the tears from her cheeks, "'cause every time I hear it from now on, I'll think of Vallie."

Wiley's heart fluttered. From this point on, every time *he* heard the song he'd remember one or another of the long conversations he'd enjoyed with Vallie—a women who was like a newborn puppy in that she marveled at every little thing. She even found the smoke from her Havana Honey cigarillos as pleasant as the smell of fresh kindling taking hold in a stove's belly.

"It was an Elvis song," Wiley said as he picked up his Roy and Trigger coffee cup. "Love Me Tender."

"I sure enough know that song," Lizzie said. "I just didn't know she liked it so."

They were quiet and a mist seemed to settle over them. Wiley lifted his chin and held his breath—was that Vallie he saw in the shadows of the large kitchen, her purple scarf tied around her riotous gray curls?

Wiley drove up to Sam in the town square as his friend sat reading the paper on an old wooden bench. "Ready to go to the funeral home," he hollered from his truck. Sam nodded. "You eat lunch?" Sam shook his head. "Let's eat at Jim's Smokin' Q. It's on the way." Sam nodded again and got in the truck.

A little way out of town, Wiley said, "You been awfully quiet. You okay."

"Just thinking about a lot of stuff that's been going on."

"Some of that wouldn't be named Eva, would it?" Sam's smile gave him away but Wiley decided to leave the issue alone. "I'm a thinkin' too. I don't want to cremate Vallie. You got any thoughts on that?"

Sam studied the fields they passed before answering. "Why not do what you think Vallie would want?"

"That's just it. What would Vallie want?"

Sam, a graduate of seminary school, had mixed thoughts on cremation. "I surely don't know what she'd want. But I think most folks in Ivy Log would like her to be in the town cemetery so they'd have a place to go and put flowers on her grave. And if you're wondering about what God has to say about it—the Bible neither condemns nor condones cremation."

Later on, when Wiley pulled into the parking lot at Jim's, a restaurant renowned for its barbeque, he said, "You done good, Sam. I believe the folks in Ivy Log would want to see Vallie buried near them, so that's what we'll do."

After some good ribs at Jim's, Wiley drove to the Mountain View Funeral Home in Blairsville. Mr. Long, who looked like every funeral director on Earth, greeted them and led them to his office. The smell in the entire place was heavily scented, a strong floral aroma that reminded Wiley of a perfume Paula wore, one he didn't like at all.

"Gentlemen," said Mr. Long, "Mountain View endeavors to answer any questions you may have regarding Ms. Thomas's remains."

Remains? Vallie Thomas's *remains*? *Remains* like in *what is left*? *Remains* like after a tornado or a fire? Wiley found himself sweating—he had never thought about the *remains* of Vallie Thomas—no, not at all. The body of Vallie Thomas lay prostrate, waiting for her loved ones to tell her goodbye. If Wiley did see her earlier in the shadows of The Boardinghouse kitchen, then she knew what he was thinking.

Wiley was candid with Mr. Long, as was his way with everyone. He squared his shoulders and used his "bullet" eye to guarantee that Mr. Long listened attentively. "I'm thinking of her as a body and not as *remains*. We'll have Vallie's *body* taken to The Church of Ivy Log and have the service at the church and then onto the graveyard at the edge of town."

Mr. Long reached for a packet of papers. "That is an acceptable decision, Mr. Hanson. All you have to do is sign a few forms. By the way, Jesse Collins sent over a certified copy of the proof of your having power of attorney over Ms. Thomas's estate. All I need is to see your driver's license to verify your identity, and all will be in order."

It was a short drive to Collins and Dyer. "You ever think about the first three letters in funeral spelling "fun," Wiley said as he grinned at Sam.

Sam chuckled. "I'll be. You're right. I guess a funeral could be fun. A lot would depend on who it's for though. Still, it would be hard to mix fun and death together. Of course, it could be done. Look at those funerals in New Orleans. You're asking about this for a reason?"

Wiley slowed his truck and eased into a parking space across the street from the attorney's office. "Music. I'm a thinkin' we ought to make Vallie's memorial service full of music—Elvis's music. That ol' woman dearly loved Elvis."

At the offices of Collins and Dyer, Wiley was welcomed by the same pretty blonde who'd greeted him and Doyce Conley the previous December when he'd worked out a loan to pay off the farmer's tractor to get him out from under a demand note held by Paula Jennings. The well-endowed young lady was wearing a tight sweater even though it was a warm spring day.

"Well, hello . . . Miss Caity, right?" Wiley held out his hand.

Caity stood and smiled as she grasped Wiley's hand. "Oh, I'm so glad you're here," she whispered. "Uncle Jess . . . sorry, Mr. Collins worked until late last night on his New York Times crossword and is totally stuck." She ducked her head. "You do remember, last time you were here you helped him out?"

Wiley winked, and she picked up her phone and pressed a button and announced that he was in the office.

"Just go on in," she said and smiled. Wiley couldn't help but notice how long Sam held his eyes on this young girl's well-proportioned body. Oh, to be eighteen again.

Once inside the cluttered office, there he was—the small man with the booming voice. Same bald head except for a few thin hairs arranged carefully crossways on his scalp as if they had been sewn on.

"Mr. Hanson," he boomed, "have you come to save me?" He laughed.

"How's that?" asked Wiley, shaking Jesse Collin's hand and introducing Sam, who followed suit.

Two old wooden chairs were positioned in front of Jesse's desk, and he motioned for each man to take a seat. "Oh, my," he said. "I worked from nine yesterday morning until six last night on one of the hardest darn New York Times crossword puzzles

I've ever seen. I didn't eat a single thing all day." He gave Wiley a devilish look. "But I did find the time to gulp down a bourbon or two."

Wiley's chest rumbled with laughter. "What's got you stumped?"

"I'm more than stumped, I'm as frustrated as can be." He spoke in hushed tones: "Well, I'll tell it like it is—I'm totally *pissed*."

"Let's hear it." Wiley sat forward in his chair and waited.

Jesse Collins shoved aside some files, a few law books, a letter opener, a pack of Ludens cough drops, and he pulled out the Saturday crossword puzzle page from The New York Times. The page had been crumpled, creased, and thoroughly abused.

"Okay, here goes." The attorney at law shoved the puzzle in front of Wiley. "Take a look at fifty-three across, The Cornish Wonder and—"

Wiley interrupted. "That would be Opie."

Jesse shuddered. "Opie?"

"That's right."

The little man, no taller than Mickey Rooney, looked sideways at Wiley. "You've seen this puzzle before?"

"'fraid not."

The man breathed in deeply. "Then how'd you get that so quick?"

Wiley shrugged. "That tidbit of information was tucked away in my brain, right next to Mayberry."

"Mayberry?" Whatever do you mean?" Jesse blinked rapidly.

"It's a mnemonic tool I use. I visualized Opie from the Andy Griffin show in the town of Mayberry riding a Cornish hen. This way, when I want to remember who the painter known as The Cornish Wonder was, I see Opie riding a big ol' Cornish hen. Opie is the painter's name. And—"

Jesse waved his hand dismissively. "Oh, never mind. What about eleven down?"

Jesse handed the puzzle page to Wiley. The clue was Schoenberg's "Moses and . . . ." Wiley didn't hesitate. "Aron. The word you want is Aron."

Silence from Jesse. He rose from the big leather chair that almost swallowed him, took the puzzle page from Wiley, and tossed it into his trashcan. He sat down and smoothed his hand across the top of his head. "Shall we get on with business?"

"I reckon we need to look at Vallie Thomas's will."

The old attorney nodded. "Been going over it this morning. Wiley, you and I have been doing business a long time. This here will is cut and dried. For an uneducated woman, Ms. Thomas did a good job of spelling out exactly what she wanted done with her estate. You, as executor, have the responsibility for assuring her will is administered appropriately. You're entitled to two percent of the total proceeds for doing this. Here's the original and my copy." He pushed the will and a copy of it toward Wiley. "Please sign in the space I've highlighted in yellow on my copy that you've received the original. I have a few other necessary papers for you to sign, and I also have several copies of her death certificate for you."

Wiley did as instructed, and when he finished he passed everything he'd signed in one pile back to the attorney, who pulled the will to him and began reading, only to stop and say, "Let's get to the meat of this thing. '. . . and I leave my entire estate to my nephew Bartholomew Thomas Hickel, the son of my deceased sister Bernice Hickel, excluding the exceptions listed below.'"

Wiley came forward in his chair. "B.T. Hickel? You got to be kiddin'. Buck Tooth and Bartholomew Thomas are the same person?"

Jesse looked over his wire-rimmed glasses, his mouth hanging open. "Who's Buck Tooth?"

"It's a long story, but they are the same person. Go on, Mr. Collins."

Jesse read silently for a moment, then picked up with the reading in the section of the will that listed the holdings of the estate. "Lost my place. Here's what goes to Mr. Hickel: 'Ten Shares of Berkshire Hathaway Class A; One-hundred Shares of Seaboard Corporation; Five-hundred Shares of Coca Cola.'" Jesse read on silently while sweat formed on his bald head and glistened like dewdrops on pink roses, then said, "'Ten St. Gauden Double Eagles.'" He looked up at the two men in front of him before returning to the papers in his hand: "'I leave my house and my forty acres of land to Wiley Hanson, my trusted friend and caretaker. To Elizabeth Lindquist, I leave my cat, Bandit, and my 45-rpm record of Elvis Presley's Love Me Tender.'" The room fell quiet. Jesse cleared his throat. "That's it. Any questions?"

Wiley looked at Sam, who was motionless as a statue, and after a nervous silence said, "No questions, I guess."

Jesse reached into a drawer. "Here's the key to her safe deposit box over at the bank. You should find the stock certificates, deed to the property, and coins in the box." Jesse opened a file folder with Vallie's name on it and pulled out an envelope with a string around it. "You'll need this too." He handed the envelope to Wiley. "You'll have to show the bank all the documentation I've given you, and the paperwork in this envelope." He handed Wiley one other envelope, which contained a half-dozen notarized death certificates.

Wiley nodded. "Appreciate your time. Just send me a bill for your services."

Jesse laughed. "No bill, Wiley. You have more than earned my services."

"How's that?"

"Opie," he said with a laugh and waved him and Sam away.

Wiley and Sam left the law offices of Collins and Dyer and walked down the street to the United Community Bank. Wiley mused over of the information regarding Vallie's will and that the boy with the buckteeth and red hair was indeed Vallie's nephew.

Sam seemed edgy as they neared the bank. Wiley gave him a good-natured poke in the shoulder. "How come you're so nervous? We ain't goin' in to rob this here bank. I saw you sittin' there as stiff as a board in Collins's office. What's got your feet stuck in the mud?"

"You don't know anything about stocks, do you?"

"Never owned the first share of anything. That Coca Cola's got to be worth something, though, right?"

Sam stopped in the middle of crossing the street and gave Wiley his own bullet eye. "I don't know about Coca Cola, but those Berkshire Hathaway shares alone are worth over two million dollars."

Wiley took a step back. "Darn. Ten little-biddy ol' shares?"

"One little-biddy ol' share of Class A Berkshire Hathaway is worth around a quarter of a million dollars on a given day."

"Forget darn. Damn."

~~~

Chapter 36

New York City, always moving and full of passion, found it-self quieted by the morning rain that fell. The streets glis-tened with the reflection of headlights sweeping down 5th Av-enue, Broadway, and Columbus Circle, everything mixing in with a steady stream of umbrellas in all different colors, and un-derneath them the souls who wanted to stay dry.

Right on time, Frandy pulled in front of the main entrance to BWM. He'd dropped Pyune off at the east entrance, with Linda waiting to take her to the photo shoot. Tess stepped out just as Frandy double-parked the limousine. He ran around to the other side of the car and opened the door for her. "Ah, Miss Starling. You are more beautiful today than yesterday." He grinned wide, his pearl-white mouth vibrant next to his dark skin.

"Thank you, Frandy. Here's my briefcase. Just put it up front with you." She slid across the leather seat.

Frandy took her briefcase and got into the car. "Where to, Miss Starling?" he asked as he looked back at her and smiled.

"The usual drive to the country. And raise that glass, please. I'm going to rest awhile. And don't sing too loudly—I can still hear you back here, even with the partition up." She wasn't smil-ing.

"Yes, ma'am. Frandy is going to be quiet like a little mouse . . . or even as quiet as a snake. You know that's why I don't like snakes. They don't bark, they don't peep . . . they be too quiet for Frandy. I wish a snake would just make a little noise when it slides along, you know when it sticks its tongue out, it could go hissssss real loud and—"

"Frandy! Raise the glass!"

The partition slid upward, and Tess closed her eyes for the half-hour ride to Mount Vernon. Frandy sped past the Time-Warner Center on Columbus Circle. He didn't need directions; he'd made the trip many times before.

Tess was very tired. There had been little sleep for her after Pyune's cocktail reception. She'd gone to bed around midnight but had tossed and turned until her alarm clock sounded at 5 a.m. At least Robert would be flying back today, and his presence would add a little calm to her life. A life that had been rather settled until the phone call from Linda the day before: "Miss Starling, can you meet at three to discuss a very important matter?" Tess had no idea the very important matter would be about Pyune EverSweet Murphy, a woman who was more than the winner of the Bakers' World Magazine grand prize. A lot more. She was her identical twin sister. This only happened in movies.

At four in the morning it had come to her. Just a simple statement Pyune had made: "I never knew my daddy. Mama said he fell off the side of the mountain when hunting for a hog that had gone missing." Pyune said that her mama had seen buzzards flying in circles above a sheer drop-off near their shack of a house, and she just knew it was Vernon they were hovering over. But they never retrieved the body, and life had gone on without him. That was the mountain way.

In the limo, Tess dozed and was awakened when the glass partition slid down and she heard: "Miss Starling, we're here." Frandy parked the car and jumped out to open Tess's door, holding a large black and white striped umbrella with BWM stamped in large letters across the top.

"Go have some lunch," she told Frandy. I'll be about an hour or so. It's ten-thirty now, meet me here at eleven-thirty." She turned away but looked back. "Thanks for letting me sleep a few minutes. Sorry I was sharp with you."

"You weren't sharp with Frandy at all." He tugged on his cap and watched Tess walk the path of colored brick pavers that led to the lobby of one of the most prestigious—and expensive—long-term-care facilities in the state. "You a worried woman,"

Frandy said softly to himself as Tess reached the entrance but stopped for a moment to pick a small pink flower.

Tess had called ahead, and she pressed in the day's entry code, smiled at the woman sitting behind a desk in the reception area, and swept through the lobby and down a long hallway that ended up in another lobby. Smaller than the main lobby, it was painted in soft hues of variegated green. Polished tables sitting against the walls held vases of fresh-cut flowers. The heady fragrance of roses filled the room and made the area seem like a lush garden. Just off the small lobby, a hall took her to the residents' rooms. She walked by the music conservatory, a magnificent mahogany concert grand piano taking its rightful place in the center of the room, with two rows of richly upholstered chairs circling it and plenty of room behind for wheelchairs and beds to be rolled in.

At Room 110, Tess stopped, the nameplate on the door reading: VERNON T. MURPHY. Everything was now fairly clear. But there were still questions. And her biggest worry was how and when to tell Pyune.

"Hello, Daddy," Tess said as she entered and found Vernon Murphy sitting in a wheelchair in front of the door to his private patio. He was wearing a light-blue sweater over a darker blue Polo shirt.

Her father looked up and grinned, pulling his glasses from his face. "Well, there's my baby girl. How are you, honey?"

Tess leaned over and kissed Vernon on top of his head and squeezed his shoulder. "Daddy, it's so good to see you. It's been a whole week, hasn't it?" She smelled Old Spice, his favorite, and he was freshly shaven. The staff at this facility was renowned for the care they took of their patients, which they strictly referred to as their residents.

"Seems like a month since you were here last. I'm so glad you've come back for a visit." His speech was clear but his eyes were cloudy. Tess wondered if his overall health might be slipping a bit. "How's Robert?" he asked. He took a newspaper from his lap and placed it on a small table nearby.

"He's in L.A. but should be back later today. I'll be sure and tell him you asked about him."

Vernon Murphy turned his wheelchair and pushed himself to the couch in his living room. "Help me up on the sofa, would you?"

Tess locked the wheels in place and steadied her father as he shifted to the sofa. On the wall, above his head, family pictures were placed in sections of three. In the middle was a picture of Tess and her mother sitting on a park bench in New York City. Tess was about two years old, curly headed and smiling, a neat row of baby teeth falling across her bottom lip.

At the far end hung a picture of her mother and father paired together, Vernon with a trimmed mustache that made him look quite distinguished. There was just one picture of Tess and her father. He was holding her in his arms, cheek to cheek, her little patent leather shoes, with their tiny buckles, falling across his stomach.

Tess removed the picture of her mother and her sitting on a park bench, and she sat beside her father. "Did you take this picture, Daddy?"

Vernon studied the picture quietly. "I'm not sure. So long ago, it's hard to say." He coughed and wiped his mouth with a crisp white handkerchief.

She asked softly, "When did you and mama meet?"

Vernon closed his eyes for a moment, and when he opened them he looked directly at Tess, a tad of irritation in his tone as he replied, "Little girl, you are asking me questions I'm having a hard time remembering the answers to. Let me think a minute."

Tess leaned back on the couch and tilted the picture upwards to reduce glare. It was taken in Central Park. She could see the old New York Coliseum in the background, which had been demolished and replaced by the Times-Warner Building in 2003. The park bench, however, was probably still in the same spot. If she was two years old at the time, the picture had been taken in 1976.

"I just can't remember anything about who took that picture, Tess. I'm sorry." He was clearly ignoring the second question by going back to the first one.

"Daddy, have you ever lived anywhere but New York City?"

Vernon's eyes roamed the room while his fingers scratched his neck. "Oh, I've been all over, I reckon."

She was certain he was dodging the question as well. He'd never demonstrated the slightest signs of memory loss, and people always remembered where they've lived. "How about Georgia? Have you ever lived in Georgia?"

"Georgia?" Vernon stared at his shoes, not at Tess. "Where's all this leading to, baby girl?"

Tess found herself unattached. She was on a quest to find the truth, and questioning her father was the only way she knew how to get there. "I think you know, Daddy."

Vernon Murphy nodded slowly. "Something must have come up?"

"It has, Daddy."

"Then I guess it's about time."

"Were you just going to die without telling me?"

Her father sighed deeply. "I could never tell you while Lula was alive. She would have left me."

Tess waited—but no other words filled the quiet. Finally, she reached over and held his hand, finding it soft and smooth. "Daddy, mama's gone. You can tell me everything right here and right now." She placed the picture in Vernon's lap and pointed to the woman who held her. "That's not my real mama, is it?"

Vernon reached out and rubbed the glass on the picture, smoothed it like it was the cheek of a baby. "That's my Lula, all right. But, no, she's not your real mama." He lifted his eyes to his daughter. "You're my baby, Tess, but you were birthed by another woman."

Tess's throat felt tight. Any words she wanted to say were locked and sitting there, not wanting to come out. If she spoke them, nothing would ever be the same. She reached up and wiped a tear from her father's cheek. "It's okay, Daddy. It's okay." She took the picture from his lap and placed it back on the wall. "What else are you going to tell me?"

Vernon shrugged his shoulders. "Everything, I guess. But where do I start?"

"In the beginning, I hope." Tess walked to her father's small kitchen and poured them both a ginger ale and returned to the couch. She noticed her father had pulled a pen from his shirt pocket and was reaching for a piece of paper.

He wrote: *Hattie Jean Murphy* on a piece of paper and held it up to her. "That's your real mama, Tess."

Tess took the piece of paper and stared at it for a long moment. She folded it gently and placed it in her handbag. At least he was telling the truth—so far. "I'm ready for the rest."

Seventy-Eight-year-old Vernon Tate Murphy began his story slowly but evenly: "I loved your mama, I really did, but somehow I got tangled up with Lula Starling, who lived right across the mountain, on the next ridge. Lula, in her younger days, was quite a gal." He craned his neck as if the memories were across the room and he could see them. "One day I was walking home from cutting firewood over by her place, and she said to come in and have a hot cup of coffee and some leftover custard pie." He smiled at the memory. "I knew she made good pies because she'd send them over to Hattie and me every now and then.

"I didn't know it at the time, but she wanted a baby real bad. Never could have any, though. She did her midwife thing all over the mountain, delivering babies, doctoring babies, holding babies, but none of them were ever her own. Her husband had run off long ago, and her life seemed to be pretty content except for that baby thing.

"She knew Hattie was going to have a baby. And when it turned out to be twins . . . well, Lula was right there for it all. She couldn't believe it when Hattie said to take one of the babies. I know Hattie meant for Lula to take one for just a short while, until she could get back on her feet, but that wasn't what happened."

Vernon's words had become gravelly, and Tess handed him a glass of the ginger ale.

"Just so happened," he continued, "I was two or three ridges away on the day you were born. Along about dark, on the way home, Lula stopped me and said Hattie had given her a baby—a little girl. Then—" Vernon faltering and finding himself trembling— "she pulled me into her cabin. Said we were going to New York together. Said she had a brother who lived there who was quite wealthy. Next thing I knew, we were on a train bound for New York." The room became hushed. Vernon neither moved nor turned his eyes toward Tess

Tess hardly breathed. "I was stolen from my real mama?"

Vernon raised his voice, "No! I was your daddy! You were mine too!"

"But you left mama." Tess stood and began pacing. "You left my mama alone." She turned abruptly and shouted, "You abandoned her and a newborn baby!"

Vernon hung his head and mumbled quietly.

"What did you say?" Tess moved closer. "I didn't hear you."

Vernon looked up. "What else could I do? Lula would have taken you, and I never would have been able to find you."

"That doesn't make sense. Didn't it ever occur to you that you had another baby back in Georgia? And a wife too."

"You don't understand. Lula would not let me go back."

Tess's head was spinning. "Daddy, my life has been a lie. Lula told me you were my stepdaddy, which until this moment I thought was the truth, while all along you were my real father and *she* was my stepmother. I even took her last name instead of yours, believing she was my mother. You helped perpetuate the lie. How could you do that? What about your other daughter? Didn't you ever think she might need you? that Hattie definitely needed you?" Her tears, as well as her anger, came in bunches.

Vernon wrung his hands. "I was so weak, Tess. It was too easy to get on that train with Lula."

Rain pelted the patio doors and thunder rumbled the glass. Tess watched a wren fly under the eaves and into the safety of a hanging flowerpot. "Well, I've got some news for you, real Daddy, your other daughter is here in New York, but she knows nothing other than the fact that I'm her sister and—"

"What? In New York?" Vernon jerked back. "How . . . how did she find you?"

"A funny thing happened. She won first prize in a baking contest for BWM and came to New York to collect the prize money. That's not all she got, though—she got me."

"Baby girl, I don't know what to say."

Tess stood silent for a time, when her words, tender like a dove's call, fell softly: "Your other daughter showing up this way was a remarkable stroke of fate, wouldn't you agree?" She slowly turned away and went into the kitchen and set her glass on the counter. "I'll be back, Daddy. But there might be two of me." She paused and stared at her father. "You ready for that?"

On his own, Vernon Murphy pulled himself from the couch and onto his wheelchair. He unlocked the brakes and wheeled himself slowly toward Tess. "Honey, I think I've been ready a long time—I just didn't know it."

But would Pyune be ready?

Frandy waited with an open umbrella at the entrance. "Miss

Starling, it's so wonderful to see you again."

"You just saw me an hour ago," she said as she ducked under the umbrella.

"Now, Miss Starling, you know very well Frandy takes care of you, and every moment I'm away from you I do worry if you're safe and sound . . . and happy." He looked at her sideways. There was no smile on her face, mascara was smeared on her cheek, and red splotches showed across her neck. "I see you're not happy. What can Frandy do to help?"

Tess snapped, "I'm fine, just fine," but her steps were rigid, her shoes splashing into a puddle and soaking her feet. She screamed, "Damn!"

"Back to BWM, Miss Starling?" he asked timidly when they were both inside the vehicle.

"Yes. And raise the window. I don't want to hear a sound except for my own breathing."

~~~

Chapter 37

Wiley and Sam spent 45 minutes at the United Community Bank of Blairsville, sorting through the contents of Vallie Thomas's safe deposit box. The more closely they examined everything, the more questions they had, the most pressing one being who *exactly* was Vallie Thomas?

Yes, who was the woman who wandered the streets of Ivy Log, a bottle of Vick's Formula 44 Cough Syrup in the pocket of a ragged purple sweater, humming randomly as she walked the sidewalks and peeked into the store windows on Main Street?

To those who might have noticed her, she appeared dried up, much like an apple that had been left in a fruit bowl and long forgotten. But on the inside she wasn't dried up at all—always full of powerful energy instead.

Regarding her finances and investments, someone had to have mentored Vallie, but it wasn't Wiley Hanson. So who was it? Could it be possible that a simple woman, who lived in near poverty yet was worth millions, had amassed this wealth on her own? Of course it was possible. *But how?*

Wiley found all the stock shares in ivory-colored jackets, and the double eagles nestled in a soft cloth bag, each coin in a holder designed specifically for protection and display. Each small sleeve was marked, and Sam said these symbols denoted the quality of the double eagle from a numismatic standpoint. He made a quick search by using his smart phone to go online and said that the price range for a single St. Gauden Double Eagle ran from $2,000 to over $1,000,000. But when he checked the year dates, each coin appeared to fall in the smaller price category. Still, ten coins meant $20,000 for B.T. Sam checked the current handle for a share of Berkshire Hathaway Class A stock, and it was $214,000.

"Tell me one more time," Wiley said as they were wrapping up everything. "One share of Berkshire Hathaway stock is worth more than two-hundred thousand dollars."

"If its Class A and not Class B." Sam pointed to the stock certificates. "You can see as plain as day that these say Class A."

"What about the Seaboard stock?"

"No idea. Don't even know what the company does." He went back to his phone and typed in the company name. Thirty seconds later he yelled, "Damn, Wiley, you aren't going to believe this, but a share of Seaboard is worth two thousand, three hundred dollars." Makes those hundred shares worth almost a quarter million."

"The Coca Cola stock?

A minute later Sam said, "This one is chump change. Forty-five dollars a share times five hundred. About twenty-two five." Sam's eyes lit up. "Add all this up, that two percent you're allowed as executor comes a pretty penny."

"I don't want any of it. I still got to figure out if I want the house."

The two men walked back to Wiley's truck and found a note stuck under the windshield wiper. Wiley read it aloud. "'*Success is counted sweetest by those who blank, blank, blank, blank succeed.*'"

Wiley glanced over at the Collins and Dyer law office. He wrote "neer" on the bottom of the note and drove over and stuck it in Jesse Collins's mailbox. He laughed as he climbed up in his truck for the ride back to Ivy Log.

The boy. The redheaded boy. Wiley would have to talk to him, tell him about Vallie, about her burial, about his inheritance. But what about a guardian? His mother had died on the mountain and left him an orphan. The skinny boy had walked through the Nantahalla Forest and ended up in Ivy Log in the middle of a horrific downpour—and was now considered in the custody of the whole of Ivy Log.

Wiley was lost in his thoughts, his tires whining as he drove

fast on the Blairsville Highway. A country song played on the radio. Something about *"sending you a big bouquet of roses . . .
one for every time you broke my heart."* Wiley reached over and
turned down the volume. "Bartholomew Thomas Hickel. Can
you believe that? Wonder if he even knows that's his real
name?"

"He wasn't bashful about telling us his name was Buck Tooth
Hickel. Maybe he didn't like the name Bartholomew. I know I
wouldn't. Plain ol' Sam is good enough for me. I sure never liked
Samuel."

"He's a strange kid. Good but strange. I think I'll take him
out to the church cemetery and explain what I'm planning for
Vallie's burial." Wiley glanced at the folder with the stock certificates and everything else Sam held in his hands. "Before that, I'll
run down to Vallie's house and look around. I told Lizzie I'd take
her over there later today and play the guitar for her. She's
grieving for Vallie, something awful. Gonna have to search for
that Elvis record, too, since it wasn't in the box."

"While you're gone, I'll get with Will and work out the
memorial service for Monday. Maybe get some ideas about
B.T.'s guardianship. As far as I can tell, he has no legal guardian
right now unless it would be Eva. If she's really his sister, then
perhaps the matter is already settled. Maybe by law B.T. is auto-
matically put into his next of kin's care. Could be some papers
need to be filled out or go before a judge, but it shouldn't be too
complicated." Sam's face turned stark. "Unless she wants to contest the will."

"I should have asked Jesse about all of this when we were
there. Eva still in Ivy Log?"

"No. She drove up to Charlotte on business, but she'll be here
for Vallie's memorial for sure." Sam leaned toward Wiley. "Eva's
a good-looking gal, isn't she? Smart too. And I don't think she'd
be interested in B.T.'s inheritance."

"Yes, she's very pretty. But this is a whole lot of money." Wiley scratched his bald head. "Dang, Sam. This is *complicated.*
You reckon we can sort all this out in an evenhanded way?"

"I don't know. I surely don't."

The miles slipped by, and it wasn't long before the men were
looking down on Ivy Log from the high ridge above the town.
The truck's engine seemed to appreciate the thrill of a 7-percent

descending slope as the vehicle zoomed down the mountain, the
tires whizzing like riled-up hornets.

"Damn," yelled Sam as he held tight to the strap above his
window. "I believe I left my stomach back there on the ridge."

Wiley laughed and eased up at the bottom of the mountain.
"You'd loved to have taken that ride in Old Blue. Now *that* was a
truck."

"Isn't Old Blue still at the bottom of Rabbit Ridge?"

"Yep. I get real sad when I pass by and see that ol' rear-end
sticking up in the air, getting all rusted and everything. Thought
maybe I'd hike down there one day, say a little prayer or something." He laughed softly. "Tell her to rest in peace." Sam chuckled and Wiley dropped him off at the parsonage.

When Wiley parked in his customary spot alongside the
woodpile at The Boardinghouse, he noticed that the resident
rooster was missing some tail feathers. He found Bandit
stretched out on the windowsill, eyeing him. "Old boy, is there
something you'd like to tell me?" Bandit swished his tail a few
times—acting as if he knew exactly what Wiley was asking him
about.

Lizzie accosted him at the back door, breathless and wring-
ing her hands. "Oh, I'm so glad you're back." Her cheeks were
flushed pink, the hair along her neck damp. "Paula done come
back over here and tried to give me a lesson on how to speak
French. I chased her away with one of Pyune's big pot lids. That
woman is going to be the death of me yet!"

"A French lesson?"

Lizzie held the door open for Wiley and grabbed the hem of
her apron and wiped her face. "That's what I said. She's got her
mind made up that The Boardinghouse is going to serve chicken
the French way."

"And how's that?"

"Heck if I know. All I know is fried chicken, chicken and
dumplings, and chicken and rice with the necks and feet and everything." She grabbed his Roy Rogers cup and filled it with
steaming coffee.

"Why don't you sit yourself down and let's go over all this,"
Wiley said as he grabbed his cup and a stool and pulled up to the
baking table. He brushed some flour away from the edge and

saw where lard had been spread out in thick gobs. *Oh, Pyune, hurry home.* "I don't think Pyune ever put chicken feet in her chicken and rice."

"She sure enough did. You just didn't know what you was eatin'."

Wiley took a deep breath and ventured away from the topic of chicken feet. "Why does Paula think you have to speak French in The Boardinghouse?"

Lizzie smacked her lips and shook her head. Her eyes and her forehead showed considerable strain. "Does that devil really need a reason for anything? Paula does whatever Paula wants to do, but I ain't havin' it. Not while Pyune is away. I feel I have to . . . to protect this place." Her lips began to tremble. "And now with Vallie gone . . . my job is double hard."

Wiley let Lizzie sniffle a moment. "Tell you what. Lunch is over and it's a few hours until supper. Let's close up and go to Vallie's for a while. I'll play some music. He stood and brushed flour from his jeans. "Put a note on the front door saying you'll be back at five o'clock. He paused. "Add this: *Buttermilk pie at six o'clock.*"

Lizzie's face screwed up. "Buttermilk pie? I ain't never made buttermilk pie in my life."

Wiley laughed. "I didn't say you had to make it. I'll make it."

Lizzie arched her gray eyebrows. "I didn't know you knew how to make buttermilk pie."

Wiley grinned real wide. "I keep some things a big secret."

"You don't say?" A smile stretched its way around the big woman's mouth. "I thought I knowed everything about you, Wiley Hansen."

"Not quite," he said. "Now write that note and let's go."

Vallie's shack of a house was on the outskirts of town, at the end of a street that was really not a street at all—merely the continuation of a paved road that had become a lane packed tight with Georgia clay. The small three-room house was partially hidden by towering ash trees whose branches were filled out with the leaves of a warm spring. The rustic house, which was actually a log cabin, was originally built by Vallie's great grandfather in 1902. Vallie's great, great grandfather had won the forty acres on which the house sat in the 1832 gold lottery. The structure, despite its age, could survive many more winters.

In the field in back of the house stood a dozen huge pecan trees that had been a source of income for Vallie. The trees had been planted to look like an arrow from the sky, and they pointed east. No one knew why this had been done, but the "arrow" could be clearly seen from the top of the main ridge overlooking Ivy Log. For the past thirty years, she had sat on her front porch shelling pecans into a large enamel pan, the past twenty of those years having Wiley drive her to the farmers market in Blairsville to sell her crop. He had spent many hours on Vallie's front porch watching her rough, wrinkled hands crack the nuts one by one and pick them out with a small tool she'd fashioned from an old can opener. The only time Vallie had ever raised her voice to Wiley was when—one time early-on`—he'd asked to help.

Wiley pulled into the side yard and sat a moment before telling Lizzie, "I brought my guitar, just like I said I would." Lizzie didn't say anything, just swallowed hard. Wiley nudged her arm gently. "Let's go sit on the porch for a spell."

Wiley believed that the rockers on the front porch had to be as old as the house. The paint had long chipped away. Vallie was not known for upgrading anything on the place. The same was true for the inside. Wiley had been inside her house only once, and that was because he hadn't seen her for a few days and decided he should check on her. He found her sprawled out on the bedroom floor. When he walked in, she raised her head and told him, "Wiley, I done had me too much Formula 44." He'd never laughed so hard in his life once he made sure she was okay.

That was long ago, and as he stepped up on the porch he heard the creaking of wood that had been hauled out of the mountains by mule and laid lovingly in a neat row. Wiley leaned his guitar in the corner and sat in one of the rockers.

"Have a seat, Lizzie, and let's you and me rock." The rocking would help soothe Wiley's mind, because he, too, had lost a good friend.

Lizzie pulled a rocker closer to Wiley and sat down. "I ain't never been here in all the years I knowed Vallie."

Wiley rested his head against the back of the rocker and closed his eyes. "That right? I'm thinkin' that's because Vallie spent most of her time in town. Even in winter. Only time she was here was at night, and that was to sleep."

He reached over and picked up his guitar and ran his fingers across the strings. He had a good ear for music, and the old Gibson had needed tuning. After he'd written Vallie's obituary the night before, he'd spent a good while getting the sound the way he wanted it.

He positioned his fingers on the neck, and in the still of the late afternoon, the sound of a well-strummed guitar lifted high in the ash trees and waited there, waited for the words that were sure to come. Wiley, his voice raspy from a deep sadness, hummed at first, then: "Love me tender, love me sweet, never let me go . . . You have made my life complete and I love you so."

The last chord was barely audible as Wiley's hand fell away from the strings. Lizzie stopped rocking and half-whispered to Wiley, "You know what I'm a thinkin'?" Wiley shook his head. "I know for sure that Vallie heard you sing and play her favorite song."

Wiley placed the guitar to the side of his rocker. "What makes you say that?"

"Well, didn't you see it?"

"See what?"

"Oh, Wiley, while you was playin' and singin,' a little hummingbird come down and fluttered by your head."

The house was musty, cluttered with all things old except the coat Paula had given Vallie the previous Christmas. It lay across a chair, the fake fur collar turned up. "Vallie left me the house and the forty acres, Lizzie."

She gasped. "Is that right?" She paused and turned to face him. "You gonna live here now?"

"I don't know. I truly don't. I love my place in the mountains. Course, I spend a lot of time at The Boardinghouse. You know, with Pyune."

She laughed. "All Ivy Log knows that." She walked over to a log mantle atop a very used fireplace in need of a major cleaning. "I wonder who's in all these pictures?" she asked. Every square inch of the mantelpiece was covered with photographs—each in a cheap frame, some without glass, some with cracked glass. Lizzie, flour stuck underneath her fingernails, picked up an 8-by-10 black-and-white photograph and pulled it closer to her face. "I do believe this here is Vallie." She held out the picture to Wiley, who examined it carefully.

"I believe you're right. She appears to be about eighteen or so. I gotta say, she was quite a looker. The person standing next to her makes me think of . . . someone." Wiley studied the image a while longer. "I'm thinkin' I know that man standing beside her, but I can't place him right now. Can you?" Wiley handed the picture back to Lizzie.

"Hmmm. He does look a might familiar." Lizzie stared a long time, her eyes squinting in the poor light. Finally, she looked up. "Could be a very young Dr. Casteel."

"That so?" Wiley took the picture again and walked over to a window with the late afternoon light streaming in from the west. A smile came to his face and he turned to Lizzie. "Why, I do believe you're right, that is Washington Casteel."

They went into Vallie's bedroom, a dismal little room with only a single bed and small, handmade dresser. Patchwork quilts were folded at the end of the bed, along with a few pillows. "Wiley, should we be here? This is Vallie's bedroom."

"Lizzie, I miss Vallie. I'm still looking for her on the streets of Ivy Log even though she's left us. I want to see her come through the door of The Boardinghouse asking for ham and eggs. And my heart squeezes every time I see Bandit looking for her. But in this house I'm near her, and it makes me feel good."

"I guess you're right." She sat on the edge of Vallie's bed and looked around the Spartan room. There were definitely no frills. Except. Except on top of her dresser lay a book with multicolored ribbons poking out from the sides. "What's that over there?" Lizzie asked as she pointed.

"Looks like an album." He reached over and picked it up and sat on the bed by Lizzie. When he opened it, an 8-by-10 glossy black-and-white photograph of Vallie—and Elvis Presley—stared up at them, each face in the picture bright and laughing.

"Looks like Vallie and Elvis is havin' a good time," Lizzie said. Vallie's hair was curled, her skin smooth and vibrant, her eyes large and round. Vallie Thomas was indeed a beautiful girl.

Next to Vallie, Elvis was sporting his half-grin and had his arm wrapped around her shoulders. A note had been written below the picture: *Carolina Theatre, Spartanburg, South Carolina*. On the next page, a short travelogue was listed. *'Drove to*

Spartanburg at 4:00 a.m. February 9 and waited in line all day to see Elvis perform. Wash Casteel, Roger Smith, Julie Stockton and I drove in Wash's car. Ate breakfast at Porky's South of the Border Truck Stop in Hamer, South Carolina. Elvis came on stage at 10:00 p.m. He wore a black shirt and black pants.

"So for sure that's Dr. Casteel in that picture on the fireplace mantle," Lizzie proclaimed.

Wiley nodded and turned the page and saw a clipping from the Spartanburg Herald-Journal with the headline: "Elvis Fans Swoon at the Carolina Theatre." Lo and behold, there was another picture of Elvis and Vallie, vibrant youth lighting their faces once more. Again, Elvis had his arm wrapped around sixteen year old Vallie, the jubilant crowd around them smiling.

The next five pages of the album were filled with black-and-white snapshots held in place by little triangular slots in which the corners of each picture fit securely. Names and dates were clearly and neatly written beneath each photograph.

Wiley turned to the last page. It was a handmade envelope that had been glued to the inside back cover of the album. His hand shaking, he pulled out a mint-condition 45-rpm record of "Love Me Tender." On the label was Elvis Presley's signature, along with the salutation: "To Vallie Thomas, prettiest Georgia peach I've ever seen!"

"Vallie left this to you, Lizzie. Looks like it was her favorite possession." Wiley hesitated. "Well, there's something else." He shifted his eyes to a faded photograph on the plain pine dresser. It was of a cat stretched out on the porch railing. "She left you Bandit too."

Wiley closed the front door to Vallie's house and slowly drove down the clay road that took them back to Ivy Log. The soft colors of a fading afternoon had always placed Wiley in a melancholy mood; which, on this day, would linger longer than usual. The whole of Ivy Log had changed in just a couple of days. Pyune had left for New York, Vallie had streaked into the heavens for adventures unknown, and a redheaded, bucktoothed boy was now a multimillionaire.

He again parked the truck by the woodpile and saw B.T. sitting on the back porch of The Boardinghouse. "Hey, young feller. Let's ride out to the church cemetery and have us a nice, long man-to-man chat."

B.T. stood, his long legs unfolding beneath him like an accordion being pulled open. "Man-to-man what?" he called out in his croaky boy-man voice as he walked toward Wiley. "Is it about my aunt's gold tooth?"

~~~

Chapter 38

New York City was home to Per Se, one of the most exquisite restaurants in the world. It was located on the fourth floor in the Times-Warner Center, behind a beckoning blue door that promised a dining delight. Stepping inside the restaurant transported discriminating gastronomes to a small café in France to enjoy chef Keller's or chef Kaimeh's glorious masterpieces. To add to the experience, owner/chef Thomas Keller wanted his patrons to know that no single ingredient was ever repeated during a meal, no matter how many courses.

Tess breezed through the entrance, Pyune by her side. She asked for her usual place in a dining room that held only sixteen tables. Per Se was made for the twin sisters, because as they swept through the dining room all heads in the room turned toward them. It was simply part of being beautiful women, and Pyune found herself liking the attention.

Both women had changed clothes after busy mornings and running in and out of the rain. Tess's silver jacket was paired with black slacks and silver strap shoes. Jewelry on her fingers and wrist was minimal, but a large silver chain fell heavily across her chest and accented her black camisole.

Pyune was wearing a spectacular ensemble, which was the final outfit she'd worn for her BWM promotional layout. The staff told her that Miss Starling had instructed them to send her out last in the midnight-blue form-hugging dress with a bright yellow scarf. Her gold drop earrings dangled elegantly as she strode beside her sister to the table.

Though it wasn't obvious to Pyune, Tess was filled with anxiety. Her exterior was cool and calm, but inside she wrangled with the knowledge that Vernon Murphy was her biological father and not her stepfather. He, along with Lula Starling, had worked together in their deceit for forty-two years. Tess could not imagine the grief Hattie Murphy must have felt after losing her baby for good to someone she thought was a dear friend.

Now, in the loveliness of a New York City spring, somehow she must be truthful with Pyune. She could not deny her newly discovered sister the knowledge of her beginnings. But how would she tell her sister that her father, along with a mountain midwife—and his lover as well—had stolen a baby from Hattie Murphy? That Pyune had grown up without the sister who had been smuggled to New York and raised as an only child by Lula Starling and Vernon Murphy?

Tess felt her chest tighten so much that she feared all air would be squeezed from her. Across the room, a vase of freshly cut red amaryllis seemed to blur, and she felt herself struggle to breathe. A waiter approached her table, and with a halting voice Tess said, "Hello, Leon, it's good to see you."

Leon was discreetly looking from one woman to the other. He stammered, "Ms. Starling and . . . and . . . Ms. . . . . . "

Tess released a charming smile. "Leon, I don't believe you've met my sister. This is Pyune."

Leon bowed slightly. "My pleasure, Pyune." He lingered, his eyes sweeping once more over Pyune and then back to Tess.

Pyune broke the spell. "What a lovely restaurant, Leon."

He nodded and regained his composure, opening the leather-bound wine list he held. "What will you be having today, Ms. Starling?"

"I'd like a glass of Riesling. You know the one." To Pyune she said, "They have a wonderful fruit tea with fresh orange slices."

"Ah, yes," said Leon. "It's a green tea with pineapple juice and a touch of grenadine as well. Very refreshing." He smiled at Pyune. "May I inquire where you are from? Your accent is not familiar to me."

"I'm from north Georgia, near the North Carolina border." Pyune glanced at Tess, a small smile beginning to sweeten her face, and added, "Maybe I should say *The South.*"

Leon seemed to comprehend a little better. "Oh, yes. Of

course, you're from the south." *The south.* The place where a woman's velvet speech hid a core of steel, and where a lady's eyes were both patient and foreboding.

Leon delivered the drinks, and the quiet of the room, as well as the subtle lighting, soothed Tess as she sipped her wine. Pyune leaned back in her chair. "I can't believe I'm here—with you. A week ago my world was so much smaller." She laughed. "Can you imagine my life in Ivy Log, the slow pace and of course the people. Everything is so different—so safe and familiar."

"You seem to have done just fine in this big city." As Tess watched her sister smooth her hair, she herself had the identical mannerism. She had noticed many little traits that were common between the two of them.

The faint strains of Puccini's "Nessum Dorma" seemed far away yet the words were clear: ". . . ma il mio mistero é chiuse . . ." Tess lifted her chin and felt the wetness of tears. "Pyune, did you ever wonder about our father? I mean . . . not knowing for sure what happened to him?"

Pyune read the emotion in her sister's question. Her dark eyes roamed Tess's face for a long moment. "I only know what my mother told me. He never returned from the woods that day —and she never saw him again."

Tess cocked her head a little, her brow wrinkling. "So you never heard your mother say anything else about him?"

Pyune found herself thinking back as far as her memory would take her. She remembered the walk into Ivy Log, holding her mother's hand, and the music and the watermelons in the town square. But it was just Pyune and her mother. That's all there had ever been.

"No, nothing. My mama was a quiet woman. She worked hard and cared for me. I felt her love. We were happy."

Tess leaned forward, her words a whisper. "And you never went back to the place where you were born? That mountain-top?"

Pyune shook her head slowly. "No. I suppose I could have, but I didn't see a reason to trudge back up that mountain. Why? Do you want to see where you were born?"

"Do you think the house is still there?"

"After forty years, probably not." Pyune thought a few moments, fiddled with her silverware, and continued, "In truth, I don't know if I could find it. After all, I was just two years old when I left. I do remember walking down the mountain, mama carrying our few belongings and me. We spent a night in some-one's old barn. She'd sat up the whole time, listening to the mountain sounds, afraid to go to sleep."

Tess felt a catch in her throat. "What if I told you our father was still alive?"

"What did you say?" The hardly discernable words had come from Pyune as if she were deep within a well. The stillness that followed seemed hollow. She became wide-eyed, picking up her napkin and holding it to her lips.

"Our father. He's alive and here in New York."

Pyune abruptly stood, dropping her napkin to the floor. "Im-possible." She turned and ran through the restaurant and into the street, her scarf falling away behind her as she slid into a taxi. "LaGuardia Airport," she shouted through her tears.

~~~

Chapter 39

"Is this Sheriff Mack Drummond . . . over in Blairsville?" Paula Jennings's words screeched into her phone.

"Yes, ma'am, what can I do for you?" a deep, calm voice replied. Mack Drummond, a life-long resident of Blairsville, the county seat of Union County, had been sheriff for two decades. His style of keeping the peace was simple. Don't break the law and everything will be just fine.

"This is Paula Jennings, in Ivy Log. We got us a runaway boy over here, about fourteen years old. He's suspicious and I think he's probably thieving around this area. He might even have a police record of arrests or something."

"That right? What's his name, and how long's he been there?"

"His name is Hickel. B.T. Hickel. He's been here three days now. Showed up at the church. Pastor Johnson took him in and has been feeding him. I wouldn't be feeding a thief if I – "

"Miss Jennings, I'll take a ride over that way this afternoon and have a talk with the young man. Did he say where he'd come from?"

"Not really. Of course, most likely everything he says is a lie if you ask me."

"So he's alone? No family?"

"Far as I know he's an orphan. Belongs in a children's home or something. Just don't want him here in Ivy Log, where he can cause trouble and maybe hurt some people."

Sheriff Drummond listened attentively. "I'm wondering if Wiley Hanson is anywhere around. If he is, tell him I'm heading to his neck of the woods."

"Sheriff, this has nothing to do with Wiley Hanson! It's about that boy!"

Paula smiled as she hung up. She had done her duty. She had taken matters into her own hands; had protected Ivy Log from the potentially horrendous acts of a runaway fourteen-year-old boy. Never mind that the young boy had sought refuge in Ivy Log during a rainstorm, was starving, his body battered from his forty-mile journey through the Nantahalla Forest.

Paula had decided that filing an official complaint with the sheriff's office, citing vagrancy and possible theft, was the responsible thing to do. Surely the boy had stolen something during his three-day stint in Ivy Log. And sleeping in the parsonage! She was certain there were lice everywhere. No doubt the pastor's residence would have to be fumigated and cleaned top to bottom.

Then there was the food this boy had eaten. The church budget for the food pantry was a paltry $200 a month. The filthy boy had likely cost the church that much or more in just the three days he'd been in Ivy Log.

Paula, riled up just thinking about the problems the boy had caused The Church of Ivy Log, tramped down the steps of her house and marched the two blocks to the parsonage. She'd make it clear to Pastor William Johnson that under no circumstances would the boy be a ward of the church or of Ivy Log.

At the parsonage, Pastor Johnson sat at his desk, notes for his Sunday sermon spread out before him, his worn bible open to the Book of John. He found joy in John's writings, the Apostle's words a reminder to the folks of Ivy Log that their benevolence toward the young boy who had sought sanctuary in The Church of Ivy Log was because of their love of God. John 3:17-18 was quite specific: *But if anyone has the world's goods and sees his brother in need, yet closes his heart against him, how does God's love abide in him? Little Children, let us not love in word or talk, but in deed and in truth.*

In deed and truth. Though William Johnson knew little of the boy, he felt strongly the lad was in the right place, with the right people. He believed that not only the citizens of Ivy Log, but that God himself, would carefully watch over the child's life. It was called *faith.*

The citizens of Ivy Log had opened their arms to B.T. Hickel, ensuring he had a warm bed and plenty to eat. Proverbs 14:31 solidified the preacher's position regarding the orphan boy who had suddenly appeared in Ivy Log: *Whoever oppresses a poor man insults his Maker, but he who is generous to the needy honors Him.*

It was during the swelling of his heart and the joy of knowing the boy was indeed loved and God's blessings were abundant that a loud banging came from the front door of the parsonage. He left his study and opened the door to a flaming Paula Jennings. Paula, with her brow perspiring from her two-block stomp to the rectory, and her eyes blazing and her vibrant red mouth screwed into a snarl, she might as well really be breathing fire, for the effect could have been no greater.

She raised herself up and looked down her nose. "Pastor Johnson, I'm here to inform you that I have taken action regarding that runaway kid—you know, that redheaded boy. The sheriff will be here this afternoon to put that child where he belongs." She didn't bother to come in, instead folding her arms across her chest, daring William Johnson to oppose her.

The reverend stood silent for a moment and found himself wondering if this woman had forgotten the teachings of Christ. A woman so involved in the church that she was president of the church's board of directors, leader of the choir, member of the visiting committee, head of a bible study group; yet here she was, heartless. Totally heartless and oblivious to her responsibilities as a Christian.

He gathered his thoughts. He was being tested, but he would not forget his Christian responsibilities. "I'm sorry you felt the need to take action, Paula. Has the boy been a bother to you?"

"Bother?" She stammered somewhat before lashing out once again. "Don't you realize that we know nothing of this boy? Came here in the middle of the night, filthy and covered in lice. Why, he could slit our throats and steal us blind before it's all over."

Pastor Johnson moved a step forward, and in his softest preacher's voice said, "There was no need to bring the sheriff into this, and you have involved yourself unnecessarily. Now, if you'll excuse me, I'm busy with Sunday's sermon." He grasped the doorknob tightly and started to pull the door shut. However, something was preventing its movement.

"Excuse me!" Paula had wedged her foot against the bottom of the door. "I happen to have the authority to do whatever I like regarding this church. My position on the board allows me to *involve* myself whenever and wherever I please."

The pastor's gaze was steady. He was surprised his words came out so cold and unrelenting: "Not in this instance, Paula."

Paula stepped back and smiled, a cunning slant to her painted lips. "May I remind you, sir, that you're still on probation as pastor of The Church of Ivy Log."

"Yes, you may remind me, Miss Jennings." She'd made the mistake of taking her foot away, so he closed the door and left a fuming Paula Jennings standing on the steps of the parsonage.

Wiley and his candy-apple-red truck pulled onto the Murphy Highway. B.T. sat beside him, the window rolled down and the April wind blowing his red hair in every possible direction. The church cemetery was only a few miles south of town, off Gum Log Road, and the future resting place of Vallie Thomas.

Vallie's wealth, when made public knowledge—which was sure to happen—would cause quite a stir in the peaceful community of Ivy Log. Things would have been rather simple had the red-headed boy not shown up on the doorstep of the Church of Ivy Log. The will would have been read, the search for Vallie's heirs begun by the state, and Ivy Log proper would not be involved.

Who could have predicted that just a day or two before her death, as though magically placed in Ivy Log by some unseen hand, the heir to the bulk of her fortune would appear? Wiley shivered. The boy who sat beside him was worth millions. And Wiley, being executor of Vallie's estate, had to advise this uneducated, inexperienced youth on how to handle his newfound wealth. To complicate matters even more, the bucktoothed boy was an orphan. The only shred of family was the possible but yet unproven relationship to a half-sister, Eva McIlwain, former governor of North Carolina.

Wiley had no idea what lay ahead—but for that matter neither did the redheaded lad who sat next to him. He turned and looked at B.T. The boy, his head out the window, spit as Wiley stopped at a crossing. "Yee haw," he hollered. "Believe I got me that road sign. You see that?"

Wiley shook his head. "What's so good about spittin'? It's as bad a habit as passin' gas. Which I'm danged happy you're controllin', by the way."

B.T. lifted his eyebrows, an incredulous expression on his face. "Ain't you ever heard of marksmanship?"

"Passin' gas is marksmanship?"

"No, but spittin' is. I reckon if you spit straight, you can shoot straight. That's how I see it."

"Ever own a gun?"

"Never owned one, but I sure did shoot one."

"Who's gun was it?"

"My mama's gun. It were a little ol' Remington rifle. Twenty-two bolt-action. Mostly for snakes and such."

"She taught you how to shoot?"

"Taught myself. Twernt nothin' to it. Just aim and pull the trigger."

Wiley wanted to keep the boy talking. "Ever shoot anything with size to it?"

B.T. seemed to think things over. "Well, once. There was this black bear messin' around in our garden."

"You shot a twenty-two at a bear?" Wiley's mouth fell open.

"Yeah. Bullet parted the hair on top a his head. He looked at me, gave out a big ol' grunt. I decided to go on back in the house."

"You only shot him once?"

"Well, sniddle-snot. I only had one bullet!"

Wiley had to look away. Soon he pulled off the Murphy Highway onto Gum Log Road, which took them to the church cemetery. A large oak tree sat to the left of the entrance and Wiley parked under it.

"So this is where them dead people from town is buried?" B.T. asked as he lifted the door handle and stepped out of the truck.

"A lot of 'em."

"Well, how come we're here? We're alive, ain't we?"

"Just follow me." Wiley began walking across the cemetery, to a waist-high fence made of flat stones laid one on top of the other. "I told you I wanted to have a man-to-man talk with you?"

"I ain't never had no man-to-man talk before."

"Well, you're getting' ready to have one now." Wiley motioned with his hand. "Come over here and sit on this fence with me."

B.T. did as he was told, hiking his lanky body onto the smooth, wide top section of the stone fence, which had to be a hundred years old. Once settled, he kicked off his boots. His socks were full of holes and both his big toes were exposed. He frowned and squinted at Wiley, the boy's mouth hanging open and his teeth protruding.

B.T. said, "I reckon you took out Aunt Vallie's gold tooth and found out it's worth a bunch a money. I need a new pair of boots. Them down there is worn out."

"Looks like you need socks, too." Wiley didn't want to even think about the condition of the boy's underwear.

"Boots is all I need. I get a new pair, I'm gonna be fine. Is the money from that tooth what you brung me out here to talk about?"

"It's a little more complicated than just money from the tooth. To be honest, I still ain't seen the tooth and probably won't, which goes for you, too."

B.T.'s face dropped and he hopped down from the fence. His movement startled some crows that were perched in a nearby tree, and they flew off.

Wiley stretched out across the top of the stone fence and propped his head in his hand. "There's some other stuff you need to know about."

"It ain't about the dang birds and bees, is it?" The boy guffawed loudly, scaring more birds, this time from the tree right next to him and Wiley. From thirty feet away, a squirrel, apparently curious, jumped onto the fence and watched them. "I know all 'bout how them babies is made."

"No, this ain't about the birds and the bees. It has to do with your Aunt Vallie."

"What about her? She done come back from the dead? Is that why I ain't gettin' that tooth."

Wiley sat up and smacked his hand on his forehead. "Would you just listen and forget about that dang tooth?"

"It don't mean nothing to you, but it can get me some new boots. If you needed boots, you'd be carin' about the tooth, I bet."

Clearing his throat, Wiley spoke in a matter-of-fact voice, "We leave here, I'm gonna buy you a new pair of boots, and some socks and underwear. So I don't want to hear one more word about boots and Vallie's tooth, okay?"

B.T. nodded, his face brightening at hearing he was getting new boots. Wiley continued, "Me and Sam drove over to

Blairsville and met with the attorney who handled your aunt's will. You know what a will is?"

B.T. shook his head. "It's a paper that says how things are to be divided up after a person dies. Your Aunt Vallie left most everything to you. But she left a few things to me and a few things to Lizzie, too."

The boy leaned back against the wall and said nothing. He closed his eyes and Wiley thought he was asleep until he sat upright. "Will I get enough—"

"Your aunt left you enough money . . . " Wiley paused, choosing his words carefully. ". . . you'll have enough money for a place to live, food and proper clothes—and braces."

B.T. whipped his head around to face Wiley. "Braces? Them wire things they put on your teeth? Why, those thangs 'll rust and —"

"Now hold on. There's a new type of braces you don't even see and—"

"I'll do just fine without 'em, thank you." B.T. pulled on his boots and began walking across the cemetery.

"Just where do you think you're goin'? We're not through with this here talk." Wiley slid from the top of the fence and followed B.T.

The boy turned toward Wiley and walked backwards as he talked, somehow missing the headstones around him. "I got it, Mr. Wiley. The gold tooth's gonna be buried with my aunt, and I gotta wear braces. Least I get a new pair a boots outta this." He stopped walking backwards. "I still get them boots, don't I?"

Wiley stood in the middle of the graveyard, frustration washing over him like muddy water—with the mud left sticking to his skin. This boy was wearing him out, shaking his bones and rattling his brain. And he still hadn't told B.T. he was rich.

~~~

Chapter 40

"LaGuardia it is!" The cabbie pulled away and the taxi sped down 42nd Street. "No luggage? Or are youse just meetin' somebody?"

"No luggage," said Pyune. *My father, no, our father, is alive and in New York. Impossible. He fell off the side of the mountain. The buzzards circled for days. Over time, animals probably scattered his bones all over the ridge. That's what mama told me.*

Pyune caught her breath, pushed back a sob and recalled Tess's words as she sat across from her at Per Se. *Alive. Her father was alive.* Forty-two years later. Forty-two years after she was born, after she and her mother had walked down the mountain and found a home in Ivy Log, Georgia. Alone, without her father, they had found happiness in the small town—a small town that gave them everything they could possibly need—everything except a father for her and a husband for her mother. Everything but a *family.* What was it that had happened so long ago which had taken her sister and her father so far away? *Did she really want to know?*

Her phone chimed. She stared at her handbag and listened to the soft notes until they faded away. Then she heard the beep denoting a message received and stored. Never mind. She was leaving New York. She'd get on the next flight and board without so much as a glance back. She wouldn't even call Wiley and tell him she was on her way home. She'd get to Atlanta and then somehow make it to Ivy Log. *Forget that damn $25,000. Forget*

New York City. Forget she had a sister. Forget the story about her father—true or not.

"What airlines, lady?" asked the cabdriver as they neared the airport. "Departures or Arrivals?"

"Delta," answered Pyune. "Departures." *Yes, departures.* She was returning to Ivy Log—and the safety of her home.

She handed the taxi driver two twenties and fled through the doors and across the terminal lobby. She had arrived in New York on Delta and would depart on Delta. Her eyes scanned the airline counters until she found the carrier's logo, which she hurried toward.

She weaved through the crowded terminal until she slammed into a tall man who then grabbed her to keep her from falling. His hands grasped her arm and held fast. He wouldn't let go. He pulled her toward him, into his chest and held her there.

"Let me go!" She tried to push him away but to no avail. It was useless to resist so she looked up and uttered the only expletive she ever said, "Dammit!" followed by another, "Let me go!"

"No, I won't," came the surprising reply.

And there, holding her, stood Monty Reynolds. It was his arms that held her; his chest that she was pressed against. "Where are you going?" he asked.

"Home! I'm going home!" Pyune relaxed her face into Monty's chest and did what she rarely did. She let someone hold her while the tears came, while her body stood weak and trembling.

"It's okay, Pyune. It's okay." Monty gently led Pyune to a row of chairs that were situated away from the crowd waiting in line for a ticket agent. "Sit down and let's talk about this."

"There's nothing to talk about." Pyune opened her handbag and pulled out a tissue and pressed it against her cheeks. "Just leave me alone." She blew her nose and swallowed hard.

"There's a lot to talk about. Tess called me and said she thought you'd probably gone to the airport after you left the restaurant. I'd had to drop off a friend, so I was already here."

"Please! Please just let me go. I can't stay in New York City another minute. I hate this place!"

Monty smiled, his face warm and consoling. "No, you don't hate it here. Things are just kind of mixed up right now."

"How do you know . . . that things are mixed up?"

"Tess told me a couple of things a long time ago—and something else just a few minutes ago. Let's go where it's quieter and talk this thing through." He reached out and she took his hand.

For some reason she didn't argue, and they went to his car in the parking garage and left LaGuardia. With the rain over, the early afternoon sun was bright, the temperature pleasant. After all, it was a zip-a-dee-doo-dah day. And there was a promise of blue birds on her shoulder and that everything would be satisfactual. *No, not true!*

"I'm not staying in New York," said Pyune.

"Of course you're not," Monty said, his assurance soothing her. He reached over and patted her hand. "Let's start at the beginning."

"What do you mean?" Pyune pulled her hand away.

"Your world was turned upside down when Tess entered your life, but she certainly didn't plan it that way. She had no say-so when she was spirited to New York by a woman who was not her mother. And your father didn't think forty-two years would pass by before he'd be able to right things. Tess just found out yesterday that the man she thought was her stepfather is in fact your and her real father."

Pyune's voice was so strained she could barely speak. "This is too much, and I don't want to be a part of it."

"But you are a part of it. You have a sister and a father. Granted, they have not been in your life until now and—"

"What do you know about it? Has Tess told you everything?"

Monty pulled through the entrance of a small park and stopped the car at a curb and turned off the engine. "I'm sure she's not told me everything. Probably far from it. But I know enough to realize that there are some things which are important to you."

"Like what?"

"Like your sister loves you."

Pyune nodded slowly. "I know. And I love her. I'm just . . . just . . . ."

"Afraid?"

The quiet lasted a long moment. When Pyune spoke, her words rang true and from the heart: "Yes, I'm afraid. I'm not sure I want to know what happened when Tess and I were born."

Monty opened his car door. "Come on. Let's go sit on that

bench over there." Tess nodded and slowly got out of the vehicle.

They walked under the shade of large oaks and maples, to a wooden bench that had been dedicated by New York City's Library Association. A small brass plate, recessed in the wood, was inscribed: "*A perfect place to read a book.*"

Pyune heard her phone again and ignored it. They sat and Pyune noticed Monty had mixed up his socks again. "You're still wearing mismatched socks," she said.

"I'm certain I am. I shall reprimand my butler when I get home."

"You have a butler?"

"No, I don't have a butler. But maybe I should. That way, perhaps my socks would match."

Across the way, a woman with two children sat and ate a picnic lunch. A fountain spewed water into the air, and it splashed down into a large ceramic bowl that surrounded it.

Monty leaned forward and placed his hands together. "I'm not saying that what happened long ago was the right thing. Far from it. I'm just saying it bears searching out the truth. You as well as Tess deserve to be sisters and in each other's lives. Please stay in New York and work through this saga of twin sisters who found each other after forty-two years."

"I just don't know," Pyune replied, looking away.

Monty lifted his hand and placed a finger under Pyune's chin, forcing her to look at him. "It can be a beautiful thing despite the circumstances," he said softly.

Pyune brushed a wisp of hair from her forehead and watched the people laughing and eating their picnic lunch. "I don't want to lose a sister I just found. I . . . I just don't know what to do regarding my father—if it's true."

"You don't have to do anything. Tess believed that the right thing was to tell you what she'd just learned. From the sound of her, she's not having an easy time with what her father just told her, but she could never continue a relationship with you if you didn't know the truth."

Pyune turned and faced Monty. "It was such a shock to hear that my father was alive after believing all these years that he was dead."

"Of course it was a shock, but the truth is important, and that's what Tess was trying to do—be truthful with you, despite that she knew it would be as upsetting for you as it was for her."

Pyune felt a large pang of guilt. "I guess it had to be a jolt to her as well. "Where is Tess now?"

"Waiting for you."

~~~

Chapter 41

Sheriff Mack Drummond was the Appalachian-born son of a family whose ancestors had migrated to North Carolina in the early 1700s from the Scottish highlands. He remembered well the usage of Gaelic by his grandparents, and even now he sometimes used a Gaelic word or two himself. Mack revered what he believed was the unique character of his ancestors. There was not a shred of elitism in his body despite his wearing a sheriff's badge the size of a Moonpie. Perhaps it was his immense bulk that caused him to walk slowly, talk quietly, and breathe softly. But let no man mistake his easy-going appearance for intelligence and good sense even though he freely subjugated both by his willingness to sit back and let others do the talking.

Such was the case when he arrived in Ivy Log and had the dubious pleasure of meeting Paula Jennings. Had he not known better, he would have thought he was a lowly cockroach being attacked by both a large flyswatter and a can of Raid. He pulled up on Main Street in his police cruiser and had barely opened the door when Paula Jennings made a beeline toward him. He felt the barrage of her barking harangue as though a dozen coonhounds had treed their quarry after an exhausting chase.

"I've been waiting for you all afternoon, sheriff. That boy has disappeared after being watched by Pastor Johnson. Guess he's hiding out somewhere." Paula took a quick breath. "In all my life, I've never known a redheaded boy who wasn't full of mischief and completely untrustworthy. And that boy is all of that!

Mack Drummond reached up and slowly pulled off his hat, revealing a rather long shock of red hair. He ran his fingers through the strands and replaced his hat, all the while searching Paula's face. Her eyes flickered for an instant, and he knew she got the message.

"You mentioned Pastor Johnson. He around?"

"The boy isn't at the church. No need to—"

"I'll visit with the pastor and see what's going on." Mack glanced at the copper-lined steeple of The Church of Ivy Log and began walking down Main Street.

"Excuse me, Sheriff Drummond. As president of the church board, I have the authority to make decisions regarding the boy's welfare, and I say he needs to be taken into custody and—"

"Believe I already have your comments, Ms. Jennings." Sheriff Drummond lingered a moment on the corner of Main and Church, pulling out a small pad and making some notes. He ignored Paula as she continued talking while he wrote. He put away everything and began ambling down Church Street. His boots had no significant heels on them—he was tall enough in his own right.

"Just a minute, sheriff," Paula said, running right up to the lawman. "That boy needs to be hunted down and—"

"Ms. Jennings, I already have your statement. I'll be in touch if I have any further questions for you." His blue eyes remained on hers until she backed away. He heard her mumble something about, "We'll see about this," as she scurried down the sidewalk.

At the parsonage, Mack knocked on the door and in moments was greeted by the pastor, who smiled warmly and noted the designation on the badge: "Hello, sheriff, I've been expecting someone from the police department. As you probably already know, I'm William Johnson. Come in, please."

Mack removed his hat and dipped his head to clear the top of the doorway. "Thanks, pastor. You can call me Mack."

"And you can call me William or Will, whichever you prefer." He led the sheriff to the kitchen and pointed to a chair. "Have a seat. I was just getting a glass of iced tea. I'll fix you one."

"I could use a cold drink." The sheriff licked his lips. "I've met Ms. Jennings. She's the one who called me about the boy. I'm not quite sure I've gotten the facts straight regarding this young man. Care to fill me in?"

"I'll be glad to." He poured the tea and placed the glass in front of Mack. "The young boy knocked on the back door of the parsonage late last Friday night. There was a terrible storm and here he was, soaked to the bone, just standing on the stoop and looking up at me. I brought him in and gave him something to eat along with a bath and a warm bed. He's been absolutely no trouble."

"What have you learned from him about his family?"

"He's not very talkative, but as I understand it, his mother died a few weeks ago and this left him alone up in the mountains where they lived. Over by Rocky Top. Two of Ivy Log's church members took him up there to see if they could find out some information about him. While they were there, they met a woman who claims she's his half-sister."

"Half-sister? What's her name?"

"Her name is Eva McIlwain."

"That name's familiar."

"She's the former governor of North Carolina. It's a long story, but a believable one."

"Is she aware of the boy's history?"

"Not really. Her story is that she and the boy had the same mother. The mother had Ms. McIlwain when she was thirteen years old and gave her up for adoption. Seems Ms. McIlwain's adoptive parents passed away recently and left her information pertaining to her adoption, which revealed her birth mother's name. That name led her to this young boy. Lots of coincidence, but so far it all seems to be true."

Mack nodded knowingly. "Looks like Ms. McIlwain might well be this boy's legal guardian."

"I'm thinking the same thing. She's in North Carolina but due back in Ivy Log tomorrow."

"I'd like to meet with her. Meantime, do you have a problem keeping the boy in your care until Ms. McIlwain states her position in this situation?"

"Not at all. In fact, the boy seems quite happy here. The citizens of this town have been very kind to him. Most, anyhow." Paula's harsh words were still ringing in his ears.

"I believe a woman named Paula Jennings is one of the dissenters," said Mack as if he could read the reverend's thoughts. "Don't let her bully you about the boy. Her kind don't readily accept that we can be generous for no other reason than God has instructed us to be this way."

"It pleases me greatly whenever a man says those words to me." There was a noise and knock at the back door. The preacher hollered, "Come in," and both men turned to see a bedraggled Wiley rush into the kitchen.

"That dang boy! He's done told Bandit 'sic em,' and that cat chased that rooster all across the yard. No wonder most of his tail feathers is missin'."

"And it's good to see you, too, Wiley." Mack reached out and shook Wiley's hand.

Wiley let out a big laugh. "Sorry, got all caught up in that boy. Mack, how you been doing? It's awhile since we seen each other. You here about that boy, I reckon. Paula done called you?"

"That she did. But don't worry. The preacher and I worked things out."

"Good. He's a fine boy."

"That's what the pastor said. Anything I can do to help?"

Wiley grinned. "Unofficially, you can tell us what Paula said."

"Unofficially, her opinion is that the boy is big trouble, and she wants him out of Ivy Log."

Wiley looked at the pastor and said, "That won't happen if we can help it."

"Ms. Jennings is quite . . . forceful." The sheriff looked at the two men with wary eyes. "So all of us will want to be cautious."

The door burst open and the lanky frame of B.T. Hickel exploded into the kitchen. "Sniddle-snot if that ain't the fastest rooster I ever did see. Bandit done chased that rooster all the way to The Boardinghouse. That cat barely missed havin' hisself a chicken dinner."

Wiley frowned. "B.T., do you realize that rooster has been in this town for years and never had his feathers removed by a cat or anything else. You come along and he's almost featherless and can hardly get to the top of the smokehouse. When Pyune gets home she's gonna have somethin' to say, you can be sure of it."

B.T. snickered. "Yeah, I guess you're right. I'll talk with Bandit 'bout him chasing that rooster." The freckles on his face glowed red. Sweat glistened across his forehead and ran into his orange eyebrows.

"Talk with Bandit? You been encouragin' that cat to create mischief. Now that Vallie's gone, he'll never behave himself."

B.T. hung his head and mumbled. "Sorry, I was just havin' a little fun." When he lifted his head he noticed the huge man in uniform. "That why that lawman's here? Gonna arrest me for eggin' on that cat to pick on that rooster?"

~~~

Chapter 42

Tess Starling sat at her desk, an untouched cup of coffee nearby. She had received Monty's text: "On the way back to your office. Both of us."

Her thoughts were many—the most prevailing involved the tragedy of the separation when she and Pyune were born. Now their fairly contented lives were being rocked with uncertainties, insecurities, and most of all a deep sorrow that they can never recoup what's been lost.

Who was to blame? What had really caused the horrendous act of separating two babies at birth? Tess felt herself succumbing to anger. She stood away from her desk and paced along the tall windows in her office.

Pyune had the benefit of a mother but she'd had no father. Tess had the benefit a father but no mother—at least not her biological mother. It was all so twisted. The woman who had raised her was not her real mother; she was a fake mother. Was her love for Tess also fake? The man who raised her was her real father—but represented as her stepfather. *Why?* Her life had been a lie. And Pyune's life? Only Pyune would be able to answer that. Vernon Murphy had told Tess the truth, though he may not have told her everything. Now, Tess, from her own lips, must tell Pyune everything she'd learned. That was the only way their lives could continue together.

Tess returned to her desk and waited. Waited and thought about what her life would have been like with a sister. She heard the elevators doors open. She rose from her desk and stood in her office doorway. As her sister walked across the lobby toward her, she felt the tears welling up. This had to be a new beginning for both of them. She opened her arms and pulled Pyune to her. They held each other and let the tears flow unabated.

"You came back. I don't know what I would have done if you hadn't." They went inside her office and collapsed in chairs. "Now that I know I have a sister, I can't bear the thought of losing you again."

Pyune managed a smile. "It's all so . . . so difficult. I still want to run away. But I can't. I can't leave you just because I don't like what happened."

"We didn't have control of what happened, Pyune. You and I aren't guilty of anything. Our only salvation now is to acknowledge the bond we have and live our lives accordingly."

"What about our father? How did all this take place?"

Tess moved closer to Pyune, her voice softening. "I'll tell you exactly what I've been told by our father." Across from her, Pyune remained still, her eyes wide and waiting.

"Lula Starling lived a short distance away from our mother and father. She was a midwife with no husband and no children of her own, and she went around the mountains delivering babies. When our mother had us, Lula was there to help with the delivery.

"Daddy told me our mother asked Lula to take one of the babies and care for it until she was on her feet. It seemed two babies were just too much for our mama at the time." Tess lowered her eyes. "Lula took me."

"Couldn't our father have helped?"

Tess shook her head. "Lula was a manipulative person from what Daddy said. He was weak or he never would have gone along with what Lula had asked him to do."

"And exactly what did she ask him to do?" Pyune asked. *How foul is this story? Do I really want to know?*

"Lula wanted a baby. She talked Daddy into leaving with her and taking me with them to New York, where her brother lived."

"So Daddy just went with her? without thinking about leaving mama and me?"

Tess took a deep breath. "Daddy was a very weak man, Pyune."

A weak man? He was more than weak. He had committed an unpardonable sin. He had abandoned his wife and child for the lust of another woman. "I can't forgive him, Tess. I'm sorry. I don't want to see him or talk to him. Ever"

Tess reached out and took Pyune's hand. "I understand how you feel. You may change your mind at some point, but right now you and I are together and that's the most important thing."

Pyune's head was swimming. "Mama never told me anything about another baby!" The tears came again and Pyune dabbed her eyes with an already wet tissue. "I wish our mother was alive to answer some of our questions."

"There's so much we don't know and will never know. So what do we do now?" Tess sat on the couch and slumped back and closed her eyes.

Unbelievably, Pyune laughed out loud and grabbed her sister. "Let's cook! I always cook when things aren't going well. Where's your kitchen?"

"You mean here? Or the Bakers' World kitchen?"

"Who cares! Let's just cook!"

"Cook what? My pantry is practically empty. All I have are eggs and a few other things." An involuntary shudder came over Tess. "You would have found out sooner or later . . . I don't cook!"

Pyune smiled. "Well, that's about to change."

A shocked Tess jumped from the couch and retrieved her phone from her desk. She punched in two numbers. "Linda! Cancel all my appointments for the afternoon! My sister and I are cooking!"

So right there in the middle of New York City, miles and miles from the peaks of the Appalachians where two babies were born, the hearts of two women were unlocked—two women who would ultimately forgive the wrongs of the past and plunge forward into the happiness of tomorrow—together.

At 2 a.m. Pyune turned out the lamp by her bed. For the third time in two days she had not called Wiley or checked her phone for messages he might have left her. He seemed so far away, as did Ivy Log and the people she loved who lived there. She held her breath, mad at herself, because for a fleeting moment she had forgot what Wiley looked like. Yet what was even more shocking, she had not thought of The Boardinghouse once since she'd been in New York. Her night was fitful. Memories she'd neglected now flickered on and off in her mind until the sun's morning rays burst through the window and warmed her bed.

~~~

Chapter 43

A t The Boardinghouse, which customarily closed after lunch for cleaning and dinner preparation, Lizzie put the finishing touches on a coconut crème pie. She'd used the recipe Pyune had given her years earlier, but her pies were never as good as Pyune's, and a taste of the filling indicated this one was even worse than most of her efforts. But she didn't really care. She was tired, her back ached, her feet hurt, but worst of all she missed Vallie.

She sat at the worktable and placed her head in her hands, flour dusting her cheeks and chin, her gray hair askew and flopping everywhere. And then it began: a soft rumble from her chest, then tears and then an all-out cry. *Vallie really was gone.* Her closest friend for over forty years, gone in just moments. One minute they sat together on the front porch of The Boardinghouse, the next minute Vallie was slumped forward. *I didn't even have a chance to say goodbye. Yet what would I have said? So long, Vallie, it's been fun. See you around, Vallie. Don't go, Vallie. Yes, that's what I would have said. Don't go. Please don't go, my friend.*

At first she didn't hear the tap on the dining room door. How could she? She was bawling loudly, with foghorn sniffs in between. She finally looked up and saw a face she'd never seen before, peeking around the edge of the door. "Excuse me," a man said. "Are you closed? I didn't see anybody out front."

Lizzie snorted and wiped her face with the bottom of her apron. "Yes, sir. We're closed. Sorry. You lookin' for somebody?"

The man, a thin fellow with short brown hair and a chin shaped carefully by a neat beard, smiled. "No ma'am. Just passing through and wanted to get a bite to eat." The man studied Lizzie's red nose and cheeks. "Is everything okay?"

Lizzie stifled a sob. "No, everything's not okay. I just lost my best friend." She threw her head back and began crying again. "And this is the most awful coconut crème pie that ever was!" In a fit of emotion, Lizzie swiped her big hand across the worktable and sent the pie sailing across the kitchen. "Hungry hogs wouldn't even eat that pie!"

The stranger stared wide-eyed at Lizzie. He hesitated in the doorway between the dining room and kitchen. Then, without a word, he walked across the floor, bent down to the scattered pie, and ran a finger through the filling. He tasted the filling on his finger and closed his eyes a moment, looking to the ceiling in obvious deep thought. "My dear, you have forgotten to put vanilla in this pie."

"Vanilla?"

The man stood up straight. "And the crust," he said, tasting a crumble he put in his mouth, "is a tad soggy. Next time, after you bake your crust, melt a little white chocolate and spread it on the crust. You will also want to put the crust in the freezer for a few minutes before you fill it. That will keep it crisp." He settled himself on the stool beside Lizzie. "Then your crème filling will sit perfectly on top of the crust." He smiled at Lizzie. "Oh, and surely you have vanilla beans available in your beautiful kitchen?"

Lizzie was paralyzed. Not a muscle moved as she stared at the man who sat beside her. Finally, in a hoarse whisper, she asked, "Who are you?"

The stranger chuckled. "Jay. Jay Metzler. Just passing through your lovely town on my way to Virginia."

"No, no. I mean . . . *who* are you? How do you know about white chocolate on piecrusts? And vanilla beans?"

"If you don't mind, I'll show you."

In a rush of hands and arms, he reminded Lizzie of the Merlin the Magician character she'd seen in a play when she was a child. After cleaning up her mess, Lizzie watched as he made the fruit-pie fillings she was working on more succulent by macerating the fruit with sugar and carefully collecting the juice and cooking it into a caramelized wonder before adding it back in each pie. She sat spellbound in front of the oven and watched puff pastry swell open and rise. It seemed alive—the right way. It really was magic.

She followed him around the kitchen as though she were on a leash and could get no more than five feet away from him. His hands enchanted her. They knew flour and sugar as though they were his best friends. He kneaded pie dough with an obvious passion for perfection.

He said, "The way to achieve flaky layers of crust is to keep the dough flat, large, and solid. Your ingredients need to be cold and you need to work quickly." He knitted his brow and added, "And keep your flour in the freezer."

Lizzie nodded, her eyes big and round. Her tears were gone. Vallie, while always in her heart, was not on her mind right now. Lizzie found herself moving around the worktable as though gliding on a cushion of air; her feet no longer aching and her back feeling strong.

"How's this?" she asked Jay after following his maceration instructions.

He leaned over and looked into a pot of pear juice that had caramelized into a rich syrup. He placed a wooden spoon in it and watched the thick liquid slowly drip back into the pot. "Perfect! Absolutely perfect."

While he busied himself chopping pecans, lyrics from "Oliver" spilled out into the kitchen: "Food. Glorious food. Hot sausage and mustard! While you're in the mood!"

Still as a statue, Lizzie squinted her eyes and quietly studied Jay. Her words were delicate, like petals falling from a spent flower. "You're a real angel, ain't you?"

Jay tilted his head at laughed. "My mother and father think so."

"I don't understand how you got here. And right when I needed you most." Lizzie slowly wiped her hands on a towel. "Can you answer that question for me? Wait, did Vallie send you?"

"Vallie?"

"Guess not. But somebody had to. How about Pyune?

He shook his head and went about this work. Soon the fragrance of freshly baked bread filled the kitchen and wafted out the screened back door into the streets of Ivy Log. Surely, every household with a window open in the cool April afternoon smelled the pies and pastry. Peace seemed everywhere. Even Bandit snoozed on the kitchen windowsill, while across the yard, atop the smokehouse, the yard rooster bathed in the afternoon sun. Jay polished a stainless steel bowl and then arranged knives along the counter as Lizzie stared at him.

"Now I believe I can answer your question," he said, brushing his hand across the top of his head and smoothing his small mustache. He came over and sat beside Lizzie as her deep brown eyes continued to study him. "Maybe God lets us fall into just the right situations sometimes. I stopped here because I was hungry." He smiled. "And you were here. Waiting." He laughed softly. "And since you weren't open, I was able to cook for myself. I've sampled a meal's worth of food and then some, haven't I?"

Lizzie nodded, not wanting to speak, not wanting to alter the magic of Jay Metzler, not wanting to realize that he was just passing through and he'd be gone at any moment—if he were really here to begin with and this weren't just an elaborate dream.

Jay shut the door on the last pie in the oven. "I take it this isn't your restaurant?"

Lizzie was shaken out of her reverie—as far as she was concerned the person sitting across from her was an angel and that was all there was to it. "Oh, no. Pyune Murphy is the owner."

"Ah, that's one of the other two names you mentioned." Lizzie nodded. "And just where is Ms. Murphy today?"

"She's in New York. She done won her a baking contest and $25,000. She's gone to collect her money. She never flew before, never been outta this little ol' town neither. She was even on 'The Today Show.'"

"My goodness. How exciting for her. So you're filling in for her?"

"Well, me and Vallie. Only Vallie done went and died on me two days ago. Left me with this here place until Pyune gets back."

"When will Pyune return?"

"Sunday." Lizzie sprang from her seat, as though she had teenage legs again, and clapped her hands. "I got me a good idea. How about you stay until she gets back? I could sure use the help, and I can tidy up the bedroom upstairs."

"I'd love to stay, but my mother is expecting me tomorrow for her birthday. I sure wouldn't want to disappoint her."

Lizzie nodded and her fingers twisted the corners of her apron. "You could spend tonight here at least. Get up and leave early in the morning. Ain't nothing like sleepin' in a little ol' town like this. Peaceful. No semi's. No drunks. No—"

The screen door slammed open and Paula's shrill voice filled The Boardinghouse kitchen. "Lizzie! What in the world are you doing? Everybody'll be wanting dinner at six, and I don't see one pot on that stove!"

The thin redhead sashayed across the kitchen, her high heels clicking like valves in a car engine needing oil. "I don't believe this!" She turned around and noticed Jay. "And who are you? the health inspector? I'll tell you right now, everything is clean as a whistle in here. No need to write out a report that's anything but perfect." She walked over and slung open the refrigerator. "Look at this refrigerator. Cleaned it myself. Immaculate!"

She put her hands on her hips. "Did you look in the stove?" She paused and studied Jay. "Well, did you? Super clean, right?"

Jay looked over the rim of his glasses at the woman in the tight skirt and with the obviously fake beauty mark above her left eye. "I'm not the health inspector. I'm just—"

"Oh, you must be—" walking closer and looking him up and down— "the delivery boy?"

"Paula, please!" Lizzie tossed aside her apron for a clean one. "He's just passing through. Leave him alone." She put on the clean apron and went over to the stove and turned on a burner.

"Just passing through? Too bad. You're a good-looking boy." Paula surveyed the kitchen, the worktable, and the counters, stopping when she came to the pies, the pastries, the breads, and cakes. "Where did all this come from?"

Lizzie, busying herself with some potatoes, said, "Me and Jay whipped up these things this afternoon."

Paula turned up her nose. "I wish you'd have called me to come over here. I could have been a big help." She eyed Jay again. "It was nice of you to do this. Guess you heard about the other lady dying who was working here. Owner of this place is in New York."

"That's what Lizzie told me. Sorry to hear about . . . Vallie, right?" Jay lifted a stockpot and filled it with water.

Paula said nothing and sauntered to the worktable and sliced off the end of a loaf of bread. "Got any coffee made, Lizzie?"

"No. Don't have time right now. I've got to get some things done first."

"So what's for dinner? Everybody'll be here in an hour or so." Paula watched Jay grating cheese into a large bowl. "What's that for?"

"Beer cheese soup."

"Beer? You're going to make soup with beer? Oh, the church folks will love that." She arched her red eyebrows. "I suggested that we turn this restaurant into a French bistro, but nobody listened to me."

"Oh, hush, Paula. Jay made all those little bread bowls and we're gonna serve the soup in them. Beer cheese soup, and potato soup with a little ham in it."

"Well now, aren't we getting fancy here?" Paula studied the tattoos on Jay's arms. "You didn't get those tattoos in prison, did you?"

Lizzie dropped a big spoon. "Paula! You get outta this here kitchen right now!" She stomped toward Paula and snapped her dishtowel like a bullwhip. "I'm telling you right now to go home. We don't need you and your French cooking ideas and smart mouth."

"Ladies! Ladies!" Jay raised his hands. "Please. The croissants are ready to come out of the oven. No loud noises!" The young man delicately opened the oven door and pulled out a pan of lemon curd croissants and spoke to them as though they were little children. "Ahhhh," he crooned, "you're going to love it when I sprinkle powdered sugar on you."

Paula sent Lizzie a sidelong glance and came back to Jay. "We don't talk to our food in Ivy Log. Something wrong with you?"

Lizzie had heard enough. A wet dishrag sailed across the kitchen, catching Paula flush across the face. "You get yourself outta here right now!" Lizzie screamed, picked up a large spatula and swiped the air with it. She moved her large body quickly, skirting the corner of the worktable and heading toward Paula. Paula screeched and shot out the back door, her skinny legs taking the back steps two at a time. Outside, the cat meowed loudly, the rooster flapped his wings, and Paula's red hair dripped with Boardinghouse dishwater as she burned her way down the sidewalk.

The Boardinghouse settled into a quiet night. The dining room, after a bustling dinner crowd that devoured everything which Jay and Lizzie had cooked, was now dark. Lizzie had collapsed in her recliner at her little house on Maple Street as Jay Metzler steered his car toward Richmond on a drive which would take the night and some of the next morning to complete. He could have arrived at his parents' home sooner, but after he'd finished helping with dinner he asked to stay on a while longer, and during this time he made dozens of lemon curd croissants, six loaves of rosemary bread, three large pans of blueberry buttermilk biscuits, two dozen almond croissants, and countless cinnamon buns.

In the wee hours of Friday morning, he drove north on the lonely, dark highway that winded its way through the Appalachians. He thought of Ivy Log, of Lizzie, of The Boardinghouse. He had meant to stop for just the time it took to eat a late lunch. Instead, he found Lizzie mourning the loss of her best friend. Now, however, he was smiling, believing that no one should go on a journey without walking arm in arm with a friend. Someday he'd come back to Ivy Log and perhaps make that walk with Lizzie again.

~~~

Chapter 44

T he stress of a Friday in a New York City media environment
became immediately apparent to Pyune. Monty, Tess and
Pyune met in the morning in Tess's office to discuss the
fundraiser scheduled for one that afternoon. Scheduled for three
hours, it would run live to raise money for New York City's homeless. A tape of the show would be aired later in the year to celebrate Bakers' World Magazine's 25th anniversary, with special
emphasis on the chef whose efforts accrued the most money during the fundraiser.

Tess began reading a copy of the show's script, scrutinizing
the setup and pace of the telecast. She raised up and said, "I want
to play devil's advocate for a moment. Why would anyone pledge
money on Pyune's behalf if she's not a celebrity chef?" Tess shook
her head. "As I've thought about this further, we're pitting an unknown against three of New York's hottest chefs. Everybody who
routinely dines out in New York City knows who they are. Who
knows Pyune?"

Monty stood and waved his copy of the script. "It's all in the
presentation. Can you imagine the underdog situation this creates? Think of a horse race. Think of Seabiscuit. He was under-
sized and knob-kneed. But he was skilled at holding to the pack
before pulling ahead with unbelievable late speed. That's how I
feel about Pyune. Yes, she's unknown. She's from a remote place
—" Monty interrupted himself, half-dancing/half-walking around
Tess's office. "I can see it now! She can win this thing. She can
take those three celebrated chefs." He retook his seat. "And an-

other thing—we've publicized the heck out of this. There's no backing out now."

Tess was unconvinced, a deep sigh falling into a half groan. "I wish I'd thought about this more before I committed Pyune." Tess bit down on a pencil. "This is all spinning into lunacy. And what about Joan Stone? I don't want to do this to Pyune. She'll be up against the bitch from hell. Joan won't give Pyune an inch. She'll eat her alive. Please, let's rearrange the lineup. We'll say Pyune became ill at the last minute, whatever."

Pyune held up her hand. "May I say something?"

A silent moment ensued. Monty smiled his movie-star smile, his teeth a shade too white to be real. Tess shrugged and nodded to Pyune.

"All this debate over a chicken potpie?"

After a few beats passed, Monty said rather sheepishly, "I guess you can look at it that way." He arched his eyebrows as if to ask for help.

"I'm wondering what the problem is," Pyune said as she stood and released a long breath. "I've cooked hundreds if not thousands of chicken potpies. I don't understand the concern?"

Tess laughed. "Dear sister, this is New York City. It's just. . . well . . . it's different here."

"But I'll be in a place I'm very familiar with, which is a kitchen. As long as I have the ingredients I need, I'll do just fine."

"Ingredients?" Monty swiveled his head to Pyune. "You mean the usual chicken, flour, salt, pepper; what else is there?"

Pyune stared at him. "For a potpie, I like to use goose fat in my crust."

Monty got wide-eyed. "Goose fat. You're kidding, right?" Pyune shook her head while Monty thumbed through the papers in his hand. He came to a page and studied it, which he subsequently waved in Pyune's direction. "Here's a list of products stored in the Bakers' World kitchen, and I hate to tell you, there's no goose fat. Guess you'll have to work without it."

Pyune, with great drama—which was not her style, but she'd learned from the queen of theatrics after being around Paula— made a big issue of looking at her watch. "Well, you've got exactly three hours to find some." Her mouth sat closed with her face unsmiling. *I'm not going to be the quiet, sweet woman from deep in the Appalachians when it comes to someone dictating how I'm supposed to cook.*

Tess began laughing loudly, slapping her hand up and down on her desk. "Goose fat. Oh, Monty, you've got two hours and fifty-nine minutes now. Better get going!" She laughed even louder. "And while you're at it, take some to loosey-goosey Joan Stone!"

Monty was not amused. He righted himself and spoke in a dignified voice to Pyune: "Is there anything else you need?"

Pyune didn't hesitate. "Yes. A bottle of Spätlese Riesling, fresh thyme and sage, fresh Italian parsley, morel mushrooms, chicken thighs with the bones in, unsalted chicken stock, and of course unsalted butter."

He began writing feverishly, and when he stopped he handed his list to Pyune to check. While Pyune looked over the ingredients, Monty asked Tess, "Where in the city do I send someone for goose fat?"

Tess thought a moment before her face lit up. "Call Eric Ripert at "Le Bernardiu"—he'll have it or know where to get it."

"I'm sure Eric will be delighted to hear that we're in need of goose fat." Monty, unsmiling, turned and headed toward the door, his feet not dancing but dragging like they were tied to concrete blocks. He stopped and slowly turned back to Pyune. "Anything else, dear lady?"

Pyune snapped her fingers once. "Yes, there is. Find me five Emile Henry four-and-one-half-inch pie dishes."

Monty added this to his list and rolled his eyes as he fell through the doorway. Tess yelled after him, "Only two-hours-and-fifty-seven minutes left, Monty!"

This year the three-hour fundraiser was slated to raise a million dollars for New York City's homeless. A trio of celebrity chefs, each of whom owned Michelin Three-Star Restaurants and had trained at the finest culinary institutes in the world, would be the headliners of the show. Their CVs showcased them as three of the world's most acclaimed chefs, their traditional tall white toques a proud indicator of their exalted status. And, in the midst of them, a woman who learned to cook on a woodstove in the remote mountains of north Georgia. Tess was right. It was all spinning into lunacy.

~~~

Chapter 45

Just after sunrise on Friday morning, a bit of melancholy fell into Wiley's walk up the mountain path that led to the ridge high above Ivy Log. He hadn't talked with Pyune in the past forty-eight hours. He had left two messages: "Hello, thinking about you. Hope all is well." And: "Hello. Mighty lonely here without you. New York is a long way away. I love you."

He'd checked his phone frequently for her calls he might somehow have missed. But none had come. He felt an emptiness that came and went and came back again, staying longer each time. High on the ridge, he found a tall elm tree and settled in beneath its cool shade. He shook his head and contemplated his feelings, enduring a heavy heart filled with sadness.

During his doldrums he checked the mileage to New York—he wanted to know exactly how far away he was from Pyune: Over 800 miles. It seemed a different world had emerged since her departure on Sunday. Nothing was the same without her. There was the arrival of the redheaded boy, Vallie's death, the reading of Vallie's will and the millions of dollars in her estate, and of course the mystery of Eva McIlwain, a former governor of North Carolina. Was she or wasn't she the bucktoothed-boy's half-sister? Would she be his legal guardian? Might she contest the will and have Wiley dragged through all sorts of court proceedings?

From atop the ridge and looking across the town square, Wiley saw Lizzie walk up the steps of The Boardinghouse. She stopped a few minutes to write the day's offerings on the old chalkboard. He hoped it was a simple menu, Lizzie's lack of culinary skills well known to all. But folks didn't seem to mind. What they craved most was small-town fellowship and the latest harmless gossip.

Wiley exhaled deeply and pulled himself up from the base of the tree and walked slowly down the mountain trail. He listened to the train whistle he heard every morning at this hour. The sound again made him think of Hank Williams singing "I Heard That Lonesome Whistle Blow." And leaving. *It was always about leaving.*

By nine that morning, every chair at The Boardinghouse was filled. Coffee had already been poured by the gallons, and there was a huge buzz about all the pastries and biscuits and breads. "Oh, my goodness, Lizzie, these croissants are fabulous!" "Those biscuits done melted in my mouth!" "My, my, Lizzie girl, them breads was delicious!" She heard the same compliments over and over.

Red-faced, Lizzie tittered around the tables, repeating, "Oh, some angel come in during the night and whipped up all them luscious things." She laughed and couldn't add often enough, "Glad y'all are enjoying everything."

At the large round table by the bay window, Wiley, Sam, the pastor, and B.T. feasted on a large basket of blueberry biscuits. B.T. had smothered his biscuits with butter, had eaten two in rapid succession, and was now slurping down a glass of milk. He had not combed his hair. In a caring gesture, the preacher reached over and smoothed his hand across the top of B.T.'s head. "Forget to comb that mop, buddy?"

"Sniddle-snot! When a man's hungry, he don't think about an unimportant thang like hair." B.T. ducked away from the preacher's hand. "Besides, your cat done slept on top of my head last night. Didn't do too much good for my hair."

The pastor laughed. "Don't you go blaming that mess on top of your head on Delilah."

Sam put down his phone. "Just heard from Eva. She's on her way. Be here in about ten minutes."

"Good," Wiley said. "We've got lots to talk about." Not the least of which would be discussing Vallie's will. But even more important was B.T.'s guardianship. If she was truly his sister, she would assume automatic custody of the underage boy since she was his only living relative. The State of Georgia would require definitive proof of her kinship, and with the amount of money now involved, a DNA test would likely be ordered.

The front doors of The Boardinghouse opened and Paula Jennings stepped inside, her lips painted red and unsmiling. She was wearing her longest false eyelashes, which fanned out at least an inch and accented her harsh turquoise eyeshadow. When her gaze caught the table by the bay window, she plunged forward, her mouth open and ready to lash out at any poor creature in her path.

"Well, there you are." She pointed at the boy. "I just got a call from Family Services in Blairsville, and they're on the way to pick you up."

"Hold on," said Sam, his words razor sharp.

Paula jerked as if a clap of thunder had hit nearby. However, she gathered herself and the red lips snarled, "Oh, please, give it up! That boy is homeless—an orphan." Her words trilled louder until hers were the only sounds in The Boardinghouse. "He belongs in a foster home somewhere and not here in Ivy Log, roaming the streets and doing all sorts of awful things."

Pastor Johnson and Sam both jumped up from the table at the same time, coffee spilling everywhere. Sam reached his arm in front of the reverend. "I've got this, Will." He moved from behind the table. "What did you do, bypass Sheriff Drummond?"

Paula raised an authoritative chin. "That man had no intention of removing that boy from Ivy Log."

"You didn't give him a chance to resolve any issues regarding the boy. He had everything under control."

Wiley pushed back his chair. "We're not going to discuss this in front of the boy." He grasped Paula by the arm and pulled her toward the door. Under his breath, he said. "Get yourself home. Now!"

Paula resisted. "What do you think you're doing? I—"

Wiley squeezed her arm tighter. "You heard me, Paula. I won't have this." His words were low and sharp but firm like the blade of a guillotine.

Paula jerked her arm free and marched through the doorway and onto the porch. At the bottom of the steps, she turned and glared at Wiley and hissed. "Just so you know, Wiley Hansen, you'll never set foot in my bedroom again."

Wiley held her stare. "I never planned to, Paula."

Eva McIlwain arrived at The Boardinghouse and squealed with joy at the lemon curd croissants. Sam poured her coffee and smiled as Eva's ponytail swung back and forth. Instead of a woman in her forties, she looked like the young woman he'd seen the first time he'd laid eyes on her. "How was your trip down?" he asked.

"It was beautiful. I love the back roads through North Carolina and into Georgia. No traffic and just beautiful mountains."

Across the table, B.T. cautiously eyed Eva. His freckles seem to fade as if in quiet remission. What he had said was true: he'd never seen that woman before in his life. He thought he was his mother's only child. Yet the woman across from him, with the shiny, laughing eyes, said she was his sister. *Well, sniddle-snot, if that was true, where has she been all my life? One good thang, though, if Mr. Wiley weren't gonna buy me new boots, and he ain't made no further mention of it this mornin', maybe she'd do it.*

B.T chewed his latest biscuit slowly and looked for freckles on Eva's smooth skin. There were only a few. *Well, that proves it. No freckles, no sister.* He felt smug and reached for the fig preserves. His long, boney fingers wrapped around the jar and he pulled it to him. He checked out Eva's hands. Her fingers were narrow and long, not boney like his. *There you go. Nope, not my sister.*

From the corner of his eye he began studying her hair. There! Not one single stand of red in it. *Ha! Told you so. Not my sister.* He stared at her nose. Petite and cute with a little dip in the middle, like a girl's. His nose was straight. Manly.

But when Eva turned her head and spoke to Sam, B.T. froze. He spotted the peanut-shaped birthmark near the bottom of her left ear. He reached up and rubbed his—which was exactly like hers. He felt his heart flutter. *Dang! Could it be?* His eyes fell to a folder she'd placed on the table. It was full of papers. *What kind of papers?* He looked up and found her watching him. He quickly looked away, his red eyelashes fluttering nervously.

"B.T., how many of those biscuits have you eaten?" she asked, her laughing eyes staying on him.

"Fi . . . five," he stuttered.

Her eyes took in his hair, his freckled face, and his protruding teeth that always seemed to rest on his bottom lip, even
when he spoke. She saw a speck of biscuit crumb on his chin.
"You probably don't know this, B.T., but I practiced law for a few
years before I entered politics." She tapped a manila folder that
lay next to her coffee cup. "I'd like you to know I have information here that I think you'll be interested in."

Wiley flicked the boy's shoulder and smiled at him. "I'm
thinking you don't need to worry about what Paula Jennings
told you, B.T."

Eva raised her eyebrows and tilted her head. "What?"

"Paula Jennings, you met her, got a little uppity and con-
tacted Family Services over in Blairsville. She was by here a little
while ago and told B.T. they were on their way to pick him up."

Eva quickly reached for her phone, left the table, and walked
outside. Everyone at the bay window saw her pace back and
forth, her hand waving, her mouth moving quickly. A short
while later she placed her phone back in her purse. She bounded
up the steps and back into The Boardinghouse, where she slid
back into her chair.

Wiley had his eyes set on Eva, who picked up the folder. "No
problem with Family Services. They're not coming to Ivy Log."

B.T.'s gaze went from the folder to the peanut-shaped birthmark on Eva's neck. "Where'd you say you was born?" He
quickly looked away as if surprised he'd spoken to her.

Eva pulled out a piece of paper with a notary seal's impression visible to all. "This document states that I was born in
Rocky Top, North Carolina."

B.T. nodded solemnly and blinked several times. "Me too."

Eva's eyes misted over, followed by a knowing grin.

~~~

Chapter 46

The commercial-size kitchen at Bakers' World had been transformed into a live studio bustling with technicians, producers, directors and enough staff to organize and run a live three-hour television show.

"Damn it," Monty yelled at a technician. "How many times have I told you, don't leave cords lying around without taping them down. Somebody's going to trip and we're going to get sued. Where's the set director?"

Four television cameras were positioned at the ready. A camera hovered above the kitchen worktables, its operator readying it for live broadcasting in only thirty minutes. A cigarette hung from the cameraman's lips. "No smoking on the set," admonished an assistant director.

The lighting was runway bright on the entire set, where a panel of five judges, three celebrity chefs, and one Pyune Ever-Sweet Murphy would perform for three long hours—all in the name of charity. A full ten-minute break was scheduled once every hour, during which time a number of New York icons would make appearances and laud his or her favorite chef in hope of spiking the donations under that person's name.

The chef who garnered the most donations would be heralded as New York City's Chef for a Day, appear on "The Tonight Show," and best of all be awarded a guest spot as the host of the wildly popular cooking show, "Dine With Me."

The meals the chefs prepared on "Dine With Me" were legendary. The chef's invited famous people to enjoy what they cooked on the show, in a lovely dining room appointed with the best of everything. Guests on the show had been numerous past and present governors of New York, Jay Leno, Barbra Streisand and James Brolin, Christy Brinkley, Cate Blanchett, and many more A-listers too numerous to name. Merchandisers flooded the show with signature china, crystal, linens, cookware and everything imaginable that promoted an elegant dining experience. Winning the competition would be an extraordinary coup for any chef, as the show had millions of viewers and consistently ranked in the top ten specials on television during a given year. The phenomenal exposure could rocket an already sterling career into the stratosphere of culinary superstardom.

And the public! They *loved* listening to celebrities' dinner conversations as well as watching them dine. It was like being invited into their homes. As for hosting "Dine With Me," this was Joan Stone's dream job. She craved the spotlight and believed that the show was her birthright and stairway to personal nirvana.

Ms. Stone, a tall blonde with a cover-girl's face and model's figure, used New York City as her playground. Anywhere excitement brewed, Joan was there. And she also well known was her disgust of traditional chef's garb while she performed as the head chef in her restaurant, Romancing The Stone, which she also owned. Rumors flew around New York that she had once ripped off her chef jacket and cooked in a lacy purple bra, much to the delight of her kitchen staff.

A New York icon, she ran the gamut of "celebrities without borders." Joan Rivers once called her a "jellyfish," which she explained to mean that Ms. Stone maintained a stinging personality while running her restaurant. Over the years employees had walked out in droves, many after spending only minutes with her,

Joan sat in the make-up artist's chair and leaned back. "Please make sure my lashes are glued well. I don't want any problems under the lights." She sipped a Perrier. "Oh, and I want my décolletage brushed with shimmering powder and—"

"But aren't you wearing a chef's jacket?" an aide for the show asked. "With a kerchief at the neck?"

"Hardly. I can't imagine being on television in a drab chef's jacket that has no color." She looked up at her hairdresser. "And

I sure as hell am not wearing a chef's hat, so work on my hair, dear."

"Briefing begins in ten minutes," Monty shouted as he walked down the hall and yelled into the rooms he passed. "Competing chefs are to meet in the conference room too. Judges also." Monty shuffled along, a clipboard in his hand. "Set director and staff, follow me, please," he called over his shoulder.

Soon chefs Whittington and Fencik made their way into the conference room, along with Pyune. The set director, Donald Jackson, followed closely behind them, as did the five judges. The room became quiet as Monty lifted his clipboard and looked around the room. "Where's Joan?"

Chef Whittington shrugged, along with the set director. Monty slapped his hand on the clipboard, irritation washing across his face. "Don, go find her!"

The room quieted and Monty took a breath. "Okay. Let's go over everything one more time. "Chefs, as you know, each of you is preparing the same dish, a chicken potpie. Each of you was responsible for assembling your own ingredients, secret or otherwise." He looked around the room. "In the end, the judges will decide whose pie wins. Of course, the dollars donated will also factor into the overall tally for the winning chef. Questions?" Monty glanced around the room. There were no questions.

He continued. "Judges, your – " Monty halted his delivery and stared above the heads of those already seated in the conference room. Joan Stone stood in the doorway and sent a tantalizing smile his way. His body sank. He immediately knew he was in trouble—in trouble with one Tess Starling. He'd promised Tess he would rein in Joan. One look at Joan made it clear he'd failed miserably.

She wore an all-black ensemble. Her top was knit, V-necked, with small cap sleeves embedded with rhinestones. The V of her neckline plummeted almost to her navel, held together by buttons that sparkled with the same rhinestones that adorned her sleeves. The air seemed to leave the room as she spoke: "So sorry I'm late, Monty. You know, girl stuff." Rather than taking a seat, she stood at the back of the room.

Monty narrowed his eyes. "All the chefs are to wear a traditional white jacket during the competition, Joan. Where's yours?"

"Oh, please, Monty. This is television, not my restaurant's kitchen. I can't believe you don't want to spice things up a little." She laughed and winked at the show's director.

Monty shook his head. "I don't know how you'll be able to cook in that outfit."

"I could cook wearing nothing . . . you know that." She sent him a man-eater smirk.

A few snickers eased around the room. Monty blushed. "We'll discuss this later."

"Yes, let's do." Joan batted her false eyelashes in a ridiculously exaggerated fashion.

"All right, judges," Monty began again. "As chefs yourselves, you know the rules. You'll judge on technique, presentation, and of course taste. There are scorecards at the judge's table for each chef. Now, let me introduce this year's competing chefs."

Monty pointed to a tall, thin man with graying hair. He was dressed immaculately in a double-breasted chef's jacket, a kerchief around his neck, and a snow-white toque sitting tall on his head. His black slacks were creased perfectly and fell into shiny black shoes. "This is chef Dick Whittington." He waited a moment while everyone in the room clapped loudly. "Chef Whittington has been in New York City for over fifteen years and is the head chef at Union Pacific.

"To my right is chef George Fencik of The Silver Spoon. You've seen his recent layout in Saveur Magazine, where his restaurant was showcased for being awarded a third Michelin Star, one of only six restaurants in New York City to hold that distinction." Again, a loud clapping of hands.

Monty hesitated when he turned to Joan. Without fanfare, he said, "And, of course, Joan Stone." Joan bowed slightly to the room, the shimmering powder on her cleavage catching the light.

Monty stepped forward and smiled from ear to ear as he lifted his hand and gestured to Pyune. "Our next competitor is a very special guest, the winner of Bakers' World Magazine's twenty-fifth annual baking contest. I give you Pyune Murphy, of Ivy Log, Georgia."

From the far back corner of the conference room, a shy Pyune EverSweet Murphy came forward, her steps hesitant, her eyes wide. The room's chatter drifted away as she moved next to Monty. Those who knew Ms. Starling were immediately aware of the striking resemblance between the two women, and looks of awe remained on the faces of those in attendance who undoubtedly thought this woman was indeed Tess.

Monty continued, "As the winner of the Bakers' World baking contest, Pyune will compete in this year's charity event as our fourth guest chef." Pyune received applause that equaled the other chefs, which she hadn't expected. Euphoria coursed through her and made her light-headed.

Monty smiled wide again. "Pyune is from a small town in north Georgia, called Ivy Log. It was her delicious lemon pudding cake that won the grand prize of $25,000, and she's gracious enough to appear in our annual charity event. Pyune now stood by Monty's side. "Anything you'd like to say, Pyune."

Pyune, as lovely as Scarlett O'Hara ever was, felt a smile tug at her lips. "I never dreamed I would be in New York and meet so many wonderful people. Thank you all for your kindness and warmth."

The softness of Pyune's words spread around the room like hot-buttered biscuits. Those who had never met her, looked at her is if to say, "*Who is this woman—this slight, gorgeous creature who speaks like an angel?*"

Joan raised her hand. "So, Ms. Murphy, you're not really a chef? I mean . . . a trained chef?" Joan lifted her chin, a challenge in her words. She took a couple of steps forward, her arms folded, the rhinestones on her top resembling the sharpness of knife points.

Monty began to speak but Pyune placed her hand gently on his arm. "Ms. Stone, what an excellent question. Thank you for an opportunity to clarify my position here at this celebrated event." The crowd hushed. They wanted to hear every single word this woman said, who softened the air by simply speaking.

"My life as a cook began at age fourteen in the remote Appalachian mountains, near the Brasstown Bald." A soft laugh. "Can you believe I learned to cook on a woodstove? How in the world I ended up with three of New York's most-renowned chefs is a miracle, and I'm so grateful."

The entire room seemed to collapse comfortably around Pyune. Joan, with words meant to decapitate, raised her voice:

"Monty, what kind of competition can this possibly be with the odds so uneven. Ms. Murphy won't have a chance against trained chefs." She shrugged her shoulders in a gesture of counterfeit helplessness. "How embarrassing it will be for her . . . her lack of training . . . and no knowledge of technique." Joan's delivery was somber but did not hide the glee in her eyes. "She has so much to overcome before she even begins to compete."

Monty jumped in, a tad of worry across his brow. "I'd like us to honor the spirit with which we will compete today, for charity, to care for New York City's homeless. Every dime earned in this fundraiser is important." He looked quickly at his watch. "Five minutes to showtime!" He grasped Pyune's arm, a move to protect her from the *jellyfish*, and pulled her under the glaring lights of the Bakers' World kitchen. "Here's your station." He added in a lower voice, "Sorry it's next to Joan's,"

"It's okay," she whispered back. "We have someone just like Ms. Stone back in Ivy Log. I'm more than used to *it*."

Soon Pyune heard, "Three, two, one! Action!"

~~~

Chapter 47

Vallie Thomas's obituary was published in the Friday edition of The Blairsville-North Georgia News. The small notice listed the date and time of her memorial service: Monday, April 25, at 1:00 p.m., at The Church of Ivy Log. Interment at the church cemetery to follow.

William Johnson sat in his office at the parsonage and read Wiley's tribute to Vallie. Indeed, Vallie had been the heart of Ivy Log. Already there were times when the pastor had found himself absentmindedly looking for her purple scarf while he walked up and down Main Street—forgetting she was gone

He leaned back and propped his feet on the corner of his desk, his mind full of tender words for the woman who lived life exactly as she pleased, with no calendars, no appointment books, no references to the future. She truly lived her days a moment at a time and relished each one as if a beautifully wrapped present.

The pastor looked up when Wiley popped his head in the doorway. "Hey!" the preacher said. "On your way to Blairsville?"

"Yep. Got to get with Jesse Collins one more time to finalize a few things. I'm taking Eva with me. Not really sure how her potential guardianship of B.T. will affect things. You know, B.T.'s inheritance."

"Didn't Eva practice law at one time?"

"Oh, yeah. Big time.

"How much does she know about Vallie's will?"

"Nothing in great detail. Just that Vallie's pretty much left everything to B.T."

Reverend Johnson cleared his throat and leaned forward. "Do you see any problems regarding the will and Eva—now that she's surfaced as B.T.'s sister?"

Wiley drummed his fingers on the doorframe and smiled as his eyes caught Delilah stretched out across the top of a bookcase. "I feel the courts will award custody of B.T. to Eva. As his guardian, she'll be responsible for overseeing his estate. Of course, she could contest the will or rob him blind later, even if the court upholds Vallie's wishes. Facts be known, I want no part of what might go on. Eva doesn't seem like the type to cause trouble, though." Wiley rubbed his bald head. "Still, it's a whole lot of money,"

William Johnson nodded as if he knew something Wiley didn't. "Let me know what Collins says."

"That I'll do. Meantime, I guess B.T. will be with you this afternoon while we're in Blairsville." Wiley walked over and handed the pastor some twenties. "Want us to bring you back some barbecue from Jim's?"

"Sure, but what's this money for?"

"You get the time, take B.T. down to the hardware store and get him some new boots. I promised him. Then buy him some underwear and socks."

"I already gave him some of my underwear. He could swim in the shorts, but they were a substantial improvement." The preacher rolled his eyes. "His socks that bad too, huh? Don't answer that."

Eva slid into the front seat of Wiley's truck, and soon he pulled onto the Blairsville Highway. "Wish you could have known Vallie, Eva. She was quite a gal."

Eva, her hair held in place with a large silver clasp, opened her window. Crisp April air swept by and carried the fragrance of blooming rhododendrons. A stray cat flitted across the road and jumped a nearby fence with ease. "I wish I could have known her too. And B.T. . . . it would have been wonderful for him to have been able to spend time with her."

"Poor young feller. But now he has you."

Eva laughed. "And now I have *him*! I always wanted a brother or a sister. But my adoptive parents seemed quite content that I'd filled their dream of having a family." She laughed again. "I guess I was enough of a family for them."

Wiley didn't want to discuss B.T.'s inheritance with her in the truck, and he sort of wished that Sam hadn't already talked with her about this. He hoped that the subject wouldn't come up until they were in Jesse Collins's office.

Wiley's wish was granted, as the conversations stayed well away from B.T.'s inheritance, and he parked in front of the Collins and Dyer law office and he and Eva walked up the wooden staircase.

A newspaper had been thrown high up the steps. When he got to it, Wiley saw it was The New York Times. "I imagine Mr. Collins will be wanting this." He laughed as he picked it up.

Inside, Caity once again greeted him. Her loveliness poured out like iced tea on a hot summer day. "Well, hello, Mr. Hanson."

"Hello, Caity. This here is Ms. Eva McIlwain." Wiley handed Caity the newspaper and smiled. "And this here is your New York Times."

"Oh, no, Mr. Hanson," she whispered. "Don't let Mr. Collins know it's here or you'll be in big trouble." She glanced toward the open door of Jesse Collins's office.

Wiley winked. "Understood."

"Go on in. Uncle Je. . . Mr. Collins is expecting you." Caity tucked the newspaper out of sight and made like she was busy at her computer.

Wiley poked his head inside the doorway. "Hey, Jesse. Caity said to barge on in."

Jesse Collins jumped out of his oversized chair, the little man rocking with energy. "Well, Mr. Hanson, twice in one week! This is a pleasure!" He smiled at Eva. "And you are?"

Eva stepped forward and shook Jesse Collins's hand. "I'm Eva McIlwain."

There was a slight pause in his movement. "Oh . . . of course I know who you are, Governor McIlwain. It's a pleasure to meet you." He made a slight bow.

Jesse returned to his purple leather chair and immediately picked up a pen. "Now, let's tackle something very important first off." He laughed and pulled a tattered page off a newspaper sitting in his middle desk drawer. "Wiley, my friend, this has been the most horrendous crossword puzzle I've ever worked, and I prayed to God that he would send you here to help me with it."

His small, thin fingers pushed his glasses up on his nose and his eyes glistened. He coughed up a laugh resembling the chattering of a squirrel and pulled the newspaper closer. His words were a whisper, his eyes narrow as a lark's as he leaned across his desk. "I am ashamed to admit that my alcohol intake has tripled in these past few days in my frustration over this puzzle." He paused and sent a half-smile. "Had you not come today, I do believe I would have jumped off the Bald."

Jesse sat up straight, apparently attempting to add a little integrity to his dedication to crossword puzzles. "You see, Ms. McIlwain, I work these puzzles to relieve my stress. But, as Wiley will attest, they seem to cause me a fair amount of anxiety on their own." He looked over his glasses. "Understand?"

Eva found herself laughing at the little man who was almost lost in his huge leather chair. "I do understand. I must confess, I'm hooked on Sudoku."

"Ah, well, then you do understand." He turned to Wiley. "Here goes." He shoved the puzzle across his desk. "See five across—town at the eight-mile mark of the Boston marathon? Well, I got that one. It's Natick. Now, seven down—Treasure Island illustrator from the year nineteen-eleven." He held his breath and intently watched Wiley's face.

The twang of the mountain man was matter-of-fact, bordering on boredom. "That would be N.C. Wyeth."

Dumbfounded silence was followed by a long sigh and then a crumbling of the newspaper. "Now, how'd you do that?"

Wiley chuckled. "Now, Mr. Collins, we all have gaps in our knowledge, whether it be art, the Bible, baseball, comics, opera, whatever. Don't you go berating yourself."

"I drank all that whiskey for N.C. Wyeth!" He threw the entire newspaper in a trashcan and pulled a folder from a pile on his desk. "Now, let's see here. You mentioned on the phone that you wanted to go over a few things that we didn't cover yesterday." He opened the file and looked up. "What exactly did you have in mind?"

Wiley moved his chair closer to Jesse's desk. "There have been a few changes since Sam Cobb and I came to see you for the reading of Vallie Thomas's will. It seems Vallie's heir, Bartholomew Thomas Hickel, has a sister."

"A sister?" Jesse Collins jerked up his head so fast that his glasses almost flew off his face.

"That's right. Miss McIlwain here is B.T.'s sister."

Jesse Collins stared hard at Eva, then his eyes darted to Wiley. "I'm afraid you're mistaken, Wiley. Miss McIlwain is not B.T.'s sister." He thumped the file folder in front of him. "Leastwise, not from what it says here."

~~~

Chapter 48

In the Bakers' World kitchens, four sets of cooking areas gleamed in the high wattage studio lights, and behind each worktable stood the competitors in the New York Cooks for Charity Fundraiser.

Monty, dressed in a tuxedo, was wired with a microphone and opened the show with a resounding welcome to the generous citizens of New York City. A live band played "New York, New York" as he smiled broadly into the cameras and said, "Hellooooooooo, New York! Thank you for joining us in our annual fundraiser for the needy citizens of New York City! I hope you'll generously support our charity!

"And you can do this by voting for your favorite celebrity chef. Your votes will transfer into dollars! Keep your eye on the leaderboard to monitor the progress of each chef. Our panel of five judges will rate each chef's cooking performance at the end of the program. Along with viewers' donations, the judges' selection as winning chef will receive an extra twenty-five thousand dollars from Bakers' World Magazine to add to his or her donation total."

Monty took a quick bow and lifted his arm toward the worktables. "And now I'd like to introduce you to our exciting celebrity chefs." A drum roll overwhelmed all other sound, as he raced over to workstation number one. "Say hello to a chef you've met before. Chef Dick Whittington is the head chef at world-famous Union Pacific and has participated in our fundraiser for the past five years. And last year he won the top position with $217,000. Welcome, Chef Whittington!" Loud applause followed and Monty moved to station two.

"And here is Chef George Fencik from The Silver Spoon, which was recently awarded Michelin's highest culinary achievement, a third star. Chef Fencik, thank you for participating in our charity event. And good luck!" Another loud round of applause, and with considerable trepidation Monty slid over to Joan's table.

Compared to the way Chef Whittington and Chef Fencik were attired, she glittered like all the gold in California. Her false eyelashes swept upward, framing the metallic eye shadow she wore. "And here we have Chef Joan Stone. Chef Stone is the owner/head chef of Romancing The Stone. Welcome, Chef Stone." During the applause that followed, Monty was careful to keep his eyes away from the plunging neckline of her black knit top. He stepped quickly to the next worktable and Pyune Murphy.

"And now, we'd like to present a very special guest. It's my pleasure to introduce the winner of Bakers' World Magazine's twenty-fifth annual baking contest. I give you Pyune Murphy, from Ivy Log, Georgia. I know you'll make her feel welcome." A loud round of applause kept up for a duration equal to what the other chefs had received, making Pyune wonder if all of it had been piped in. Monty placed his arm around Pyune and looked into the camera. "This is Pyune's first time in New York City—so what do you say we show her how generous we can be!"

More applause, but of shorter duration, and a bell rang and a camera panned to a ticking clock before returning to Monty, who said, "Each of our chefs will prepare a chicken potpie using his or her own special recipe. Everyone will use the first segment of the show to prep. We'll break for ten minutes, then return at the top of the hour with celebrity guests who will cheer for their favorite chef. So, without further ado, lettttttt's get started."

The band played "Red, Red Wine" by UB40, and all four chefs delved into what each hoped would be the winning chicken-potpie recipe.

No, I can't be here. Not the little girl who'd walked barefoot down the mountain so many years ago. Not Pyune EverSweet Murphy, the woman who'd lived in small-town Ivy Log for forty years and had never imagined herself anywhere else. But, here she was—in a place called New York City, in a place where there seemed to be magic everywhere she went.

She blinked several times. No, she wasn't dreaming. This was real. Television cameras zoomed in on her hands. *What am I doing? I'm chopping food. Why would anyone want to see me chopping celery and onions? No one watched me at The Boardinghouse.*

She looked up and saw herself on the monitor, at least she thought is was her, as perspiration had lightly formed on this woman's forehead and the red lipstick she wore might as well be flashing like the lights on a fire truck. Her dangling gold earrings caught the lights no matter how slightly she moved. Then she noticed her eyelashes. Yes, it was her. *Oh, dear. My lashes are so long. What kind of mascara did they put on them? And is that a beauty mark painted on my cheek?* She had just one tiny, barely noticeable mole, but not *that* big and certainly not *that* dark. Whack! *Is that blood on my finger?* The camera quickly moved away.

"Pyune! You've cut yourself!" Monty rushed to her workstation and examined her hand.

"It's just a little nick." Pyune reached for a nearby paper towel.

Monty took the towel from her and carefully wiped away the blood and examined her finger. "It's more than a little nick. Let's get some ointment and a big Band-Aid on it." He hurried away and left Pyune frowning. This was the first time in years that she'd cut herself while cooking.

To her right, Joan stepped next to Pyune and whispered, "Oh, what we do for a little extra attention. No one told me you were such a drama queen. The viewers will love the poor little cook from Georgia who cut her finger." She walked away, her black slacks hugging her perfect derriere.

Monty returned with some Neosporin and a Band-Aid and administered to Pyune's finger. "Does it hurt?" he asked after he finished.

Pyune shook her head. "No, it's fine. Thanks for being such a good nurse." She smiled at Monty and picked up a knife and began chopping carrots. She gave Joan a side-glance. Apparently not everyone in New York was impressed with the woman who had learned to cook on a woodstove in the Georgia mountains.

At the end of the first fifty-minute segment, the leaderboard flashed with the donation totals. Contributions had been brisk: Chef Whittington led with $36,650; Chef Fencik next with $23,500; followed by Joan at $19,300; and Pyune with $11,700.

During the ten-minute break, Chef Whittington wiped his brow and gulped a bottled water, remarking, "Whew, those lights are hotter than last year!" An assistant brought him a fresh chef's coat and hat.

Another assistant reapplied Joan's lipstick and dusted her nose with powder. "Look at mountain woman over there, would you," Joan said, loud enough so Pyune and everyone else nearby could hear her. "Got a big fat bandage on her finger, looking for sympathy. Thinks it'll get her more votes." Joan laughed and pushed the assistant's hand away. "Enough." She leaned on her worktable and watched Pyune open a bottle of wine. "What's that wine for?"

Without looking at Joan, Pyune poured two cups of the wine in a measuring cup. "My pie filling."

"Oh? Guess you don't know that wine will glob up your butter. Well, since you're not a trained chef, I guess you wouldn't know, would you." She rolled her eyes and turned away.

Glob up the butter? What is she talking about? When Pyune placed the wine aside, she noticed her hand shaking. She heard the set director yell, "Ten seconds and we're live!"

Immediately a flourish of activity occurred, all of which Pyune was unprepared for. From all directions celebrities flooded the set. Kathy Lee Gifford rushed to Chef Whittington and hugged him. "Vote for my favorite chef," she beamed into the cameras.

At worktable two, Chef Fencik was assailed good-naturedly by Tina Fey, who boogied around him and yelled, "This is my guy! Vote for George!" Chef Fencik blushed and pumped his fist in the air.

Joan Stone gushed when Mathew Broderick grabbed her hand and held it in the air as if she had just won a boxing match. "Best chef in New York," he crooned. Noticeably missing was someone lobbying for Pyune.

Monty Reynolds made the rounds and gave the guest celebrities a quick interview and thanked them for their appearances. The band played the theme from "Chariots of Fire" as the cooking competition resumed.

A bell next to the leaderboard clanged loudly whenever the dollars moved upward in dramatic fashion. This was now occurring with frequency, and as the money was pouring in the judges took notes on the chefs' techniques. As a by-product, the aromas associated with the delicious baking filled the air.

At worktable four, Pyune Murphy had stood quietly and watched the glitterati of New York City champion everyone but her. There had been no celebrity guest visit her workstation, nor did her numbers move upward at the pace of the others. Her finger throbbed, and all she could think about was the wine globbing up the butter. She glanced at Joan and wondered how the woman could cook with such long fingernails. Pyune slipped on a pair of latex gloves. She didn't want the Band-Aid on her finger ending up in her chicken potpie.

~~~

Chapter 49

Jesse Collins thumped the top of the file folder again—a very serious thump this time. The discussion of crossword puzzles was long over. It was time to get down to business. *Real business.* He frowned at Wiley and Eva. "I repeat, you are mistaken, Ms. McIlwain is not Bartholomew Hickel's sister."

Wiley, his calm demeanor ever-present, nodded. "That so?"

"That's so," said Jesse Collins, attorney at law, sort of a solver of crossword puzzles, and mean as a snake when challenged in the courtroom or out. Despite his small stature, he could tangle with a rabid dog and come out clean and freshly pressed every time.

Wiley, however, was not one to be intimidated. He fixed Jesse Collins with his bullet eye, the same eye that stared down a two-hundred-pound black bear in the mountains of Appalachia when he was only eight years old. "You thumped that folder twice now," Wiley said. "You gonna show us what's in it?" His words were gruff, coming up from deep in his chest and not mixing well in the stuffiness of the small room.

"I plan to," said Jesse. "But first I'd like to ask Ms. McIlwain a question or two." He cleared his throat and leaned back in his tufted-leather chair. The chair seemed to scream when Jesse's bright orange shirt touched its eggplant color. "Ms. McIlwain, is it your belief that your mother and B.T.'s mother are one and the same?"

"Yes. I am sure of it." Eva's words were smooth, confident, and she held a hint of amusement on her face.

"What do you base that on, Ms. McIlwain?"

"I was adopted by Earl and Sally McIlwain when I was a new-born. They recently passed away and left me records of my birth and adoption."

"And those records stated?"

Wiley was about to say something. Surely this wasn't a court-room with Eva's being under examination. But she sensed his discomfort and shook her head at him when Jesse Collins briefly looked away. She said, "The documents stated that I was born in Rocky Top, North Carolina, in 1970, and given to Earl and Sally McIlwain, a young couple who'd visited the Rocky Top Baptist Church. The minister of the church handled everything. Then, my adoptive parents processed a formal adoption when they moved to Raleigh, North Carolina."

"I see," said Jesse. "Did any of those documents state the name of your birth mother?"

Eva faltered. She folded her hands and took a moment to an-swer. "No. The information stated that the birth mother was thirteen years old and unmarried and the daughter of John and Evelyn Thomas."

Jesse Collins rocked his chair back and forth for a moment. He stopped and placed his hand on what was now becoming an ominous-looking folder. "How were you able to locate Bartholomew Hickel?"

"I searched the obituaries of North Carolina, looking for John and Evelyn Thomas of Rocky Top, North Carolina. In the process, I found an obituary for Bernice Thomas Hickel of Rocky Top, North Carolina. Upon further research, I determined she was the daughter of John and Evelyn Thomas and born in 1956. I learned she'd later married and then had Bartholomew Thomas Hickel in 2002 at the late age of forty-six. This makes him my brother . . . . "

Eva's voice caught. She had long dreamed of her birth mother. And, here she was, being challenged by a small-town at-torney who was wrecking her dream. Though she learned her birth mother was deceased, in her research she'd discovered she had a brother—or half-brother—but a brother nevertheless. It seemed Mr. Collins was trying to take her joyous discovery away from her. If he tapped that folder one more time, she was going to jump over the desk and slap him.

She felt Wiley's hand on her arm. "Wha . . . yes?"

She turned to Wiley and saw his bullet eye on her. Wiley shot a look at Jesse Collins and came back to Eva. "Let's hear what Mr. Collins has in that folder of his."

Jesse Collins sat straight up in his chair, but he was still only a foot or so above the top of his desk. "First, I must apologize to you, Wiley. Last year, after Vallie Thomas had me draw up her will and I duly recorded it, I went on a trip with my darling wife, Estelle. While I was absent, Vallie came back over to Collins and Dyer, and since I was unavailable she filed a notarized document with my law partner, Charles Dyer." He paused. "Wiley, your daddy went huntin' with Charlie's daddy, Clyde—you might remember him?"

Wiley barely nodded.

"Anyway, when Charlie read the obituaries this morning in the Blairsville-North Georgia News, he saw Vallie's obituary and remembered he had a file on her that contained an affidavit. He had totally forgotten about it. Therefore, he never passed it on to me as Vallie's attorney. He rushed into my office first thing this morning and gave it to me." A long, quiet moment followed until Jess continued. "He felt really bad about forgetting about that file for a whole year. But that's okay. We attorneys are—"

"An affidavit for what?" Eva demanded. "I'm an attorney myself, and I'd like to get down to what this is all about."

"I didn't know you were an attorney too. Well, it's a formal affidavit, witnessed and notarized. I think it's time I read it to you." Jesse held the document in front of him, and with a reverent voice began to read:

"My name is Vallie Thomas. I was born in Rocky Top, North Carolina, on April 26, 1957. Though never married, I gave birth to a baby girl in 1970, on November 9. My mother and father gave her to a man and woman who visited our church, the Rocky Top Baptist Church. My baby was only three days old.

Though I have searched for her for over forty years, I have not been able to find her. My sister, Bernice, and I have shared this knowledge all of our lives. The purpose of this affidavit is twofold:

1. If my daughter ever surfaces, I wish her to know I never stopped loving her, and I did try to find her af-

ter I was grown.

  2. If by chance my daughter finds her way to the reading of this revised will, she is to inherit one-half of my estate, and this document supersedes all codicils in my earlier will except for what I give to Lizzie Lindquist. Sorry Wiley.

Signed: Vallie Thomas, Ivy Log, Georgia
Date: June 30, 2015
Witness: Charles R. Dyer, Blairsville, Georgia
Witness: Dorothy Harrell, Blairsville, Georgia

Wiley leaned over to Eva. "Looks like you got yourself a new cousin, Ms. McIlwain."

~~~

Chapter 50

Since the judges for the 2016 New York Cooks for Charity Fundraiser were all chefs, it was their expertise that was to be used to evaluate the four participants in the charity cook-off. While each chef prepared what he or she hoped would be a prize-winning chicken potpie, the judges found themselves drawn to Pyune Murphy, who at the moment was making the pastry for her pie. She worked quickly. She used goose fat, and fresh thyme that was finely chopped. Judge Gerri Boyce edged over to Pyune's workstation and watched with her mouth agape. She kept mumbling "goose fat" as if these were words from another planet.

From the top of the Bakers' World Building, Tess Starling had just turned on the television and with rapt intensity was watching the fundraiser. Robert had returned home, and he'd been occupying her time, so she was just now catching up with how the fundraiser was progressing. When she caught a glimpse of the leaderboard, she yelled and Robert ran into the living room, thinking something had happened to her. Pyune was lagging behind in the donations—dead last by a large margin. Tess grabbed her phone and sent a text to Monty. PYUNE'S IN LAST PLACE. WHAT CAN WE DO?

On the set, Monty read Tess's text and shrieked, "Damn!" He looked at the clock and saw a ten-minute break was coming up, followed by another round of celebrity guests, whose appearances would spike the numbers. He had just minutes to find a celebrity guest for Pyune EverSweet Murphy.

He left the stage for a quiet corner of the conference room, where he pressed a number into his phone. "Are you too busy to make an appearance at The New York Cooks For Charity Fundraiser?"

"Never too busy for you, Monty!"

"Well, how about in ten minutes?"

"Ten minutes! You've got to be kidding!"

"No, I'm not. I need you here bad. I also need you to support a particular chef who's in the competition. Here name is Pyune Murphy."

"Pyune Murphy, huh. You doing this again from your building?"

"Thirtieth floor."

"Let me wrap up something, and I'll get there as soon as I can."

"I'll be waiting. Ten minutes, okay?"

"I might not be able to make it that fast, but I'll be there!"

At 2:50, the television station went to a series of commercials, referred to in the trade as a hard break. The four chefs grabbed water bottles, wiped their respective brows, and took deep breaths. Again, Chef Whittington changed his chef's coat, kerchief, and toque. Chef Fencik pulled off his jacket and ripped off his undershirt. "Too hot under these lights!" He stood barechested and fanned himself before slipping on a fresh white jacket, sans an undershirt.

As her assistant began dabbing her brow and touching up her make-up, Joan Stone took a dainty sip from her water bottle. Joan was unaffected by the lights or the cameras. A coolness emanated from her, an aloofness that exuded an air of superiority. She fluffed her assistant away and looked over to station four, where Pyune Murphy leaned against her worktable and changed the Band-Aid on her injured finger.

"Poor widdle cook from the mountains gettin' tired?" Joan tossed her head back and laughed. "Why don't you bow out now —you're out of your league and you know it." She glanced at the leaderboard. "You're not doing too well. Just over fourteen-thousand dollars at this stage is not a heck of a good showing." She snapped her fingers. "Hey! I'm talking to you!"

Pyune turned to Joan and smiled. The blond woman was immaculate, not a hair out of place, not a speck of flour on her racy, all-black outfit. Pyune wondered if her heart was black too. In her softest voice, Pyune said. "I don't know about you, but I'm here because I love to cook." She held Joan's stare. "Do you like to cook? Or do you cook because you like the pressure?"

Joan sent a sly smile. "No pressure here. I think the pressure is on you, Ms. Murphy."

A bell rang. The set director held up three fingers. "Three, two, one. Live."

Pandemonium broke out across the Bakers' World kitchen as the band played the signature slap-bass theme from "The Jerry Seinfeld Show" as Jerry himself casually walked up to Chef Whittington. "Hello, my man. How's it goin'?"

"Going great, Jerry. Thanks for coming by."

The cameras zoomed in. Jerry picked up a piece of carrot and popped it in his mouth. While chewing, he waved to the camera. "Let's send this guy to the top, New York!" He saluted to the camera and was gone.

Sarah Jessica Parker swished around workstation two and left red lipstick on Chef Fencik's cheek. She smiled into the camera and held up her index finger. "Number one," she said, breathlessly. "Let's make this darling chef number one! I love New York!" In a flash she was gone.

At her station, Pyune wiped her worktable and rearranged her ingredients. The final segment of the cooking competition would have everyone's creation in the oven and baking for the judges to sample when ready.

The timeslot for celebrity appearances for this section of the show was long over, but she heard some commotion and when she looked up she noticed a sizable entourage moving toward her. The man in the center looked familiar but she couldn't quite place him. He was tall, rather flamboyant in his style, had a lot of hair, and was smiling broadly—at her.

She heard a gasp from Joan Stone, who stepped out from her station to greet the man, who breezed by her and reached for Pyune's hand. "My dear, thank you so much for your participation in this wonderful event. Let me tell you, I've heard great things about you." The cameras covered Donald Trump from every angle. Monty shoved a microphone toward the always-ebullient New Yorker.

"Ah, Mr. Trump. Thanks so much for coming by."

"I'm sorry I'm a little late, but I'm delighted to support Ms. Murphy, and I'm placing my money on her to win this competition!" He reached his arm around Pyune and looked down at her. "What are you preparing today, Pyune?"

The cameras zoomed in for close ups. Pyune, in her soft southern voice, picked up an Emile Henry pan. "In just a few moments, I'm going to fill this pan with the most delicious chicken potpie you've ever tasted—it's my grandmother's recipe."

Donald Trump reached up and brushed flour off Pyune's cheek. "Did you put lots of sage in it? I love sage!"

Pyune laughed warmly and lifted a spoon of the pie filling to Donald Trump. He tasted it and smacked his lips. "Wow! Absolutely perfect!" He found the camera lens and spoke directly to the television audience. "Take it from me—this is the best chicken potpie I've ever tasted." He hugged Pyune and briskly walked away, waving to everyone he saw but ignoring a wordless Joan Stone as he left the kitchen.

"And there you go, folks! Jerry Seinfeld, Sarah Jessica Parker, and Donald Trump—each cheering for his or her favorite chef."

The bell rang and Monty announced the beginning of the last segment of the competition. "Okay, New York, let's meet our goal of one million dollars! Support your favorite chef by keeping those votes coming!"

From her station, Joan Stone studied the scoreboard and watched silently— an ever-increasing frown etching itself on her forehead—as Pyune's donations shot up and surpassed everyone else's.

~~~

Chapter 51

An April shower skirted its way along the Appalachians, moving east, filling the streams with cold rushing water and sending great booms of thunder across the peaks. With no umbrella, Wiley and Eva dashed to Wiley's truck just before a heavy downpour hit Blairsville. They left Jesse Collins standing under the overhang. Wiley couldn't help but notice perspiration rings had soaked through Jesse Collins's orange shirt. The little guy had struggled with Vallie Thomas's document.

Their session with the Blairsville attorney had been enlightening. Eva's mother was Vallie Thomas, the enigmatic woman who touched everyone's lives in Ivy Log. Bernice Thomas Hickel was Eva's aunt; her son was B.T., who had evolved as Eva's cousin in the grand scheme of things. And Eva was a millionaire if she weren't one already. Best of all, as far as Wiley was concerned, he wouldn't have to deal with a potentially contested will involving millions of dollars. His losing the cabin and the forty acres meant nothing to him. He was just happy it was all settled.

However, in just a few moments everything had turned upside down and all around for Eva, leaving her to ponder B.T.'s future as well as her own. She'd been considering another run at public office, perhaps the senate this time, or returning to her career as an attorney, her future sitting on the edge and in need of some life decisions.

Wiley began feeling great sadness as he drove along the Blairsville Highway on the way back to Ivy Log. He said to Eva, "You would have loved Vallie. She was eccentric in many ways, but her heart was as good as gold." He felt his throat tighten. "She would have been a . . . very good mama to you."

The from-the-heart catch in Wiley's voice made Eva tear up. "You knew my mother for a long time, but she never mentioned having a baby?"

Wiley deliberated before answering, slowing the truck when the rain became heavier and a strong wind shook the vehicle. "Vallie was a very private person. A good ol' soul who kept to herself. She never even allowed Lizzie in her house but a single time in forty years. I had to break in once just to check on her." He glanced at Eva and laughed. "Your mama smoked Havana Honey cigarillos. Can you believe that?"

"Really? Tell me more about her." Eva settled back, seeming to be lulled by the steady hum of the truck's tires and the pelting rain on the windshield.

"Your mama was a hoot! She had more fun in a day than most people do in their entire lives. There was just something about her that everybody liked."

Wiley turned on his fog lights as he climbed the ridge above Ivy Log. "Tell you what. Tomorrow, let's go over to Vallie's house. There are some things I'd like to show you."

"I'd like that very much." Eva's words were husky, from a place of regret. She had been so close. Had Vallie Thomas hung onto life just a little longer, mother and daughter surely would have met.

A short while later, the sky was clearing in the west, a late sun peeking through the now thinning clouds. Wiley left Eva to her thoughts. He looked down the mountain, just below the ridge, and watched Ivy Log easing into what would soon be dusk. The lights in The Boardinghouse windows beckoned, and he felt his heart ache for Pyune, for the smell of vanilla on her, for the sound of her humming as she kneaded biscuits or iced a cake.

New York City had captured her, he was sure of it. He had let her go, encouraged her to sprout her wings, never imagining it was possible she would not return. What if Paula were right? He slipped his hand in his pocket and looked at his phone. No messages.

Eva interrupted his thoughts. "I'm thinking I ought to sit down with B.T. and let him know everything.

"There's a lot to discuss."

"Like where we'll live, his education, and a million other things."

"Like a million dollars." Both of them laughed. "He wanted a new pair of boots. I asked the preacher to take him out today and get him a pair."

"You pay for that?"

"No matter. Least I can do for the boy. Kinda like him. Reminds me a lot of me when I was his age." Wiley felt his heart skip a beat. "So, you're planning on you and B.T. being together . . . as a family?"

"Of course. I can't imagine it any other way, can you?" She slapped the dashboard. "That redheaded witch would have had him sent to reform school if she'd had her way."

They rode in silence for a few minutes, Wiley's thoughts on the gray-headed woman with the gold tooth and not on Paula. What if Vallie's parents had told her they would care for the child? What if they had not given the baby to the strangers who had visited their church? But that was not what had happened. God must have had a reason.

"I was thinking, Eva. You and B.T. could live here in Ivy Log. We don't have an attorney, so folks would really appreciate having you. Besides that, you and B.T. could live in a town that knew and loved your mama."

"You know what?"

"What?"

"That's not a half-bad idea."

Wiley chuckled. "I know Sam would like that."

"Sam?"

"Oh, you can't tell me you haven't seen him eyeballin' you."

"I'm surprised." Wiley gave her his bullet eye. "Okay, not really."

Wiley eased his truck behind The Boardinghouse and turned off the motor. "Let's take B.T. with us when we go over to Vallie's tomorrow. Oh, shoot, I forgot to stop at Jim's Smokin' Q for some food for the pastor. Maybe we'll find some leftovers inside. Lizzie might still be here. If she is, I'll go get the preacher."

Bandit was stretched out across the back steps and flicked his tail in the air as if to say he wasn't moving—they'd have to step over him. And they did.

Inside The Boardinghouse kitchen, Lizzie wasn't there, but they didn't have to go far to find the preacher.

Pastor Johnson and Sam were bellied up to the worktable, eating lima beans and ham, a pan of hot cornbread nearby. Sam jumped up and placed two more stools at the table. "Hey! Just in time for some good vittles."

Wiley nodded to Sam and said to the pastor. "We got tied up in Blairsville, and I plum forgot to get you the food I promised. Glad y'all made it over here." He looked around. "Where's Lizzie?"

"Went out. She told Pastor Will and me that some beans and ham on the stove just needed to be heated up, and to help ourselves. So here we are."

"Where's B.T.?"

"He was tuckered out," the pastor said. "I made him take a bath, and I left him watching TV." He buttered a piece of cornbread. "Come and sit down, Eva. Believe it or not, Lizzie did a fine job on this pot of ham and beans."

Eva slid in between Sam and the reverend. "It smells good. Wiley promised me Jim's Smokin' Q, too, but whizzed right by the place. I'm starving."

"B.T. get him some new boots?" Wiley asked the pastor as he ladled out a plate of food.

"Eighty-five dollars worth. Took care of the underwear, too, but he wanted the kind hunters wear, so that's what I got him. With the socks, cost almost as much as the boots. You still got some money coming back, though. I've got it at the parsonage."

"Put what's left over in the collection plate this Sunday."

Late in the evening, Wiley left The Boardinghouse, crossed over Main Street, and ambled up the path that led to the top of the ridge. The view of a sleeping Ivy Log soothed him but did not diminish his worried mind. There was only one thing to do. The woman he loved was in New York City— and that's were he was going.

~~~

Chapter 52

"**D**addy, turn on the television and you'll see your other daughter," Tess said softly to her father, who was on the other end of the line.

"That right?" Vernon Murphy pushed his wheelchair to the table and punched the power button on the remote. "What channel?"

"NBC."

Tess heard her father's breathing. If Pyune didn't want to meet him, at least he could see her—even if it wasn't in person.

"Ah, there she is," Vernon Murphy said. "Looks just like you, sweetie. Just like you." He laughed and Tess could hear the joy in his voice. "Sure would like to be with her a few minutes. You know, explain some things to her and . . . ." His words faltered and he coughed.

"Not yet, Daddy. She's not ready. Give her some time."

They talked a moment longer, Tess saying goodbye just as the camera zoomed in on her sister. Pyune was beautiful, a serene beauty whose warmth radiated from within and touched everyone around her. Tess slumped into her chair. Her throat ached and the tears came. She'd already forgiven her father; she wondered if Pyune ever would.

The numbers on the leaderboard climbed upward. Monty zipped from one chef to the next, encouraging viewers to support their favorite. Chef Whittington spooned his potpie into five servings and placed a sprig of rosemary on the edge of the bowl and stood back. He smiled at the judges and waved, adding, "Bon appétit."

Chef Fencik browned his pie under the broiler for a moment, then placed it onto his worktable, steam escaping from the slits in the crust. He raised his hands in the air, removed his toque and took a slow bow. "I give you my masterpiece," he said in his strong Slovakian accent.

Across from him, Joan Stone placed fine china bowls on chargers, along with gleaming silver spoons. Her black ensemble had not one speck of flour on it, not a hair was out of place, and her long nails shined bright red as she lifted one of the bowls and tilted it toward the camera.

Pyune kept her potpies in the individual Emile Henry pie dishes. She had baked her top piecrusts separately, along with a small crust in the shape of a chicken. She'd placed the delicate crusts on top of the dishes, following this by gently setting a chicken-shaped piece atop each crust and letting everything bake some more. She stood back and laughed into the cameras. Flour dusted her cheeks, a lock of hair hung across her forehead, and her chef's coat was smeared with goose fat. She picked up a piece of leftover crust and plopped it in her mouth! "Yummm-mmm." She grinned toward the judges.

A bell rang. Monty raced to the judges' table. "Here we go, folks. The final segment of our fundraiser." He pointed to the board showing donation totals for each chef. Chef Whittington $283,650; Chef Fencik $256,500; Chef Stone $273,000; Pyune Murphy $284,900. "Remember, the winning chef receives twenty-five thousand dollars that will be added to his or her to-tal!"

Joan pranced around and stood in front of her table, her hand on her hip, her sultry smile beckoning as she, in studio talk, made love to the camera. Next to her, Pyune brushed the flour from her jacket and pulled a stray piece of piecrust from it as well.

Monty nodded. "Judges, are you ready?" A drum roll filled the air as each judge stood and walked down the line of tables, beginning with Chef Dick Whittington. Monty said, "Chef Whit-tington, thank you for your participation." Each judge sampled the beaming chef's creation. They nodded and sampled another spoonful, made notes on their clipboards, and continued to Chef

Fencik's station.

Chef Fencik, his mustache perfectly twirled, placed his hands behind his back. A toque soared above the short man's head as he rocked back and forth on his heels. The judges picked up their spoons and dipped into the luscious pie, placing a few spoonfuls on their small plates.

The chef's eyes narrowed when the judges wrote on their clipboards. He clicked his heels together and bowed again when they moved to Joan Stone's station.

The titillating blonde came from behind her workstation, her cleavage shining from the overhead lights, and she welcomed the judges with a wave of her hand. Each judge picked up a dainty china bowl and lifted bites of potpie with their silver spoons. "Hmmmmmm," said judge number one, a chef known for his love of women, especially blondes. He winked at Joan and she winked back. The five judges made entries on their clipboards and continued in their quest to determine the winner of the culinary contest.

At her worktable, Pyune fiddled with a row of spices, aligning each one perfectly, her hands shaking. *What am I doing here? I have no training, no education in the culinary arts, and here I am amid some of the finest chefs in the world. I learned to cook on a woodstove.* She felt her throat tighten. She wished the cameras and hot lights were not bearing down on her.

Licking her lips, she smiled when the judges approached her station. The judges introduced themselves and studied the Emile Henry pie dishes.

One judge remarked, "I like the cutout of the piecrust into the shape of a chicken. How clever."

"Thank you. My mother taught me everything I know about piecrust."

The judges all nodded and began tasting the individual pies Pyune had prepared for each of them. "Excuse me, Ms. Murphy, have you made this recipe often?" judge Claire Engle, a short, stout chef with legs like fireplugs asked as she stared at Pyune and held her spoon in midair.

"Why, yes, many times. It's the only way I make chicken potpie." Pyune found the woman's stare intimidating. She looked away and saw Joan smirking at her.

"The chicken is quite tender and tasty," judge Engle said.

"Thank you, and it can be even better because I normally soak the chicken in buttermilk overnight. The acidity of the buttermilk acts as a tenderizer and also makes the meat more flavorful." The judges were all listening attentively.

"The morel mushrooms are luscious," Judge Engle said after she took another bite of the potpie. "Didn't I also see you with a bottle of Spätlese Riesling?"

"After I reduce the stock, I add the wine and reduce again." Pyune became excited and looked into the camera, talking directly to the viewers. "Oh, before I forget, use chicken thighs with the bone in them. Debone them after cooking and cut them into one-inch pieces. The dark meat of the chicken has the best flavor."

Pyune clapped her hands as though in a classroom setting. Her excitement bubbled over as if she were the pie itself with juices steaming upward from her. "I bake the pastry tops separately, place them on top of the pie and bake another five minutes." She stood back and silently watched all the judges sample more of her individual potpies.

The judges made notes on their clipboards, said thank you, and briskly left the stage while the band's drummer simulated a ticking clock. The cameras zoomed to Monty, who hammed it up for the television audience and announced, "So, here we are at the end of our marvelous fundraiser, and thanks to you folks we have surpassed our $1,000,000 goal and ended up with $1,092,150. Thank you, New York!

"In just a few minutes, we'll have the winner of our 2016 New York Cooks for Charity Fundraiser, and as I've mentioned several times during this telecast, the winning chef will have twenty-five thousand dollars added to his or her total.

"Now, I'd like to thank our wonderful cheerleaders who took time to visit our set and encourage their favorite chef. Thank you Kathy Lee Gifford, Tina Fey, Jerry Seinfeld, Mathew Broderick, Sara Jessica Parker, and of course Donald Trump."

The theme from "Rocky" erupted from the band and the crowd in the room went wild. The lights on the leaderboard flashed, bells rang, and finally the judges returned to the stage. Not a whisper could be heard as the judges assembled behind their tables. Monty projected his deepest voice, low and serious: "Judges, do you have a winner?"

The head judge, Chef Billie Hausen, held up an envelope and passed it to Monty. Monty grinned into the camera. "All of you have been waiting for this, and so have I." He opened the envelope, and a look of enormous pleasure crossed his handsome face. "Congratulations Pyune Murphy of Ivy Log, Georgia! You are our winner!"

Pyune squealed with joy; Joan shrieked in horror. The entire stage exploded into an enthusiastic round of applause, with Joan clearly painfully going through the motions. Monty shoved the microphone toward Pyune. "Ms. Murphy, is there anything you'd like to say?"

A dazed Pyune, mouth open, said nothing. All she could hear was music, the deafening applause, and the earsplitting sound of ringing bells. The lights on the leaderboard flashed off and on. The sum of $25,000 was added to her total as hundreds of balloons fell from the ceiling. Monty Reynolds put his arm around her, squeezed her shoulders, and spoke into her ear, "I do believe I told you, my dear, that you'd become the toast of the town." He kissed her cheek. "And Monty Reynolds is never wrong when it comes to knowing a winner when he sees one."

Tess Starling turned off the television. She had purposefully not visited the set of the New York Cooks for Charity Fundraiser. She had wanted Pyune to experience the excitement of being in front of the cameras, the competition; and, if it happened, the thrill of winning something this prestigious without her presence. She also didn't want to have to deal with the obvious issues of both woman looking identical and Tess ruining the contest.

She and Monty had been right. Pyune EverSweet Murphy had charmed the television audience and judges into making her the winning chef. She was magical. She had enchanted and delighted the strangers who had watched her performance, and their donations had put her on top—beating out three celebrated chefs from New York City.

Her phone rang. *Monty.* She answered. "I know what you're going to say."

"You do?"

"Yes, I do. You're going to say that my sister is a star, and we've got to figure out a way to keep her in New York City."

There was a long silence—an empty moment that they both

knew was necessary. They would each work day and night to en-
tice the woman from Ivy Log, Georgia, to become a New Yorker.

Tess sighed and leaned her head into her hand. "You know,
Monty. I've been without my sister for forty-two years. I'm not
about to let her go back to Ivy Log." She closed her eyes. "Trouble is, I don't know how to prevent it."

~~~

Chapter 53

The Saturday-morning breakfast crowd drank gallons of coffee, ate dozens of biscuits, and consumed platter upon platter of eggs. Ham slices as big as a farmer's hand lay on heavy plates along with thick slabs of bacon the flavor of apple wood. Two pots of cheese grits simmered on the back burners of the big gas stove on which Lizzie flipped pancakes the size of sunflowers.

Lizzie smelled *her* perfume. A moment later Paula poked her head in the back door. "Lizzie, I'd like to come inside and help—if you promise not to hurt me."

Lizzie glared at Paula. "As long as you don't talk about anything French, you can come in." The stack of pancakes Lizzie was working on was twelve inches high. "Why don't you warm some maple syrup for me? I got four more orders for pancakes." She looked up and down at Paula. "You ain't gonna be able to work in them heels." Her eyes found Paula's face. "You forgot to put on that black beauty mark thing this morning."

Paula, dressed in a frilly yellow blouse and tight white slacks, scrunched her face. "I sure don't want to get syrup on my clothes."

Lizzie stomped her foot. "Do you want to help me or not? You know where the aprons are." Lizzie shuffled through the doorway to the dining room, her hands full of plates of pancakes. Two high-school kids were busy bussing tables. Two more from the school were off to the side, washing dishes.

"I hate that woman," said Paula as she looked for an apron to complement the color of her yellow blouse. She dug deep in a drawer, rummaging through a dozen aprons with varying patterns, but all of them clashed with her $80 designer-blouse knock-off. Then, she remembered her chef's coat, the one with the words *Chef* and *Paula* embroidered on the left lapel. *Hot diggity!*

She ran to the pantry and there it was—hanging on a hook. She slipped it on and frolicked around the kitchen, her high heels clicking across the wooden floor, and she broke into song: *"I feel pretty! Oh, so pretty! I feel pretty and witty and bright! And I pity any girl who isn't me tonight . . . ."* She bellowed out the last line and threw her arms wide. *"I feel charming! Oh, so —"*

"What in the hell are you singing? Get that damn chef's coat off and get outta here!" Lizzie, as frumpy as she was, moved with speed across the kitchen, grabbing a broom that quickly became a weapon."

Paula scampered a few feet away from her and spun around. "Lizzie Lindquist, you are a mean old woman."

"Out!" She raised the broom and took a menacing step forward. Paula ran out the back door and down the steps, Lizzie yelling after her, "Keep your skinny behind away from this place, Paula, or I'll have Wiley set you straight."

Wiley? Where was Wiley? Lizzie went back into the dining room and called to Sam and the pastor, whose plates showed the remnants of pancakes, "Where's Wiley this morning?"

"Haven't seen him," Sam replied. "We thought maybe he ate early."

"Nope. Hasn't been in at all. Roy and Trigger's still on the shelf." Lizzie wiped her hands on her apron and returned to the kitchen.

"That's odd," Sam remarked to Will. "Wiley never misses breakfast." He pulled out his phone and punched in Wiley's number.

After three rings: "Hey, Sam. Saw it was your number."

"Hey, Wiley. If you don't hurry up, you're going to miss breakfast. Where are you?"

"I'm on the Interstate, halfway to Atlanta."

"Atlanta? What's happening in Atlanta?"

"I got an eleven-twenty flight to catch."

"A flight? Where to?" Sam shrugged his shoulders at Will.

"New York."

"New York! You know that Vallie's memorial is Monday, right?"

"That I do." Wiley increased his speed to eighty miles an hour.

"What's going on in New York?"

"That's what I want to find out," said Wiley, and he ended the call.

~~~

<h1 style="text-align:center">Chapter 54</h1>

They celebrated until the wee hours of Saturday morning, the bright lights of Manhattan even more luminous as Tess, Monty and Pyune walked the streets, popping in and out of famous hangouts that catered to New York's elite. They ended up in Tess's apartment, exhausted but happy. In just three days, Pyune EverSweet Murphy had captured the hearts of New Yorkers, had mesmerized "The Today Show" audience, smashed the fundraiser records, and triumphed as the city's new darling. And she had accomplished this by just being herself.

Tess peered at Monty over her wine glass, a slight slur in her words: "I'm not going to let you get away with Joan Stone."

Monty ducked as if she might shoot him. "It was pretty awful, wasn't it?"

"I was appalled. Why couldn't she wear a chef's jacket like everyone else? *Really*? She doesn't show that much cleavage when she wears a cocktail dress. What was she thinking?"

Monty chuckled. "It's all about brand, Tess. You know that better than anyone. Joan has a certain image she wants to portray at all times, and it's that image which gives her the edge." He glanced at Pyune. "Maybe she's insecure. Or maybe she just wants attention. I truly don't know."

"Did you say anything to her?"

Monty chuckled, some of his drink spilling he laughed so hard. "Are you kidding? I'd be committing professional suicide."

"Well, her ensemble did nothing to promote her skill as a chef, which I will admit, she definitely possesses." Tess laughed.

"At least her cleavage didn't push her over the top with donation dollars."

Monty chuckled again, the abundance of drinks throughout the evening clearly getting to him as well. "We really don't know if her donations were because of her culinary skill or her boobs. What do you think, Pyune?"

Her exposure to Joan had been interesting, reminding her very much of Paula—except that even the New York vixen was not in the same league as the woman from Ivy Log. "People who seek attention in the way Joan obviously does believe they're always on a stage of some sort. They constantly create images that will get them the attention they crave to balance their insecurity."

Tess and Monty gasped. "What an incredibly acute analysis of Joan," Tess said as she held her glass toward Monty, who dutifully refilled it with her favorite Riesling. "I'm amazed at your sense of understanding."

Pyune dipped her head, not proud of what she was going to say next. "We have people like Joan in Ivy Log too. Or at least one person for sure." Her normally gentle countenance waxed stern, and she handed her glass to Monty. "More ginger ale, please."

"Enough about Joan—or anyone else," Tess said. "I'm sorry I brought her up." She smiled at Pyune. "Let's talk about you, Sister. The 'Dine With Me' show is one of the most popular on the food channel—so popular that it was picked up for a seventh season, beginning in September."

"You can begin your television career on the very first show," said Monty, sending out a message to Pyune that it was a foregone conclusion she would be the show's new head chef. He reaffirmed what Tess had just said: "The 'Dine With Me' series is one of the most coveted positions for any chef in New York—"

Tess broke in, saying, "The concept of the show is this: You, as the star of the show, will prepare a meal for a celebrity guest— or guests as the case may be. At the end of your meal's preparation, you'll sit at a beautifully appointed table and dine with your guests. You'll discuss the dishes you've prepared, and the celebrity in turn will provide you with comments. It will be twenty-two minutes of dining and chit-chat with some of the most loved and admired celebrities in the country—as well as our adored star chef."

Tess leaned back and sipped her wine. Across from her, Pyune had listened attentively, nodding now and then but saying nothing. Tess couldn't wait any longer. "So what are your thoughts, Pyune? Of course, for the most part the show will require you to be here in New York City."

Tess found herself anxious, her heart racing. She'd made the last remark ". . . require you to be in New York," as casually as she could. ". . . require you to be in New York," was meant to be as mundane as if she'd said, "It's a pretty day, and I think I'll take a walk in the park and look at the flowers."

Monty and Tess exchanged quick glances. Pyune seemed far away, not in New York City, not with her newly found sister and newly acquired fame, and certainly not excited by the extraordinary opportunity that had been presented to her. Perhaps her thoughts were on Ivy Log, the only place she had ever known, and with the people she always considered her family.

She sighed deeply and smiled faintly. "I am very tired. Can we discuss this tomorrow?"

Her room was dark except for a sliver of light coming from below the door. She slipped her cell phone under her pillow. Once again she had let the events of the day take precedence and had neglected to call Wiley.

~~~

Chapter 55

In extraordinary times men do extraordinary things. Wiley Hanson, at forty-eight-years old, was an extraordinary man. He had killed a wild bear when he was eight years old, earned a Ph.D. in environmental engineering, walked the Appalachian Trail from start to finish, and despite the lack of hair on his head was as handsome as any movie star. Some folks thought of him as a bald Clark Gable. That he had gotten up in the middle of the night, thrown some clothes and toiletries in a bag, and was now driving lickety-split down I-85 to the Atlanta airport, fell into the category of extraordinary times.

Pyune was the sole reason for his hurry. He loved her; she knew that. He wanted to marry her; she didn't know that. He had never experienced a separation from her. She had always been there when he needed her. He would scream it from the mountaintop: He loved Pyune, and without her he would be a failure. Methodically his thoughts went from the knowns to the unknowns, but the one thing glaringly obvious to him was that he did not want a life without Pyune EverSweet Murphy in it.

At the Atlanta airport, he made his way through the madhouse called the terminal. His jeans and plaid shirt were commonplace, as were his boots. The only thing out of place was his Stetson. He uncomfortably bumped along with the throng of people in his security line, but he managed to arrive at his gate on time. Wiley was a prompt man, prone to order, sometimes a little too much so, oddly enough due to chopping wood. The logs had to be precisely twenty inches long, a hard thing to achieve, even with a sharp axe.

While hardly methodical, he was precise about making love as well. Slow and easy. Always slow and easy, especially in the early mornings. Especially in the wintertime. Especially when the fireplace had gone cold, and moving under heavy quilts was the perfect thing to do to create warmth.

He felt an ache in his heart. He would be 2 hours and 14 minutes in the air to New York City. The plane would land at 12:59. Then what? He knew what. He'd find Pyune. But then what? The same person who had killed a bear, possessed a Ph.D., and walked the Appalachian Trail, had absolutely no idea.

~~~

Chapter 56

On Saturday morning, the residents of New York City awoke slowly, sliding into their New York Times over leisurely cups of coffee and warm Danishes, jogging in Central Park, and observing a mass of cooing pigeons shuffling their little pink feet along the marble rim of Carnegie Hall. However, even at half-past seven, the blare of a taxi horn mixed in with the faint sound of the bells from St. Patrick's Cathedral.

On 5th Avenue, the pungent smell of duck fat heating for Shady Dawg's fried potatoes filled the air, softened somewhat by the aroma of sizzling hot dogs. Thirty-two stories above those bustling about on the pavement below, Pyune and Tess drank coffee on the apartment terrace, both women overcome with giddy happiness, hair uncombed, and last-night's makeup smearing their cheeks.

"Joan Stone left a scathing message for me," Tess said as she slapped her forehead, laughing all the while. "Said she was certain, since I was your sister, that you had an unfair advantage in the competition. I'd skewed the numbers in your favor." Tess poured more coffee. "She's never been a good loser."

Pyune smiled. "She's not the sweetest person I've ever met. But I found her quite interesting. Her outfit alone was a—."

"Speaking of outfits, we've got to find something for you to wear for the awards banquet tonight. After breakfast, let's spend some time in my closet." Just as Tess finished speaking, her husband joined them on the terrace.

Pressed for time, Robert Larson had said just a few words to Pyune previously, and he now spent a pleasant and unhurried half-hour with her. Robert seemed very down to earth, and he kept saying how thrilled he was that Tess had a sister. Over and over he commented on their identical appearance, and he laughed when he noticed that they held their coffee cups the same way and blotted a napkin to their lips in a comparable manner. Indeed, they were twins in many ways beyond their looks.

When Pyune walked into Tess's mammoth closet, she couldn't believe her eyes. Everything Tess owned seemed to be from a famous designer's line, and she was willing to share any one of her outfits with Pyune—her small-town sister. "Before I forget," Pyune said as she held up a snow-white moiré Valentino shift she just loved, "Monty is picking me up at one for lunch and a tour of the city. I've not seen much of it in the daylight."

"Oh, you'll love that. Robbie and I have a few things we've got to attend to today, so this will work out perfectly, as you won't be left alone with nothing to do."

"Tell me what all is going to be happening tonight. I mean . . . it's not a really big deal, is it?"

"Oh, Pyune, I'm sorry, but it is a big deal. We're celebrating the twenty-fifth year of Bakers' World Magazine, and you're our newest star. You're shining white hot, and now you'll be hosting 'Dine With Me' and—"

"Tess! I'm just not sure it's what I want to do."

"I know, it's daunting. But you'll handle it all beautifully, just like you did with the fundraiser." Tess patted her sister's arm. "All I can think about is having a sister and doing wonderful things with you. It's like . . . it's like starting life all over again."

Pyune let out a long breath and nodded slowly. "I feel the same way, but you have to remember that I had a life before I met you—in Ivy Log. And I'm very happy where I am." She took Tess's hand. "I love you, and appreciate everything you want to do for me, but The Boardinghouse is my life."

Tess studied her sister's face. She had never thought of herself as really beautiful until she saw Pyune. It embarrassed her to think she looked this good. "You know, there's one thing we haven't talked about at all during these past three days?"

"What?"

"Men. You must tell me, do you have a man in your life?"

"I do have a man." Pyune's face now shone like bright sunlight on fresh snow. "I have a wonderful man in my life, named

Wiley. Wiley Hanson."

"So tell me about this Wiley." Tess tilted her head, a mischievous grin filling her face as she looked at Pyune.

A clear sense of yearning came to Pyune's eyes. "Ah, Wiley. Wiley is everything to me. I've known him most of my life and we're . . . we're . . . just together. That's all. Together."

"Does he make you happy?"

"Oh, my, yes. There's no one like my mountain man. Like I said, he's everything to me."

"Ever thought of marriage?"

Pyune looked sharply at Tess. "Ha! It seems we've evolved into a comfortable twosome, with no demands on the other."

"Is that all you need . . . and want?"

Pyune contemplated Tess's question with a pause that was so long it became awkward. She forced a smile, "I haven't thought about it much. Our life in Ivy Log is truly calm, and, for lack of a better word, measured. We just roll along, day to day." She laughed loudly. "It's not New York City, Tess."

"You wouldn't be giving up Ivy Log or Wiley. You could commute back and forth. Spend three days filming 'Dine With Me' and four days in Ivy Log. You and I could spend time together while you're in New—"

"Please, no more right now. Before I fly out tomorrow, we can talk about this again."

"So you're not saying no to the idea of doing the show?"

Pyune turned away, but when she came back to Tess there was no hesitation in her voice: "I've been very happy with my life in Ivy Log. And now my life has you in it, and I'm very happy with this too. So, I don't know what I'm going to do." She sighed. "At this minute, however, I'd just like to decide on what to wear tonight."

~~~

Chapter 57

The plane to New York City soared through a cloudless April sky. Wiley leaned back in his seat and placed his hat over his face. The previous night had been sleepless, a journey into a fretful place that kept him tossing and turning until he pulled himself out of bed at 3 a.m. and began his race to get to Pyune.

He slept under his hat, in a darkness that was soothing. He dreamed that he and Pyune were catching the winds high above the mountaintops and spiraling in the downdrafts to the valleys below. In the dream, they held hands and danced upon the clouds. They collapsed in laughter as the clouds gave way and they plummeted to the earth below. It was the way it had always been between them, two self-sufficient souls who'd found each other one early morning so long ago.

The clunk of the landing gear sounded against the belly of the plane and Wiley shot forward, confused at first. *Where am I? Oh, yes. On a plane.* When they landed, he grabbed his small bag from the overhead bin. In just moments, for the first time ever, he'd be planting his feet in New York City.

At the curb outside the terminal, he walked to the cab queue and was quickly on his way to the Marriott Marquis in Manhattan, where he'd booked a room. The cabbie chattered in a language Wiley didn't understand, so he just nodded now and then as he scanned the expanse of tall buildings until they entered the Queens Midtown Tunnel. They took the ramp for East 37th Street, made a right on 3rd Avenue and a left on 45th to 7th Avenue, where the hotel stood in the middle of Times Square.

"Thanks," said Wiley, paying the driver, and grabbing his bag. He stood a moment on the sidewalk and looked up and down Broadway. *How close am I to Pyune?*

Inside the hotel, the desk clerk pulled up his reservation, and he checked in. "May I leave a message for Ms. Murphy?" Wiley asked.

"Ms. Murphy? What's her first name please?"

"Pyune." Wiley spelled it.

A young man, the clerk clicked a few keys on his computer. "I'm sorry, there's no Ms. Pyune Murphy registered. Are you sure you have the right hotel?"

Wiley looked sharply at the slicked-up fellow. From under the brim of his hat, he said, "I have the right hotel. You mind checking again?"

A shrug and a few clicks of the computer keys. "No Ms. Murphy, sir."

Wiley nodded a thank you and went to a bank of elevators. A subtle dinging buzz, if there was such a thing, and soon he was gliding upward, a long, smooth ride in a glass enclosure that Wiley didn't particularly enjoy. He exited on the 16th floor and made his way to Room 1620. Once inside, he pulled his cell phone from his pocket and called Pyune. No answer. He left a message: "Miss hearing from you. Love you. Wiley."

~~~

Chapter 58

Pyune and Tess began trying on outfits, both women fiercely hunting for the *perfect* dress for each other to wear to tonight's gala. They tried on a myriad of ensembles before deciding on something. Collapsing from sheer exhaustion, the sisters fell on the bed in unison. Soon, however, they made miraculous recoveries when Tess suggested they begin the process of selecting shoes, purses, and jewelry. The sisters had discovered each other in the most delightful way: clothes and accessories.

Around noon, Tess dressed for lunch with Robert, and Pyune put on a simple dress and comfortable shoes for her tour of New York City with Monty. They would all be back at four, as the BWM cocktail party would get underway at six sharp, followed by an awards dinner attended by the chefs and judges from the fundraiser, who would be joined by other renowned New York City chefs and well-known restaurateurs.

The elusive $25,000 check was getting nearer and nearer. Pyune's entry into one of the most storied cities in all the world had been phenomenal. The same city that hosted the skyscraper from which King Kong tumbled had also opened its arms wide for the unpretentious woman from the Appalachian mountains. Her appearance on "The Today Show" had sparked a flurry of interest among viewers, who saw her as unflawed, fresh—and, oh, so beautiful.

The New York Cooks for Charity Fundraiser had catapulted Pyune from obscurity to stardom. In hours she had become New York City's darling. But regardless of the celebrity, her heart remained in Ivy Log, in The Boardinghouse kitchen, where for years she labored lovingly over the simmering soups and roasting meats, not once thinking of a life anywhere but in her beloved mountains.

At 1 o'clock Pyune rode the elevator down to the lobby of BWM and found Monty waiting for her. "Hello!" he called out as the elevator door opened. "I see you've recovered from your wild night of bar hopping." Monty placed his arm around Pyune's shoulders.

"I finally got into bed around two this morning, and then I was up again bright and early."

"If you're too tired, we don't have to do this." His tone hadn't indicated much conviction for his remark.

"No, no, I want to go. I'm excited about seeing New York City just like a tourist would."

Monty smiled wide and led Pyune to the parking garage and his car. "Frandy wanted to drive us around, but I thought it would be fun to take my car." A minute later he pulled into traffic and they were off to see the sights.

~~~

Chapter 59

After settling in his room, Wiley exited the Marriott Marquis lobby onto 7th Avenue, his hat keeping the noonday sun off his eyes. The ever-scurrying New York City crowds passed by him as if in a blur. He looked up and down the street. *What a city—both brutal and beautiful.* He breathed in the big-city air, which reminded him of Atlanta, and began the ten-block walk to Bakers World Magazine—and he hoped Pyune.

"Hey, buddy!" A very thin man with an unkempt beard reached out and touched Wiley on the arm. "Got a cigarette?"

"No, I don't. Sorry." Wiley moved on before the man had the opportunity to ask for money, which was sure to come next. Wiley crossed 46th Street, the noise deafening as an earsplitting cacophony of horns, traffic, people, and worst of all a jackhammer, filled the air. He willed himself to another place; a place where the air was pure and cool; a place where the smell of the earth infused itself with peace of mind and set everything on a course of truth and enlightenment.

At 58th Street, he leaned back and saw the letters "BWM" across the top of a tall building. When he crossed the street, he found himself at the entrance and large glass double doors that swung open upon entry. Once inside, he heard the chirping of birds and the flutter of wings. A whiff of popcorn met him as well, and right away he spotted a vendor dispensing bags of the treat to a crowd of children.

At that moment, across the enormous lobby, the elevator doors opened and from one hundred feet away he saw Pyune.

His heart leapt and he took a step forward, lifting his hand to wave. His arm froze in midair. The man next to Pyune leaned over and kissed her. Smiling, she placed her arm around him and pulled him toward her. They kissed again and exited the building from a side door, laughing and holding hands.

Wiley stood motionless, a ringing in his ears. Unable to speak, he stared and watched the pair through the glass until they disappeared into the New York masses.

Wiley Hanson, mountain man, felt his knees weaken as he walked to a nearby chair. The ringing in his ears continued while the birds flew back and forth across the aviary in slow motion, their beaks opening in soundless chirps.

The airport. He would get his things from the Marriott and catch the next flight to Atlanta. He would return to Ivy Log. Without Pyune.

"Hey, mon! I think I know you."

Wiley looked up from under the brim of his hat. A tall, uniformed fellow with a cap on his head leaned over him.

"What did you say?" His words were hoarse, barely audible. Wiley shifted his hat lower and blocked the man from his view except for his shiny black patent-leather shoes.

"I know you, mon," the affable fellow repeated.

Wiley tapped his hat back on his forehead. The face looking at him was smiling, the teeth white against the jet-black color of his skin. "Don't believe you have the right guy," said Wiley, standing up and brushing past the man.

"Well, I thought mountain folks were a little friendlier than this," the man called after him.

Wiley hesitated and turned around to face the tall man. He narrowed his eyes and studied the face. It was unfamiliar. "How did you know I was from the mountains?"

"Ha! Frandy knows everything. I'm de man. I be handsome. I be smart. I be Frandy."

"Frandy?"

"You got it! And you must be Wiley, mon. Wiley from de mountains." Frandy shuffled his feet. "You come to see Pyune? Eh?"

Wiley jerked back. The big man would not stop smiling. "Who are you?" he asked, not concealing his irritation in the least.

Frandy folded his arms across his chest. "I told you I was 'de man.' You don' believe me, eh?"

"Oh, I believe you. How do you know me? And how do you know Pyune?"

"Ah, mon, you are finally realizing how brilliant I truly am." Laughter came from deep inside his chest. "I pick up your Pyune at the airport. I am BWM's limousine driver."

"She told you about me?" Wiley was getting more irritated by the second.

"Ah, that she did. She described you to a T. That's how I knew it was you, mon."

Wiley nodded, deciding he'd heard enough. "Well, I'll be seeing you. I'm headin' back to Atlanta."

Frandy crunched his brow. "What about Pyune?"

"What about her?"

"You came to see her?"

A stuttering. A hesitation. "I've already seen her." He shook his head once, fast and hard. "Gotta get to the airport." He turned and faced the lobby doors.

Frandy watched him for a few seconds before calling out as Wiley started to step through the doorway. "Frandy take you to the airport."

Wiley looked over his shoulder. "No thanks."

Frandy yelled louder. "You no like Frandy?"

Wiley stopped and turned around. He examined the man who spoke with such bluntness. "Okay, you can drive me to the airport."

Frandy jumped forward and his large hand found Wiley's back. "Ah, you smart man, Wiley Hanson."

In the parking garage, Frandy opened the limousine door. "Here. You sit by Frandy." They pulled out of the parking garage and into what was relatively light traffic for Manhattan.

"I gotta stop by the hotel. Pick up my things."

"What hotel?"

"Marriott Marquis. Be just a few minutes."

"Frandy will wait for the mountain man."

They rode in silence to the hotel. Wiley, numb with the realization that Pyune was smitten with another man, stared ahead, oblivious to his surroundings. The airport. The plane. Atlanta. Ivy Log. If he kept his mind on those four things, he would survive the day.

At the Marriott, Wiley rode the elevator to the 16th floor, re-trieved his bag, and checked out. Frandy cruised around the block and picked him up at the hotel entrance. "Hello, mountain Wiley. I am back, you see. Frandy is known for his promptness and reliability. Eh?"

Wiley threw his bag in the back and climbed in the front seat, and the sleek black limo headed for LaGuardia. Frandy waited patiently before asking, "So, what do you think?"

"About what?" Wiley asked, without the slightest bit of inter-est.

"About Pyune, of course. She is a star, you know. Love that woman! She swooped down on New York and nobody have a chance, mon. Oh, no. She stole our hearts the first day she here." Frandy rocked in his seat, calypso music in the background as WVIP 93.5 played through the speakers.

The limo glided through the Queens Midtown Tunnel and onto 495 towards LaGuardia. Clouds had moved across the sky from the west and blocked out the afternoon sun. Traffic slowed at the exit to LaGuardia. "She wowed everyone on 'The Today Show,'" Frandy said. "I hear that the phones lit up so much that the network could not handle the calls. Everyone love Pyune."

"Delta," said Wiley. He pulled three twenties from his shirt pocket and flipped them to Frandy. "Appreciate it." Frandy stopped at the curb and Wiley opened his door. "Let me grab my bag." He yanked the back door open and took his bag from the back seat. "Thanks, again."

Frandy glanced at Wiley. "Tess, she is just elated about it all."

"Who's Tess?" Wiley asked, not concerned about the answer; just wanting to get the hell away from the car and New York City.

"You funny, mon. Pyune's sister, Tess,"

"Pyune doesn't have a sister." Wiley tuned out Frandy and his chatter; his thoughts only on getting home as fast as he could.

"Eh? What you say, mon? Pyune didn't tell you about Tess? Tess Starling?"

Wiley raised his voice, "What are you talkin' about?"

Frandy frowned. "Didn't you say you talked with Pyune?"

"No, I didn't say that. I said I saw Pyune. I didn't get to talk with her."

A stunned Frandy stared at Wiley. "So, you know nothing?"

A confused Wiley slammed the car door and began walking toward the terminal. Frandy pressed the button to lower the window and yelled to Wiley's back. "Pyune has a twin sister who looks just like her, mon! Didn't she tell you?"

Wiley skidded to a stop and spun around.

~~~

Chapter 60

Pyune and Monty ended up along 44th Street, where he parked and they walked around Midtown Manhattan. "You've never seen a Broadway play." It was a statement, not a question. Monty lamented that this lovely woman had never traveled outside of Ivy Log. Never experienced the center of the cultural universe that was New York City.

"Maybe one day," Pyune said, a wistful sigh escaping her as she stared at a poster of "Hello, Dolly" starring Bette Midler.

"This is the Shubert Theatre," Monty said. "The three Shubert brothers began producing plays early in the twentieth century. "Hello, Dolly" will start its run next year. Should be a long one."

They meandered the streets without talking. For Pyune, New York City had become a bittersweet journey. It had changed her life. They crossed 8th Avenue and circled the block. Pigeons scattered and flew above them. They passed a deli where the aroma from hot pastrami made her smile.

Monty said, "You know, Pyune, I am a firm believer that life is just one big adventure. You never really arrive and you're constantly evolving. New York City has been an adventure for you—and you've been exposed to many new things. You don't have to say no to those new things."

Pyune walked a few steps and lingered under the shade of a large green-and- white-striped awning, where in the display window she saw the reflections of a tall handsome man—and a woman who didn't know what she was going to do. She deliberated a few moments before turning to Monty. "I believe in what you're saying, but I also believe that life is full of compromises."

Monty smiled at Pyune. "Am I being selfish?"

"No, not at all. I understand your position. As producer of 'Dine With Me,' of course you want another successful season. But it's such a wonderful show concept, I think anyone would be a good host."

"That may be true to a certain degree. But it's you who can guarantee its success for another season." Monty began gesturing as if a bee had stung him. "Look at the response you had from your appearance on 'The Today Show'! And what about the fundraiser? You were an unknown who wowed the public into donating hundreds of thousands of dollars just to see you win. They loved you, and obviously the judges loved your cooking." Monty placed his arms at his side and sent a pensive look Pyune's way. "You're a star, Pyune. Whether you like it or not, you're a star."

~~~

Chapter 61

Unbelievable! Pyune had a sister! Not only that, a twin sister! Wiley asked, "Since Frandy knows everything, how about telling me *everything you know*?"

Frandy laughed heartily. "Ah, the mountain man has finally found trust in this handsome Jamaican. Eh?"

The limo rocketed from the curb and Frandy began telling Wiley *everything he knew*. Tess Starling was the CEO of Bakers' World Magazine and the overseer of the baking contest that was won by Pyune. Upon Pyune's arrival in New York, Frandy had met her at the airport and went into absolute denial that the woman standing before him was none other than Tess Starling. It was a total fluke, a chance occurrence, a wobble in the universe that had turned everything upside down.

"So, mon, when are you going to tell Frandy why you run back to the airport, back to the mountains?"

A reticent silence filled the space between Wiley and Frandy. *Why was I fleeing New York City? The thought of losing Pyune was too much to bear.*

Wiley shook his head and pulled out his phone. Still no message from Pyune.

"Frandy give this mountain man some good advice, eh?" The handsome Jamaican began to rock slowly in his seat. "But first Frandy has to sing this song." "No Woman, No Cry" drifted from the radio and the big limo seemed to sway with the smooth tones of Bob Marley. Frandy's high tenor overwhelmed the car. "So dry your tears," he sang. "I say no woman, no cry. Little darlin'—don't shed no tears."

On the ramp for 37th street, Wiley could wait no longer. His words roared inside the limo: "Let's hear that advice, mon." Wiley laughed, something just fifteen minutes earlier he didn't think he'd ever do again.

A slow bubbling lilt came from Frandy's throat. "Oh, mon, it is so simple to Frandy." Another song came on the radio, and Frandy's shoulders began to rock back and forth once more.

"Dang it, Frandy!" Wiley reached over and turned off the radio. "Do you have any advice or not?"

"Do not be impatient with Frandy. Music is important to this island man." He grinned and slowed for a traffic light. "This is Frandy's advice: the mountain man must find the mountain woman and give her a big kiss. Eh?"

"You've got to be kiddin'! That's your advice? A kiss isn't going to fix this. I saw Pyune with another man!"

Frandy braked hard and pulled to the curb. "What man, you say?"

"The man I saw kissing her in the lobby of the Bakers' World Building!"

Frandy scratched his smooth chin. "Describe this man to Frandy."

Wiley sputtered. "Well . . . tall feller, black hair, medium build. Good lookin', I guess."

Frandy leaned over and squared his eyes with Wiley's. "You have just described Mr. Robert Larson, Tess's husband." His body began to shake with laughter. "Ah, Frandy says the mountain man is not so smart after all. Eh?"

Frandy had stopped the limo in traffic and Wiley opened his door. "You're getting on my nerves, Frandy. Be seeing you." Grabbing his bag, Wiley slammed the car door and headed into the heart of Manhattan.

Frandy watched for a moment before pulling the car beside him, to an open space along the curb. The window down, Frandy said, "It's thirty blocks back to BWM. Frandy give you a ride. Promise not to sing Bob Marley."

Wiley got in, and the sleek limo cruised along for five more blocks. "I take you to Pyune if you be nice to Frandy."

Wiley glared at Frandy. "No singing. No advice."

"If you say so, mon."

~~~

Chapter 62

Monty dropped Pyune at the curb. "See you at six," he said.

Pyune waved goodbye and found the elevators that would take her to Tess's floor. The swish of the elevator was the only noise. For the first time in four days, she was alone. Why had it been so difficult to say yes to New York, to "Dine With Me," to the excitement of her newly acquired fame?

By the time she reached her floor she'd made a decision. She rushed inside the apartment and called out. She found no one there. Five o'clock. Where was Tess? She called out again for Tess. No answer.

In her room, Pyune threw her belongings into her luggage. She quickly wrote a message to Tess: "Dearest Sister, I'm not leaving you. I'm leaving New York to go home. I long for Wiley and Ivy Log. I will be back. Love, Pyune."

But she was saying no to New York, no to the $25,000, no to the celebrity life-style that had been thrown at her in just a few short days. What waited for her was Wiley and Ivy Log. That's all she wanted.

She'd packed in a frenzy. In a half-run, she exited the elevator, almost spearing a surprised Frandy with her handbag. "Oh!" she yelped.

Frandy, his legs spread wide, folded his arms across his chest, a solid barrier that thwarted Pyune's rush from the building. "Miss Murphy, Frandy wants to know where you are going?"

"Oh, Frandy, you must take me to the airport!" Pyune was breathless, her face flushed. "I want to go home."

The tall man grinned. "Frandy will take you to the airport, but you'll have to ride with another fare. Eh?"

"That's okay. Let's go!" She rushed ahead of him, but with one big step he caught up with her and took the suitcase from her.

Through the darkened windows of the limo, Wiley saw Pyune. Saw the woman he loved. He reached for the door and pushed it open. "Pyune," he called, a tremble in that one soft word.

"Wiley!" she breathed. She fell into the back seat of the limo, into his arms, and never wanted him to let go.

"Oh, Pyune. Let me hold you." He rocked her and smoothed her hair away from her face. "My love."

Pyune nestled into Wiley's neck, her eyes closed. She smelled his aftershave, felt his heartbeat and the warmth of his body. "Let's go home," she mumbled.

"Home?" Wiley gently pushed her shoulders back and looked into her glistening rum-colored eyes. "What about the awards dinner tonight?" He sounded legitimately confused. "And that check?"

"Forget that check! We're going home!" Pyune pressed the window button and called to Frandy, who was standing near the limo, "Frandy, let's go!"

Frandy jumped to attention and placed his cap on his head. "Frandy, he move like lightening!" The Jamaican slid behind the wheel and in moments they were on their way.

Wiley reared back and gave Pyune his bullet eye. "Now, Pyune, The Boardinghouse needs a new refrig—"

"Wiley, I'm not staying in New York another minute. Not even for twenty-five thousand dollars."

Wiley yelled to the front of the limo, "Frandy, pull over until we work this thing out." Frandy slowed the limo and the glass between Frandy and the back seat glided upward. He parked at the curb, and without a word left the limo and walked slowly along the sidewalk, his hands in his pockets, his shoulders slumped. The Jamaican had nothing to sing about.

A cajoling Wiley pulled Pyune's hands into his. "Let's be smart about this. Twenty-five thousand is a lot of money, and you could use it for the things you need for The Boardinghouse. Let's just spend a few more hours in New York City, and then we'll go home together." He knew of a reason beyond money that Pyune should stay, with her sister's being that reason. Wiley Hanson, a master of reason, calmly put his finger under Pyune's chin and her eyes found his. "I'll be with you the whole way."

She blinked, and the tears that had welled up in her eyes slid down her cheeks. How many times had she tried to leave during these past few days but couldn't?

Frandy drove back to BWM at slow pace, his music turned down low. Now and then his shoulders jerked to a beat, his head rocking slowly up and down while the rest of his body moved in a gentle sway. The Jamaican was back on the island, near the blue seawater, under a big yellow umbrella, his toes in the sand. And right beside him Bob Marley strummed his red Gibson guitar.

In the back of the limo, Wiley and Pyune talked in a whisper, a smile from Wiley occasionally necessary to reassure Pyune. At her insistence, in just a few hours he was to attend the awards dinner with her. What he was to wear was undecided. Pyune's full-blown meltdown over clothes to take to New York was fresh on his mind. He calmly discussed the comparative value of jeans and a flannel shirt over a tuxedo with all the trimmings. He lost the debate before he could even say, "Now, Pyune."

They moved smoothly through the Queens Midtown Tunnel, and in just minutes the limo pulled into the BWM parking garage. Frandy jumped out and opened the limo door. "Frandy did it again" he announced, his big smile swallowing his face. "He take you safely home. I be so careful with my people. Eh?"

"You're a fine feller, Frandy," Wiley said, and meaning it. "I think you would have made a great mountain man."

Frandy pretended to shudder and convulse. "Frandy no like snakes. He stay in the big city."

The elevator ride took Wiley and Pyune to the apartment on the top floor, a journey that lasted only a minute but was filled with trepidations that caused the back of Wiley's neck to tingle, a sure sign that trouble lay ahead. Pyune, her face flushed with nervous apprehension, grasped Wiley's hand tightly. They could not turn back now.

Before they could knock, the apartment door swung open. A

wobbly Tess stood in the doorway, Robert at her side. Tess held the note Pyune had written. Her makeup was streaked with tears. Tess gasped, "Pyune!" She lunged forward and pulled Pyune inside, a stricken Wiley following close behind, stunned to see a perfect match of the woman he loved.

After a few minutes of formal introductions and cursory explanations, Wiley, with a calmness he gathered from someplace deep inside him, asked, "Y'all know anywhere I can rent a tuxedo in a hurry so I can accompany Pyune to the awards dinner?"

All four collapsed in laughter, their individual joy tainted with palpable relief all around. Robert looked closely at the bearded man who sat in front of him and sipped a root beer. Both men were about the same height, but Robert Larson was at least thirty pounds heavier. However, Robert said, "Follow me," and Wiley did as requested.

~~~

Chapter 63

New York shimmered with light in the coolness of an April night, the heart of the city thumping with music and sounds of laughter that floated in the same air that carried the fresh aroma of freshly baked pastries and sizzling steaks. The streets were awash with the gaiety of the city's nightlife, and right in the middle of it was a horribly overdressed mountain man. Ridiculous!

Wiley, brushed and shining and smooth, walked down 7th Avenue, his suit tailored by Desmond Merrion—a London tailor who spent an average of 200 hours making a single suit. The suit, on loan from Robert Lawson, had spawned a little bit of jive in Wiley's walk. The suit had been made twenty years earlier, when Robert was a lot slimmer. He'd kept a great many of his older clothes, always hoping he'd someday lose the weight he'd gained and once again be able to get into the outfits. Wiley's boots, however, were a problem, and his feet were much larger than Robert's. Leave it to Frandy to come to the rescue, as he provided a brand-new pair of black patent-leather shoes—he'd received as a present but had not yet worn—that looked as though they'd been acquired specifically to go with the suit Wiley wore.

The suit and shoes, along with the other habiliments Robert provided, gave Wiley a strong sense of confidence, something he'd never lacked to begin with. Thus, Wiley Hanson, already the most confident, most well-rounded man in the universe, wore the outfit proudly. Many believe that the image of a man in a finely tailored suit is instant seduction. Maybe that's why women of all ages turned their heads as the debonair mountain man strolled the streets of New York City.

As they walked together, Pyune's beauty settled alongside Wiley like a kiss blown into a soft breeze. Wiley could not quiet the throbbing of his heart every time he looked at her. She was exquisite, her Giorgio Armani black dress sparkling with a row of rhinestones at the neck, as at the last minute she'd made a complete switch from the Valentino. She didn't want the white to clash with Wiley's all-black outfit.

From far off they heard the bells of a cathedral. Wiley believed that the laughter of angels must sound like this. They passed a homeless man who hovered in the shadow of an alley. When Wiley saw him his confident gait faltered. There was no dark side to a mountain moon; the streams ran clear and the rhododendron were always in bloom. It was the mountains that existed with no heartache, and he became sadly aware of how far he was from his beloved peaks. He walked back to the man and gave him two twenties.

In front of them, Frandy pulled the limo to the curb and the two couples slid inside and were off to the Bakers' World Magazine gala.

Wiley, for the first time since he'd met Tess at the door of her apartment, studied the woman who sat across from him. He casually glanced at Pyune. No doubt about it, the women were twins. But how? Questions tumbled in his head. The same questions Tess and Pyune had undoubtedly posed to themselves.

"Wiley, how long have you known my sister?" Tess's question had come out of nowhere and surprised Wiley.

"From when I first got to Ivy Log. About thirty years ago." He smiled and took Pyune's hand. "It's a small place. Everyone knows everybody else."

Pyune straightened her jewelry. "I threw a hard biscuit at Wiley when he walked down the streets of Ivy Log for the first time."

"What a memorable introduction that must have been," Robert said and laughed.

Wiley rolled his eyes. "It was unforgettable."

"We have arrived," said Frandy, putting a halt to the conversation. He pulled along the curb and jumped out of the limo, his cap firmly on his head. He opened the doors wide and the two couples walked up the storied steps of the Villard Mansion on Madison Avenue, and into the Villard Ballroom.

Several hundred people had gathered in the grand oval-shaped ballroom, a room right out of New York's gilded age. The historic room carried the scents of the finest perfumes, lavish jewelry sparkled from all corners as if constellations all their own, and the air was indeed infused with the rich aroma of money. Almost immediately Monty Reynolds was at Tess's side, his charm spewing forth in a fountain of grace and dignity. "Good evening, everyone," he said, clearly enamored with his role as the toastmaster of this show.

Tess leaned her cheek toward him and he kissed it sweetly. Without a thought, he leaned over and kissed Pyune's cheek. It was then that he noticed the tall, bearded man at her side. He reached out his hand. "Have we met?"

Wiley, a twinkle forming in his eyes, shook Monty's hand. "Not unless you drove the cab that got me here from the airport?"

Tess laughed so loud it belied her ladylike stature. "Monty, this is Wiley Hanson." Monty didn't say anything, so Tess added, "From Ivy Log."

"Oh, my. Pyune's . . . Pyune's . . . ." A slight blush came to Monty's cheeks.

"Pyune's feller," said Wiley, cocking his head.

Monty nodded quickly. "Of course. Let me show everyone to your table. It's right up front."

The small group meandered through the crowd, Tess and Monty stopping frequently to say hello to friends and business acquaintances, and introducing Pyune and Wiley as they moved along. Tess found her way to the podium, where her notes had been placed earlier, thanks to Monty. She looked over the crowd and saw most tables were filling up quickly. It was 7:30. They'd missed the cocktail party that began at 6:00 because she was too distraught over the note Pyune had written. Now, her eyes on her sister, things were all aligned where they should be. They were together.

In the background, the music of "New York, New York" added to the festive evening. Tess stepped to the side and left it up to Monty to welcome everyone and begin the program.

Monty's flamboyant personality was ideal at large events, validating his reputation as Mr. New York, perhaps second only to Donald Trump in the realm of charisma.

A ruckus at the table behind them began with "Shit!" followed by the sound of breaking glass and someone saying, "Sit down, Joan!" A hand reached up and grabbed Joan Stone's arm and pulled her into her chair.

It was inevitable—the woman was trouble. Had Tess been able to prevent her attendance at this Restaurant and Chef Awards dinner, she would have done so. But that would not have been possible. Joan stumbled to their table and plopped herself down beside Wiley, in the chair Tess had just vacated. "Well, hello," she said, toppling her drink onto Wiley's slacks as she leaned into him. "I like your beard," she said, low and sensual.

"Thank you," said Wiley. "I like your earrings. Did you know they don't match?"

"Whaaa . . . . " Joan pulled them off and compared the two pieces of jewelry. They were thin, simple strands of gold. And identical!

She narrowed her eyes at Wiley. "They're a perfect match."

Wiley leaned closer and spoke in a conspiratorial whisper. "Yes, the earrings match each other—but they don't match you. They are plain and you are exquisitely beautiful."

A soft intake of breath filled Joan's lungs as she contemplated the handsome, bearded man who spoke so eloquently to her. Her lips eased into a smile.

Wiley carefully picked up the earrings, and his big hand returned each one gently to her ears. "Now, my dear woman, I want you to go back to your table and sit there, knowing you are as lovely as a mountain spring."

For a moment, Wiley let his eyes hold Joan's. And, as though his arms were carrying her, she returned to her table and sat primly with her hands in her lap, thinking about mountain springs and exactly how lovely they were.

At exactly 8 o'clock the ballroom lights dimmed. Monty began singing the lyrics along with the "New York, New York" instrumental, and his trained voice filled the ballroom: "Start spreading the news, I'm leaving today." He danced across the stage with a beautiful, long-legged blonde who wore silver heels and moved with the speed of lightning and the grace of a gazelle.

Monty left the blonde at the edge of the stage and streaked back to the podium in time to sing the finale of the powerful middle verse: "And if I can make it there, I'll make it anywhere. It's up to you, New York . . . New York."

The crowd jumped to its feet and wildly applauded while Monty bowed and walked along the stage. Panting, but holding his composure like the professional he was, he came back to the podium, took a deep breath, and announced, "Ladies and gentlemen, this is what we've all been waiting for—a night to honor New York's finest chefs and restaurateurs. But, first, I'd like to introduce the sponsor of these awards, Tess Starling of Bakers' World Magazine."

The spotlight moved the short distance to Tess, who waved to the audience, saying, "Thank you, thank you!"

At that the festivities began. Award after award, acceptance speeches, recognitions for contributions to the New York Cooks for Charity Fundraiser, all leading up to the announcement of Bakers' World Magazine's annual contest winner. The room quieted as Tess took the microphone for what would be the last time that evening.

"For twenty-five years, Bakers' World Magazine has held its annual baking contest and operated its test kitchens for many projects, one of which has been the New York chefs' charity event that feeds the homeless. This year marks the twenty-fifth anniversary of Baker's World Magazine, and I'm proud to be associated with such a loving and giving group of employees as well as the citizens of New York who contribute hugely to so many philanthropic projects."

Tess paused and looked across the crowd. "Tonight . . . tonight is rather special for me. When the thousands of recipes were received at Bakers' World for our annual contest, I never dreamed the winner would be . . . be known to me." Her voice faded. She searched through the lights for Pyune and found her looking up at her, a face that matched her own. "What can I say? A miracle is a miracle. And that's what happened. When the winner of this year's contest arrived in New York, I never dreamed she . . . she would be a . . . a sister I didn't know I had."

The room, as if alive, seemed to be holding its breath. Tess walked to the edge of the stage and reached out her hand. "I'd like to introduce this year's winner. From Ivy Log, Georgia, I give you my sister, Pyune EverSweet Murphy."

The spotlights swirled around the room and settled on Pyune. Wiley reached over and squeezed her hand. Monty rushed to her table. "Come, Pyune. This is your moment." Pyune took Monty's hand and followed him to the stage. There was a roar of applause mixed in with whistles and cheers.

Pyune EverSweet Murphy. Her name was written on mountain peaks. And on the trees and the streams and in the fragrance of the earth that permeated all things good. Her name was written on the small town that opened its arms and took her in. Her name was on every pie, every jar of jelly, and every piece of wood she fed the old woodstove in the back of The Boardinghouse kitchen. Pyune EverSweet Murphy was on a stage in New York City, but her heart was—and would always be—in the Appalachian mountains.

"Thank you so much," Pyune said as the sisters held hands and let the joy of the moment wash over them. The long applause finally quieted, and Tess took the microphone again.

"Pyune's winning recipe was for a lemon pudding cake, a family recipe she's been making all her life. You'll see the recipe in our anniversary issue of Bakers' World Magazine." Tess picked up a check from the podium. "Pyune, it is my pleasure, as well as the pleasure of Bakers' World Magazine, to present you with a check for twenty-five thousand dollars as winner of the silver anniversary of our annual baking contest."

Pyune held out her hand and Tess placed the check in it. "Thank you so much," Pyune said. She looked over the crowd. "I never imagined I would win this contest. The people in New York City have been so kind to me, and I am so grateful." She turned to Tess. "You'll never know how much everything has meant to me."

Wiley watched the stage and the two women who stood next to each other. He felt an ache in his throat: the two women belonged together. How could he take Pyune away from the only family she had? With tears in his eyes, he saw Tess reach out and clasp Pyune's hand into hers. Sisters. Together at last.

Cheers from the crowd lasted until Pyune stepped from the stage, the check in her hand and a smile on her face. She looked for Wiley at their table but didn't see him. She turned around and searched the throngs of people. *Where is Wiley?* She rushed across the room, through the large doorways, and into the lobby. A hallway stretched in each direction, from her left and then her right. There was no tall, bearded man in a tuxedo. She ran to the entrance and there stood Frandy, holding a sign that read: "Miss Murphy."

Pyune shrieked. "Frandy, what are you doing?"

"Ah, Miss Murphy. Frandy has been instructed to find you and take you to the limo." The Jamaican rocked his shoulders and shuffled out the door. Pyune followed behind him, confused, her eyes still searching for Wiley.

At the curb, Frandy opened the limo door and pointed inside. "It's Wiley. He changed into his jeans and is ready to go to the airport. He wants to know if you got the check."

"The check?" Pyune fell into the limo and squealed at seeing Wiley, who was tightening his belt. "Yes, I have the check. Why?"

"Then let's go to the airport."

"The airport?"

"Yes, the airport. I can't ask you to marry me while we're still in New York City. The sooner we get home to Ivy Log, the sooner I can ask you and we can get married."

"Get married?" She squealed even louder. "Wait! What about Tess?" Pyune pulled away, her worried look exaggerated by the city lights.

Wiley guffawed. "Tess? Ha! She's the one who put me up to this. She and Robert will be at our weddin'."

Pyune lay her head on Wiley's shoulder while the limo sped through New York on the way to LaGuardia. This time Pyune was really leaving. Frandy turned his music low; low and sweet like the island he loved.

"Oh, Wiley, I'm so tired. I'm so ready to get home. Tell me about Ivy Log." Her eyes closed and images of her green mountains played like a symphony in her head.

Wiley, his eyes also closed, leaned over and smelled Pyune's hair and pressed his lips to her cheek. Yes, he would tell her about their beloved Ivy Log. He'd tell her about the passing of Vallie, the woman they all loved—the woman who had searched her entire life for a daughter she'd given away. He'd tell her about the bucktoothed boy with hair as red-orange as a Crayon, and who'd become a multimillionaire in just a matter of days—

but was now just a millionaire. And that he had new boots because of Wiley.

And Eva, the woman who thought B.T. was her half-brother, only to discover he was her cousin and that the mother she had been looking for—was none other than Vallie Thomas.

And Lizzie. The lumbering woman had met the challenge of cooking stews, making biscuits, and frying bacon—and the folks in Ivy Log had loved her for it. In Pyune's absence, Lizzie had protected the character of The Boardinghouse with a fierce vengeance despite Paula Jennings's misguided quest to turn it into a French bistro. Yes, Paula, who rallied around God's words but whose actions bespoke the devil at every turn. Her attempts to send the mountain boy to a reformatory had failed. Ivy Log's pastor and its citizens would never allow such a thing to happen, and neither had Eva McIlwain, the cousin B. T. didn't know he had.

And beautiful Ivy Log. The little hamlet had fared well, had opened its loving arms to the wayward boy, grieved over the death of an eccentric woman, and lovingly cared for her orphaned cat. The town waited for the return of Pyune EverSweet Murphy, their shining star who had come to them so long ago and taught them the joys of hot peach pies with whipped cream, of heavenly pot roast, and of course her prize-winning lemon pudding cake. But it really wasn't about pies and cakes and simmering roasts—not at all. It was about *love*.

THE END

AUTHOR SUE CHAMBLIN FREDERICK. She is known as a sweet Southern belle, a woman whose eyelashes are longer than her fingers, her lips as red as a Georgia sunset. Yet, behind the feminine facade of a Scarlett-like ingénue lies an absolute and utterly calculating mind – a mind that harbors hints of genius – a genius she uses to write books that will leave you spellbound.

A WARNING! She's dangerous – when she writes spy thrillers she's only six degrees from a life filled with unimaginable adventures – journeys that will plunge her readers into a world of breath-taking intrigue. Put a Walther PPK pistol in her hand and she will kill you. Her German is so precise she'd fool Hitler. *Her amorous prowess?* If you have a secret, she will discover it – one way or the other.

When she writes romance, her readers swoon and beg for mercy as they read her seductive stories about luscious characters. Be sure to have a glass of wine nearby as you snuggle up to her books about *love*.

The author was born in north Florida in the little town of Live Oak, where the nearby Suwannee River flows the color of warm caramel, in a three-room, tin-roofed house named "poor." Her Irish mother's and English father's voices can be heard even today as they sweep across the hot tobacco fields of Suwannee County, "Susie, child, you must stop telling all those wild stories."

She lives with her Yankee husband in the piney woods of north Florida, where she is compelled to write about far away places and people whose hearts require a voice. Her two daughters live their lives hiding from their mother, whose rampant imagination keeps their lives in constant turmoil with stories of apple-rotten characters and plots that cause the devil to smile.

Pyune has shared her prize-winning lemon cake recipe for each of you. Pyune said, *"make sure your beaters and bowl are completely free of grease"* when you beat the egg whites. And, *"absolutely no egg yolk can mix in with the whites when you separate the eggs."*

Pyune EverSweet Murphy's
LEMON PUDDING CAKE
FROM
THE IVY LOG SERIES

INGREDIENTS:
3 large lemons
½ cup all-purpose flour
3/8 teaspoon salt
1 cup plus 2 tablespoons sugar
3 large eggs (room temperature), separated
(Ask Paula how to separate the eggs.)
1 1/3 cups whole milk
l ½ tablespoons lemon zest
½ cup fresh lemon juice

PREPERATION:
1. Zest lemon to make 1 ½ Tbs. Squeeze lemons to make ½ cup.
2. Whisk together flour, salt and ¾ cup **plus 2** tablespoons sugar in large bowl.
3. Whisk together egg yolks in a small bowl. Add milk, lemon zest and lemon juice and whisk together. Add to flour mixture, mixing until just combined.
4. Beat egg whites in a large bowl with electric mixer until soft peaks form. Beat in ¼ cup of sugar, a small amount at a time and continue to beat until peaks are stiff and glossy. Whisk ¼ cup of egg whites into batter. Fold in remaining egg whites gently, but thoroughly.
5. Pour into buttered 1 ½ quart shallow baking dish. Place baking dish into a shallow pan. Pour boiling water into the pan until ¾ inch from the top of the baking dish with the cake batter.

<u>BAKE AT:</u>
350 degrees.   About 45 minutes.   Serves 6. *Dust with confectioner's sugar when served.

* Pyune serves her famous lemon pudding cake on The Boarding House's fine china.
– *Old French Saxon,* the *Morning Glory* pattern.

Coming Summer 2017

The Front Porch Sisters

By Sue Chamblin Frederick

From the front porch of their ancestral home in the sprawling fields of Madison County, spinster sisters Essie and Jewel reminisce about times gone by – neighbors no longer come to their front porch for lively conversations or Jewel's buttered rum pound cake. The sisters felt it was just a matter of time before they were forgotten, ending up in the Mt. Horeb cemetery and remembered only as the Donnelly sisters who never married. Before it was too late, they decide to alter the course of their lives, never dreaming they would change their small town forever.

23140336R00167

Made in the USA
Columbia, SC
04 August 2018